THE TRIUMPH OF THE SUN

Volume 2

Wilbur Smith

WINDSOR
PARAGON

First published 2005
by
Macmillan
This Large Print edition published 2005
by
BBC Audiobooks Ltd by arrangement with
Macmillan

ISBN 1 4056 1148 0   (Windsor Hardcover)
ISBN 1 4056 2135 4   (Paragon Softcover)

British Library Cataloguing in Publication Data available

Printed and bound in Great Britain by
Antony Rowe Ltd., Chippenham, Wiltshire

This book is for my helpmate, playmate, soulmate, wife and best friend, Mokhiniso Rakhimova Smith

The earth burns with the quenchless thirst of ages, and in the steel blue sky scarcely a cloud obstructs the relentless triumph of the sun.

The River War, Winston S. Churchill, 1905

They had ridden five days in the vast assembly of men and animals. It rolled ponderously northwards across the desert. Penrod Ballantyne swivelled on the saddle of his camel to look back. The dust of their progress reached the horizon and rose to the sky.

Fifty thousand fighting men? he wondered. But we will never know for sure—nobody can count them. All the emirs of the southern tribes and all their warriors. What power does this man Muhammad Ahmed wield that he can bring together such a multitude, made up of tribes that for five hundred years have been riven by feud and blood feud?

Then he turned back in the saddle and looked to the north, the direction in which this vast host was riding. Stewart has only two thousand men to oppose them. In all the wars of all the ages did odds such as these ever prevail?

He put aside the thought, and tried to work out how far back Yakub and he were from the vanguard of this mighty cavalcade. Without drawing attention to themselves they had to work their way gradually to the front. It was only from that position that they could break away and make a final dash for the Wells of Gakdul. The Dervish were pacing their camels, not driving them so hard that they would be unfit to take part in the battle ahead. That they were moving so quietly and not rushing into battle reassured Penrod that Stewart must still be encamped there.

They passed slowly through another loose formation of Dervish. These were hard desert

1

tribesmen with swords and shields slung across their backs. Most were mounted on camels, and each led a string of pack camels carrying tents and ammunition cases, cooking pots, food bags and waterskins. Trailing along behind them were the traders and petty merchants of Omdurman, their camels also heavily laden with trade goods and merchandise. After the battle, when the Ansar were rolling in loot, there would be rich profits.

At the head of this formation rode a small group of Ansar on fine Arab steeds, which had been lovingly curried until their hides shone in the sunlight like polished metal. Their long silky manes had been combed out and plaited with coloured ribbons. Their trappings and tack were of painted and beautifully decorated leather. The horsemen sat upon their backs with the panache and studied arrogance of warriors.

'Aggagiers!' Yakub muttered, as they drew closer. 'The killers of elephant.'

Penrod drew the tail of his turban closer over his mouth and nose so that only his eyes showed, and edged aside his camel to pass the group at a safe distance. As they drew level with them they saw the horsemen staring across at them. They were animatedly discussing the two strangers.

'Damn Ryder Courtney for his taste in camel flesh.' For the first time since leaving Khartoum, Penrod bemoaned the quality of their mounts. They were magnificent creatures, more befitting a *khalifa* or a powerful emir than a lowly tribesman. Even in this vast assembly they stood out as thoroughbreds. Yakub urged his camel forward at a faster clip, and Penrod cautioned him sharply: 'Gently, fearless Yakub. Their eyes are upon you.

When the mice run the cat pounces.'

Yakub reined in, and they continued at more leisurely pace, but this did not deter the aggagiers. Two broke away from the group and rode across to them.

'They are of the Beja,' Yakub said hoarsely. 'They mean us no good.'

'Steady, glib and cunning Yakub. You must deceive them with your ready tongue.'

The leading aggagier came up and reined his bay mare down to a walk. 'The blessings of Allah and His Victorious Mahdi upon you, strangers. What is your tribe and who is your emir?'

'May Allah and the Mahdi, grace upon him, always smile upon you,' Yakub responded, in a clear untroubled voice. 'I am Hogal al-Kadir of the Jaalin, and we ride under the banner of the Emir Salida.'

'I am al-Noor, of the Beja tribe. My master is the famed Emir Osman Atalan, upon whom be all the blessings of Allah.'

'He is a mighty man, beloved of Allah and the Ever Victorious Mahdi, may he live long and prosper.' Penrod touched his heart and his forehead, 'I am Suleimani Iffara, a Persian of Jeddah.' Some Persians had fair hair and pale eyes, and Penrod had adopted that nationality to explain his features. It would also account for the slight nuances and inflections in his speech.

'You are a long way from Jeddah, Suleimani Iffara.' Al-Noor rode closer and stared at him thoughtfully.

'The Divine Mahdi has declared *jihad* against the Turk and the Frank,' Penrod replied. 'All true believers must hearken to his summons and make

3

haste to join up with him, no matter how hard and long the journey.'

'You are welcome to our array, but if you travel under the banner of Emir Salida, you must ride harder to catch up with him.'

'We are solicitous of the camels,' Yakub explained, 'but on your advice we will move faster.'

'They are indeed magnificent beasts,' al-Noor agreed, but he was staring at Penrod and not at his mount. He could see only his eyes, but they were the eyes of a jinnee and disconcertingly familiar. Yet it would be a deadly offence to order him to unveil his features. 'My master Osman Atalan has sent me to enquire if you wish to sell any. He would pay you a good price in gold coin.'

'I have the utmost respect for your mighty master,' Penrod replied, 'but rather would I sell my firstborn son.'

'I have said before and I say again that they are magnificent creatures. My master will be saddened by your reply.' Al-Noor lifted his reins to turn away, then paused, 'There is aught about you, Suleimani Iffara, your eyes or your voice, that is familiar. Have we met before?'

Penrod shrugged. 'Perhaps in the mosque of Omdurman.'

'Perhaps,' al-Noor said dubiously, 'but if I have seen you before I will remember. My memory is good.'

'We go on ahead to find our commander,' Yakub intervened. 'May the sons of Islam triumph in the battle that looms ahead.'

Al-Noor turned to him. 'I pray that your words may carry to the ear of God. Victory is sweet, but death is the ultimate purpose of life. It is the key to

Paradise. If the victory is denied to us, may Allah grant us glorious martyrdom.' He touched his heart in farewell salute. 'Go with the blessings of Allah.' He galloped away to rejoin his squadron.

'The Emir Atalan,' Yakub whispered in awe. 'We ride in the same company as your most deadly enemy. This is the same as carrying a cobra in your bosom.'

'Al-Noor has granted us permission to leave his banner,' Penrod reminded him. 'Let us make all haste to obey.'

They stirred up the camels with the goad, and pushed them into a trot. As they pulled away Penrod looked across at the distant group of aggagiers. Now that he knew what to look for he recognized the elegant figure of Osman Atalan in a bone-white *jibba* with gaily coloured patches that caught the eye like jewels. On his lovely pale mare he was riding a few lengths ahead of the rest of his band. He was staring at Penrod, and even at that distance his gaze was disturbing.

Behind his master, al-Noor drew his rifle from its boot under his knee and pointed it to the sky. Penrod saw the spurt of blue powder smoke a few seconds before the report reached his ears. He lifted his own rifle and returned this *feu du joie*. Then they rode on.

They were challenged several times during the rest of the day. The quality of their camels and their obvious haste marked them out even among this huge gathering of animals and men. Each time they asked for the red banner of Emir Salida of the Jaalin, they were told, 'He leads the vanguard,' and they were pointed ahead. Penrod pushed on rapidly: ever since the meeting with al-Noor he had

5

felt uneasy.

They paused in their journey only once more. One of the petty traders who followed the armies called to them as they passed. They turned aside to inspect his wares. He had rounds of dhurra bread, roasted in camel's milk butter and sesame seeds. He showed them also dried dates and apricots, and goat's milk cheese, whose high aroma started their saliva. They filled their food bags, and Penrod paid the exorbitant prices with Maria Theresa dollars.

When they rode on the merchant watched them until they were well out of earshot, then called his son who handled the pack donkeys. 'I know that man well. He marched with Hicks Pasha to El Obeid, at the start of the war of *jihad*. I sold him a gold inlaid dagger, and he bargained shrewdly. I would never mistake him for another. He is an infidel and a Frankish *effendi*. His name is Abadan Riji. Go, my son, to the mighty Emir Osman Atalan, and tell him all these things. Tell him that an enemy marches in the ranks of the warriors of Allah.'

*   *   *

The sun was sinking towards the western horizon and the elongated shadows cast by their camels flitted across the orange yellow dunes when at last Penrod made out the streaming red banner of Emir Salida through the dustclouds ahead.

'This is the front rank of the army,' Yakub agreed. He rode close to Penrod's right hand so that he did not have to raise his voice: other riders were within earshot. 'Many of these men are Jaalin. I have recognized two who carry a blood feud

6

against me. They are of the family who drove me out of my tribe, and made me an outcast. If they confront me I will be honour-bound to kill them.'

'Then let us part company with them.'

The Nile was only a mile distant on their left hand. The whole army had been following the course of the river since they had joined it at Berber. At this late hour of the day many other travellers were turning aside to water their animals on the riverbank. They were too intent on their own affairs to remark the presence of the two strangers among them. Nevertheless Penrod contrived to keep well clear of them.

The grazing closer to the riverbank was dense and luscious. The grass reached as high as the knees of their camels. Suddenly there was an explosion of wings from under the front pads of Yakub's mount, and a covey of quail rocketed into the air. These were the Syrian Blue variety of their breed, larger than the common quail and highly prized for the pot. Yakub swivelled in his saddle and, with a whipping motion of his right hand, threw the heavy camel goad he carried. It cartwheeled through the air and smacked into one of the birds. In a burst of blue, gold and chestnut feathers the quail tumbled to earth.

'Behold! Yakub, the mighty hunter,' he exulted.

The rest of the covey swung across the nose of Penrod's camel and he made his throw. The goad clipped the head off the leading cock bird, and spun on with almost no deflection. It thumped into a plump young hen and snapped her near wing. She came down heavily and scuttled away through the tall grass.

Penrod jumped from the camel's back and

chased her. She jinked and fluttered up, but he snatched her out of the air. Holding her by the head he flicked his wrist and broke her neck. He retrieved his goad and the cock's carcass, then ran back to his mount and swung up into the saddle. 'Behold! Suleimani Iffara, the humble traveller from Jeddah, who would never boast of his prowess.'

'Then I will not embarrass him by speaking of it,' Yakub agreed ruefully.

So they came down to the river. Hundreds of horses and camels were spread out along the bank, drinking. Others were grazing on the green growth that bordered it. Men were filling their waterskins, and some were bathing in the shallows.

Penrod picked out a spot on the bank that was well away from any of these people. They hobbled the camels and let them drink while they filled the waterskins and cut bundles of fresh grass. They turned the hobbled camels loose to graze, and built a small cooking fire. They roasted the trio of quail, golden brown and oozing fragrant juices. Then Yakub went to the cow camel and milked her into a bowl. He warmed the milk and they washed down with it a round of dhurra bread topped with a slice of the cheese, which reeked more powerfully than the goat that had produced it. They ended the meal with a handful of dates and apricots. It was tastier fare than Penrod had ever enjoyed in the dining room of the Gheziera Club.

Afterwards they lay under the stars with their heads close together. 'How far are we from the town of Abu Hamed?' Penrod asked.

With his spread fingers Yakub indicated a segment of the sky.

'Two hours.' Penrod translated the angle to time. 'Abu Hamed is where we must leave the river and cut across the bight to the Wells of Gakdul.'

'Two days' travel from Abu Hamed.'

'Once we pass the vanguard of the Dervish, we will be able to travel at better speed.'

'It will be great pity to kill the camels.' Yakub rose up on one elbow and watched them grazing nearby. He whistled softly and the cream-coloured cow wandered over to him, stepping short against her hobble. He fed her one of the rounds of dhurra cake and stroked her ear as she crunched it up.

'O compassionate Yakub, you will cut a man's throat as happily as you break wind, but you grieve for a beast who was born to die?' Penrod rolled on to his back and spread his arms like a crucifix. 'You stand the first watch. I will take the second. We will rest until the moon is at its zenith. Then we will go on.' He closed his eyes and began almost at once to snore softly.

When Yakub woke him, the midnight chill had already soaked through his woollen cloak and he looked to the sky. It was time. Yakub was ready. They stood up and, without a word, went to the camels, loosened the hobbles and mounted up.

The watchfires of the sleeping army guided them. The smoke lay in a dense fog along the wadis, and concealed their movements. The pads of the camels made no sound, and they had secured their baggage with great care so that it neither creaked nor clattered. None of the sentries challenged them as they passed each encampment.

Within the two hours that Yakub had predicted they passed the village of Abu Hamed. They kept well clear, but their scent roused the village dogs,

9

whose petulant yapping faded as they left the river and struck out along the ancient caravan route that crossed the great bight of the Nile. By the time dawn broke they had left the Dervish army far behind.

In the middle of the next afternoon they couched the camels in the lengthening shadow of a small volcanic hillock and fed them on the fodder they had cut on the riverbank. Despite the severity of the march the camels ate hungrily. The two men examined them at rest but found no ominous swellings on their limbs or shale cuts on their pads.

'They have travelled well, but the hard marches lie ahead.'

Penrod took the first watch and climbed to the top of the hillock so that he could overlook their back trail. He panned his telescope over the south horizon in the direction of Abu Hamed, but could pick out no dustcloud or any other sign of pursuit. He built a knee-high wall of loose volcanic rocks to screen himself in this exposed position, and settled comfortably behind it. For the first time since they had left the Nile he felt easier. He waited for the cool of the evening, and before the sun reached the horizon he sat up and once more glassed the southern horizon.

It was only a yellow feather of dust, small and ephemeral, showing almost coyly for a few minutes, then dissipating and fading away as though it were merely an illusion, a trick of the heated air. Then it materialized again, and hovered in the heat, like a tiny yellow bird. 'On the caravan road, fairly on our tracks, the dust rises over soft ground and subsides again when the trail crosses shale or lava beds.' He explained to himself the intermittent appearance of the dustcloud. 'It seems that al-Noor's memory has returned at last. Yet these cannot be horsemen. There is no water. Camels are the only animals that can survive out here. There are no camels in the Dervish army that can run us down. Our mounts are the swiftest and finest.'

He stared through the lens of his telescope but could make out nothing under the dust. Still too far off, he thought. They must be all of seven or eight miles away. He ran down the hill. Yakub saw him coming and could tell from his haste that trouble was afoot. He had the camels saddled and loaded before Penrod reached them. Penrod jumped into his saddle and his mount lurched up, groaning and spitting. He turned her head northwards, and urged her into trot.

Yakub rode up alongside him. 'What have you seen?'

'Dust on our backtrail. Camels.'

'How can you tell that?'

'What horse can survive so far from water?'

'When the aggagiers are in hot pursuit of either elephant or men, they use both their camels and their horses. At the beginning of the hunt they ride the camels, and also use them to carry the water. That is how they save the horses until they have their quarry in sight. Then they change to them for the final chase. You have seen the quality of their horses. No camel can run against them.' He looked back over his shoulder. 'If those are the aggagiers of Osman Atalan, they will have us in sight by dawn tomorrow.'

They rode on through the night. Penrod gave no thought to conserving the water in the skins. A little before midnight they stopped just long

11

enough to give each animal two bucketfuls of water. Penrod stretched out on the ground and used an inverted milk bowl as a sounding board to pick up the reverberation of distant hoofs. When he placed his ear against it, he could hear nothing. He did not allow this to lull him into complacency. Only when they sighted the pursuers at dawn would they know how far they were trailing behind them. They wasted no time and padded on through the desolation and the hissing silence of the desert.

As the first soft light of dawn gave definition to the landscape Penrod halted again. Once again he was prodigal with the remaining water, and ordered Yakub to give each of the camels two more buckets and the remainder of the fodder.

'At this rate, we will have emptied the skins by this evening,' Yakub grumbled.

'By this evening we will either have reached the Wells of Gakdul, or we will be dead. Let them drink and eat. It will lighten their load, and give strength to their legs.'

He walked back a hundred yards and once again used the milk bowl as a sounding cup. For a few minutes he heard nothing, and grunted with relief. But some deep instinct made him linger. Then he heard it, a tremble of air within his eardrum, so faint it might been a trick of the dawn breeze sweeping over the rocks. He wetted his forefinger and held it up. There was no wind.

He lowered his head to the bowl, cupped his hands round his ear and closed his eyes. Silence at first. He took a deep breath and held it. At the outer reaches of his hearing there was a susurration, like fine sand agitated gently in a dried gourd, or the breathing of a beloved woman sleeping at his side in the watches of the night. Even in this fraught situation an image of Rebecca flared in his memory, so young and lovely in the bed beside him, her hair spread over them both like cloth of gold. He thrust away the picture, stood up and went back to the camels. 'They are behind us,' he said quietly.

'How far?' Yakub asked.

'We will be able to see them clearly in the first rays of the sun.' They both glanced into the east. The sun cast a nimbus around a distant hilltop, as though it were the rugged head of an ancient saint.

'And they will see us just as clearly.' Yakub's voice was husky and he cleared his throat.

'How far to the Wells of Gakdul?' Penrod asked.

'More than half a day's ride,' Yakub answered. 'Too far. On those horses they will catch us long before we reach the wells.'

'What terrain lies ahead? Is there a place for us to take cover where we might evade them?'

'We approach the Tirbi Kebir.' Yakub pointed ahead. 'There is good reason why it is called the Great Graveyard.' This was one of the most formidable obstacles along the entire crossing of the bight. It was a salt pan twenty miles across. The surface was level as a sheet of frosted glass, unmarred by a single ripple or undulation, other than the broad indentation of the caravan road. Both its verges were outlined by the skeletons of the men and camels who, over the centuries, had perished along the way. The noon sunlight reflecting off the diamond white salt crystals lit the noonday sky with a glare that could be seen from many leagues in every direction. A camel standing in the centre of this great white place could be

13

clearly recognized from the perimeter. The unrelenting sunlight, reflected and magnified by the shining surface, could roast man and beast like a slow fire.

'There is no other way forward. We must go on.' They put the camels to the crossing. Refreshed by the copious draughts of water and the fodder they had eaten they paced out strongly. As the daylight strengthened, the sky ahead became incandescent, like a metal shield raised to white heat in the forge of Vulcan. Abruptly they left the area of dunes and undulated gravel hills, and rode out on to the pan. With theatrical timing the sun soared out above the eastern hills and struck into their faces with its stinging lash. Penrod could feel it sucking the moisture from his skin and frying the contents of his skull. He groped in his saddlebag and brought out a piece of curved ivory into which he had carved horizontal eye slits so narrow that they blocked out most of the reflected glare. He had copied this from an illustration in the book of Arctic travel by Clavering and Sabine that depicted a native Eskimo of Greenland wearing such a contrivance, carved from whalebone, to ward off snow blindness.

Under the goads, the camels broke into the gait that the Arabs called 'drinking the wind', a long striding trot that sent the miles swiftly behind them. With every few strides either Penrod or Yakub swivelled round and stared back into the shimmering glare.

When the enemy came it was with shocking suddenness. At one moment the pan behind them was bare and white with not the least sign upon it of man or beast. At the next the Dervish column

14

poured out from among the gravel hills and rode on to the white expanse. The weird play of sunlight created an illusion of perspective and foreshortened distances. Although they were still several miles away, they seemed so close that Penrod fancied he could make out the features of each individual.

As Yakub had predicted they were riding camels, pack camels: the aggagiers sat up in front of the huge balloon-like waterskins. Each rider led his horse behind him on a long rein. Osman Atalan was on the leading camel. The folds of his green turban covered his lower face, but his seat in the saddle was unmistakable, head held high and shoulders proud. Beside him rode al-Noor. Bunched up behind the leading pair Penrod counted six more aggagiers. Both sides spotted each other in the same instant. If the pursuers shouted it was too far for the sound to reach him.

Without undue haste the aggagiers dismounted from their camels. Two men were acting as camel-handlers and they gathered up the reins. Osman and each of his men led out a horse and watered it. Then the aggagiers tightened the girths and swung up into the saddle. This changeover took only the time that a Red Sea diver might hold his breath when he goes down to fill his net with pearl oysters from the deep coral reef. Then the horsemen bunched up and came across the shimmering salt surface at an alarming pace.

Penrod and Yakub leant forward in their saddles and, with thrusting movements of their hips, urged their mounts to the top of their speed. The camels reached out in a long-legged gallop. For a mile and then another the two bands raced on, neither gaining nor faltering. Then Hulu Mayya, Osman's cream-coloured mare, broke from the pack. She came on with her mane and long golden tail floating in the wind, a pale wraith against the dazzling plain of salt.

Penrod saw almost at once that no camel could hold off this horse over any distance, and he knew the tactics Osman would adopt: he would ride up behind them and hamstring their camels on the run. Penrod tried to conjure up a plan to counter this. He could not rely on a lucky bullet to bring down the mare. Perhaps instead he should let her come close, then turn back unexpectedly, taking Osman by surprise, and use his camel's height and weight to rush down on the mare. He might be able to force a collision that would inflict such injury on her that she would be out of the race. In truth, he knew that such a plan was futile: the mare was not only fleet but nimble; Osman was probably the most skilled horseman in all the Dervish ranks. Between them they would make a mockery of any clumsy charge he could mount. If by some remote chance he succeeded in crippling the mare, the rest of the Beja aggagiers would be upon them in the next instant, their long blades bared.

The tail of the green turban had blown clear of Osman's face and now he was so close that Penrod could make out his features clearly. The crisp curls of his beard were smoothed back by the wind of the mare's run. His gaze was locked on Penrod's face.

'Abadan Riji!' Osman called. 'This is our moment. It is written.'

Penrod drew the Martini-Henry carbine from its boot under his knee, and half turned in the saddle. He could not make the full turn and face his enemy

16

to mount the rifle to his shoulder, without throwing his camel off balance. He swung up the rifle with his right hand, as though it was a pistol and tried to settle his aim. The camel lurched and jerked under him, and the rifle barrel made wild and unpredictable circles. At the full reach of his right arm the muscles strained and tired swiftly. He could hold his aim no longer, and fired. The recoil jarred his wrist and the trigger guard smashed back into his fingers. His aim was so wild that he did not mark the flight or strike of the bullet. Osman's replying laughter was natural and easy. He was so close now that his voice carried over the sound of hoofs and the rush of the wind.

'Put up your gun. We are warriors of the blade, you and I.' His mare came on apace, now so close that Penrod could see the white froth flying from the snaffle between her jaws. The scabbard of Osman's broadsword was trapped under his left knee. He reached down and drew out the blade, then held up its shining length for Penrod to see. 'This is a man's weapon.'

Penrod felt the strong temptation to respond to his challenge and take him on with the sword. But he knew that more was at stake than pride and honour. The fate of an army of his countrymen, the city of Khartoum and all within the walls—Rebecca Benbrook too—hung on the outcome of this race. Duty dictated that he must eschew any heroics. He ejected the empty case from the breech of his rifle, and took another round from his bandolier to replace it. He locked the breech-block but before he could turn back to fire again, Osman Yakub called to him in urgent tones. He glanced at him, and saw that he was pointing ahead, standing high

17

in the saddle, waving his arms above his head, screaming in wild excitement.

Penrod followed the direction of his finger and his heart bounded. Out of the white glare of the salt pan ahead a squadron of mounted men appeared, their camels racing towards him on a converging track. There was no mistaking that their intentions were warlike. How many? he wondered. In the clouds of white dust it was impossible to guess but they came on, rank upon rank. A hundred, if not more, he realized, but who were they? Not Arabs! That's certain. Hope stirred. None of them wore the *jibba*, and their faces were unbearded.

They rushed towards each other, and Penrod saw the khaki of their tunics and the distinctive shape of their pith helmets. 'British!' he exulted. 'Scouts from Stewart's Camel Corps.'

Penrod swivelled in the saddle and looked back. Osman was standing tall in his stirrups, peering at the approaching ranks. Behind him his aggagiers had reined down from the charge and were milling in confusion. Penrod looked ahead again and saw that the commander of the Camel Corps had ordered a halt. His men were dismounting and couching their camels to form the classic square. It was done with precision. The camels knelt in an unbroken wall, and behind each crouched the rider, with rifle and bayonet presented across his animal's back. The white faces, although tinted by the sun, were cleanshaven and calm. Penrod felt a breathtaking surge of pride. These men were his comrades, the flowering of the finest army on earth.

He ripped the turban from his head to show

18

them his face, then waved the cloth over his head. 'Hold your fire!' he yelled. 'British! I am British!' He saw the officer standing behind the first rank of troopers, with drawn sword, step forward and give him long, hard scrutiny. Now he was only a hundred and fifty paces from the square. 'I am a British officer!'

The other man made an unmistakable gesture with his sword, and Penrod heard his order repeated by the sergeants and non-commissioned officers: 'Hold your fire! Steady, the guards! Hold your fire.'

Penrod looked back again, and saw that Osman was close behind him. Although his aggagiers were still in confusion, he was charging alone into the face of a British square.

Again Penrod raised the carbine and aimed at Osman's mare. He knew that this was the one thing that might turn him aside. Now they were no more than three lengths apart, and even from the unstable back of a galloping camel Penrod's carbine was a deadly menace. Nevertheless, if he had aimed at the man, Osman would not have been daunted by it. But by this time Penrod had learnt enough about him to know that he would not push the mare into the muzzle of the rifle.

Osman reined back, his face furrowed with rage. 'I was wrong about you, coward,' he shouted.

Penrod felt his own rage flare. 'There will be another time,' he promised.

'I pray God that it is so.' Within sixty yards of the British square Osman turned. He brought the mare down to a trot and rode away to rejoin his aggagiers.

The square opened to let in Penrod, Yakub

following. He rode up to the officer and slid to the ground.

'Good morning, Major.' He saluted, and Kenwick stared at him in astonishment.

'Ballantyne, you do turn up in odd places. You might have got yourself shot.'

'Your arrival was at a most appropriate moment.'

'I noticed you were having a spot of bother. What in the name of the Devil are you doing out here in the middle of the blue?'

'I have despatches from General Gordon for General Stewart.'

'Then you are in luck. We are the advance guard. General Stewart is with the main body of the relief column, not more than an hour behind us.' He looked out over the camels and the kneeling men at the front of his square. 'But first things first. Who was the Dervish bounder chasing after you?'

'One of their emirs. Fellow called Osman Atalan, head of the Beja tribe.'

'My solemn oath! I've heard of him. He's a nasty piece of work, by all accounts. We had better deal with him.' He strode away towards the front of the square. 'Sergeant Major! Shoot that fellow.'

'Sir!' The sergeant major was a burly figure with a magnificent pair of moustaches. He picked out two of the his best marksmen. 'Webb and Rogers, shoot that Dervish.'

The two troopers leant across the backs of their couched camels and took aim. 'In your own time!' the sergeant major told them.

Penrod found he was holding his breath. He had told Kenwick of Osman's position and rank to discourage just such an order. He had vaguely hoped that some chivalrous instinct might have dissuaded Kenwick from shooting down an emir. At Waterloo, Wellington would never have ordered his sharpshooters to make Bonaparte their target.

One of the troopers fired but Osman was riding steadily away and the range was already over five hundred yards. The bullet must have passed close for the mare swished her tail as though to drive off a tsetse fly. But Osman Atalan did not deign even to look back. Instead he deliberately slowed his horse to a walk. The second trooper fired and this time they saw dust fly. Again the bullet had missed by very little. Osman continued to walk the mare away. Each marksman fired two more shots at him. By then he was out of range.

'Cease firing, Sergeant Major,' Kenwick snapped. Then, in an aside to Penrod, 'Damned fellow has the luck of the fox,' he was smiling thinly, 'but you have to admire his cool performance.'

'We will almost certainly be treated to other virtuoso performances in the near future,' Penrod agreed.

Kenwick glanced at him, sensing the note of censure in his tone. 'A sporting sentiment, Ballantyne. However, I do believe that one should not accord too much respect to the enemy. We must bear in mind that we are here to kill them.'

And vice versa. But Penrod did not say it aloud.

In the distance they watched Osman Atalan join up with his aggagiers and ride away southwards towards Abu Hamed.

'Now,' said Kenwick, 'General Stewart will probably be pleased to see you.'

21

'And vice versa, sir.' This time Penrod voiced the thought.

Kenwick scribbled a note in his despatch book, tore out the page and handed it to him. 'If you wander around the countryside dressed like that, it's likely you'll be shot as a spy. I shall send young Stapleton back with you. Please inform General Stewart that we're making good progress and, apart from this Atalan fellow, we have made no other contact with the enemy.'

'Major, please do not be lulled into believing that happy state of affairs will persist much longer. For the last several days I have been riding in company with a vast concourse of the Dervish. All of them are coming this way.'

'How large a force?' Kenwick asked.

'Difficult to say for certain, sir. Too many to count. However, I would estimate somewhere between thirty and fifty thousand.'

Kenwick rubbed his hands with glee. 'So, all in all, you might say that we are in for an interesting few days.'

'You might indeed, sir.'

Kenwick called over a young ensign, the lowest rank of commissioned officer. 'Stapleton, go back with Captain Ballantyne, and see him through the lines. Don't get him or yourself shot.'

Percival Stapleton gazed at Penrod with awe. He was not much more than seventeen, fresh-faced and eager as a puppy. The two rode back, with Yakub, along the ancient caravan road. For the first few miles Percy was struck dumb with hero-worship. Captain Ballantyne was a holder of the Victoria Cross, and to have the honour of riding with him was the pinnacle of his sixteen months of military experience. Over the next mile he summoned up his courage and addressed a few respectful remarks and questions to him. He was highly gratified when Penrod responded in a friendly fashion, and Percy became relaxed and chatty. Penrod recognized him as a prime source of information, encouraged him to speak freely, and quickly picked up most of the regimental gossip from him. This was highly coloured by Percy's pride in the regiment, and his almost delirious anticipation of going into action for the first time.

'Everybody knows that General Stewart is a fine soldier, one of the best in the entire army,' the youngster informed him importantly. 'All the men under his command have been drawn from the first-line regiments of guards and fusiliers. I am with the Second Grenadiers.' He sounded as though he could hardly believe his good fortune.

'Is that why General Gordon has been waiting so long in Khartoum for your arrival?' Penrod needled the boy with surgical skill.

Percy bridled. 'The delay is not the general's fault. Every man in the column is as keen as mustard, and spoiling for a fight.' Penrod lifted an eyebrow, and the boy rushed on hotly: 'Because of the haste with which the politicians in London forced us to leave Wadi Halfa, we were obliged to wait at Gakdul for the reinforcements to reach us. We were less than a thousand strong and the camels were sick and weak from paucity of fodder. We were in no fit state to meet the enemy.'

'What is the position now?'

'The reinforcements arrived only two days ago from Wadi Halfa. They brought up fodder, fresh camels and the provisions we were lacking. The general ordered the advance at once. Now we have men enough to do the job,' he said, with the sublime confidence of the very young.

'How many is enough?' Penrod asked.

'Almost two thousand.'

'Do you know how many Dervish there are?' Penrod asked, with interest.

'Oh, quite a few, I shouldn't wonder. But we are British, don't you see?'

'Of course we are!' Penrod smiled. 'There is nothing else to say, is there?'

They topped the next rise and on the stony plain ahead appeared the main body. It was advancing in a compact square formation, with the pack camels in the centre. There appeared to be many more than two thousand. They came on at a good steady rate, and it was clear that they were under firm command.

With young Percy in uniform to smooth the way, the pickets let them into the marching square. A party of mounted staff officers was coming up behind the front rank. Penrod recognized General Stewart. He had seen him at Wadi Halfa, but had not been presented to him. He was a handsome man, stiff-backed and tall in the saddle, exuding an air of confidence and command. Penrod knew the man at his side rather better: he was Major Hardinge, the Camel Corps senior intelligence officer. He pointed at Penrod and spoke a few words to the general. Stewart glanced in Penrod's direction and nodded.

Hardinge rode over. 'Ah, Ballantyne, the traditional bad penny.'

'Penny now worth at least a shilling, sir. I have despatches from General Gordon in Khartoum.'

'Have you, my goodness? That's a guinea's worth. Come along. General Stewart will be pleased to see you.' They rode back to join the staff.

General Stewart motioned to Penrod to fall in alongside his own camel. Penrod saluted. 'Captain Penrod Ballantyne, 10th Hussars, with despatches from General Gordon in Khartoum.'

'Gordon is still alive?'

'Very much so, sir.'

Stewart was studying him keenly. 'Good to have your confirmation. You can hand over the despatches to Hardinge.'

'Sir, General Gordon would not commit anything to paper in case it fell into the hands of the Mahdi. I have only a verbal report.'

'Then you had best give that to me directly. Hardinge can take notes. Go ahead.'

'My first duty, sir, is to inform you of the enemy order of battle, as we are aware of it.'

Stewart listened intently, leaning forward in the saddle. His features were lean and suntanned, his gaze steady and intelligent. He did not interrupt Penrod while he reported the condition of the defenders in Khartoum. Penrod ended the first part of his report succinctly: 'General Gordon estimates that he can hold out for another thirty days. However, the food supplies have been reduced to well below survival level. The level of the Nile is falling rapidly, exposing the defences. He asked me to emphasize to you, sir, that every day that passes renders his position more precarious.'

Stewart made no effort to explain the delays he had encountered. He was a man of direct action,

25

not one who made excuses. 'I understand,' he said simply. 'Go on, please.'

'General Gordon will fly the flags of Egypt and Great Britain from the tower of Mukran Fort, day and night, while the city is still being defended. With a telescope the flags can be seen from as far downstream as the heights of the Shabluka Gorge.'

'I hope shortly to verify that for myself.' Stewart nodded. Although he listened to Penrod with attention, his eyes were constantly busy, watching over the orderly formation of his square as it moved steadily southwards.

'My journey from the city brought me through the midst of the enemy formations. I can give you my own estimate of their dispositions, if you consider that might be of use, General.'

'I am listening.'

'The commander of the Dervish vanguard is the Emir Salida, of the Jaalin tribe. He has probably fifteen thousand warriors under his red banner. The Jaalin are the northernmost tribe of the Sudan. Salida is a man in his late sixties, but he has a formidable reputation. The commander of the centre is the Emir Osman Atalan of the Beja.' Stewart narrowed his eyes at the name. Obviously he had heard it before. 'Osman has brought approximately twenty thousand of his own men from the siege of Khartoum. They have Martini-Henry rifles, captured from the Egyptians, and a great store of ammunition. As I am sure you are well aware, sir, the Dervish prefer to get to close quarters and use the sword.'

'Guns?'

'Although they have Nordenfelts, Krupps and plentiful supplies of ammunition in Omdurman, I

26

have seen none being brought north with this wing of their army.'

'I know you're an old hand at Arab fighting, Ballantyne, where will they meet us, do you suppose?'

'I believe that they will want to deny you the water, sir,' Penrod replied. In the desert everything came down sooner or later to that. 'The next water is at the Wells of Abu Klea. It is sparse and brackish, but they will try to prevent you using it. The approach to the wells is through a rocky defile. I would guess that they will offer battle there, probably as you debouch from the narrow way.'

Hardinge had the map ready. Stewart took it and spread it on the front of his saddle. Penrod pressed close enough to read it with him.

'Point out to me the spot where you think they may attack,' Stewart ordered.

When Penrod did so Stewart studied it for a short while. 'I had planned to bivouac tonight on the north side of Tirbi Kebir.' He placed his finger on the spot. 'However, in the light of this new information it may be better to force march today, and reach the head of the defile before dark. This will place us in a flexible position in the morning.'

Penrod made no comment. His opinion had not been asked. Stewart rolled the map. 'Thank you, Captain. I think you will be most useful with the vanguard under Major Kenwick. Will you ride forward again and place yourself under his command?'

Penrod saluted, and as he rode off Stewart called after him, 'Before you join Kenwick, go back and see the quartermaster. Get yourself a decent uniform. From here you look like a bloody Dervish

27

yourself. Somebody is going to take a pot at you.'

*   *   *

In the early-morning light, Osman Atalan and Salida sat at the top of the burnt-out hills of Abu Klea. From this vantage-point they overlooked a deep defile. They were seated on a fine woollen carpet, laid on the edge of the dragon's back ridge of black basalt rock. An almost identical ridge of the same dark rock faced them across the pass. At its narrowest point it was some four hundred paces across.

The Emir Salida of the Jaalin had known Osman since he was a stripling of seventeen. At that age Osman had ridden into Jaalin territory from the east with his father's raiding party. They had killed six of Salida's warriors and driven off sixty-five of his finest camels. Osman had killed his first man on that long-ago raid. The Beja had also abducted twelve Jaalin girls and young women, but these in Salida's eyes were insignificant against the loss of his camels. In the twelve years since then their blood feud had run red and rank across the desert.

Only since the Divine Mahdi, may he ever triumph over his foes, had called all the tribes of the Sudan to unite in the holy *jihad* against the infidel had Osman and Salida sat at the same campfire and shared the same pipe. In *jihad* all personal feuds were suspended. They were united by a common enemy.

A slave girl set the hookah between them. With silver tongs she lifted a live coal from the clay fire pot and placed it carefully on top of the black tobacco packed into the bowl of the pipe. She

28

sucked on the ivory mouthpiece until the smoke was flowing freely. She coughed prettily on the powerful fumes, and passed the mouthpiece to Salida, a mark of respect for his years. The water in the tall glass jar bubbled blue as he drew the smoke through it, held it in his lungs and passed the mouthpiece to Osman. The Mahdi had forbidden the use of tobacco but he was in Omdurman, and Omdurman was far away. They smoked contentedly, discussing their battle plans. When there remained only ash in the pipe bowl, they knelt and prostrated themselves in the ritual of morning prayers.

Then the girl lit another pipe, and at frequent intervals one of their sheikhs came up the ridge to report to them on the enemy movements and the disposition of their own regiments.

'In God's Name, the squadron of Sheikh Harun is in position,' reported one.

Salida looked at Osman from under hooded, sun-freckled eyelids. 'Harun is a fine fighting man. He has two thousand under him. I have placed him in the wadi where the buzzard perched yesterday evening. From there he will be able to rake the enemy rear when they come out on to the plain.'

A short while later another junior sheikh came up the steep slope. 'In the Name of God and the Victorious Mahdi, the infidels have sent forward their scouts. A patrol of six soldiers rode through the pass as far as the mouth. They gazed through their long glasses at the palm grove of the wells, then rode back. As you ordered, mighty Emir, we let them go unhindered.'

An hour after sunrise the final report came in, and all the Dervish forces were in the positions allotted to them.

'What of the infidel?' Salida asked, in his rusty high-pitched voice.

'They have not yet broken camp.' The messenger pointed to the head of the long defile. Salida offered his elbow to Osman, and his erstwhile enemy helped the old man to his feet. His joints were lumpy with arthritis, but once in the saddle he could ride and ply the sword like a young warrior. Careful not to show a silhouette against the early-morning sky, Osman led him solicitously to the edge of the cliff and they looked down.

The infidel camp was in full view less than two miles away. The previous evening the soldiers had thrown up a zareba of stones and thornbush around the perimeter. As always the camp was in the shape of a square. They had placed a Nordenfelt gun at each of the four corners, so it could throw down enfilading fire on the outer walls of the stockade.

'What machines are those?' Salida had never fought the Franks. The Turks he knew well for he had slaughtered them in their hundreds with his own hands. But these big, red-faced men were a different breed. He knew nothing of their ways.

'Those are rifles, which fire very fast. They can lay down fields of dead men, like grass under the scythe, until they grow hot and jam. It is necessary to feed them corpses to stop up their mouths.'

Salida cackled with laughter. 'We will feed them well today.' He made a wide gesture, 'The feast is ready. We await the honoured guests.'

The hills, valleys and narrow gullies appeared barren and deserted, but in truth they were alive with tens of thousands of men and horses, sitting on their shields, waiting with the patience of the hunter.

'What are the infidels doing now?' Salida asked curiously as his attention went back to the enemy camp.

'They are preparing for our attack.'

'They know that we are here, waiting for them?' al-Salida enquired. 'How do they know that?'

'We had a spy in our ranks. A *ferenghi* officer. A clever, crafty infidel. He speaks our sweet mother tongue, and passes readily as a son of the Prophet. From Berber he rode northwards with our array. Doubtless, he has counted our heads, divined our intentions and gone into the infidel camp.'

'What is his name? How do you know so much about him?'

'His name is Abadan Riji. He gave me the wound at El Obeid that almost carried me to my grave. He is my blood enemy.'

'Then why have you not killed him?' Salida asked, in a reasonable tone.

'He is slippery as a river eel. Twice he has wriggled through my fingers,' Osman said, 'but that was yesterday. Today is today, and we shall count the dead at the setting of this sun.'

'The infidel may not offer us battle this day,' Salida demurred.

'Look!' He passed Salida his telescope. The old man held it the wrong way round and peered through the large lens. Though he could see nothing but a vacant blue sky, he looked wise. Osman knew that he understood little of these infidel toys, so to spare him embarrassment he described the scene in the British camp for him.

'See how the quartermasters are passing down

31

the ranks handing out extra ammunition.'

'By God, you are right,' Salida said, and the telescope wavered several degrees in the wrong direction.

'See how they are bringing in the Nordenfelts.'

'In the saintly name of the Mahdi, you are right.' Salida bumped his eyebrow on the brass frame of the telescope, and lowered it to rub the spot.

'See how the infidel mounts up, and you can hear the bugles sound the advance.'

Salida looked up and, without the hindrance of the lens, saw the enemy clearly for the first time, 'By the holy name of the Mahdi, you are right!' said he. 'Here he comes in full array.'

They watched the British break camp and ride out. Their orderly ranks immediately assumed the dreaded square formation. They moved deliberately into the mouth of the defile, and no gaps appeared in their lines. Their discipline and precision were chilling, even to men of Osman's and Salida's temperament.

'For them there is no turning back. They must win through to the water or perish as other armies have done, swallowed by the desert.'

'I will not leave them for the desert,' declared Salida. 'We will destroy them with the sword.' He turned to Osman. 'Embrace me, my beloved enemy,' he said softly, 'for I am old and tired. Today seems a good day to die.'

Osman hugged him and kissed his withered cheeks. 'When you die, may it be with your sword in your hand.' They parted and moved down the back slope of the ridge to where the lance-bearers held their horses.

*   *   *

Penrod looked up at the stark black cliffs that rose on each side of them. They were barren as ash heaps from the pit of hell. As they moved into the gut of the defile the cliffs compressed and deformed their formations. But no gaps appeared in the sides of the square. Carefully Penrod scanned the cliffs. There was no sign of life, but he knew this was an illusion. He glanced across at Yakub. 'Osman Atalan is here,' he said.

'Yes, Abadan Riji.' Yakub smiled and his right eye rolled out of kilter. 'He is here. There is the sweet perfume of death in the air.' He drew a deep breath. 'I love it even more than the smell of fresh quimmy.'

'Only you, lascivious and bloodthirsty Yakub, could combine love and battle in the same thought.'

'But, Effendi, they are one and the same.'

They moved on down the narrow defile. Fear and excitement coursed like intoxicating wine through Penrod's veins. He looked around at the bluff, honest faces that surrounded him and was proud to ride in their company. The quiet orders and responses were given in the familiar accents of home, so diverse that they might have been different languages: the sounds of the Scottish Highlands and the West Country, of Wales and the Emerald Isle, of York and Kent, of the Geordies, the Cockney, and the elegant drawl of Eton and Harrow.

'They will be waiting for us on the far side of this pass,' Yakub said. 'Osman and Salida will want to work their cavalry in the open ground.'

33

'Salida is the emir of your tribe so you understand his mind well,' said Penrod.

'He was my emir, and I rode in his raiding parties with him and ate at his fire. Until the day his eldest son ravished my little sister and I took the dagger to them both, for it was she who enticed him. Now there is blood between me and Salida. If he does not kill me first, one day I will kill him.'

'Ah, patient and vengeful Yakub, this may be that day.'

They rode on through the narrow neck of the pass and the sides opened like the jaws of a monster on each side of them. Still there was no sign of life on the dead, seared hills, not a bird or a gazelle. The bugle sounded the halt, and the distorted square came to a jerky stop.

The sergeants rode down the ranks to redress them. 'Close up on the right!'

'Keep your spacing in the ranks.'

'Wheel into line on the left.'

Within minutes the integrity of the square was restored. The corners were at meticulous right angles and the spacings were precise. The lines of bayonets glittered in the relentless sunlight, and the faces of the waiting men were ruddy with sweat, but not one unhooked a water-bottle from his webbing. In this thirsty wilderness, to drink without orders was a court-martial offence. From the back of his camel Penrod surveyed the ground ahead. Beyond the funnel of hills it opened into a broad, level plain. The earth was carpeted with white quartz pebbles and studded with low, sun-blackened salt scrub. At the far end of this bleak expanse stood a tiny clump of palm trees that seemed to have fossilized with age.

Good cavalry country, Penrod thought, and turned his full attention back to the trap of hills on either hand. Still they were devoid of all life, yet seemed charged with menace. They quivered in the heat mirage like hunting hounds brought up short by the scent of the quarry, waiting only the slip to send them away in full tongue.

The cliffs were riven by gullies and wadi mouths, by rocky salients and deep re-entrants. Some were choked with rock and scree, others coated with sand like the floor of a bullring. Yakub giggled softly and indicated the nearest of these with the point of his camel goad. There was no need for him to speak. The tracks of a thousand horses dimpled the surface of the sand. They were so fresh that the edge of each hoofprint was crisply defined and the low angle of the sun defined it with bold blue shadow.

Penrod raised his eyes to the serrated tops of the hills. They were sharp as the fangs of an ancient crocodile against the eggshell blue sky. Then something moved among the rocks and Penrod's eye pounced upon it. It was a tiny speck and the movement was no more striking than that of a flea crawling in the belly fur of a black cat.

He brought his small telescope out of the leather saddlebag and focused on it, then saw the head of a single man peering down on them. He wore a black turban and his beard was black, blending well with the rock around him. It was too far to recognize his features but the man turned his head, perhaps to give an order to those behind him. Another head appeared beside his, and then another, until the skyline was lined with human heads like beads on a string.

35

Penrod lowered the glass and opened his mouth to shout a warning, but at that moment the air throbbed with the gut-jarring beat of the Dervish war drums. The echoes rebounded off the facing cliffs, and now the host of the Mahdi appeared, with miraculous suddenness, upon all the ledges, galleries and crests of the pass. The central figure stood clear upon the utmost pinnacle. His *jibba* sparkled white in the sun, and his turban was dark emerald green. He lifted his rifle with one hand and pointed it at the sky. The grey gunsmoke spurted high into the air like the breath of a breaching sperm whale, and the sound of the gunshot followed seconds later. A mighty shout went up from the serried Dervish ranks: '*La ilaha illallah!* There is but one God!'

The echoes shouted back: 'God! God! God!'

The bugle in the centre of the British square sang on a wild, urgent note, and the troops reacted with smooth, practised precision. Down went the camels, kneeling in orderly lines, forming at once the outer ramparts of this living fortress. The baggage animals and their handlers moved back and couched in a dense mass in the centre. They were the inner keep. Swiftly the gunners unloaded the Nordenfelt machine-guns from the pack-camels and staggered with them to the four corners, from where they could lay down enfilading fire along the front of each wall of the square. General Stewart and his staff stood in a group just within the front wall. The runners knelt close at hand, ready to race to any corner of the square with the general's orders.

A deadly silence fell upon this assembly of warriors. The Dervish ranks stared down upon

36

them, and time seemed frozen. Then a single Dervish horseman rode out from the stony mouth of the main wadi. At extreme rifle range, he stopped, facing the square. He raised the curved ivory war clarion, the *ombeya*, and its clear, deep voice resounded along the cliff.

From the mouth of every wadi and combe poured the Dervish host, rank upon rank, thousand upon thousand, camels and horses. They kept coming, wheeling into loose squadrons, facing the little square. Few man were dressed or armed in the same way: lance and spear, axe and round leather targe, rifle, jezail and the dreadful broadsword were poised. The drums started again, a slow rhythmic beat and the Dervish ranks started forward.

'Wait for 'em, lads.' The sergeants strolled down behind the front wall of the square.

'Hold your fire, boys.'

'No hurry. There's enough for everybody.' The voices were calm, almost jocular.

The drums beat faster and the Dervish lines broke into a trot, the Ansar in the front beginning to jostle each other to be first into the square. Faster still, and the dense, savage masses seemed to fill the valley floor. Drums crescendoed and hoofs thundered. The dust rose in a choking miasma. The war cries were shrill.

'Steady, boys, steady!' Calm English voices, responding to the pagan shrieks.

'Hold your fire, chaps!' Penrod recognized Percy Stapleton's clear, boyish voice as he called to his platoon. He was having great difficulty restraining his eagerness. 'Steady, the Blues!'

The scamp thinks it's the boat race. Penrod

smiled to himself. The drums pounded feverishly, and the *ombeyas* squealed and sobbed. Like the flood from a burst dam, the Dervish cavalry came straight at the British square.

'Get ready! Rolling volleys, lads,' called the sergeants.

'By the book now, my boys. Remember your drills.'

'Rolling volleys! Make each shot tell.'

Penrod was watching a sheikh on a rangy ginger camel. He had forced his way well ahead of the front rank of the charge. His mouth was wide open as he screamed, and there was a black gap in the line of his front teeth. He was a hundred yards from the face of the square, then seventy, then fifty, and coming on at a wild gallop.

The bugle rang out sweet and high.

'Rolling volleys. Front rank, fire!'

There was that brief pause, characteristic of highly trained troops, as each man steadied his aim. Penrod picked out the gap-toothed sheikh. The volley crashed out, astonishing the ear. The front rank of the charge shuddered to the shock. Penrod's man took the heavy bullet squarely in the chest, and flipped backwards from his high saddle. His camel slewed round and crashed into the two horses coming up behind it, bringing one down heavily.

'Second rank, rolling volleys. Fire.' Again the rifles crashed out. The bullets struck flesh with the sound of wet clay slung against a brick wall. The Dervish charge wavered, and lost impetus.

'Third rank, rolling volleys,' sang out the sergeants. 'Fire!' The bullets churned the Dervish into confusion. Riderless animals milled and shied.

Bearded warriors swore and struggled to break clear. Corpses and wounded men were trampled and kicked beneath the hoofs. At that moment the Nordenfelts added their spiteful chatter to the uproar. Their fire hosed down the line. Like a barracuda driving through a shoal of pilchards, it split them into small, isolated groups.

'Front rank, rolling volleys. Fire!' The orders were repeated. The troopers reloaded, aimed and fired, with the oiled precision of rows of bobbins on a carding machine. The charge stalled, broke, and the survivors streamed towards the cliffs. But before they reached them the drums called to them and the *ombeyas* sang: 'Go back! For Allah and the Mahdi, go back into the battle!'

Fresh squadrons streamed out from the rocks to swell their depleted ranks. They massed, shouted to God, and came again, tearing across the trampled field where so many of their comrades already lay. Charging in to break the British square.

But a British square does not break. The sergeants called the timing of those regular rolling volleys. The barrels of the Nordenfelt machine-guns began to glow like horseshoes in the blacksmith's forge.

Osman Atalan had told Salida, 'It is necessary to feed them corpses to stop up their mouths.'

The Nordenfelts gorged on human flesh, choked on it and one after another jammed. As their staccato chatter ceased so the Dervish cavalry pressed closer, right on to the thicket of bright bayonets. Still the volleys crashed into them. They struggled forward and were chopped down, until even their courage and resolve were exhausted. At last they shrank away and rode back to the cliffs.

* * *

Salida looked down on the unbroken square from the heights. 'These are not men,' he said, 'they are jinn. How does a man kill a devil?'

'With courage and the sword,' replied Rufaar, his eldest surviving son. Two other sons older than him had been killed in raids and tribal warfare, and one had died in a feud over a woman. That death was still to be avenged.

Rufaar was thirty-three, a child of the warrior blood. With his own sword he had killed fifty men and more. He was as his father had been at the same age: his ferocity was unquenchable. Three of his younger brothers stood behind him. They were of the same brood, and in their veins also Salida's blood ran true.

'Let me lead the next charge, revered father,' Rufaar pleaded. 'Let me shatter these pig-eaters. Let me cauterize this festering sore in the heart of Islam.'

Salida looked upon him, and he was pleasing to a father's eye. 'Nay!' He shook his head. The single word of denial cut deeper than any enemy blade ever had. Rufaar winced with the pain of it. He went down on one knee and kissed his father's dusty foot. 'I ask no other boon but this. Let me lead the charge.'

'Nay!' Salida denied him a second time, and Rufaar's expression darkened. 'I will not let you lead, but you may ride at my right hand.' Rufaar's face cleared. He jumped to his feet and embraced his sire.

'What of us?' His other three sons joined the chorus. 'What of us, beloved father?'

'You puppies may ride behind us.' Salida glowered at them to hide his affection. 'Perchance Rufaar and I may throw you some scraps from the feast. Now fetch my camel.'

*   *   *

'Stretcher-bearer!' The call came from a half-dozen points around the outer wall of the square, where troopers had been hit by random Dervish fire. Quickly the wounded were carried into the centre and the gaps were closed. The doctors operated amid the dust and flies, sleeves rolled to the elbow, blood clotting swiftly in the heat. The wounded who could still stand came back in their bandages to take their places in the square once more.

'Water-boys!' The shout went around the little square. The boys scurried about with the skins and spilled water into the empty felt-covered bottles.

'Ammunition here!' The quartermasters moved along the sides of the square, doling out the cardboard packets.

The gunners struggled to clear the blockages of the machine-guns. They splashed precious water over the barrels to cool them. It boiled off in clouds of hissing steam, and the metal crackled and pinged. But the actions were locked solidly, and though they hammered and heaved they would not budge.

Suddenly in the midst of all this frantic activity the bugle rang out again. 'Stand to!' shouted the sergeants.

'They are coming back.' The Dervish cavalry rode out from the fastness of the hills. Like a great wave building up beyond the surf, they lined up again along the foot of the hills, facing the square.

'There is your enemy.' Penrod murmured to Yakub. The red banner waved in the centre of the line, carried by two Dervish striplings.

'Yes.' Yakub nodded. 'That is Salida in the blue turban. The mangy jackal beside him is his son, Rufaar. I must kill him also. Those are some of his other brats carrying his flag. There will be no honour in killing them, no more than popping fleas between the fingernails, but it must be done.'

'Then we still have much work to do.' Penrod smiled as he broke open another paper box of cartridges and filled the loops of his bandolier.

'Salida is a clever old jackal,' Yakub murmured. 'By the sweet breath of the Prophet, he learns quickly. He saw how we broke their first charges. Look! He has hardened his centre.'

Penrod saw what he meant. Salida had changed his formation. His line was not evenly distributed. The flanks were only two ranks deep, but in his centre Salida had formed a hammer, a solid knot of six closely packed ranks.

*   *   *

On the other side of the square General Sir Herbert Stewart studied the emir through the lens. 'He appears very old and frail.'

'He is old, but not frail, sir.' Hardinge assured him. 'With only fifty men, he led the charge that broke up Valentine Baker's Egyptians at Suakin. That was less than two years ago. The old dog still

42

has teeth.'

'Then we shall have to draw them for him,' Stewart murmured.

'Here he comes, sir.'

'Here he comes indeed,' Stewart agreed.

*   *   *

The Dervish ranks rolled forward, the horses trotting and the camels pacing steadily, the men upon their backs brandishing their weapons and chanting their war cries. The dust storm trailed behind them. They crossed the half-way line, and broke into a canter. The lines bunched up like a clenching fist. Ahead the ground was littered with their own dead. They lay thickly as cherry blossom beneath the windblown trees of an orchard. Their harlequin *jibbas* bore fresher, darker stains than the decorative patches, and the blue flies rose in a cloud as the thunder of the charge shook the earth. The hoofs of the front rank trampled the corpses, scattering the bloody heaps into fresh confusion, and they came on without check.

In the centre Salida leant forward in the saddle of his grey camel. His rifle was still in its boot beneath his knee, but he handled the heavy broadsword as lightly as if it were a toy. He shouted no war cry, reserving his scant breath for the main business. His expression was ecstatic; the rheum from his bloodshot eyes ran down his cheeks into his silver-grey beard. He was an obvious target for the rifles that lay ahead. The first volley crashed into them, and men and animals were shot down. But Salida and his sons rode on untouched. Men pushed forward from the rear ranks to fill the gaps, and they were just in time to receive the next volley, and the next. But Salida rode on.

On the left flank a Nordenfelt machine-gun opened up, slicing through the front of the Dervish charge with bullets. Then, almost immediately, it jammed again and fell silent. But the Martini-Henrys crashed out in unison, keeping their terrible unhurried beat. Camels bellowed as they were hit and went down. Horses plunged, reared and fell backwards, crushing their riders. But in Salida's centre new men rode forward, keeping up the impetus of the charge. Salida reached the point twenty feet in front of the wall of the square where each of the previous charges had failed and floundered. Rufaar's knee touched his own, his other sons backed him almost as closely. Although three ranks of the Dervish centre had been shot away, brave men still poured forward to give the hammer weight as it swung towards the frail wall of the square.

'This time we will break these dogs.' Rufaar laughed.

But the British line never breaks. Now it gave a little, as a blade of Damascus steel will bend, but it did not shatter. A wave striking the solid coral reef, they washed over the front rank. Khaki-clad figures fell under the swinging blades, and the Dervish fired down into them from the backs of the camels. But gradually Salida's hammer lost its momentum. It slowed and stalled and at last spent its weight and fury against the second rank of the little square. The big men in sweat-soaked khaki tunics held them, then hurled them back.

The Dervish cavalry turned and streamed away towards the cliffs.

Salida was reeling on the saddle. A bayonet thrust had gone in deep above his hip bone. He might have fallen, but Rufaar reached across and, with one arm around his shoulders, steadied him and led him back to the shelter of the wadi. 'You are sore wounded, Father.' He tried to lift him to earth.

'The battle has only just begun.' Salida struck away his son's hands. 'Help me bind up this little cut, then we will ride back and finish the task that God and the Mahdi have set us.'

With his own long blue turban they bound up the old man's wound, so tightly that the flow of blood was stopped; and the bandages stiffened his back so that he could sit tall in the saddle once again.

'Start the drums,' said Salida. 'Sound the *ombeya*. We are going back.'

Osman Atalan rode up on Sweet Water, Hulu Mayya. His Beja division had been waiting in reserve, ready to ride in and exploit when Salida and his Jaalin forced the breach. 'Revered and warlike Emir, you have done more than any man before you. Now let me take in my Beja to finish the work you have begun so well.'

'I will force the opening,' Salida told him firmly. 'You can follow after me, as we agreed.'

Osman looked into that haughty face, and saw that there was no merit in argument. If they delayed here another minute the day was lost. The British wall had almost broken. If they struck again in the same place before it could recover, perhaps they could carry it away.

'Ride then, noble Emir. I will follow close behind you.'

The entire Dervish army, two full divisions,

poured out from the hills and advanced upon the little cluster of men on the open plain. In the van rode the emaciated figure in a bloody *jibba*, bareheaded, his grey hair covering his shoulders. His eyes glittered feverishly, like those of a saint or a madman.

*　　　*　　　*

'Gentlemen,' Stewart addressed his staff, 'we will move our station across to meet these fine fellows. I had not expected them to pound away at our rear wall like this. However, it seems that they are coming back for more of the same.'

They moved off in a group, just as Hardinge rode up to report. 'The Dervish did some damage with that last charge, sir. We suffered fifty-five casualties all told. Three officers killed—Elliot, Cartwright and Johnson. Another two were wounded.'

'Ammunition?'

'Still in good supply, but all four of the Nordenfelts are out of action.'

'Damned rubbish. I asked for Gatlings. What about the water?'

'Running low, sir. We must reach the wells before nightfall.'

'That is my intention.' Stewart pointed at the massed Dervish cavalry drawn up along the foot of the hills. 'It looks as though they are about to attack with everything they have. A last desperate throw of the dice. I want you to pass the order to the three other walls to have the quarter columns standing in reserve. Just in case these fellows get inside.'

'Oh, they'll never get in, sir.'

'Of course they won't, but see to the quarter columns nevertheless.'

During the battle the Dervish had hammered away at the northern wall of the square. The men in the other three walls had received only the very first charge. Since then they had taken little part. They were restless and frustrated. Now, in the face of this new threat, the sergeants strode down the ranks detailing the quarter columns. If the enemy broke one wall, the square must not be allowed to collapse in upon itself. The other three walls must stand firm, while every fourth man, the quarter columns, rushed to stop the gap and shore up the broken wall. Before they were ready the war drums began their frenetic rhythm, and the *ombeyas* brayed and blared. The Dervish cavalry rolled forward yet again.

With no troops under his direct command Penrod had time enough to squint up at the height of the sun through slitted lids. It's after noon, he thought, amazed. We have been in play for three hours and more.

Beside him Yakub was fretting: 'If Salida does not come to me, someone else will kill him first.'

'That will never do, gentle Yakub.' Penrod lifted his helmet, swabbed his brow with his kerchief and settled the helmet again at a rakish angle. Then he looked ahead as the rumble of hoofs and the babble of Arab voices swelled into the deafening overture of battle. They swept up to the threshold of the square.

'First rank, rolling volleys. Fire.' The sergeants began their chant and at regular intervals the massed gunfire thundered out. The ranks of

47

cavalry shuddered and shook as the volleys raked them, and their advance slowed under the dreadful punishment, but they came on and on, struggling over the last few yards until they struck the wall for the second time. Like raging bulls the two sides locked horns, swayed and pushed, thrust and hacked.

The British gave a little, then heaved themselves back. The white soldiers were adept with the bayonet. These weapons were longer reaching and quicker to recover than the swinging broadswords. For the second time that day Salida's division began to crumple. The soldiers plied the bayonets at close quarters, and some went down under the heavy crusader blades, but the rest tightened their grip and the Dervish gave ground more rapidly.

Then Osman Atalan rode in at the head of his fresh reserves. He came up behind Salida, and threw his full weight into the balance. His Beja were an avalanche and nothing could stand before them.

'They are in!' Along the British ranks a terrible shout went up. The unthinkable had happened. A British square had broken. The Dervish poured in exultantly. They drove back the khaki line and chaos descended on the dense maul and ruck of struggling men. Isolated British soldiers dropped and died under the Dervish blades, and were trampled beneath the hoofs.

'There is but one God!' the aggagiers shouted, as they killed and killed again.

The troopers of the shattered north wall were swiftly broken up into tiny groups of three and four men under the weight of Osman Atalan's aggagiers. As they were pushed back, Penrod ran forward to meet them, and gathered some of the strays to his own command. 'Form on me, lads. Back to back, shoulder to shoulder,' he shouted.

They recognized his authority and presence, and fought their way to him. As they came together they hardened into a cohesive whole, a prickly hedgehog of bayonets in the fluid fury of the fight.

Other officers were rallying the scattered troopers. Hardinge had gathered up a dozen, and the two bands melded. They were no longer a pair of tiny hedgehogs, but a fierce porcupine rattling steel quills.

An Arab on a tall black camel smashed into them, and before they could cut him down, he had lanced Hardinge through the belly. Hardinge dropped his sword and seized the lance shaft in both hands. The Arab still had hold of the butt. With a single heave Hardinge plucked him off his saddle. They fell in a tangle together. Penrod snatched up the sword Hardinge had dropped and rammed the point between the Dervish's shoulder-blades. Hardinge tried to rise, but the lance tip was deep in his guts. He tried to pull it out, but the barb held. He sank down again, bowed his head and closed his eyes, clutching the shaft with both hands.

Penrod stood over him to protect him and his troopers closed the gaps on either hand. It was good to have a fine sabre in his hand again. The blade had wonderful balance and temper: it came to life in Penrod's hand. Another Dervish rushed at him, swinging overhand with the broadsword. Penrod caught the heavy blade high in the natural line, and deflected it past his shoulder. It sliced open Penrod's sleeve but did not break the skin beneath. Before the Dervish could recover Penrod

49

killed him with a thrust through the throat. He had a moment to glance round: his little group was standing firm. Their bayonet blades were dulled, and their arms black with clotted Arab blood. 'Forward, lads,' Penrod called to them. 'Close the breach!'

'Come on, boys. Let's see these fellows off!' a familiar voice piped at Penrod's elbow. Percy Stapleton was beside him. He had lost his helmet and his curly hair was dark with dust and sweat, but he was grinning like a demented ape as he cut and thrust at another Dervish then hit him cleanly in the chest. Penrod saw at once that Percy was a practised natural swordsman. When a Dervish swung low at his knees, Percy jumped lightly over the blade and cut the Arab across the side of the neck, half severing it. The man dropped his broadsword and tried to grab at his throat with both hands. Percy killed him with a quick thrust.

'Well done, sir.' Penrod was mildly impressed.

'You are too kind, sir.' Percy flicked his hair out of his eyes, and they both looked round for another opponent.

But, quite suddenly, the Dervish charge ran out of momentum. It slowed and hesitated, heaved forward again, then ran up against the mass of couched camels of the British baggage train, and stopped dead. The two opposing sides clinched and leant against each other like exhausted boxers in the tenth round, too weary to throw another punch.

'Quarter columns, forward!' General Stewart took command of his reserves at this crucial moment when all hung in such fine balance. They wheeled in behind him. Sword in hand, he stalked ahead on long legs like a marabou stork. He led them round the bulwark of kneeling baggage camels and they took the stranded Dervish in their left flank. The scattered and exhausted bands of British troopers saw them coming, took new heart and hurled themselves back into the fray. The ruptured square began to contract, and repair the tear in its outer fabric.

Osman Atalan, with the sure instinct of the warrior, recognized the moment when the battle was lost. He turned his mare back, then he and his aggagiers fought themselves clear before the jaws of the trap could close on them. They galloped away to the safety of the hills and left Salida and his sons enmeshed in the British square.

Salida was still sitting high on his camel. But the wound above his hip had burst open again and blood was streaming down his legs. His face was yellow as the mud of a sulphur spring and the sword had fallen from his trembling hand. Rufaar sat up behind him and, with an arm round his waist, held him upright, despite the camel's terrified plunges. Salida was dazed by the lethargy of his wounds, and the shock of watching his younger sons die under the British bayonets He looked for them in childlike bewilderment, but their broken bodies were lost under the trampling hoofs.

Yakub saw an opening in the Dervish ranks as they turned to meet Stewart's reserves. 'I have private affairs to attend to, Effendi,' he called to Penrod, but Penrod and Percy Stapleton had found three more maddened Dervish to deal with and did not notice as he slipped away.

As Yakub ran up behind Salida's camel he scooped up a broadsword from the hand of a dead Arab. The animal was kicking and plunging, but

Yakub dodged the flying hoofs, which might have delivered a killing blow. With a powerful double-handed swipe he cut through the tendons in one of the beast's hind legs. It bellowed and lurched forward on three legs, but he ran after it and hacked through the other hamstring. The camel collapsed on to its hindquarters. Salida and Rufaar were hurled violently from its back. Rufaar kept hold of his father and tried to break his fall as they struck the ground at Yakub's feet.

Rufaar looked up and recognized him. 'Yakub bin Affar!' he said, and the bitter hatred of the blood feud roughened his voice. But he was holding his father with both hands and unable to defend himself.

'Mine enemy!' Yakub acknowledged, and killed him. He left the broadsword buried to the hilt in his chest, and drew his dagger. He caught a handful of Salida's silver beard and pulled his head back, exposing his throat. He did not hack at the windpipe, but drew the razor edge of the dagger across the side of the wattled throat. It sliced through the carotid artery under Salida's ear, and Yakub made no effort to avoid the jet of bright blood that spurted over his hands and arms.

'She is avenged,' he whispered as he daubed the blood on his forehead. He would not utter his sister's name for she had been a whore, and many good men had died because of her. He let go of Salida's beard and let his face flop into the dust. He left him lying beside his son and ran back to Penrod's side.

The breach in the British square closed on the Dervish like the mouth of sea anemone on a small fish that had swum into its tentacles. The Dervish asked no quarter. Martyrdom was the way to eternal life, and they welcomed it. Stewart's men knew that they would not surrender. Like a poisonous serpent with a broken back, they would strike at any hand extended to them, no matter how compassionately.

Relentlessly the soldiers plied the bayonet and the sword, but it was dangerous, bloody work, for each Dervish had to be surrounded and cut down. While there was life in them they fought on. The slaughter went on through the afternoon, raging at first, then gradually subsiding.

Even when it seemed to be over, it was not. Among the mounds of corpses individual Ansar were feigning death, poised to leap on any unwary victim. They lost a half-dozen more men to these furtive assassins before General Stewart ordered the advance. They gathered up their own casualties, and there were many. They took with them ninety-four wounded and seventy-four British corpses, wrapped in their own blankets, as they marched away towards the palm grove at the limit of the plain that marked the Wells of Abu Klea.

Among the palms they threw up a zareba, and buried their dead, laying them gently in rows in the shallow communal grave dug hastily in the sandy earth. It was evening before Penrod could go to find Hardinge in the hospital bivouac. 'I have come to return your sword, sir.' He proffered the beautiful weapon.

'Thank you, Ballantyne,' Hardinge whispered weakly. 'It was a gift from my wife.' His face was as pale as candlewax. They had moved his stretcher close to the fire, because he had complained of the cold. He reached out painfully and touched the blade, as if in farewell. 'However, I doubt I shall have much further use for it. Keep it for me, and use it as you did today.'

'I will not accept that, sir. You will march with us into Khartoum,' Penrod assured him, but Hardinge sagged back on to the stretcher.

'I think not,' he murmured. He was right: he was dead before daybreak.

The rest of the men were too exhausted to move on. Although he was haunted by thoughts of the great and lonely man waiting for them in Khartoum, Stewart could not drive them on in their present state. He gave them that night and most of the next morning to recover. They rested until noon in the scanty shade of the palm grove around the wells. The water was filthy, almost as salty as seawater. They boiled it with black tea and the last of the sugar.

In the enervating heat of midday Stewart dared delay no longer. He gave the order to continue the march. They loaded the seriously wounded on to the camels, and when the bugler sounded the advance they toiled away across the burning land. They marched on through the rest of that day, then on again through the night. They had covered twenty-three miles before sunrise, and then they stopped. They could go no further. They were utterly exhausted. There remained only a few cupfuls of water for each man. The camels were all played out: even though they could smell the river ahead, they could not go on. The wounded were in desperate straits. Stewart knew he would lose most of them unless he could bring them to the water. He sent a runner to summon Penrod. 'Ballantyne, I have need of your local knowledge again. How far is it to the river?'

'We are very close, sir, about four miles. You will be able to see it from the next ridge.'

'Four miles,' Stewart mused. He looked back over the exhausted British formation. Four miles might as well have been a hundred for all the hope he had of getting them there. He was about to speak again, but Penrod interrupted him.

'Look ahead, sir.'

Upon the ridge of higher ground that lay between them and the river a small band of fifty or so Dervish had appeared. All the officers reached for their telescopes. Through the lens Penrod at once recognized the banner of Osman Atalan. Then in the centre of the band he picked out his tall lean figure on the back of the cream-coloured mare.

'Not too many of them,' said Sir Charles Wilson, Stewart's second-in-command, but his tone was dubious. 'We should be able to brush them aside without too much trouble. I don't think they will have the temerity to come at us again, not after the lesson we gave them at the wells.'

Penrod was about to contradict him. He wanted to point out that Atalan was a clever tactician: he had pulled his men out of the lost battle at Abu Klea before they were utterly destroyed. During the previous day and night, his scouts must have shadowed the battered British square, waiting for this moment when they had used up all their strength and endurance and their camels were finished. With an effort Penrod bit back the words.

'You wanted to say something, Ballantyne?' Stewart had not lowered his telescope but he had been aware of Penrod's reaction.

'That is Osman Atalan himself on the cream horse. I think there are more than just that one troop. He got off comparatively lightly at Abu Klea. His divisions are almost intact.'

'You are probably right,' Stewart agreed.

'There is dust on the right,' Penrod pointed out. All the telescopes turned in that direction, and another group of several hundred more Dervish cavalry appeared upon the ridge. Then there was more dust further to the left. Swiftly the numbers of the enemy swelled from fifty to thousands. Their sullen squadrons stood squarely across the road to the Nile.

Stewart lowered his telescope and snapped it shut. He looked directly at Sir Charles Wilson. 'I propose to laager the baggage and the wounded here in a zareba, and leave five hundred able-bodied men to protect them. Then with a flying column of eight or nine hundred of the fittest men we shall make a run for the river.'

'The camels are done in, sir,' Wilson cut in quickly. 'They will never make it.'

'I am aware of that,' said Stewart, crisply. Privately he had come to think of his second-in-command as a man who could smell the dung in a bed of roses. 'We will leave the camels here with the wounded and proceed on foot.' He ignored the shocked expressions of his staff and looked at Penrod, 'How long would it take you lead us to the river, Ballantyne?'

'Without the wounded and the baggage I can have you there in two hours, sir,' Penrod answered, with all the confidence he did not feel.

'Very well. The company commanders will select their strongest and fittest men. We will march in forty minutes' time, at fifteen hundred hours precisely.'

*   *   *

'What kind of men are these?' al-Noor asked with wonder, as they sat on their horses and watched the depleted British square form up and march out of the zareba. 'They have no animals and no water and still they come on. In God's Holy Name, what kind of men are they?'

'They are descendants of the men who fought our ancestor Saladin, Righteous of the Faith, eight hundred years ago before Jerusalem,' Osman Atalan replied, 'They are men of the Red Cross, like the crusaders of old. But they are only men. Look upon them now and remember the battle of Hattin.'

'We must always remember Hattin,' agreed his aggagiers.

'At Hattin Saladin trapped an exhausted, thirst-crazed army of these men and destroyed it at a single blow. So great were the losses he inflicted upon the infidel that he tore from their bloody hands the entire kingdom of Jerusalem, which they had stolen from the faithful and held for eighty-eight years.' Osman Atalan rose in his stirrups and pointed the blade of his broadsword at the band of marching men, so tiny and insignificant on the stony grey plain. 'This is our field of Hattin. Before the setting of the sun we will destroy this army. Not one will reach the river alive. For the glory of Allah and his Mahdi!'

His aggagiers drew their swords. 'The victory belongs to God and his Mahdi,' they cried.

57

As the slow-moving British square climbed the gentle slope towards them the Dervish disappeared behind the ridge. The British toiled on. Every few hundred yards they halted to preserve the order of the wavering ranks and bring in their stragglers. They could not leave them for the Dervish and the castrating knife. Then they started again. In one of the pauses Stewart sent for Penrod. 'What lies beyond the ridge? Describe the ground ahead,' he ordered.

'From the ridge we should overlook the town of Metemma on the near bank,' Penrod assured him. 'There is an intervening strip of heavy scrub and dunes about half a mile wide, then the steep bank of the Nile.'

'Please, God, from the ridge let us also see Gordon's steamers moored against the bank and waiting to take us up to Khartoum.' As Stewart said it the ridge ahead was transformed. The entire length was sown with bright white puffs of powder gun-smoke, like a cotton field with ripe pods bursting open in the hot sunlight. The Boxer-Henry bullets began to whip around them, ploughing up the red earth and whining off the white quartz rocks.

'Should we not return their fire, sir?' Wilson asked. 'Clear that ridge before we move on?'

'No time for that. We must keep stepping out,' Stewart snapped. 'Pass the word for my piper.'

General Sir Herbert Stewart's personal piper, like his master, was a Highlander. His tartan was the hunting Stewart and he wore his glengarry at a jaunty angle, the ribbons dangling down his back.

'Give us a good marching tune,' Stewart ordered.

'"The Road to the Isles", sir?'

'You know my favourites, don't you, young Patrick Duffy?'

The piper marched twenty paces ahead of the front wall of the square, his kilt swinging and his pipes skirling the wild, outlandish music that inflames the warlike passions of all men who hear it. The bullets still whipped around them. Every few minutes a man was hit and went down. His comrades lifted him and carried him forward. The Dervish snipers retreated before the resolute advance until at last the ridge was silent and deserted. The square marched on towards it.

Suddenly the drums hidden behind the ridge began a deep bass beat that made the air tremble. Then the ground seemed to tremble in sympathy. To the rumbling thunder of hoofs, the Beja cavalry swept over the skyline ahead.

The square halted and tightened its formation, and the horde of horsemen rode into the first blast of gunfire and reeled back. The second and third volleys decimated them and they turned and galloped away.

The soldiers picked up their wounded comrades and started forward again. The next Beja charge thundered over the skyline. The drums thudded and *ombeyas* shrieked. The British laid down their wounded and dead, and formed up in the impenetrable walls. The charge broke against them and, like a retreating wave, fell back. The weary march resumed. They passed over the fallen Dervish, and to forestall the treacherous suicidal attack of the warriors feigning death, they bayoneted the living and dead bodies as they stepped over them.

At last, the front rank came out on the skyline. A hoarse cheer issued from their parched throats and they grinned with cracked, bleeding lips. Before them lay the broad sweep of the Nile. The surface of the river splintered the sunlight into myriad bright reflections like spinning silver coins. There, against the far bank, lay the pretty little steamers of Gordon's flotilla, waiting to take them upriver to Khartoum.

Some of the men sank to their knees, but their comrades hauled them to their feet and held them erect. Penrod heard a youngster croak, 'Water! Sweet God, water!' But his voice was gagged by his swollen purple tongue.

The corporal who supported him answered, 'The bottles are dry, but there is all the water you can drink down there. Brace up, lad! We're going down to fetch it. Ain't no blackamoor going to stop us either.'

'No stopping, lads,' the sergeant major called to them. 'Not until you wash off the stink of your sweat in yon wee stream.'

Those who were still able to laughed, and with a new lift in their weary stride they started down towards the Nile. Ahead stood an undulating series of low dunes, the last barrier before the river. The sands were multi-hued: cinnamon and chestnut, puce and chocolate. The hollows between them were thick with thorn scrub and saltbush.

Beyond the dunes, along the riverbank, lay the labyrinthine native town of Metemma. The narrow winding alleys, huts and hovels pressed right up to the water's edge. It was silent and deserted as a necropolis.

'The town is a trap, sir.' Penrod offered his

opinion diffidently. 'You can be certain that it is teeming with Dervish. If the men get into those alleys they will be cut to shreds.'

'Quite right, Ballantyne,' Stewart grunted. 'Make for the open stretch on the bank below the town.' The Dervish harassing fire still spurted and smoked from the tops of the dunes and from among the thick scrub in the hollows below them. Stewart took one step forward, then spun round as a heavy bullet thudded into him. He went down in a broken heap. Penrod knelt beside him and saw that the bullet had struck him in the groin, shattering the large joint of the femur. Shards of bone stuck out of the churned flesh, and blood bubbled over them. It was a wound that no man could survive.

Stewart sat up and thrust his clenched fist into the gaping hole in his flesh. 'I am hit,' he called urgently to Sir Charles Wilson. 'Take command, and keep the regiment pushing hard for the river. Let nothing stand in your way. Drive for the river with everything you have got.'

Penrod tried to lift him and carry him forward. 'Damn you, Ballantyne. Do your job, man. Let me lie. Take them on. You must help Wilson to get them to the river.'

Penrod stood up and two burly troopers rushed to the general.

'Good luck, sir!' Penrod said, and left him. He hurried to catch up with the front rank and lead them down into the dunes.

It did not seem that a squadron of cavalry could conceal itself in that low scrub, but as they came off the ridge, the bush ahead came alive with horses and figures in speckled *jibbas*. Within seconds the two sides were once more locked in savage, bloody conflict. Every time the soldiers drove them back with those flailing volleys, they reassembled and charged again. Now some of the white men in the front rank of the mangled British square were dropping, not from their wounds but from heat exhaustion and that terrible thirst. The men on each side hoisted them up again and pushed them forward.

The sweat dried in salt-ringed patches on their tunics; their bodies could no longer sweat. They reeled like drunks and dragged their rifles with the last of their strength. Penrod's vision wavered and darkened with cloudy shapes. He blinked eyes to clear his eyes, and each step was a monumental labour.

Just when it seemed that mortal man could endure no longer, the dense scrub ahead rustled and shook and out came the horsemen yet again. Riding at the head of the charge was the familiar figure in the green turban. The coat of the cream-coloured mare under him was dulled with sweat, her long mane matted and tangled. Osman Atalan recognized Penrod in the front rank of the square, turned the mare with his knees and rode straight at him.

Penrod tried to steady himself for his legs were rubbery under him. His light cavalry carbine seemed to have been transmuted to lead. It needed a painful effort to lift it to his shoulder. Even though they were still separated by fifty paces the image of his enemy, Osman Atalan, seemed to fill the field of his distorted vision. He fired. The sound seemed muted, and everything around him moved with dreamlike slowness. He watched his bullet strike the mare high in the forehead above the level of her magnificent dark eyes. She flung her head back and went down, struck the earth and rolled in a cloud of sand with her legs kicking spasmodically. She came to rest with her neck twisted back under her body.

With feline grace, Osman kicked his feet from the stirrups as she fell and sprang from her back to land lightly in balance. He stood and glared at Penrod with an expression of deadly hatred. Penrod tried to reload the rifle, but his fingers were numb and slow, and Osman held his eyes with a mesmeric spell. Osman stooped and picked up his broadsword from where he had dropped it. He ran towards Penrod. At last Penrod managed to guide the cartridge into the open breech and closed the block. He lifted the weapon and his aim wavered. He tried desperately to steady it, and when, for an instant, the bead of the foresight lay on Osman's chest he fired. He saw the bullet graze the emir's sword arm, and leave a bloody line across the muscle of his biceps, but Osman neither flinched nor lost his grip on the hilt of the broadsword. He came on steadily. Other troopers on either side of Penrod turned their rifles on him. Bullets kicked up sand or snapped through the scrub around him. But Osman's life seemed charmed.

'Kill that man!' shouted Wilson, his tone strident and nervous.

The rest of the Arab horsemen had seen their emir go down and their ranks broke up. One of his aggagiers swerved towards Osman's isolated figure. 'I am coming, master.'

'Let me be, Noor. It is not yet finished,' Osman shouted back.

'It is enough for this day. We will fight again.'
Without slowing his mount al-Noor leant out of the
saddle, linked arms with him and swung him up
behind his saddle.

As he was carried away into the dense scrub,
Osman glared back at Penrod. 'It is not finished. In
God's Name, this is not the end.' Then he was
gone. The rest of the Dervish cavalry disappeared
as swiftly, and an eerie silence fell over the field.
Some of the exhausted men in the British line sank
to the earth again, their legs no longer able to
support them, but the cries of the sergeants roused
them: 'On your feet, boys. There is the river in
front of you!'

Stewart's piper puffed up his bag and 'Scotland
the Brave' shrilled on the desert air. The men
shouldered their weapons, picked up their dead
and the square moved forward yet again.
Staggering along in the front rank, Penrod licked
the salt and dried blood from his cracked lips, and
the last few drops of his sweat burned his bloodshot
eyes as he searched the scrub ahead for the next
wave of savage horsemen.

But the Dervish had gone, blown away like
smoke. The British came out on to the high bank of
the Nile, and waved and shouted to the steamers
across the river. They were pretty as model boats
floating on the Serpentine on a bright Sunday
morning in London Town.

They had won through. They had reached the
river, and a hundred and fifty miles to the south in
Khartoum, General Charles Gordon still endured.

*　　*　　*

64

Osman Atalan waited in the village of Metemma for shattered divisions of his Jaalin allies to reassemble, for their sheikhs to come to him and place themselves under his command. But their own emir, Salida, and all his sons were dead. So brave when he led them, they were now like children without a father. Allah had deserted them. The cause was lost. They disappeared back into their desert fastnesses. Osman waited in vain.

At first light the next morning he called for the master of the pigeons. 'Bring me three of your fastest and swiftest birds,' he ordered. With his own hand he wrote out his message for the Mahdi in triplicate, one copy to be carried by each bird. If falcons or other misfortune struck one or even two, the vital message would still reach the holy man in Omdurman.

'To the Mahdi Muhammad Ahmed, may Allah protect and cherish him. You are the light of our eyes, and the breath of our bodies. My shame and sadness is a great rock in my belly, for know you that the infidel has prevailed in battle against us. Emir Salida is dead, and his division destroyed. The infidel has reached the Nile at Metemma. I am returning in all haste with my division to Omdurman. Pray for us, Holy and Mighty Mahdi.'

The pigeon-master tied the folded messages to the legs of the birds, replaced them in their basket and carried them to the riverbank. Osman went ahead of him. The pigeon-master handed the birds to him one at a time. Before he launched them, Osman held each in his cupped hands and blessed it. 'Fly swiftly and straight, little friend. May Allah protect you.' He tossed the bird into the air, and it rose on the clatter of wings, circled the little village of Metemma, then picked up its bearings and shot away on rapid wingbeats into the south. He let each pigeon get well clear before he sent away the next, lest they should form a flock that would attract the attention of the predators.

When they were gone he walked back to the village and climbed the mud dome of the mosque. From the top balcony of the prayer tower, whence the muezzin called the faithful to their devotions, he had a full view of both banks of the river. The cluster of small white steamers was still anchored downstream in the Pool of the Crocodiles. They were beyond his reach, for he had no artillery with which to attack them. Instead he turned his attention to the British camp. With the naked eye he could make out the men within the walls of their hastily constructed zareba. They had not yet made any effort to begin loading the steamers with either men or equipment. He wondered at their curious lethargy. It was much at variance with the energy and urgency they had displayed until now. If their goal was still to reach and relieve Khartoum as swiftly as possible they should have left their wounded on the riverbank, embarked their fighting men and sailed southwards without an hour's delay.

'Perhaps Allah has not yet forsaken us. Perhaps He will help me to reach the city ahead of these unpredictable men,' he murmured.

He went down from the tower to where the remnants of his division were waiting for him on the outskirts of the village. The horses and camels were already saddled and loaded, and al-Noor held his new steed. It was a big black stallion, the strongest animal in his string. Osman stroked the white blaze on his forehead. His name was al-Buq, the War Trumpet.

'You are without vice, Buq,' he whispered, 'but you could never match Hulu Mayya.' He looked back up the dunes to where she had fallen. The vultures and the crows still circled over the ridge. Will there ever be another animal as noble as she? he wondered, and the black tide of his anger flooded the depths of his being. Abadan Riji, you have much to atone for.

He swung up into the saddle and raised his clenched right fist. 'In the Name of Allah, we ride for Omdurman!' he cried, and his aggagiers thundered after him.

*   *   *

Khartoum lay in a torpor of despair, weak with plague and deprivation. The girls' voices were in penetrating contrast to the brooding silence around them.

'There's one coming.' Saffron sang out.

'I know. I saw it long ago,' Amber chanted.

'That's a lie. You never did!'

'I *did*!'

'Stop that squabbling, you two little harridans,' David Benbrook ordered sternly, 'and point it out to me.' Their young eyes were sharper than his.

'Over there, Daddy. Straight above Tutti Island.'

'Just to the left of that little cloud.'

'Ah, Yes. Of course,' David said, slipped the butt of the shotgun under his right armpit and turned to line up with the approaching bird. 'I was just testing you.'

'You were not!'

'Tut, tut. A little more respect, please, my angel.'

Nazeera heard their voices. She was on her way back to the kitchen carrying a pitcher of water that she had drawn from the well in the stableyard. She had been going to boil and filter it, but the voices distracted her. She set the pitcher on the table beside the front door next to the cluster of glasses on the silver tray, crossed to the window of the dining room and looked out over the terrace. The consul stood in the middle of the brown, burnt-out lawn. He was staring up into the sky. There was nothing unusual in this behaviour. For many weeks now he had spent each afternoon on the terrace watching for any bird to come within range of his shotgun. She turned back to the kitchen, but absentmindedly left the pitcher of unboiled water on the table with the glasses. Behind her she heard the thud of the gun and more excited squeals from the twins. She smiled fondly and closed the kitchen door behind her.

'You got him, Daddy!'

'Oh, clever paterfamilias!' This was Saffron's latest addition to her vocabulary.

The pigeon tumbled in the air as the pellets plucked a burst of feathers from its chest. It fluttered down and crashed into the top branches of the tamarind tree above the palace bedrooms. It stuck there, thirty feet above the ground. The twins raced each other to the base of the tree and clambered up it, arguing and pushing each other.

'Be careful, you little demons!' David called anxiously. 'You're going to hurt yourselves.'

Saffron reached the bird first. She was the tomboy. She balanced on the branch and stuffed the warm body into the front of her bodice and started down again.

'You are always so overbearing,' Amber accused her.

Saffron accepted the compliment without protest and jumped the last few feet to the ground. She ran to her father. 'It's got a note!' she shrilled. 'It's got a note just like the others.'

'Goodness gracious me, so it has,' David agreed. 'Aren't we lucky? Let's see what the gentlemen across the river have to say for themselves.' The twins danced after him as he carried the dead pigeon into the hall. He propped the shotgun against the wall and fumbled in his coat pocket for his *pince-nez* and clipped it on to the end of his nose. Then with his penknife he cut the thread that held the tiny roll of paper, and spread it carefully on the table beside the pitcher and the glasses. His lips moved silently as he deciphered the Arabic script, and slowly his benign expression changed. It became alert and businesslike.

'This is the most wonderful news. The relief column has smashed up the Dervish army in the north. Now they will be here within days. I must take this note across to the general right away,' he told the twins. 'Go in and ask Nazeera to pour your bath now. I will be a while, but I will come to your room to say goodnight.' He clapped his hat on to his head and set out down the terrace towards Gordon's headquarters.

Saffron snatched up the shotgun before Amber could reach it. She held it tantalizingly, like another trophy under her sister's nose.

'That's not fair, Saffy. You always do everything.'

'Don't be a baby.'

'I'm not a baby.'

'You are a baby, and you're sulking again.'

69

Saffron carried the shotgun across the lobby and into her father's gunroom. Amber watched her go with her clenched fists on her hips. Her face was flushed and her hair was sticking to her forehead with perspiration. She saw the pitcher on the side table where Nazeera had left it. With an angry flourish she poured herself a glass of water, drank it and pulled a face. 'It tastes funny,' she complained. 'And I'm not a baby and I'm not sulking. I'm just a bit cross, that's all.'

*   *   *

Ryder Courtney knew that his stay in Khartoum was drawing to an end. Even if the relief column arrived before the city fell, and was able to evacuate them all safely, the city would belong to the Dervish. He was clearing out the compound, ready to pull out at the first opportunity. Rebecca had volunteered to help him draw up an inventory and bills of lading for everything that was being loaded on board the *Intrepid Ibis*.

Ryder had become increasingly aware of the emotional turmoil she was going through. The uncertainty was wearing away at everyone's nerves, as conditions in the city deteriorated. The menace of the great army of the Dervish besiegers seemed to grow as the will of the trapped population declined and the relief column did not arrive. It had been ten months since the city had been invested by the Mahdi. A long time to live under the threat of horrible death.

Ryder knew how the responsibility of caring for her little sisters weighed upon Rebecca Her father was little help in this regard: he was amiable and affectionate but, like the twins, he relied on her with almost childlike faith. None of the Sudanese women had returned to work since the mob attack on the compound. The running of the little green-cake kitchen had devolved almost entirely upon Rebecca. The twins were willing helpers, but the grinding labour was beyond their strength and endurance. Ryder's admiration and affection for her were enhanced as he watched her struggle to take care of her family. He considered once again the fact at barely eighteen she had been saddled with this heavy load of responsibility. He understood how alone and isolated she felt, and tried to give her the help she needed. However, he was aware that his ill-considered unrestrained behaviour had damaged her trust in him. He had to be careful not to frighten her again, yet he longed to take her in his arms, comfort and shield her. He felt that since Penrod Ballantyne had left Khartoum he had made good progress in repairing their damaged relationship: she seemed so much easier in his company. Their conversations were more relaxed and she did not avoid him so obviously as before.

They were in the blockhouse, sitting at his desk across from each other. They were counting the piles of silver dollars into heaps of fifty, then wrapping them into rolls of parchment and packing them into wooden coffee chests, preparatory to taking them on board the *Ibis*. From the corner of his eye Ryder watched her brush back a strand of that beautiful silken hair. His heart ached as he noticed the calluses on her hands, and the little lines of worry and hardship at the corners of her eyes. A complexion like hers was more suited to the pleasant climes of England than to scorching sunlight and burning desert airs. When this is over, I could sell up here, and take her back to England, he thought.

She looked up suddenly and caught his eyes upon her. 'What would we do without you, Ryder?' she said.

He was astonished by the words and the tone in which they were spoken. 'My dear Rebecca, you would do well in any circumstances. I claim no credit for your strength and resolve.'

'I have been unkind to you.' She ignored his denial. 'I behaved like a little girl. You of all people I should have treated more kindly. Without you we might long ago have perished.'

'You are being kind to me now. That makes up for everything,' he said.

'The green-cake is just one of your valuable gifts to my family. I do not think it an exaggeration to say that with it you have saved our lives. We are healthy and strong in the midst of starvation and death. I can never repay you for that.'

'Your friendship is all the payment I could ask for.'

She smiled at him and the worry lines were smoothed away. He wanted to tell her how beautiful she was, but he bit back the words. She reached across the desk, spilling a stack of silver coins, and took his hand. 'You are a good friend and a good man, Ryder Courtney.'

For the first time she studied his face quite openly. He is not as beautiful as Penrod is, she thought, but he has a strong, honest face. It's a face one could see every day and not grow tired of. He would never leave me, as Penrod has. There would be no native girls hiding in a back room. He is a man of substance, not ostentation or pretence. There would always be bread on his table. He is a rock of a man and he would shelter his woman. The hand holding hers was powerful and competent, hardened with work. His bare arm reaching towards her was like the pillar of a house. His shoulders under the cloth of his shirt were broad and square. He was a man, not a boy.

Then, suddenly, she remembered where they were. Her smile crumpled. The precariousness of their lives rushed back upon her. What would happen if Ryder sailed away in the *Ibis* and left her and the twins here? What would happen to them when the Mahdi and his murderous army stormed into the city? She knew what they did to the women they captured. Tears swamped her eyes and clung to her lashes. 'Oh, Ryder, what will become of us all? Are we all going to die in this awful place? Dead before we have lived?' She knew in her woman's heart that there was only one certain way that she could bind a man like him to herself for ever. Was she ready to take that step?

'No, Rebecca, you have been so brave and strong for so long. Don't give up now.' He stood up and moved quickly round the desk.

She looked up at him as he stood over her, and the tears ran down her cheeks. 'Hold me, Ryder. Hold me!' she pleaded.

'I do not want to give you offence again.' He hesitated.

'I was a child then, a mindless girl. Now I am a woman. Hold me like a woman.'

He lifted her to her feet and took her gently in his arms. 'Be strong!' he said.

73

'Help me,' she answered and pressed close to him. She buried her face against his chest and inhaled his scent. Her terrors and doubt seemed to recede into insignificance. She felt safe. She felt his strength flowing into her, and clung to him with quiet desperation. Then, slowly, she was aware of a new, pleasant sensation that seemed to emanate from the centre of her being. It was not the divine and consuming madness that Penrod Ballantyne had evoked. It was, rather, a warming glow. This man she could trust. She was safe in his arms. It would be easy to do what she had contemplated.

This is something I must do not only for myself but for my family. Silently she made the decision, then said aloud, 'Kiss me, Ryder.' She lifted her face to him 'Kiss me as you did before.'

'Rebecca, my darling Becky, are you sure what you are about?'

'If you can speak only to ask daft questions,' she smiled at him, 'then speak not at all. Just kiss me.'

His mouth was hot and his breath mingled with hers. Her lips were soft and she felt his tongue slip between them. Once that had frightened and confused her, but now she revelled in the taste of him. I will take him as my man, she thought. I reject the other. I take Ryder Courtney. With that level-headed decision she let her emotions take control. She slipped the leash on all restraint as she felt something clench deep in her belly. It was a sensation so powerful that it reached the edge of pain. She felt it throbbing inside her.

It is my womb, she realized, with amazement. He has roused the centre of my womanhood. She pushed her hips hard against his, trying to ease the pain or aggravate it, she was not certain which. The last time Ryder had embraced her she had not understood what she had felt swelling and hardening. Now she knew. This time she was not afraid. She even had a secret name for that man's thing. She called it a tammy, after the tamarind tree outside her bedroom, which Penrod had climbed that first night.

His tammy is singing to my quimmy, she thought, and my quimmy likes the tune. Her mother, the emancipated Sarah Isabel Benbrook, had taught her the quaint word. 'This might be the last day of our lives. Do not waste it,' she breathed. 'Let us take this moment, hold it and never let go.' But he was diffident. She had to take his hands and place them on her breasts. Her nipples seemed to swell and burn with his touch.

She twisted the fingers of one hand into the hair at the back of his head to pull it down, and with the other hand she opened the hooks down the front of her bodice. She freed one of her breasts and as it popped out she pressed it into his mouth. She cried out with the sweet pain of his teeth on her tender flesh. Her essence welled inside her and overflowed.

She was overcome with a desperate sense of urgency. 'Quickly—please, Ryder. I am dying. Do not let me die. Save me.' She knew she was babbling nonsense, but she did not care. She clasped both her arms round his neck and tried to climb up his body. He reached behind her, took a double handful of the hem of her skirt and lifted it up round her waist. She wore nothing beneath it, and her buttocks were pale and round as a pair of ostrich eggs in the gloom of the shuttered room. He cupped them in his hands and lifted her.

She locked her thighs round his hips, and felt him burrowing into the silken nest of curls at the fork of her legs. 'Quickly! I cannot live another moment without you inside me.' She pressed down hard, screwing up her eyes with the effort, and felt all her resistance to him give way. She dug her fingernails into his back and pushed down again. Then nothing else in the world mattered: all her worries and fears dissolved as he glided in, impaling her deeply. She felt her womb open to welcome him. She thrust against him with a kind of barely controlled desperation. She felt his legs begin to tremble, and stared into his face as it contorted in ecstatic agony. She felt his legs juddering beneath them, and she thrust harder and faster. He opened his mouth and when he cried out, her voice echoed his. They locked each other in a fierce paroxysm that seemed as if it would bind them together through eternity, but at last their voices sank into silence, and the rigid muscles of his legs relaxed. He sank to the floor on his knees, but she clung to him desperately, clenching herself round him so that he could not slip out and leave her empty.

He seemed to return at last from a faraway place, and stared at her with an expression of awe and wonder. 'Now you are my woman?' It was half-way between a question and a declaration.

She smiled at him tenderly. He was still deep inside her. She felt marvellously powerful, deliciously lascivious and wanton. She tightened her loins, and gripped hard. She had not realized she was capable of such a trick. He gasped and his eyes flew wide. 'Yes,' she agreed, 'and you are my man. I will hold you like this for ever, and never let you go.'

'I am your willing captive,' he said. She kissed his lips.

When she broke off to draw breath he went on, 'Will you do me the great honour of becoming my wife? We do not want to shock the world, do we?'

Suddenly it was all happening very swiftly. Although this had been her intention, she could not think of a response both demure and yet binding upon him. While she considered it there was a loud knock on the blockhouse door. She pushed him away and hurriedly stuffed her breasts back into her bodice, looking anxiously towards the door. 'It is locked,' he reminded her in a whisper. With hundreds of pounds in coin lying on his desk, he had taken no chances. Now he raised his voice: 'Who is it?'

'It is I, Bacheet. I have brought a news bulletin from Gordon Pasha.'

'That is not important enough to worry me when I am busy,' Ryder retorted. Gordon issued his bulletins almost daily. They were designed to comfort the populace of the city and to bolster their will to resist. Thus his compositions were subject to wide literary licence, and were often separated from the truth by a considerable distance.

'This one is important, Effendi.' Bacheet's tone was excited. 'Good news. Very good news.'

'Push it under the door,' Ryder ordered.

He stood up and lifted Rebecca to her feet. They both adjusted their clothing: he buttoned the front of his breeches and she straightened her skirts. Then Ryder went to the door and picked up the crudely printed bulletin. He scanned it, then

77

brought it to her.

DERVISH ARMY ROUTED.
THE ROAD TO KHARTOUM IS OPEN.
BRITISH RELIEF COLUMN WILL ARRIVE WITHIN DAYS.

She read it twice, the first time swiftly, the second deliberately. At last she looked up at him. 'Do you think it is the truth this time?'

'It will be a cruel hoax if it is not. But Chinese Gordon is not renowned for his restraint or his consideration for the delicate feelings of others.'

Rebecca pretended to reread the bulletin, but her mind was racing. If the relief column was truly on its way, was the need for a permanent relationship with Ryder Courtney really so pressing? As his wife she would be doomed to spend the rest of her days in this wild, savage land. Would she ever again see the green fields of England and have the society of civilized people? Was there any desperate urgency to marry a man who was pleasant and would care for her, but whom she did not love?

'True or not,' Ryder went on, 'we shall find out very soon. One way or the other you will still be my fiancée. There is a full head of steam in the *Ibis*'s boiler and her hold is loaded with every stick of cargo it can carry—' He broke off and studied her face quizzically. 'What is it, my darling? Is something worrying you?'

'I have not yet replied to your question,' she said softly.

'Oh, if that is all, then I shall repeat it and hope for your formal response,' he said. 'Will you, Rebecca Helen Benbrook, take me, Ryder

Courtney, to be your lawful wedded husband?'

'In all truth, I do not know,' she said, and he stared at her, appalled. 'Please give me a little time to think about it. It is a momentous decision and not one I can rush into.'

In this pivotal moment on which so much depended, a thought suddenly occurred to her: If the relief column arrives the day after tomorrow, will Penrod Ballantyne be with them? Then she thought, It is of no account, one way or the other, for he no longer means anything to me. I made a mistake in trusting him, but now he can go back to his Arab girls and his philandering ways for all I care. But she found herself unconvinced by this, and the image of Penrod persisted in her mind long after she had left Ryder's compound and was on her way back to the consular palace.

*   *   *

It took Sir Charles Wilson several days to bring in all his wounded, the baggage and the camel string. In the meantime he fortified the camp on the riverbank below Metemma, siting the Nordenfelt machine-guns to cover all the approaches, and he raised the walls of the zareba to a height of six feet.

On the third day after the battle the chief regimental surgeon reported to him that General Stewart's wound had developed gangrene. Wilson hurried down to the hospital tent. The rotten sweet smell of necrotic flesh was nauseating in the heat. He found Stewart lying in a bath of his own sweat under a mosquito net over which the huge hairy blue flies crawled, searching for some point of entry to reach the irresistible odour of the wound.

It was covered with a field dressing, heavily stained with a custard-yellow discharge.

'I have managed to remove the bullet,' the surgeon assured Wilson, then lowered his voice to a whisper that the stricken man could not hear: 'The gangrene has a firm hold, sir. There is little or no hope, I am afraid.'

Stewart was delirious and mistook Wilson for General Gordon as he stooped over the camp bed. 'Thank God we were in time, Gordon. There were times when I feared we would be too late. I offer you my congratulations for your courage and fortitude, which saved Khartoum. Yours is an achievement of which Her Majesty and every citizen of the British Empire will be justly proud.'

'I am Charles Wilson, not Charles Gordon, sir,' Wilson corrected him.

Stewart stared at him in astonishment, then reached through the mosquito net and seized his hand. 'Oh, well done, Charles! I knew I could trust you to do your duty. Where is Gordon? Ask him to come to me at once. I want to congratulate him myself.'

Wilson freed his hand and stood back from the bed. He turned to the surgeon. 'Are you sedating him sufficiently? It will do him no good to become so agitated.'

'I am administering ten grains of laudanum every two hours. But there is little pain in the site of a wound once the gangrene takes hold.'

'I will place him on the first steamer that departs downriver for Aswan. That will probably be in two or three days' time.'

'Two or three days?' Stewart had only picked up the last few sentences. 'Why are you sending

Gordon down to Aswan, and why two or three days? Answer me that.'

'The steamers will set off for Khartoum imminently, General. We have run into unforeseen but unavoidable obstacles.'

'Gordon? But where is Gordon?'

'We must hope he is still holding out in Khartoum, sir, but we have had no news of him.'

Stewart looked around the tent with a wild, bewildered expression. 'Is this not Khartoum? Where are we? How long have we been here?'

'This is Metemma, sir,' the surgeon intervened gently. 'You have been here four days.'

'Four days!' Stewart's voice rose to a shout. 'Four days! You have thrown away the sacrifice made by my poor lads. Why did you not push on with all speed to Khartoum, instead of sitting here?'

'He is delirious,' Wilson snapped at the surgeon. 'Give him another dose of laudanum.'

'I am not delirious!' Stewart shouted. 'If you don't set out for Khartoum immediately, I will see you court-martialled and shot for dereliction of your duty and cowardice in the face of the enemy, sir.' He choked and fell back, spent and muttering, on his pillows. He closed his eyes and was quiet.

'Poor fellow.' Wilson shook his head with deep regret. 'Completely out of his head and hallucinating. No appreciation of the situation. Look after him and make him comfortable.'

He acknowledged the doctor's salute, and ducked out through the fly of the tent. He blinked in the bright sunlight, then scowled as he realized that a small group of officers was standing rigidly to attention nearby. They had certainly heard every word that had been spoken. Their expressions left no doubt of that.

'Have you gentlemen nothing better to do than laze about here?' Wilson demanded. They avoided his eyes as they saluted and walked away.

Only one stood his ground. Penrod Ballantyne was the junior officer in the group. His behaviour was impudent. He was walking the tightrope across the lethal chasm of insubordination. Wilson glowered at him. 'What are you about, Captain?' he demanded.

'I wondered if I might speak to you, sir.'

'What is it, then?'

'The camels are fully recovered. Plenty of water and good feed. With your permission I could be in Khartoum within twenty-four hours.'

'To what purpose, Captain? Are you proposing a one-man liberation of the city?' Wilson allowed his scowl to change to an amused smirk—an expression that was no great improvement, Penrod thought.

'My purpose would be to take your despatches to General Gordon, and inform him of your intentions, sir. The city is sore pressed and at the limit of its endurance. There are English women and children within the walls. It can be only days before they fall into the clutches of the Mahdi. I was hoping I might be allowed to assure General Gordon that you have his plight and that of the populace in mind.'

'You disapprove of my conduct of the campaign, do you? By the way, what is your name, sir?' Of course Wilson knew his name: this was a calculated insult.

'Penrod Ballantyne, 10th Hussars, sir. And no,

sir, I would not presume to remark on your conduct of the campaign. I was merely offering, for your consideration, my local knowledge of the situation.'

'I shall be sure to call upon you if I feel in need of your vast wisdom. I will mention your subordinate conduct in the despatches I shall write at the conclusion of the campaign. You are to remain in this camp. I shall not detach you on any independent mission. I shall not include you in the force that I shall lead to the relief of Khartoum. At the first opportunity you will be sent back to Cairo. You will take no further part in this campaign. Do I make myself clear, Captain?'

'Abundantly clear, sir.' Penrod saluted.

Wilson did not return his salute as he stamped away.

Over the days that followed, Wilson spent most of his time in his headquarters tent, busying himself with his despatches. He ordered an inventory of the remaining stores and ammunition. He inspected the fortifications of the zareba. He drilled the men. He visited the wounded daily, but General Stewart was no longer conscious. The steamers waited at their moorings with full heads of steam in their boilers. A mood of indecision and uncertainty descended on the regiment. Nobody knew what the next step would be, or when it would be taken. Sir Charles Wilson issued no orders of consequence.

On the evening of the third day Penrod went down to the camel lines and found Yakub. While he made a pretence of inspecting the animals, he whispered, 'Have the camels ready and the waterskins filled. The password for the sentries when you leave the zareba will be Waterloo. I will meet you at midnight by the little mosque on the far side of Metemma village.' Yakub looked at him askance. 'We have been ordered to take messages to Gordon Pasha.'

Yakub was at the rendezvous, and they set out southwards at a rate that would take them beyond pursuit by dawn.

Two days to Khartoum, Penrod thought grimly, and my career in ruins. Wilson will throw me to the lions. I hope Rebecca Benbrook appreciates my efforts on her behalf.

*   *   *

Osman Atalan, riding hard with a small group of his aggagiers, left the main body of his cavalry many leagues behind. He climbed up through the gut of the Shabluka Gorge. On the heights, he reined in al-Buq and leapt on to the saddle. Balancing easily on the restless horse, he trained his telescope on the City of the Elephant's Trunk, Khartoum, which lay on the horizon.

'What do you see, master?' Al-Noor asked anxiously.

'The flags of the infidel and the Turk are flying on the tower of Fort Mukran. The enemy of God, Gordon Pasha, still prevails in Khartoum,' said Osman, and the words were bitter as the juice of the aloe on his tongue. He dropped back onto the saddle and his sandalled feet found the stirrups. He gave the stallion a cut across the rump with the kurbash, and al-Buq jumped forward. They rode on southwards.

When they reached the Kerreri Hills they met the first exodus of women and old men from

84

Omdurman. The refugees did not recognize Osman with his black headcloth and unfamiliar mount, and an old man called to him as he cantered by, 'Turn back, stranger! The city is lost. The infidel has triumphed in a mighty battle at Abu Klea. Salida, Osman Atalan and all their armies have been slain.'

'Reverend old father, tell us what has become of the Divine and Victorious Muhammad, the Mahdi, the successor of Allah's Prophet.'

'He is the light of our eyes, but he has given the order for all his followers to leave Omdurman before the Turks and the infidels arrive. The Mahdi, may Allah continue to love and cherish him, will move into the desert with all his array. They say he purposes to march back to El Obeid.'

Osman threw back the headcloth that covered his face. 'See me, old man! Do you know who I am?'

The man stared at him, then let out a wail and fell to his knees. 'Forgive me, mighty Emir, that I pronounced you dead.'

'My army follows close behind me. We ride for Omdurman. The *jihad* continues! We will fight the infidel wherever we meet him. Tell this to all you meet upon the road.' Osman thumped his heels into al-Buq's flanks and galloped on.

He found the streets of Omdurman in turmoil. Heavily armed Ansar galloped down the narrow streets; wailing women were loading all their possessions on to donkey carts and camels; crowds hurried to the mosques to hear the imams preach the comforting word of Allah at this terrible time of defeat and despair. Osman scattered all before his horse, and rode on towards the mud-walled palace of the Mahdi.

He found the Mahdi and Khalifa Abdullahi on the rooftop, under the reed sunscreen, attended by a dozen young women of the harem. He prostrated himself before the *angareb* on which the Mahdi sat cross-legged. He had agonized over his decision to ride for Omdurman and face the successor to the Prophet of Allah, rather than taking his aggagiers and disappearing into the eastern deserts of the Sudan. He knew that if he had taken that course the Mahdi would certainly have sent an army after him, but in his own territory he would prevail against even the largest and most skilfully led host. But to wage war on the Mahdi, the direct emissary of Allah on earth, would have meant the end of him as a Muslim. The risk of death he ran now was preferable to being declared by the Mahdi an unbeliever, and having the gates of Paradise closed to him through all eternity.

'There is only one God, and no other God but Allah,' he said softly, 'and Muhammad, the Mahdi, is the successor to his Prophet here on earth.'

'Look in my face, Osman Atalan,' said the Mahdi. Osman looked up at him. He was smiling, the sweet smile that showed the small, wedge-shaped gap between his front teeth. Osman knew, with the cold hand of death laid upon his heart, that this did not mean he was forgiven. The Mahdi was certainly infuriated by his failure to stop the relief column. It was necessary only for him to raise his hand and Osman would suffer death or mutilation. Often the Mahdi would offer the condemned man his choice. On the long ride up from Metemma Osman had decided that if the choice were offered him he would choose beheading, rather than the amputation of his hands and feet.

'Will you pray with me, Osman Atalan?' the Mahdi asked.

Osman's spirit quailed. This invitation was ominous, and often preceded the sentence of death. 'With all my heart and the last breath of my body,' Osman responded.

'We will recite together the *al-fatihah*, the first *sura* of the Noble Koran.'

Osman adopted the appropriate first prostration position, and they recited in unison: 'In the name of Allah, the Most Gracious, the Most Merciful,' then went on through the remaining four verses, ending, 'You alone we worship, and you alone we ask for help, for each and everything.' When they had finished, the Mahdi sat back and said, 'Osman Atalan, I placed great faith in you, and set a task for you.'

'You are the beat of my heart, and the breath in my lungs.' Osman thanked him.

'But you have failed me. You have allowed the infidel to triumph against you. You have delivered me up to mine enemy, and it is all finished.'

'Nay, my master. All is not finished. I have failed in this one thing, but not in all.'

'Explain your meaning.'

'Allah has told you that it will not be finished until a man brings you the head of Gordon Pasha. Allah told you that I, Osman Atalan, am that man.'

'You have not fulfilled that prophecy. Therefore you have failed your God as well as his prophet,' the Mahdi replied.

'The prophecy of God and Muhammad, the Mahdi, can never be brought to naught,' Osman replied quietly, feeling the breath of the dark angel upon his neck where the executioner's blow would fall. 'Your prophecy is a mighty rock in the river of time that cannot be washed away. I have returned to Omdurman to bring the prophecy to fruition.' He pointed across the river to the stark outline of Fort Mukran. 'Gordon Pasha still awaits his fate within those walls, and the time of Low Nile is upon us. I beseech you, give me your blessing, Holy One.'

The Mahdi sat silent and unmoving for a hundred of his rapid heartbeats while he thought swiftly. The Emir Osman was a clever man and an adroit tactician. To refuse his plea was to admit that he, Muhammad, the Mahdi, was fallible. At last he smiled and reached out to lay his hand on Osman's head. 'Go and do what is written. When you have fulfilled my prophecy, return to me here.'

*   *   *

An hour before midnight a small felucca lay in the eastern channel of the Victoria Nile. It was hove to against the night breeze and the current, with sail skilfully backed. Al-Noor sat beside Osman Atalan on the thwart. Both men watched the Khartoum bank. Tonight the rocket display was extravagant. Since the onset of darkness a continual succession of fireworks had soared into the sky and burst in cascades of multi-coloured sparks. The band was playing with renewed alacrity and verve, and at intervals they heard singing and laughter, carried faintly across the dark waters.

'Gordon Pasha has heard the news of Abu Klea,' al-Noor whispered. 'He and his minions rejoice in their heathen hearts. Hourly they expect the steamers to appear from the south.'

It was long after midnight before the sounds of celebration slowly subsided, and Osman gave a quiet order to the boatman. He let the lateen sail fill, and they felt their way in closer to the shore below the walls of Khartoum. When they reached a point opposite the maidan, al-Noor touched his master's arm and pointed at the tiny beach, now exposed by the retreating waters. The wet mud glittered like ice in the starlight. Osman spoke a quiet word to the boatman, who tacked and sailed in closer still. Osman moved up to the bows and used one of the punt poles to take soundings of the sloping bottom as they crept along the beach. Then they sat quietly, listening for the sentries doing their rounds, or other hostile movements. They heard nothing except the hoot of an owl in the bell tower of the Catholic mission. There was lamplight within the upper floor of the British consular palace which faced on to the river, and once they saw shadowy movement beyond the window casement, but then all was still.

'After their victory, the infidel is lulled. Gordon Pasha is not as vigilant as he was before,' al-Noor whispered.

'We have discovered the beach on which we can land. We can return to Omdurman now to make our preparations,' Osman agreed. He gave a quiet command to the boatman, and they headed back across the river.

When Osman and al-Noor reached his double storeyed house in the south quarter, which lay between the Beit el Mal, the treasury, and the slave market, dawn was breaking and a dozen of his aggagiers were sitting in the courtyard being fed by the house slaves a breakfast of honey-roasted lamb and dhurra cakes with steaming pots of syrupy black Abyssinian coffee. 'Noble lord, we arrived at dusk last night,' they told him.

'What kept you so long on the road?' he asked.

'We do not ride horses like al-Buq, who is the prince of all horses.'

'You are welcome.' Osman embraced them. 'I have more work for your blades. We must retrieve the honour that was stripped from us by the infidel on the plains of Abu Klea.'

*   *   *

David Benbrook insisted that he should host a victory party to celebrate the battle of Abu Klea, and the imminent arrival of the relief column in the city. Because of the paucity of food and drink, Rebecca decided on an al fresco dinner, rather than a formal display of silver and crystal in the dining room. They sat on folding canvas campaign chairs on the terrace overlooking the maidan, and listened to the military band, joining in with the better-known choruses. In the intervals, while the band regained their breath, they toasted the Queen, General Wolseley and, for the benefit of Consul Le Blanc, King Leopold.

After much inner communication with his conscience, David decided to bring up from the cellars the single case of Krug champagne that he had been hoarding all these months. 'A little premature perhaps, but once they arrive we will probably be too busy to think about it.'

This was the first time that General Gordon had

accepted one of Rebecca's invitations to dinner and entertainment. He wore an immaculate dress uniform with a red fez. His boots were polished to a high gloss and the Egyptian Star of Ishmael glinted on his breast. He was in a relaxed, expansive mood, although Rebecca noticed the nervous tic below his eye. He nibbled a minute portion of the food on offer: green-cake, dhurra bread and cold roast bird of indeterminate species, which had been gunned down by the host. He chain-smoked his Turkish cigarettes, even when he stood to make a short speech. He assured the company that the steamers crammed with British troops were racing even at that hour up against the rapids of the Shabluka Gorge and that he confidently expected them to reach the city by the following evening. He commended the other guests and the entire populace, of every colour and nationality, for their heroic resistance and sacrifice, and gave thanks to Almighty God that their efforts had not been in vain. Then he thanked the consul and his daughters for their hospitality and took his leave. The mood of the remaining guests was at once much lighter.

The twins were given special dispensation to delay their bedtime until midnight, and were allowed a sherry glass of the precious champagne. Saffron quaffed hers like a sailor on shore leave, but Amber took a minute sip and made a face. When Rebecca was looking the other way, she poured the rest into her twin's glass, much to Saffron's glee.

Amber was becoming increasingly quiet and wan as the evening progressed. She took no part in the singing, which Rebecca thought odd. Amber had a sweet, true voice and loved to sing. She refused when David asked her to dance the polka with him. 'You are so quiet and subdued. Are you feeling unwell, my darling?'

'A little, Daddy, but I do love you so much.'

'Would you like to go up to bed? I will give you a dose of salts. That will fix it.'

'Oh, no. Goodness me, no! It is not that bad.' Amber forced a smile, and David looked worried but did not pursue the matter. He went off to dance with Saffron instead.

Consul Le Blanc also noticed Amber's unusual behaviour. He came to sit beside her, held her hand in an avuncular manner and launched into a long, complicated joke about a German, an Englishman and an Irishman. When he reached the climax he doubled over with laughter and tears ran down his pink cheeks. Although she saw nothing funny in the story Amber laughed dutifully, but then stood up and went to Rebecca, who was dancing with Ryder Courtney. Amber whispered in her elder sister's ear, and Rebecca left Ryder, took the younger girl's hand and hurried indoors with her. David saw them leave and he and Saffron followed. When they reached the foot of the staircase, Rebecca and Amber were on the first landing above them.

'Where are you going?' David called after them. 'Is anything the matter?'

Still holding hands Rebecca and Amber turned to face him. Suddenly Amber groaned and doubled over. With an explosive rush of gas and liquid, her bowels started to empty. It poured out of her like a yellow waterfall, and went on and on, forming a deep, spreading puddle at her feet.

David was the first to recover his wits. 'Cholera!' he said.

At that dread word Saffron thrust the fingers of both hands into her mouth and screamed.

'Stop that!' Rebecca ordered, but her own voice was almost a scream. She tried to lift Amber, but the yellow discharge was still spurting out of her and splattered down the front of Rebecca's long satin evening dress.

Ryder had heard Saffron scream and ran in from the terrace. He took in the scene almost instantly. He dashed back to where they had dined and swept the heavy damask cloth off the long table, sending silver candlesticks and table ornaments crashing to the floor. He raced up the stairs.

Amber was still voiding copiously. It seemed impossible that such a small body could contain so much liquid. It was running down the staircase in a rivulet. Ryder shook out the damask like a cape, and enfolded her in it, lifted her as though she were a doll and ran with her up the stairs.

'Please put me down, Ryder,' Amber begged. 'I will dirty your lovely new suit. I cannot stop myself. I am so ashamed.'

'You are a brave girl. There is nothing to be ashamed of,' Ryder told her. Rebecca was at his side. 'Where is the bathroom?' he asked her.

'This way.' She ran ahead and threw open the door.

Ryder carried Amber in and laid her in the galvanized bath. 'Get her soiled clothes off her and sponge her down with cool water,' he ordered. 'She is burning up. Then force her to drink. Weak warm tea. Gallons of it. She must keep drinking. She has to replace every drop of the fluid she has lost.' He

93

looked at David and Saffron in the doorway. 'Call Nazeera to help you. She knows about this disease. I must go back to the *Ibis* to fetch my medical chest. While I am gone, you must keep her drinking.'

Ryder raced through the streets. He was fortunate that for this one night General Gordon had relaxed the curfew so that all the populace might celebrate the relief of the city.

Bacheet had stowed the medical chest in its usual place under his bunk in the main cabin of the *Ibis*. He rummaged through it swiftly, searching for what he needed to staunch Amber's diarrhoea and replace the mineral salts that she had lost. He knew he had little time. Cholera is a swift killer. 'The Death of the Dog,' they called it. It could kill a robust adult in hours, and Amber was a child. Already her body had been stripped of fluid. Soon every muscle and sinew would scream for liquid, terrible cramps would twist her, and she would die a desiccated husk.

For a dreadful moment he thought that the vital packets of dirty white powder were missing, then remembered that he had moved them to the lockers in the galley for safety. In the cholera-torn city they were worth more than diamonds. The powder was packed in a woven sisal bag. There was enough to treat five or six cases. He had bought it at a usurious price from the abbot of a Coptic monastery deep in the gorge of the Blue Nile. The abbot had told him that the chalky powder was mined by his monks from a secret deposit tucked away in the mountains. Not only did it have a powerful binding effect on the bowels, it was also close in character and composition to those minerals purged from the human body by the disease. Ryder had been sceptical until Bacheet had been struck down with cholera, and Ryder had pulled him through with liberal doses of the powder.

He stuffed everything he needed in to an empty dhurra sack and ran back to the consulate. When he climbed the stairs to the bathroom he found that Amber was still in the bath. She was naked, and Rebecca and Nazeera were sponging her from the basin of warm soapy water that Saffron held. David hovered ineffectually in the background holding a tin mug of warm black tea. The stench of vomit and faeces still hung heavily in the room, but Ryder was careful not to show disgust.

'Has she vomited?'

'Yes,' replied David, 'but only some of this tea. I don't think she has anything else inside her.'

'How much has she drunk?' Ryder demanded, as he snatched the mug from the other man's hand and poured a handful of the powder into it.

'Two mugs and a bit,' said David, proudly.

'Not enough,' Ryder snapped. 'Not nearly enough.'

'She won't take any more.'

'She will,' said Ryder. 'If she can't drink it, I will give it to her with an enema tube.' He carried the mug to the bath. 'Amber, did you hear what I said?' She nodded. 'You don't like enemas, do you?' She shook her head vehemently, and her sodden curls dangled in her eyes. 'Then drink!' He placed one hand behind her head and held the cup to her lips. She gulped it down painfully, then lay back gasping. Already wasted by prolonged starvation, her body was now dehydrated and skeletal. The

95

change that had taken place in the hour he had been away was dramatic. Her legs were as thin as those of a bird, her ribs as distinct as the fingers of a hand. The skin on her sunken moon-pale belly seemed translucent so that he could see the network of blue veins under it.

Ryder poured another handful of powder into the mug, and filled it with warm tea from the kettle that stood close at hand. 'Drink!' he ordered, and she choked it down.

She was panting weakly, and her eyes had sunk into plum-coloured sockets. 'I have no clothes on. Please don't look at me, Ryder.'

He stripped off his moleskin jacket and covered her. 'I promise not to look at you if you promise to drink.' He refilled the mug and poured the powder into it. As she drank it, her belly bulged out like a balloon. The gases in it rumbled, but she did not void again. Ryder refilled the mug.

'I can't drink any more. Please don't make me,' she begged.

'Yes, you can. You made me a promise.'

She forced down that mug and another. Then there was a strong ammoniac odour and a yellow trickle of urine ran down the bottom of the bath to the plug-hole. 'You've made me wet myself like a baby.' She was weeping softly with shame.

'Good girl,' he said. 'That means you are making more water than you are losing. I am so proud of you.' He understood the trespasses he had already made on her modesty, so he stood up. 'But I am going to let Rebecca and Saffy look after you now. Don't forget your promise. You must keep drinking. I will wait outside.'

Before he left the bathroom he whispered to

96

Rebecca, 'I think we may have beaten it. She is out of immediate danger. But the cramps will begin soon. Call me at the first sign. We will have to massage her limbs or the pain will become unbearable.' From his sack he handed her the bottle of coconut oil he had brought from the *Ibis*. 'Tell Nazeera to take this down to the kitchen and warm it to blood heat, no more than that. I will stay close.'

The other dinner guests had left hours ago, and everything was quiet. Ryder and David settled down to wait on the top step at the head of the staircase. They chatted in a desultory fashion. They discussed the news of the relief column, and argued about when the steamers would arrive. David agreed with Chinese Gordon's estimate, but Ryder did not: 'Gordon is always conservative with the truth. He says whatever suits his purpose best. I will believe in the steamers when they tie up in the harbour. In the meantime I will keep up steam in the *Ibis*.'

Out in the night an owl hooted mournfully, then again, and a third time. Restlessly David stood up and went to the window. He leant on the sill and looked down on the river

> 'When the midnight owl hoot thrice.
> To-wit-too-woo, with one breath,
> Then in a trice
> It heralds death.'

'That's superstitious nonsense,' said Ryder, 'and, what's more, it does not scan.'

'You are probably right,' David admitted. 'My nursemaid repeated it to me when I was five, but

97

she was the wicked witch in person and loved to frighten us children.' Then he straightened up and peered down towards the riverbank. 'There's a boat out there, close in to the beach.'

Ryder went across to join him at the window. 'Where?'

'There! No, it's gone now. I swear it was a boat, a small felucca.'

'Probably a fisherman laying his nets.'

From the bathroom they heard Amber cry out in anguish. They rushed back to her. She was curled into a ball. The wasted muscles in her limbs were like whipcords as the spasms tightened them almost to snapping point. They lifted her out of the bath and laid her on the clean towels that Rebecca and Nazeera spread on the tiled floor.

Ryder rolled up his sleeves and knelt over her. Nazeera poured warm coconut oil into the cup of his hands and he began to massage Amber's twisted legs. He could feel the ropes and knots under the skin. 'Rebecca, take the other leg. Nazeera and Saffy, her arms,' he ordered. 'Do it this way.' While they worked, David dribbled more of the tea mixture into their patient's mouth. Rebecca watched Ryder's hands as he worked. They were broad and powerful, but gentle. Under them Amber's muscles gradually relaxed.

'It's not over yet,' Ryder warned them. 'There will be more. We must be ready to start again as the next spasms seize her.'

What depths there are to this man, Rebecca thought. What fascinating contradictions. Sometimes he is ruthlessly resourceful, at others he is filled with compassion and generosity of spirit. Would I not be foolish to let him go?

Before the hour was up the next cramps had locked Amber's limbs so they fell to work on her again, and were forced to keep it up through the rest of the night. Just before daybreak, when all were reaching their own limits of exhaustion, Amber's limbs gradually straightened and the knots softened and relaxed. Her head rolled to one side and she fell asleep.

'She has turned the corner,' Ryder whispered, 'but we must still take care of her. You must make her drink the powder mixture again as soon as she wakes. She must eat also. Perhaps you might feed her a porridge of dhurra and green-cake. I wish we had something more substantial, like chicken broth, but that is the best we can do. She will be weak as a newborn infant for days, perhaps weeks. But she has not scoured since midnight, so I hope and believe that the germs, as Joseph Lister is pleased to call the wee beasties that cause the trouble, have been purged from her.' He picked up his damp, soiled jacket from the floor. 'You know where to find me, Rebecca. If you send a message I will come at once.'

'I will see you to the door.' Rebecca stood up. As they went out into the passage, she took his arm. 'You are a warlock, Ryder. You've worked magic for us. I don't know how the Benbrook family can ever thank you.'

'Don't thank me, just say a prayer for old Abbot Michael who robbed me of fifty Maria Theresa dollars for a bag of chalk.'

At the door she reached up and kissed him, but when she felt his loins stir, she pulled away. 'You are a satyr as well as a warlock.' She managed a faint smile. 'But not now. We shall attend to that

99

business at the first opportunity. Perhaps tomorrow after the relief force arrives, when we are all safe from the evil Dervish.'

'I will hold myself on a short rein,' he promised, 'but tell me, dearest Rebecca, have you given any further thought to my proposal?'

'I am sure you will agree, Ryder, that at this dire time in our lives, my first thoughts must be for Amber and the rest of my family, but each day my affection for you increases. When this dreadful business is over, I feel sure that we will have something of value to share, perhaps for the remainder of our days.'

'Then I shall live in hope.'

*   *   *

Osman Atalan picked out two thousand of his most trusted warriors for the final assault on Khartoum. He marched them out of Omdurman, making no effort to conceal his movements. From his roost on the parapets of Fort Mukran, Gordon Pasha would observe this exodus, and take it as another indication that the Mahdi was abandoning the city and fleeing with all his forces to El Obeid. Once his men were behind the Kerreri Hills, where they were concealed from the prying telescopes on the towers and minarets in Khartoum, Osman divided them into five battalions of roughly four hundred men.

A large assembly of boats on the Omdurman bank would warn Gordon Pasha that something was afoot. If he attempted to take such a large force across the river in a single wave, it would overcrowd the tiny landing beach below the maidan, and in the darkness create chaos and confusion. He decided to use only twenty boats for the crossing of the river, each vessel could carry twenty men safely. Once they had landed the first wave of four hundred men, the boats would return to the Omdurman bank to take on board the following battalions. The first wave of attackers would get off the beaches as soon as they could, and leave the way clear for the next. Osman estimated that he would be able to transport his entire force across the Nile in little more than an hour.

He knew his men so well that he gave simple orders to the sheikhs he placed in charge of each battalion, orders that they would not forget in the passion of battle and the heady excitement of looting the city.

Dervish spies within the city had drawn detailed maps of the exact layout of Gordon Pasha's defences. The Gatling guns were Osman's prime targets. The memory of his last encounter with those weapons was etched deeply on his mind. He wanted no recurrence of that slaughter. The first battalion ashore would go straight for them, and put them out of action.

Once the guns had been captured or destroyed, they could roll up the fortifications along the waterfront, then wipe out the Egyptian troops in the barracks and the arsenal. Only then would it be safe to turn his men loose on the populace.

The previous night Muhammad, the first Prophet of Allah, had visited Muhammad, the Mahdi, his successor. He had brought a message directly from Allah. It was decreed that the faith and devotion of the Ansar should be rewarded.

Once they had delivered to the Mahdi the head of Gordon Pasha, they must be allowed to sack the city of Khartoum. For ten days the sack would be allowed to run unchecked. After that the city would be burned and all the principal buildings, particularly the churches, missions and consulates, would be demolished. All traces of the infidel must be eradicated from the land of Sudan.

At nightfall Osman marched his two thousand back from the Kerreri Hills to Omdurman. Across the river in the city of Khartoum, Gordon's nightly firework display and the recital of the military band were more subdued than they had been the previous evening. There was widespread disillusionment that the steamers had not yet arrived. When the rocket display fizzled out, and silence settled on the city, Osman led his first battalion down to the riverbank, where the twenty boats were moored. This small flotilla was an eclectic collection of feluccas and trading dhows. The crossing of the Nile through banks of river mist was conducted in an eerie silence. Osman was the first man to wade ashore. With al-Noor and a dozen of his trusty aggagiers close on his heels, he raced up the beach.

The surprise was total. The Egyptian sentries were sleeping complacently, in the certainty that dawn would show the steamers of the relief force anchored before the walls. There was no challenge, no shot or shouted warning, before Osman's aggagiers were into the first line of trenches. Their broadswords rose and fell in a dreadfully familiar rhythm. Within minutes the trenches were clear. The dead and wounded Egyptian troops lay in heaps. Osman and his aggagiers left them and raced for the arsenal. They had not reached it before the second battalion landed on the beach behind them.

Suddenly a rifle shot clapped on the silence, then another. There were shouts, and a bugle sounded the call to arms. Erratic and isolated gunfire built into a thunderous fusillade, and the ripples and echoes spread across the city as the startled Egyptians blazed away at shadows or cravenly fired into the air. Down near the little beach an *ombeya* howled and a war drum boomed as another battalion landed and rushed through the breach into the city.

'There is only one God and Muhammad, the Mahdi, is his prophet.' The war chant was carried through the city, and suddenly the streets and alleys were alive with running, struggling figures. Their screams and entreaties rose in a babble of terror and anguish like voices from the pit of hell.

'Mercy in the Name of Allah!'

'Quarter! Give us quarter!'

'The Dervish are within! Run! Run or die!'

All Gordon's famous forts and redoubts were sited to cover the river approaches. Taken in the rear they were swiftly overwhelmed. Osman's aggagiers massacred the stunned defenders in their trenches or hounded them through the streets and alleyways, rabbits before the wolf pack.

*   *   *

David was at his desk, working on his journal. He had kept it up to date faithfully throughout the ten long months that the city had been under siege. He knew that it was an invaluable document. With the promise of relief so near, it could only be a matter of weeks before he and his girls were aboard a P&O steamship on their way back to England. One of the first goals he had set himself on arrival was to work up his journal into a full-length manuscript. The public appetite for books of adventure and exploration in the Dark Continent seemed insatiable. Baker, Burton and Stanley had each made several thousands of pounds from their publications. Sam Baker had even received a knighthood from the Queen for his literary efforts. Surely David's own first-hand memoirs of the valiant defence of the city would please many, and his account of the bravery and suffering of his three girls would tear at the heartstrings of every lady reader. He hoped he might have the book ready for the publishers within a month of reaching England. He dipped the nib of his pen in to the silver inkwell, and wiped off the excess carefully. Then he stared dreamily into the flame of the lamp on the corner of his desk.

It might bring in fifty thousand. The thought warmed him. Dare I hope for a hundred thousand? He shook his head. Too much by far, I would settle happily for ten thousand. That would help immeasurably with re-establishing ourselves. Oh! It will be so good to be home again!

His musings were interrupted by the sound of a rifle shot. It was not far off, somewhere down by the maidan. He tossed down his pen, splattering the page with a blob of ink, and strode across his office to the window. Before he reached it there were more shots, a volley, a crackling storm of gunfire.

'My God! What is happening out there?' He

threw open the window and stuck out his head. Close at hand a bugler played the shrill, urgent notes of 'stand to arms'. Almost immediately there came a faint but triumphant chorus of Arab voices: '*La ilaha illallah!* There is but one God!' For a brief moment he was rooted to the spot, too shocked to draw breath, then he gasped. 'They are in! The Dervish have broken into the city!'

He ran back to the desk and swept up his journal. It was too heavy to carry so he crammed it into the safe that was concealed behind the panelling of the back wall. He slammed the steel door and tumbled the combination of the lock, then closed the panelling that concealed it. His ceremonial sword was hanging on the wall behind his desk. It was not a fighting weapon and he was no swordsman, but he buckled it round his waist. Then he took the Webley revolver from his desk drawer and thrust it into his pocket. There was nothing else of value in the room. He ran out into the lobby and up the stairs to the bedrooms.

Rebecca had moved Amber into her own room so that she could care for her during the night. Nazeera was sleeping on an *angareb* in the far corner. Both women were awake, standing indecisively in the middle of the room.

'Get your clothes on at once!' he ordered. 'Dress Amber too. Don't waste a moment.'

'What is happening, Daddy?' Rebecca was confused.

'I think the Dervish have broken in. We must run to Gordon's headquarters. We should be safe there.'

'Amber cannot be moved. She is so weak it might kill her.'

'If the Dervish find her she will fare far worse,' he told her grimly. 'Get her up. I will carry her.' He turned to Nazeera. 'Run to Saffron's room, quick as you can. Get her dressed. Bring her here. We must leave immediately.'

Within minutes they were ready. David carried Amber, and the other women followed at his heels as he went down the stairs. Before they reached the bottom, there came the crash of breaking glass and splintering wooden panels from the main doors, and savage shouts of Arab voices.

'Find the women!'

'Kill the infidel!'

'This way,' David snapped, and they ran into the back rooms. Behind them came another thunderous clap of sound as the front door was torn from its hinges and fell inwards. 'Keep close to me!' David led them to the door into the courtyard. Gordon's headquarters were on the far side. He lifted the locking bar and pushed it open a crack. He peered out cautiously. 'The coast is clear, for the moment at least.'

'How is Amber bearing up?' Rebecca whispered anxiously.

'She is quiet,' David answered. Her body was as light as that of a captured bird. She did not move. She might already have been dead, but he could feel her heart beating under his hand, and once she whimpered softly.

Gordon's headquarters were only a hundred paces or so across the courtyard. The main gate at the opposite end was bolted. There were open staircases on the side walls leading up to the second store, where General Gordon had his private rooms. There was no sign of any Egyptian troops.

'Where is Gordon?' David asked, in consternation. It did not seem there was any shelter for them even in the general's stronghold. At that moment the main gates shook, and heavy blows resounded on the outside. A terrible chorus of Dervish war cries swelled the uproar. While David tried to make up his mind as to what he should do next, three Egyptian troopers emerged from the headquarters building and ran across the courtyard to the main gates. They were the first David had seen.

'Thank God! They are waking up at last!' he exclaimed, and was about to lead the women out through the door when, to his amazement, he saw the soldiers lifting the heavy locking bars. 'The craven bastards are surrendering, and letting in the Dervish without a fight,' he barked.

Now the soldiers shouted, 'We are faithful to the Divine Mahdi.'

'There is one God, and Muhammad, the Mahdi, is his prophet.'

'Enter, O ye faithful, and spare us, for we are your brothers in Allah.'

They swung open the gates and a horde of *jibba*-clad figures swarmed in. The first of the Dervish warriors chopped down the Egyptian traitors ruthlessly, and their bodies were trampled by the rush of hundreds of feet as the courtyard filled with the attackers. Many were carrying burning torches and the flickering yellow light of the flames lit up the horrific scene. David was about to shut and bolt the door before they were discovered, but at that moment a solitary figure appeared at the head of the stone staircase that overlooked the courtyard. Fascinated, David continued to peer through the chink.

General Charles Gordon was in full dress uniform. He prided himself on his ability to impress the savage and the barbarian. He had taken time to dress even when he heard the pandemonium in the streets. He wore his decorations but carried no weapon other than a light cane: he was fully aware of the danger of antagonizing the men he was trying to placate.

Calmly, the hypnotic gaze of those sapphire eyes glinting in the torchlight, he held up his hands to quell the uproar. To David this seemed futile but, astonishingly, an unnatural quiet descended on the courtyard. Gordon kept both arms raised, like a conductor controlling an unschooled orchestra. His voice was strong and unruffled, as he spoke good but heavily accented Arabic: 'I wish to speak to your master, the Mahdi,' he announced.

The listeners stirred like a field of dhurra when a breeze sweeps through it, but nobody answered him. His voice was sharper and more masterful when he spoke next—he had sensed he was taking control. 'Who among you is your leader? Let him step forward.'

A tall, strikingly handsome figure stepped from the mob. He wore the green turban of an emir, and mounted the first step of the staircase. 'I am the Emir Osman Atalan of the Beja, and these are my aggagiers.'

'I have heard of you,' Gordon said. 'Come up to me.'

'Gordon Pasha, you will give no more orders to any son of Islam, for this is the last day of your life.'

'Utter no threats, Emir Atalan. The thought of death troubles me not at all.'

'Then come down these stairs and meet it like a man, and not a cringing infidel dog.'

For another few seconds Chinese Gordon stared down at him haughtily. Watching from the darkness of the doorway, David wondered what was going on in that cold, precise mind. Was there not, even now, a shadow of doubt or a flutter of fear? Gordon showed neither emotion as he started down the staircase. He stepped as precisely and confidently as if he were on a parade ground. He reached the step above Osman Atalan and stopped, facing him.

Osman studied his face, then said quietly, 'Yes, Gordon Pasha. I see you are indeed a brave man.' And he thrust the full length of his blade through Gordon's belly. In almost the same movement he drew it out again, and changed to a double-handed grip. The pale blue light in Gordon's eyes flickered like a candle flame in the wind, his cold granite features seemed to fall in upon themselves like melting beeswax. He struggled to remain upright, but the flame of his turbulent life was flickering out. Slowly his legs gave way under him. Osman waited for him with the sword poised. Gordon sagged forward from the waist and Osman swung his sword two-handed, aiming unerringly at the base of his neck. The blade made a sharp snick as it parted the vertebrae and Gordon's head fell away like the heavy fruit of the durian tree. It struck the stone stair with a solid thump, and rolled down to the courtyard. Osman stooped, took a handful of the thick curls and, ignoring the blood that splashed down the front of his *jibba*, held the head aloft to show it to his aggagiers. 'This head is our gift to the Divine Mahdi. The prophecy is fulfilled.

109

The will and the word of Allah govern all of creation.'

A single abrupt roar went up to the night sky: 'God is great!' Then, in the silence that followed, Osman spoke again: 'You have made a gift to Muhammad, the Mahdi. Now he returns a gift to you. For ten days this city, all its treasures and the people in it are yours to deal with as you wish.'

David waited to hear no more, and while the full attention of the Dervish was on their emir, he closed and bolted the door. He gathered the women about him, settled Amber's head more comfortably against his shoulder and led them back through the scullery, past the pantries and the entrance to the wine cellars to the small door that led to the servants' quarters. As they hurried along they could hear behind them the crash of breaking furniture. The women looked up fearfully at the sound of running footsteps from the floor above as the Dervish rampaged through the palace. David struggled briefly with the servants' door before he could open it and lead them out into the night air.

They reached the entrance to the reeking sanitary lane that ran along the back wall of the palace. Along it stood stacks of the night-soil buckets. They had not been collected for months and the odour of excrement was overpowering. This was a place so unclean that any devout Muslim would avoid it assiduously so they could afford to pause for a few moments. While they regained their breath, they heard gunfire and shouting in the streets beyond the boundary wall, and in the palace they had just left.

'What shall we do now, Daddy?' Rebecca asked.

'I do not know,' David admitted. Amber groaned

and he stroked her head. 'They are all around us. There does not seem to be any avenue of escape.'

'Ryder Courtney has his steamer ready in the canal. But we must go quickly, or he will set sail without us.'

'Which road to reach him is safest?' David's breathing was laboured.

'We must keep clear of the waterfront. The Dervish will certainly be looting the big houses along the corniche.'

'Yes—of course. You are right.'

'We must go through the native quarter.'

'Lead the way!' he said.

Rebecca grabbed Saffron's hand. 'Nazeera take the other.'

The women ran down the narrow alley between the buckets. David ploughed along heavily behind them. When they reached the far end of the lane Rebecca paused to make certain that the street ahead was empty. Then they ran to the next corner. Once more she checked the ground ahead. They went on like this, a stage at a time. Twice, Rebecca spotted groups of rampaging Dervish coming towards them, and was just quick enough to lead them down a side alley. Eventually they came out behind the rear of the Belgian consulate. Here they were forced to a halt to avoid another gang of Dervish, who were breaking into the building. They were using a pew from the Catholic cathedral as a battering ram. The tall carved doors gave way and the Dervish burst in.

Rebecca looked around for another escape route. Before she could find one the aggagiers dragged the portly figure of Consul Le Blanc through the shattered doors into the street. He was squealing like a piglet on its way to the abattoir. Although he fought and struggled, he was no match for the lean and sinewy warriors. They pinned him down on his back in the middle of the road, and ripped off his clothing. When he was naked one knelt beside him with a drawn dagger. He took a handful of Le Blanc's hairy scrotum, and stretched it out as though it was india-rubber. With one stroke of the dagger he sliced it away, leaving a gaping hole in the base of the pale, pendulous belly. Roaring with laughter the men who held him forced Le Blanc's jaws open with the handles of their daggers and stuffed his testicles into his mouth, gagging his shrieks. Then they completed the ritual mutilation by lopping off his hands and feet at wrists and ankles. When they were finished with him, they left him writhing on the ground, and rushed back into the consulate building to join the pillage. Le Blanc struggled up and sat like some grotesque statue of Buddha, clumsily trying to remove the flaccid sack of his scrotum from his mouth with his bleeding stumps.

'Sweet Jesus, how horrible!' Rebecca's voice was husky with pity. 'Poor Monsieur!' She started to go to his aid.

'Don't! They will have you also.' David's voice was choked not so much with pity, as with the brutal effort of running so far with Amber in his arms. 'There is nothing we can do for him. We can try only to save ourselves. Becky darling, we must keep going. Don't look back.'

They ducked down another alley, forced ever deeper into the warren of huts and hovels of the native quarter and further off the direct route to Ryder Courtney's compound. After another few hundred yards David came up short, like an old stag run to a standstill by the hounds. His face was twisted with pain and sweat dripped from his chin.

'Daddy, are you all right?' Rebecca had turned back to him.

'Just a little winded,' he gasped. 'Not as young as I once was. Just give me a moment to get my breath back.'

'Let me take Amber from you.'

'No! Little mite that she is, she is still too heavy for you. I will be all right in a few seconds.' He sank to the ground, still holding Amber tenderly to his chest. The other three women waited with him, but every time there was another outburst of gunfire or shouting they gazed around fearfully and huddled closer together. From the direction of the Belgian consulate, flames towered into the sky, and illuminated the surroundings with a yellow, flickering light. David heaved himself back to his feet, and stood swaying. 'We can go on now,' he said.

'Please, let me take Amber.'

'Don't be silly, Becky. I am perfectly all right. Go on!'

She peered closely at his face. It was pale and shining with sweat, but she knew that to argue with him would be a dangerous waste of time. She took his arm to steady him and they went on, but their pace was slower now.

After another short distance David had to stop again. 'How far to where the *Ibis* is moored now?'

'Not far,' she lied. 'Just beyond that little mosque at the end of the road. You can do it.'

'Of course I can.' He staggered forward again. Then, from behind, they heard a shout and the

113

baying of Arab voices. They looked back. There was another pack of Dervish down the road behind them, at least two dozen, brandishing their weapons and hooting with wild excitement as they saw the women.

Rebecca dragged David to the corner of the nearest building. For a moment they were out of sight of their pursuers. David leant heavily against the wall. 'I can't go any further.' He handed Amber to Rebecca. 'Take her!' he ordered. 'Take the others with you and run. I will hold them here while you get away.'

'I cannot leave you,' said Rebecca, staunchly. Her father tried to argue but she ignored him and turned to Nazeera. 'Take Saffron and run. Don't look back! Run for the boat.'

'I'll stay with you, Becky,' Saffron cried.

'If you love me, you will do as I say,' Rebecca told her.

'I love you, but—'

'Go!' Rebecca insisted.

'Please, Saffy, do as she says.' David's voice was rough with pain. 'For my sake.'

Saffron hesitated only a moment longer. 'I will always love you, Daddy, and Becky and Amber,' she said, and grabbed Nazeera's hand. The two dived down the alley. David and Rebecca turned back to face the Dervish as they poured round the corner. Their *jibbas* and the blades of their swords were wet with blood, their faces were mad with blood lust. David drew his sword. He pushed Rebecca and Amber behind him to protect them.

The Dervish formed a half-circle facing him, just out of reach of his sword. One darted forward and feinted at his head. When David slashed back at

114

him he shouted with laughter and jumped away. David tottered unsteadily after him. The others joined in the sport. They baited him, just out of reach of his blade, forcing him to turn from one side to the other.

While the others kept him in play, one circled and came up behind Rebecca. He seized her round the waist with one arm, and with the other hand pulled up her skirts. She was naked below the waist and the other Arabs roared with approval, as their comrade butted his hips against her buttocks in a copulatory display. Rebecca shrieked with outrage and tried to break away but she was hampered with Amber in her arms. David staggered back to try to protect them.

The Dervish released Rebecca. 'We will all mount her like that and she will bear us twenty fine Muslim sons.' He laughed and leered.

David was maddened by the pain in his chest and the taunts they shouted at him. He charged again and again, but they were swift and nimble. Blinded by his own sweat, and crippled by the pain that was building swiftly in his chest, the sword slipped from his hand at last and he sank to his knees in the dirt. His face was swollen and contorted, his mouth was open and he gulped like a stranded fish. One of the aggagiers stepped up behind him and, with a surgeon's skill, sliced off one of his ears. Blood poured down his shirt but David did not seem to feel the pain.

Rebecca was still holding Amber, but she rushed to her father and knelt beside him. She placed an arm round his shoulders. 'Please!' she said in Arabic. 'He is my father. Please spare him.' The blood from David's wound sprinkled them both.

The Dervish laughed. 'Please spare him!' they mimicked her. One grabbed a handful of her hair, and dragged her away. He threw her full length in the dust.

She sat up, holding Amber in her lap. She was weeping wildly. 'Leave him alone!' she sobbed.

With a shaking hand David reached into the pocket of his jacket and drew out the Webley. He waved it in vague circles. 'Stand back or I shall fire.'

The aggagier who had cut off his ear stepped in again, and with another quick, controlled cut lopped off David's outstretched hand at the wrist. 'Spare us, O mighty infidel, for we are in great terror of you,' he jeered. David stared at his severed wrist from which spurted a jet of arterial blood.

Rebecca cried out, 'Oh, what have they done to you?'

David clutched the stump to his chest with the other hand, then bowed his head over it, in an attitude of devout prayer. The Arab swordsman stepped up to him again and lightly touched the back of his neck with the blade, measuring the distance for a clean blow. Rebecca shrieked with despair as he lifted the sword, then swung back into the stroke. It cut through David's neck without sound or check, and his head dropped free of his shoulders. His headless body collapsed and his legs kicked in a brief convulsive jig.

The Arab picked up the head, holding it by a handful of its grey hair. He came to where Rebecca crouched and thrust her father's head into her face. 'If he is your father, then kiss him farewell before he goes down to boil in the waters of hell through all eternity.'

Although Rebecca was sobbing hysterically she tried to cover Amber's eyes with one hand and keep her face averted. But Amber twisted back, and screamed as she looked into her father's face. The tip of David's tongue protruded between slack lips, and his eyes were open, but blank and sightless.

At last the Dervish lost interest in such mild sport. He threw aside the head, and wiped his bloody hands on Rebecca's bodice. Then, through the cloth, he pinched and twisted her nipples, laughing when she cried out at the pain. 'Take them!' he ordered. 'Take these two filthy infidel whores to the pen. They will be taught to serve the needs and pleasures of their new masters.'

They pulled Rebecca to her feet, still with Amber in her arms, and dragged her away towards the waterfront.

*   *   *

Saffron crouched in the angle of one of the ruined shacks. Nazeera was beside her as they stared back down the alley and watched the Dervish tormenting her father and Rebecca. Saffron was too shocked to speak or weep. When the executioner stepped up to David and held the sword over him she covered her mouth with both hands to prevent herself uttering a sound that might betray them but she could not tear her gaze away from the harrowing sight. When the Dervish made the fatal stroke and her father's corpse fell forward, Saffron was at last released from the spell. She began to sob silently.

She watched them tormenting Amber with their

father's head, and could not control her tears. When at last they dragged Rebecca and Amber towards the waterfront, Saffron jumped to her feet and took Nazeera's hand. The two ran on towards Ryder Courtney's compound.

Dawn was breaking when they reached it, and the light was growing stronger. The gates of the outer compound stood wide and the buildings were deserted. The Dervish had not yet spread out from the centre of the town as far as this. They ran on across the inner courtyard. Saffron paused long enough to peer through the open door of the blockhouse. It was empty, stripped of every item of value. 'We are too late! Ryder has gone!' she cried to Nazeera. With a despairing heart she ran on towards the canal gates. They were closed but unbarred. It required their combined efforts to push them open. Saffron was the first through. Then she stopped abruptly. The *Intrepid Ibis*'s mooring was empty, and the steamer was gone.

'Where are you, Ryder? Where have you gone? Why have you left me?' She gasped for breath and fought back the dark waves of panic. Once she had gathered herself, she turned and raced along the canal towpath towards its juncture with the Blue Nile. She had not covered more than half the way to the first bend in the canal before she smelt the woodsmoke from the *Ibis*'s funnel. 'He can't be too far ahead,' she told herself, and her spirits soared. She pulled quickly ahead of Nazeera, who was struggling to keep pace with her. When she reached the first bend in the canal and came round it she screamed at the top of her voice, 'Wait for me! I am coming. Wait for me, Ryder!' The *Ibis* was two hundred yards ahead. She was puffing away down the channel towards the open river. Saffron summoned every last ounce of strength, and raced after it. The little steamer was not yet under full power, but was easing her way carefully down the shallow, winding canal. With this last burst of speed Saffron began to overhaul it.

'Wait! Ryder, wait!' In the glowing sparks from the smoke stack she could just make out Ryder's dark figure in the angle of his bridge, but he was looking ahead. The pumping steam cylinders drowned her voice.

'Ryder!' she screamed. 'Oh, please, look round.' Then she saved her breath and ran with all her heart. Ahead of her the *Ibis* reached the entrance to the river, and increased her speed, pulling out into the stream of the Nile current. Saffron came up short on the edge of the bank. She cried out again, danced up and down and waved both hands over her head. The *Ibis* drew away rapidly into the softly swirling banks of silver mist that hung low on the water. Saffron dropped her arms and stood still. Nazeera came up beside her and the two hugged each other in despair. Suddenly a rifle shot rang out on the towpath behind them. They spun round and saw four Dervish running towards them. One halted and levelled his rifle. He fired another shot. The bullet kicked dust from the towpath at their feet and ricocheted across the river. Saffron turned back towards the rapidly departing shape of the *Ibis*.

The rifle shot had alerted Ryder and he was staring back at them. Saffron was lifted on a new wave of hope: she shrieked again and waved her arms. Then Ryder was bringing the little steamer round in a tight circle, and heading towards them.

119

She looked back at the Dervish. All four were running towards her in a bunch. She saw at once that they would be upon her before the *Ibis* could reach the entrance to the canal.

'Come!' she called to Nazeera. 'We must swim.'

'No!' Nazeera shook her head. 'Al-Sakhawi will take care of you. I must go back to look after my other girls.' Saffron would have argued, even though the pursuers were closing in swiftly, but Nazeera forestalled her protests and ducked off the towpath. She disappeared into the swamp reeds that grew along the verge.

'Nazeera!' Saffron shouted after her, but the yells of the Dervish were louder still. She pulled off her shoes, tucked up her skirts and ran to the edge of the canal. She drew a deep breath and dived in. When her head broke the surface she launched out towards the approaching steamer in a determined dog-paddle.

'Good girl!' She heard Ryder's voice and kicked wildly with both legs, pulling at the water with her cupped hands. Behind her she heard another shot and a bullet kicked up a fountain that showered her head and ran into her eyes.

'Come on, Saffy.' Ryder was leaning over the side of the steamer, ready to grab her. 'Keep swimming.' At last she felt the current catch her and push her faster. Then she saw his face above her and reached up to him.

'Got you!' Ryder said. With a single heave he plucked her out of the river, as though she was a drowning kitten, and swung her up on to the deck. Then he shouted to Bacheet, 'Take her out again.'

Bacheet spun the wheel and the deck canted over into the turn. Once more they headed out into mid-stream. The Dervish was still firing at them from the towpath, but swiftly the river mist closed around them, and although the bullets still splashed about them or pinged off the steel superstructure the man had lost sight of them. At last the gunfire petered out.

*   *   *

'What happened to you, Saffy?' Ryder carried her down the deck to the cabin. 'Where are the others? Where are Rebecca and Amber, and your father?'

She tried to stop herself blubbering at his questions and put her arms round his neck, 'It's just too horrid to say, Ryder. Terrible things have happened. The very worst things ever.'

He sat her on his bunk in the cabin. Her distress touched him and he wanted to give her a few moments to recover. He handed her a dry but grubby towel. 'Very well. We'll get you tidied up first. Then you can tell me about it.' He pulled a faded blue shirt off the clothes-line above the bunk. 'Hang your dress up there. Put this shirt on when you're dry, and come to the bridge. We can talk up there.'

The tails of his shirt reached below her knees. It served well enough as a loose shift. She found one of Ryder's neckties in the drawer under the bunk, and tied it round her waist as a belt. She used his tortoiseshell comb to tidy her damp hair, then twisted it into a single pig-tail. A few minutes later, she went up to the bridge. Her eyes were pink and swollen with grief. 'They have killed my father,' she said hopelessly, and ran to Ryder.

He caught her up and hugged her hard. 'It can't

be true. Are you sure, Saffy?'

'I saw it. They cut off his head, just like they did to General Gordon. Then they took Rebecca and Amber away.' She fought back another sob. 'Oh, I hate them. Why are they so cruel?'

Ryder lifted her up and sat her on the coaming of the engine-room hatch. He kept one arm round her. 'Tell me everything, Saffy, every detail.'

Jock McCrump heard her voice and came up from the boiler room. He and Ryder listened in silence to her account. By the time she had finished, the top rim of the sun was showing above the horizon, and the river mist was burning off. The city was slowly revealed in all its stark detail. Ryder counted eight burning buildings, including the Belgian consulate. Thick smoke drifted across the river.

Then he turned his telescope on the square silhouette of Mukran Fort. The flags had been pulled down and the flagstaff was as bare as a gallows. Slowly he panned his lens across the rest of the city. Crowds of the faithful were dancing through the streets, and crowding the corniche in their brightly patched *jibbas*. There were outbursts of gunfire, black powder smoke spurting into the air, salvoes of *feu de joie* from the victors. Many were carrying bundles of loot. Others were rounding up the survivors of the attack. Ryder picked out small groups of women prisoners being herded towards the Customs House.

'What colour dress was Rebecca wearing?' he asked Saffron, without lowering the glass. He did not wish to look upon her anguish.

'Blue bodice, with yellow skirts.' Although he stared until his eye ached, he could not pick out a

122

blue and yellow dress, or a head of golden hair among the captive women. But they were far off, and the smoke from the burning buildings and the dust from all the wild activity ashore confused the scene.

'Where will they take the women, Bacheet?' he demanded.

'They will pen them up like heifers in the cattle market until first the Mahdi, then the *khalifa* and the emirs have time to look them over and take their pick.'

'Rebecca and Amber?' he asked. 'What will happen to them?'

'With their yellow hair and white skin they are a great prize,' Bacheet answered. 'They will certainly be selected by the Mahdi. They will go to him as prime concubines.'

Ryder lowered the telescope. He felt sick. He thought of Rebecca, whom he loved and had hoped to make his wife, reduced to a plaything for that murderous fanatic. The thought was too painful to bear, and he forced it to the back of his mind. Instead he thought of sweet little Amber, whom he had nursed and saved from cholera. He had a vivid image of her pale childish body, the same body he had massaged back to life, being mounted and violated, sweet flesh torn and alien seed flooding her immature loins. He felt vomit rising to the back of his throat.

'Take us in closer to the shore,' he ordered Bacheet. 'I must see where they are so I can plan a rescue.'

'Only Allah can save them now,' said Bacheet softly. Saffron overheard, and fresh tears oozed down her cheeks.

'Damn you, Bacheet, do as I say,' Ryder snarled.

Bacheet turned across the current and they eased in towards the city waterfront. At first they attracted little attention from the shore. The Dervish were too preoccupied with the sack of the city. An occasional shot was fired in their direction, but that was all. They steamed downstream as far as the confluence of the two great rivers, then turned back, cruising in close to the Khartoum waterfront. Suddenly there was the boom of a cannon shot, and a Krupps shell burst the surface ahead of the bows. The spray flew back across the deck. Ryder saw the gun smoke on the harbour wall. The Dervish had turned the captured guns on them. Another Krupps in the redoubt below the maidan came into action and the shell screeched over the bridge and burst in the middle of the river.

'We are not doing much good here, except giving them artillery practice.' Ryder glanced at Bacheet. 'Turn back into mid-stream and head on upriver. We'll find a quiet place to anchor until we can gather more news and find out what they have done with Rebecca and Amber. Then I can plan more sensibly for their rescue.'

For miles up the Blue Nile both banks were deserted. Ryder headed for the Lagoon of the Little Fish in which he had transhipped the cargo of dhurra from Ras Hailu's dhow. When he reached it he anchored in a stand of papyrus, which hid the *Ibis* from curious eyes on the shore.

As soon as they had made everything onboard shipshape, he called Bacheet to the engine room where they could talk without being overheard by the rest of the crew. He wasted no time but put it to Bacheet straight and unadorned.

'Do you think you would be able to go back among the Dervish and discover what has become of al-Jamal and al-Zahra without arousing the suspicions of the Ansar?'

Bacheet pursed his lips and puffed out his cheeks, which made him look like a ground squirrel. 'I am as they are. Why should they suspect me?'

'Are you willing to do it?'

'I am not a coward, but neither am I a rash man. Why would I be willing to do something as stupid as that? No, al-Sakhawi. I would not be willing. I would be extremely reluctant.' He tugged unhappily at his beard. 'I will leave at once.'

'Good,' Ryder said. 'I will wait for you here, unless I am discovered, in which case I will wait for you at the confluence of the Sarwad river. You will go into the city and, if necessary, cross to Omdurman. When you have news for me, you will return to give it to me here.'

Bacheet sighed theatrically and went to his own tiny berth in the forecastle. When he emerged he was dressed in a Dervish *jibba*. Ryder refrained from asking where he had obtained it. Bacheet dropped over the side of the *Ibis* and waded to dry ground. He set off along the bank towards Khartoum.

*   *   *

On the waterfront Nazeera mingled unobtrusively with the milling crowds. There were as many Dervish women as men in the throng, and she was no different from them in her black ankle-length robes and the headcloth covering half of her face.

125

The other women had come across from Omdurman as soon as they had heard that the city had been taken. They had come for the excitement of the triumphal celebrations, the loot, and for the thrill of the executions and torture that must surely follow the victory. The wealthy citizens of Khartoum would be forced to reveal the hiding-places of their valuables, their gold, jewellery and coin. Obtaining information was a skill that the Dervish women had learnt from their own mothers and honed to a high art.

Nazeera was part of the jostling, cavorting, ululating river of humanity that flowed along the corniche above the river. Ahead the crowd parted to allow a line of chained Egyptian soldiers through. They had been stripped of their tunics, then beaten until their bare backs looked as though they had been savaged by angry lions. The blood from the whip weals soaked their breeches and dripped down their legs. As they shuffled past on their way to the beach, the women rushed forward to beat them again with any weapon that came to hand. The Dervish guards chuckled indulgently at the women's antics, and when a prisoner fell under the blows they prodded him to his feet again with a sword point.

Although Nazeera was desperate to find where her charges had been taken, she was trapped in the mass of women. She could see down on to the beach where lines of rickety gallows of roughly trimmed poles were being hastily erected. Those that had been completed were already buckling under the weight of the bodies that dangled from them, and more captives were being dragged forward with nooses round their necks. In groups

126

they were prodded by the executioners on to the *angarebs* placed as steps beneath the gallows. When the nooses had been fastened to the crosspiece the *angareb* was pulled away and the victims were left swinging and kicking in the air.

This was slow work, and further along the beach another gang of executioners was hastening the business with the sword. They forced their victims to kneel in long lines with their hands tied behind their backs, their necks stretched forward. Then two headsmen started at opposite ends of the line and moved slowly towards each other, lopping off heads as they went. The watchers shouted as each head fell into the mud. When one of the executioners, his sword-arm tiring from the work, missed his stroke and only partially severed his victim's neck they clapped and hooted derisively.

At last Nazeera extricated herself from the press of bodies and made her way towards the British consular palace. The gates were open and unguarded. She slipped through them into the grounds. The palace was extensively damaged, window-panes smashed and doors torn off. Most of the furniture had been thrown out of the upper-floor windows. She went stealthily to the front terrace, and found more devastation. Terrified that she might run into a looter she crept in through the french windows and made her way through the wreckage to David Benbrook's study. Papers and documents were strewn across the room.

However, the oak panelling on the walls was intact. She went quickly to one panel and pressed the hidden spring built into the carving of the architrave. With a soft click it jumped back to reveal the door of the large safe. Her father had allowed Rebecca to keep her jewellery there, and Rebecca had taught Nazeera how to tumble the combination so that she could fetch and return the pieces she needed. The combination numbers were Rebecca's birthdate. Now Nazeera fed them into the lock, turned the handle and swung open the door.

On the top shelf lay David's leatherbound journal. The lower shelves were filled with family valuables, including the jewellery that Rebecca had inherited from her mother. It was all packed into matching red-leather wallets. There were also a number of canvas money-bags, which held over a hundred pounds in gold and silver coins. It was too dangerous to carry all of this with her. Nazeera returned all of the jewellery and most of the cash to the safe, then relocked the door and closed the secret panel. This would be her secret bank when she needed money. She placed a few small coins in her sleeve pocket for immediate use, then lifted her robe and strapped a canvas bag with more round her waist, then smoothed her shapeless skirts over it.

She left the study and climbed the stairs to the second floor. She went to Rebecca's bedroom, and stopped involuntarily in the doorway as she saw the extent of the damage. The looters had smashed every stick of furniture, and scattered books and clothing across the floor. She went in and searched through the mess.

She was almost in despair when at last she spotted the sisal bag lying under the overturned bed. The drawstring had burst open and much of the cholera remedy had spilled out. Nazeera squatted, scooped it up and poured it back into the bag. When she had salvaged as much as she could, she knotted the drawstring securely and tied it round her neck so that it hung down inside her robe. She gathered up a few other feminine trifles that might be useful and hid them about her person.

She went back downstairs, and stole out of the palace. She left the gardens through the small gate at the end of the terrace and lost herself in the Dervish victory celebrations. It did not take her long to discover where the women prisoners had been taken: the news was being shouted in the streets and people were flocking to the Customs House. Many had climbed up the walls and were clustered at the windows to peer in at the captives. Nazeera tucked up her skirts and scrambled up one of the buttresses until she reached the highest row of barred windows. She elbowed two small urchins out of her way. When they protested she unleashed a torrent of abuse that sent them scampering off. Then she gripped the bars and pressed her face to the square opening.

It took a minute for her eyes to adjust to the dim light inside. The Egyptian women prisoners were the wives and daughters of Gordon Pasha's officers, who were probably now lying headless on the river beach or dangling from the gallows. The women were squatting in miserable groups, with their children huddled around them. Many were spattered with the dried blood of their murdered menfolk. Among them were a few white women, the nuns from the Catholic mission, an Austrian lady doctor, the wives of the few Occidental traders and travellers who had been trapped in the city.

Then Nazeera's heart bounded: she had spotted

Rebecca sitting on the stone floor with her back against the wall and Amber on her lap. She was bedraggled and filthy with dust and soot. Her hair was lank and matted with sweat. Her father's blood had dried in black stains down the front of her yellow skirt. Her feet were bare and dusty, scratched and bruised. She sat aloof from the others, trying to fight off the waves of despair that threatened to overwhelm her. Nazeera recognized the stoic expression that concealed her courageous spirit, and was proud of her.

'Jamal!' Nazeera called to her, but her voice did not carry. The other women and their brats were making a fearful racket. They were weeping and wailing for their murdered menfolk, praying aloud for succour, entreating their captors for mercy. Above all else they were calling for water.

'Water! In the Name of Allah, give us water. Our children are dying. Give us water!'

'Jamal, my beautiful one!' Nazeera screamed to her, but Rebecca did not look up. She went on rocking Amber in her arms.

Nazeera broke a chip of plaster from the rotten windowsill, and threw it down through the bars. It struck the ground just short of where Rebecca was sitting, but skidded across the stone flags and hit her ankle. She lifted her head and looked around.

'Jamal, my little girl!'

Rebecca raised her eyes. She stared at the head in the window high above her, and her eyes flew wide in recognition. She looked around her quickly, to make certain that the Dervish guards at the doors had noticed nothing. Then she stood up and crossed the floor slowly, carrying Amber, until she stood directly under the high window. She

130

looked up again, and mouthed a single word: '*Mayya!* Water!' She lifted Amber's face and touched her chapped, swollen lips. 'Water!' she said again.

Nazeera nodded and climbed down the wall. She pushed her way through the crowds, searching frantically until she found the old woman with the donkey she had noticed earlier. The animal was so heavily laden with waterskins and bags of dhurra bread that its legs splayed outwards. The old woman was doing a thriving business with the hungry and thirsty crowds along the waterfront.

'I wish to buy food and one of your skins, old mother.'

'I still have a little bread and dried meat to sell, and for three *pice* you may drink your fill, but I will never sell one of my waterskins,' said the woman firmly. She changed her mind when Nazeera showed her a silver dollar.

With the small waterskin slung over her shoulder, Nazeera hurried back to the front entrance of the Customs House. There were five guards at the main door. They stood with drawn swords, holding the curious throng at a respectful distance. Nazeera saw at a glance that they were all men of her tribe, the Beja. Then, with a twinge of excitement, she recognized one. He was of the same clan and had been circumcised at the same time as her dead husband. They had ridden beneath the banner of the Emir Osman Atalan, before the rise of the Mahdi when their world had been sane and sensible, not yet maddened by the new fanaticism.

She sidled closer to the doors, but the man she knew made a threatening gesture with his sword, warning her to come no closer.

'Ali Wad!' Nazeera called in a low tone. 'My husband rode with you on the famous raid to Gondar when you slew fifty-five Christian Abyssinians and captured two hundred and fifty fine camels.'

He lowered the sword and stared at her in astonishment. 'What is your husband's name, woman?' he demanded.

'His name was Taher Sherif, and he was killed by the Jaalin at Tushkit Wells. You were with him the day he died.'

'Then you are the Nazeera who was once reckoned beautiful.' His stern expression relaxed.

Her old feelings of affection for him stirred. 'When we were all young together,' she agreed, and lowered the headcloth so he could see her face. 'It seems to me, Ali Wad, that you have become a man of great power. One who could still light the flame in any woman's belly.'

He laughed. 'Nazeera of the silvery tongue. The years have changed you little. What is it you seek from me now?' She told him and his smile faded. The scowl reappeared. 'You ask me to risk my life.'

'As my husband gave his life for you . . . and as, once, his young widow risked more than her life for your pleasure. Have you forgotten?'

'I have not. Ali Wad does not forget his friends. Come with me.'

He led her in through the main door, and the guards within deferred to him respectfully. She followed him, and Rebecca ran to her. They embraced ecstatically and tearfully. Even in her extremity Amber recognized her and whispered to her, 'I love you, Nazeera. Do you still love me?'

132

'With all my heart, Zahra. I have brought water and food.' She led them to a corner of the hall and they huddled close together. Nazeera mixed some of the powder with water in the mug she had brought from the palace. She held it to Amber's lips. She drank greedily.

While this was going on Ali Wad glowered at the other prisoners. 'These three women,' he indicated Nazeera and her charges, 'are under my protection. Interfere with them at your peril, for I am a man of ugly moods. It gives me great pleasure to beat women with this kurbash.' He showed them the wicked hippo-hide whip. 'I love to hear them squeal.'

They cringed away from him fearfully. Then he stooped and whispered in Nazeera's ear. She cast down her eyes and giggled coquettishly. Ali Wad stalked back to his post at the door, grinning and stroking his beard.

The water revived Amber miraculously. 'What has happened to my sister?' she whispered, 'Where is Saffy?'

'She is safe with al-Sakhawi,' Nazeera assured her. 'I saw her go on board his steamer before I returned to you.' At this wonderful news Rebecca was too overcome with relief to speak. Instead she threw her arms round Nazeera and hugged her.

'You must stop weeping now, Jamal,' Nazeera told her sternly. 'We must all be clever, strong and careful, if we are to survive the difficult days that lie ahead.'

'Now that you are back with us, and I know Saffy is safe, I can face whatever comes. What will the Dervish do with us?'

Nazeera did not answer at once but glanced

133

significantly at Amber. 'First you must eat and drink to remain strong. Then we shall talk.'

She gave them a little of the dhurra bread. Amber managed a few mouthfuls, and kept them down. Nazeera nodded with satisfaction, and took her on to her own lap to allow Rebecca a chance to eat and rest. She stroked Amber's hair and crooned softly to her. The child fell asleep almost at once. 'She will be well again within days. Young ones have the most resilience.'

'What will happen to us?' Rebecca repeated her question.

Nazeera pursed her lips as she considered how much she should say. As much of the truth as is good for her, she decided. 'You and all these women are part of the spoils of war, as much as horses and camels.' Rebecca glanced at the sorry creatures around her, and felt momentary pity for them, until she remembered that she and Amber were in the same predicament. 'The Dervish will use them as they wish. The old and ugly will become house and kitchen slaves. The young and nubile will be used as concubines. You are young and surpassingly beautiful. Your hair and pale skin will intrigue all men.'

Rebecca shuddered. She had never imagined what it might be like to fall under the power of a man of different race. Now the thought sickened her. 'Will they draw lots for us?' She had read in Gibbon's *Decline and Fall of the Roman Empire* that that was what soldiers did.

'No. The Dervish leaders will select those they want. The Mahdi will choose first, then the others in order of their rank and power. The Mahdi will choose you, there is no doubt of that. And it is good. He is the best for us, far better than any of the others.'

'Tell me why. Explain this to me. How can you know what he is like in his *zenana*?'

'He already has over three hundred wives and concubines, and his women talk. It is widely known where his tastes lie, what he likes to do with his women.'

Rebecca looked puzzled, 'Don't all men do the same thing, like—'

She broke off, but Nazeera finished the question for her: 'You mean the same as Abadan Riji and al-Sakhawi have done to you?'

Rebecca blushed scarlet. 'I forbid you to speak to me like that ever again.'

'I shall try to remember,' Nazeera replied, with a twinkle in her eye, 'but the answer to your question is that some men want different things from their women.'

Rebecca thought about that, then lowered her eyes shyly. 'Different things. What is the different thing that the Mahdi wants? What will he do to me?'

Nazeera glanced down at Amber to make sure she was asleep, then leant closer to Rebecca, cupped her hand to her ear and whispered. Rebecca jerked back. 'My mouth!' she gasped. 'That is the most disgusting thing I have ever heard.'

'Nay, silly girl. Think a moment. With a man you do not love, or one you hate, it is quicker, easier and less uncomfortable. You do not lose your precious maidenhead, or if you have already done so, nobody is any the wiser. Even more important, there are no undesired consequences.'

'I can see that with certain men this might be preferable.' Then another thought struck her, and her expression changed again. She looked intrigued. 'What is it like . . . to do that to a man or let him do it to you?'

'First, remember this. With the Mahdi you obey him in all things with every semblance of pleasure and joy. Only one thing is vitally important. With the Mahdi you must never display repugnance. He is divine, but in these matters he is as vain as all other men. Unlike other men, however, he has in his hands the power of life and death, and he does not hesitate to employ it on all who displease him. Thus the next thing to bear closely in mind is not to gag or spit. To reject and expel his essence would be a mortal insult to him.'

'But, Nazeera, what if I do not like the taste? What if I cannot help myself?'

'Swallow quickly and have done. In all events you will grow accustomed to it. We women learn and adjust very quickly.'

Rebecca nodded. Already the idea was not so shocking. 'What else must I remember?'

'There is no doubt in my mind that the Mahdi will choose you. You must greet him as the Chosen of God and the successor to His Prophet. You must tell him what a deep joy and honour it is to meet him at last. You can add whatever else you wish—that he is the light of your eyes and the breath of your lungs. He will believe this. Then you must tell him that al-Zahra is your orphan sister. The holy law places a duty on him to protect and care for the orphan, so she will not be parted from you. There are quotations from the holy writings about orphans that you must learn by rote so that you are

136

able to repeat them to him. I will teach them to you.' Rebecca nodded, and Nazeera went on, 'There is one other thing more important than all else. You must do or say nothing that might cause the Mahdi to pass you by. Show no anger, or resentment or disrespect. If he should reject you, the next choice will fall to his Khalifa Abdullahi.'

'Would that be worse?'

'Abdullahi is the cruellest, most wicked man in Islam. Better we should all perish than he take you or al-Zahra as his concubine.'

Rebecca shivered. 'Teach me the quotations.'

She was a quick learner and, before Amber woke, Nazeera was satisfied that she would acquit herself properly in the presence of the prophet of God.

*   *   *

Osman Atalan returned across the Nile from the city he had conquered. He came in glory at the head of the flotilla of boats that had carried his army to Khartoum. Every man, woman and child who could walk, toddle or totter came down to the riverbank to greet him. The war drums boomed and thumped and *ombeyas* blared. One groom held his weapons, his lance, spears and broadsword. Another groom held his warhorse al-Buq for him, fully caparisoned, with his rifle in the scabbard behind the saddle.

When Osman stepped ashore from the dhow he was preceded by al-Noor who carried over one shoulder a leather dhurra bag, whose bottom was stained a dark wine colour. The crowds shouted when they saw it, for they guessed the contents.

They shouted again at the sight of Osman, so tall and noble in his gleaming white *jibba* decorated with the brightly coloured patches.

Osman mounted al-Buq and processed through the town. The crowds lined both sides of the narrow, winding streets, and the road was strewn with palm fronds. The children ran ahead of his horse and the women lifted their infants high so that they could look upon the hero of Islam and tell their own children that they had seen him. Brave men and mighty warriors tried to touch his foot as he swept past, and the women ululated and called his name.

At the Mahdi's palace, Osman dismounted and took the stained dhurra bag from al-Noor. He climbed the outside staircase to the flat-roof terrace where the prophet of Allah sat cross-legged on his *angareb*. He made a sign to the young women who attended him, and they prostrated themselves quickly before him, then moved gracefully backwards, leaving the terrace to the two men.

Osman went to the Mahdi and placed the sack before him. He knelt to kiss his hands and feet. 'You are the light and the joy of our world. May Allah always smile upon you, who are his chosen one.'

The Mahdi touched his forehead. 'May you always please God, as you have pleased His humble prophet.' Then he took Osman's hand and raised him up. 'How went the battle?'

'With your presence watching over us and your face before us, it went well.'

'What of my enemy and the enemy of Allah, the crusader, Gordon Pasha?'

'Your enemy is dead and his soul boils eternally in the waters of hell. The day you had foreseen has arrived, and those things you had prophesied have come to pass.'

'All that you tell me, Osman Atalan, pleases God. Your words are as honey on your lips and sweet music in my ears. But have you brought me proof that what you say is true?'

'I have brought you proof that no man may doubt, proof that will resound in the heart of every son of the Prophet throughout all Islam.' Osman stooped, gripped the corner seams of the dhurra bag and lifted it. The contents rolled out on to the mud floor. 'Behold the head of Gordon Pasha.'

The Mahdi leant forward with his elbows on his thighs and stared at the head. He was no longer smiling. His expression was cold and impassive, but there was such a glow in his eyes that struck fear even into Osman Atalan's valiant heart. The silence went on, and the Mahdi did not move for a long time. Then at last he looked up again at Osman. 'You have pleased Allah and his prophet. You shall have great reward. See that this head is placed on a spike at the gates of the great mosque that all the faithful may look upon it and fear the power of Allah and his righteous servant, Muhammad, the Mahdi.'

'It shall be done, master.' For the first time Osman used the title *'Rabb'*, which was more than 'master'. It meant 'Lord of all things'. 'Rabb' was also one of the ninety-nine beautiful names of Allah. Had his praise exceeded the limits of flattery? Was this not blasphemy? Osman was immediately stricken by his own presumption. He bowed his head and waited for the Mahdi to rebuke him.

He need not have feared. His instinct had been flawless. The serene smile blossomed once more on the Mahdi's beloved face. He held out his hand to Osman. 'Take me to the city you have won for the glory of Allah. Show me the spoils of this great victory that brings the *jihad* to its full flowering. Take me across the river Nile and show to me all that you have achieved in my name.'

Osman took his hand and brought him to his feet. They went down to the riverbank and embarked in the dhow that was waiting for them. They crossed the flow and went ashore in the harbour of Khartoum. When he walked along the corniche to the governor's palace the crowds spread before him bolts of looted silk, fine linen and wool so that the Mahdi need not soil his feet in the dust and filth of the captured city. The chorus of prayer and praise that went up from the prostrating crowds was deafening.

In the governor's audience hall the Mahdi took his place beside Khalifa Abdullahi, who was working with four black-robed *kadi*, the Islamic judges. They were questioning the wealthy citizens of Khartoum who had been brought before them in chains. They were asked to reveal where they had hidden their treasures. This was a protracted process, for it was not enough simply to reveal all one's wealth at the outset. The Khalifa Abdullahi and his *kadi* had to ensure that the victims were holding back nothing. The full answers were extracted with fire and water. The branding irons were heated in charcoal braziers and when the tips glowed red they were used to burn the texts of appropriate *sura* from the Koran into the naked bellies and backs of the victims. Their agonized shrieks echoed from the high ceilings.

'Let your cries be heard as praise and prayers to Allah,' the Mahdi told them. 'Let your riches be offerings that you render to His glory.'

When there was no space left on their blistered skin for further religious texts to be inscribed, the red-hot irons were applied to their genitals. At last they were carried to the water fountain in the middle of the atrium of the palace. There they were strapped to a stool and tipped backwards over the wall of the fountain until their heads were below the surface of the water. When they lost consciousness, they were tipped forward, mucus streaming from their mouths and noses. They revived, and were immersed again. Before they expired the judges were well satisfied that they had revealed all their secrets.

Abdullahi led his master to the governor's robing room, which they were using as a temporary treasury, and showed him all that they had collected so far. There were bags and chests of coin, piles of plate and chalices of silver and gold; some were even carved from pure rock crystal or amethyst and encrusted with precious and semi-precious stones. There were heaps of silk and fine wool in bolts, satins embroidered with gold thread, more chests of jewellery, fantastic creations from Asia, India and Africa, earrings, necklaces, collars and brooches set with fiery diamonds, emeralds and sapphires. There were even statuettes in images of the old gods, fashioned thousands of years previously and plundered from the tombs of the ancients. The Mahdi frowned angrily when he saw these. 'They are an abomination in the sight of

God, and every true Muslim.' His usually mild tones thundered through the halls so that even the *khalifa* trembled. 'Take them hence, smash them into a hundred pieces and throw the fragments into the river.'

While many men scrambled to obey his order, the Mahdi turned to Osman and smiled again. 'I think only what Allah wishes me to think. My words are not my own words. They are the very word of God.'

'Would the blessed Mahdi care to see the women prisoners? If any please him, he might take them into his *zenana*.' The *khalifa* sought to placate him.

'May Allah be pleased with you, Abdullahi,' said the Mahdi, 'but first I wish some refreshment. Then we shall pray, and only thereafter will we go to view the new women.'

Abdullahi had prepared a pavilion in the governor's garden at a spot that overlooked the river and the beach beside the harbour on which the gallows had been erected. Under a tent of plaited reed matting, which was suspended on bamboo poles and open on all sides to allow a cooling breeze to blow through, they reclined on splendid rugs of the finest wool and pillows of silk. From clay pitchers that allowed the liquid to permeate through and cool the rest of the contents, they sipped the Mahdi's favourite beverage of date syrup and ground ginger. In the meantime they watched, with mild interest, the execution of Gordon's men. Some of the victims were cut down from the scaffold while they still writhed in the noose and thrown into the river, hands bound behind their backs.

'It is a pity that so many are of Islam,' said

Osman, 'but they are also Turks, and they opposed your *jihad.*'

'For that they have paid the price, but in as much as they were of the true faith let them find peace,' said the Mahdi, and extended the forefinger of his right hand in blessing. Then he stood up and led them towards the Customs House.

When they entered the main hall the captured women had been lined up against the far wall. They prostrated themselves as the Mahdi entered and sang his praises.

The guards had erected a dais at the opposite side of the hall to where the women knelt. This was covered with Persian carpets. The Mahdi took his seat upon them, then motioned for his *khalifa* to sit at his right hand and the Emir Osman Atalan to sit on his left. 'Let them bring the captives forward, one at a time.'

Ali Wad, who was in charge of the women, presented them in inverse order of their appeal to masculine taste. The old and ugly to start with, and the younger and prettier to follow. The Mahdi dismissed the first twenty or so, who interested him not at all, with a curt gesture of his left hand. Then Ali Wad led forward a young Galla girl. The Mahdi made a sign with his right hand. Ali Wad lifted her robe over her head and she was naked. The three great men leant forward to examine her. The Mahdi made a circular movement with his right hand, and the girl revolved before them to display all her charms, which were considerable.

'She is, of course, too thin,' the Mahdi said at last. 'She will have eaten little in the last ten months, but she will plump up prettily. She is pleasing, but she has a bold eye and will be difficult. She is of the kind that causes trouble in the *zenana*.' He made the left-hand sign of rejection, then smiled at his *khalifa*. 'If you decide she is worth the trouble, you may take her, and I wish you joy of her.'

'If she makes trouble in my harem, she will have stripes on her lustrous buttocks to show for it.' The Khalifa Abdullahi flicked her with his fly whisk on the threatened area of her anatomy. At the sting she squeaked and stotted in the air like a gazelle ewe. Abdullahi made the right-hand sign of acceptance and the girl was led away. The selection went on at a leisurely pace, the men discussing the females in explicit detail.

The daughter of a Persian trader caught their particular attention. They all agreed that her features were unattractively bony and angular, but the hair of her head was red. There was some discussion about its authenticity, which the Mahdi settled by having Ali Wad remove her garments. The gorgeous ruddy tone of her dense, curling nether bush dispelled their doubts.

'There is every hope that she will bear red-headed sons,' said the Mahdi. The first Prophet Muhammad, of whom he was the successor, had possessed red hair. Thus she was highly valuable as a breeder. He would give her to one of his emirs as a mark of his divine favour. It would reinforce the emir's loyalty and strengthen the bonds between them. He made the right-hand sign.

Then Ali Wad led forward Rebecca Benbrook. Nazeera had covered her head with a light shawl. Amber had just enough strength to totter at her elder sister's side, clinging to her hand for comfort and support.

'Who is the child?' demanded Khalifa Abdullahi. 'Is she the woman's daughter?'

'Nay, mighty *khalifa*,' Ali Wad replied, as Nazeera had coached him. 'It is her little sister. Both girls are virgins and orphans.'

The men looked interested. A maidenhead was of great value, and bestowed a magical and beneficial influence on the man who ruptured it. Then, as Nazeera had told him, Ali Wad drew off the shawl that covered Rebecca's head. The Mahdi drew a sharp breath, and both the *khalifa* and Osman Atalan sat straighter as they stared in astonishment at her hair, which Nazeera had combed out carefully. A beam of sunlight through one of the high windows transformed it into a crown of gold. The Mahdi beckoned Rebecca to come closer. She knelt before him. He leant towards her and fingered a lock. 'It is soft as the wing of a sunbird,' he murmured in awe.

Rebecca had been careful not to look directly into his face, which would have been a gesture of disrespect. With her eyes still lowered, she whispered huskily, 'I have heard all men speak of your grace and of your holy state. I have longed for sight of your beautiful face, as a traveller in the great desert longs for his first glimpse of Mother Nile.'

His eyes opened a little wider. He placed one finger beneath her chin and lifted her face. She saw at once that what she had said had pleased him. 'You speak good Arabic,' he said.

'The holy tongue,' she agreed. 'The language of the faithful.'

'How old are you, child? Are you virgin, as Ali Wad has told us? Have you ever known a man?'

145

'I pray that you might be my first and my last,' she lied, without a tremor, knowing just how much depended on his choice. She had been watching the *khalifa* during the selection of the other women and sensed that all Nazeera had told her was true: he was as slippery as a slime-eel and as venomous as a scorpion. She thought that it would be better to be dead than to belong to him.

When he whispered to the Mahdi his voice was oily and unctuous. 'Exalted One, let us have sight of this one's body,' he suggested. 'Is the bush of her loins of the same colour and texture as the hair on her head? Are her breasts white as camels' milk? Are the lips of her quimmy pink as the petals of a desert rose? Let us discover all these sweet secrets.'

'Those sights are for my eyes alone to gaze upon. This one pleases me. I will keep her for myself.' With his right hand he made the sign of acceptance over Rebecca's head.

'I am overcome with joy and gratitude that you have found me pleasing, Great and Holy One.' Rebecca bowed her head. 'But what of my little sister? I pray that you will take her under your protection as well.'

The Mahdi glanced down at Amber, who shrank from him and clung to Rebecca's dusty, bloodstained skirt. She stared back at him in trepidation and he saw how young she was, how weak and sickly she appeared. Her eyes were sunk into bruised-looking cavities, and she had barely the strength to stand upright. The Mahdi knew that a child in her condition would be a nuisance and the cause of disruption in his household. He was not lubriciously attracted to children, either male or female, as he knew his *khalifa* was. Let him have

146

this wretched creature. He was about to make the left-hand gesture of rejection, when Rebecca forestalled him. Nazeera had coached her in what she must say. She spoke up again, clearly this time.

'The saint Abu Shuraih has reported the direct words of the Prophet Muhammad, the messenger of Allah, may Allah love him eternally, who said, "I declare inviolate the rights of the weak ones, the orphans and the women." He said also, "Allah provides for you only in as much as you protect the orphans among you."'

The Mahdi lowered his left hand, and looked at her thoughtfully. Then he smiled again, but there was something unfathomable in his eyes. He made the right-hand sign of acceptance over Amber and said to Ali Wad, 'I place these women in your charge. See that no harm befalls them. Convey them to my harem.'

Ali Wad and ten of his men escorted Rebecca, Amber and the other women chosen by the Mahdi to the harbour. Without drawing attention to herself, Nazeera followed them. When they were placed on board a large trading dhow to be carried across the Nile to Omdurman, she went on board with them, and when one of the crew questioned her presence Ali Wad snarled at him so belligerently that he scurried away to attend to the hoisting of the lateen sail. From then on Nazeera was accepted as the servant to al-Jamal and al-Zahra, the concubines of the Mahdi. The three squatted together in the bows of the dhow.

While Nazeera made Amber drink again from the waterskin, Rebecca asked fretfully, 'What am I going to do, Nazeera? I can never allow myself to become the chattel of a brown man, a native who is not a Christian.' The full extent of her predicament began to dawn on her. 'I think I would rather die than have that happen to me.'

'Your sense of propriety is noble, Jamal, but I am brown and a native also,' Nazeera replied. 'Also, I am not a Christian. If you have become so fastidious, then perhaps it would be better if you sent me away.'

'Oh, Nazeera, we love you.' Rebecca was immediately contrite.

'Listen to me, Jamal.' Nazeera took Rebecca's arm and forced her to look into her eyes. 'The branch breaks that will not bend with the wind. You are a limber young branch. You must learn to bend.'

Rebecca felt as though she were being crushed beneath a great weight. Wherever her mind turned it encountered only sorrow, regret and fear. She thought of her father, and touched the black stains of his blood on her bodice. She knew that the terrible moments of his beheading were engraved on her memory for the rest of her life. The sorrow was almost unsupportable. She thought of Saffron and knew she would never see her again. She held Amber close to her heart, but wondered if she would survive the disease that had already damaged her fragile body. She thought of the future that awaited them all, and gaped before her, like the black, insatiable maw of a monster.

There is no escape for any of us. As she thought it, there was an urgent shout from one of the crew. She looked about her as though she had been rudely awakened from a nightmare. The dhow had reached the middle of the river, and was sailing along on the light breeze. Now the entire crew was agitated. They crowded the weather rail, and gabbled at each other, pointing downstream.

A cannon boomed out across the water, then another. Soon every one of the Dervish guns were blazing away from both banks. Rebecca handed Amber to Nazeera and jumped to her feet. She gazed in the direction in which everybody was staring and her spirits lifted. All her dark fears and uncertainties fell away. Close at hand she saw the Union Flag of Great Britain flying bravely in the bright sunlight.

Quickly Rebecca pulled Amber to her feet, held her close and pointed downriver. Less than half a mile away a squadron of ships was steaming towards them down the middle of the channel. Their decks were crowded with British soldiers.

'They are coming to rescue us, Amber. Oh, look.' She turned Amber's head. 'Is it not the finest sight you have ever seen? The relief column has arrived.' Now, for the first time, she allowed herself to succumb to her tears. 'We are safe, darling Amber. We are going to be safe.'

*   *   *

Penrod Ballantyne kept at a safe distance from the river as they rode the last few miles along the eastern bank of the Nile towards the smoke-hazed city of Khartoum on the horizon. Every mile they covered confirmed what was already a certainty in his mind. The flags on the tower of Mukran Fort were gone. Chinese Gordon had been overwhelmed. The city had fallen. The relief column was too late to save them.

He tried to arrive at some decision as to what he

149

should do now. Every one of his calculations up to this point had depended on the survival of the city. Now there seemed to be no reason or logic in going on. He had seen a city captured and sacked by the Dervish. By the time he arrived the only living things inside the walls of Khartoum would be the crows and vultures.

But something drew him onwards. He tried to convince himself that this course of action was dictated by the fact that the doors behind him were shut. He had compounded the charge of insubordination that hung over him by disobeying Sir Charles Wilson's direct orders to stay in the camp at Metemma. There seemed little merit in turning back now to face the court-martial with which Sir Charles Wilson would welcome his return.

'On the other hand, what merit is there in going forward?' he asked himself. There were others who might still be alive and in need of his assistance: General Gordon and David Benbrook, the twins and Rebecca. At last he was honest with himself. Rebecca Benbrook had loomed large in his consciousness ever since he had ridden away from Khartoum. She was probably the true reason he was there. He knew he must find out what had become of her, or for the rest of his life her memory would haunt him.

Suddenly he reined in his camel and cocked his head towards the river. The sound of gunfire was close and clear. It mounted swiftly from a few random shots to a full artillery barrage. 'What is it?' he called to Yakub, who rode close behind him. 'What are they shooting at now?'

There was a scattered grove of thorn acacia and

150

palms growing along the bank, obscuring their view of the river. Penrod turned his camel and urged it into a gallop. They rode through the intervening belt of trees and came out abruptly on the bank of the Nile. A forlorn and desperate sight lay before him. The steamers of Wilson's division were struggling upstream towards the city of Khartoum, whose skyline was clearly visible before them. From their mastheads they flew the red, white and blue Union Flag. Their decks were crammed with troops, but Penrod knew that between them they could not carry more than two or three hundred men. Most of the faces he could see through the lens of his telescope were those of Nubian infantrymen. There was a cluster of white officers on the bridge of the leading steamer. They all had their telescopes raised and were peering upstream. Even at this distance Penrod could pick out the tall, awkward figure of Wilson, his craggy features hidden by his large pith helmet.

'Too late, Charles the Timid,' Penrod whispered bitterly. 'If you had done the right thing, as General Stewart and your officers urged, you might have been in time to tip the scales of Fate and save the lives of those unfortunates who waited ten months for you to come.'

The Dervish shot began falling more heavily around the little vessels, and hordes of Arab cavalry came galloping down the banks from the direction of Omdurman and Khartoum to intercept the flotilla. The Dervish riders fired from the saddle as they kept pace with Wilson's steamers.

'We must join them!' Penrod shouted to Yakub, and they raced forward to mingle with the Dervish. It was the perfect cover for them. They were soon

151

lost in the dust and confusion of the Arab squadrons. Penrod and Yakub fired as enthusiastically as all the riders around them, but they aimed low so that their bullets whacked harmlessly into the river.

The surface of the water all around the two steamers was lashed by musketry, and the leaping fountains of spray kicked up by the Krupps guns. The white hulls were quickly pockmarked by the bullets that hammered against the steel plate. The thinner steel of the funnels was riddled with holes. Suddenly there was a louder explosion and a cloud of silver steam flew high into the sky above the second vessel. The Dervish riding around Penrod howled triumphantly, and brandished their weapons.

'One of the Krupps has hit her cleanly in the boiler,' Penrod lamented. 'By all the gods of war, this day belongs to the Mahdi.'

With steam still erupting from her, the stricken vessel swung helplessly across the stream and began to drop back downriver. Almost immediately Wilson's leading vessel slowed and turned back to render assistance, and the rest of the squadron followed him round.

The Arab riders with Penrod shouted threats and derision at the two vessels: 'You cannot prevail against the forces of Allah!'

'Allah is One! The Mahdi is his chosen prophet. He is omnipotent against the infidel.'

'Return to Satan who is your father! Return to hell, which is your home!'

Penrod shouted with them, and exhibited the same jubilation, firing his rifle into the air, but inwardly his anger and contempt for Wilson seethed. What a fine excuse to break off your determined attack and betake your craven buttocks back to a comfortable chair on the veranda of the Gheziera Club in Cairo. I doubt, Sir Charles, that we shall be seeing much more of you in these latitudes.

In the hope that the crippled vessel would be carried on to the bank, hundreds of Dervish riders followed the squadron downstream, keeping up a rattling fusillade. The crews struggled to pass a towline between them. As the steamers drifted in towards the opposite bank, and out of rifle range, many riders gave up the chase and turned back towards Omdurman. Penrod moved along with them and his presence was unremarked in the effusive mood of victory and triumph. It took almost an hour to reach Omdurman. This gave him plenty of opportunity to listen in on many shouted conversations, all of which were discussions of the devastatingly successful night attack on Khartoum, led by the Emir Osman Atalan, and the subsequent sack and looting. At one point he overheard some discussing the captured white women whom they had taken to the Customs House in Khartoum.

They must be talking about Rebecca and the twins. His hopes were resuscitated. Apart from them there were hardly any white women remaining in Khartoum, except the nuns and the Austrian doctor from the leper colony. Please, God, let it be Rebecca they are speaking about. Even if that means she is a prisoner at least she has survived.

Among the long, haphazard ranks of riders Penrod and Yakub rode into Omdurman. Yakub knew of a small caravanserai on the edge of the

153

desert, which was run by an old man of the Jaalin tribe, a distant relative to whom he referred as Uncle. This man had often given him shelter and shielded him from the blood feud with the other powerful members of their tribe. Although he looked curiously at Penrod he asked no questions and placed at their disposal a filthy cell with one tiny high window. The only furniture was a rickety *angareb* covered with coarse sacking in which numerous blood-sucking insects had already set up home. They seemed to resent any human intrusion into their territory.

'To reward you for your service to me over the years, Yakub the Faithful, I shall allow you to sleep upon the bed while I make do with the floor. But tell me how much we can trust our host, this man Wad Hagma.'

'I think my uncle suspects who you are, for I told him once, long ago, that you were my lord. However, Wad Hagma is of my clan and blood. Although he has sworn the oath of Beia to the Mahdi, I believe he did so with his mouth only, not his heart. He would not betray us.'

'He has an evil cast in his eye, Yakub, but that seems to run in the family.'

By the time they had watered and fed the camels and penned them in to the kraal at the back of Wad Hagma's caravanserai, darkness had fallen and they wandered into the sprawling warren of the holy city, seemingly without purpose but in reality to find some news of the Benbrook family. After dark Omdurman was still a holy city and under the Mahdi's strict moral code. Nevertheless, they found a small number of dimly lit coffee shops. Some offered in the back rooms a hookah pipe and the company of a young, beautiful woman or, should their tastes lean in that direction, an even more beautiful boy.

'It has been my experience that in any foreign town the most reliable sources of information are always the women of pleasure.' Yakub volunteered his services.

'I know that your motives are praiseworthy, Yakub the virtuous. I am grateful for your self-sacrifice.'

'I lack only the few paltry coins required to perform this onerous task for you.'

Penrod pressed the room price into his hand, and ensconced himself in a dimly lit corner of the coffee shop from where he was able to eavesdrop on several conversations between the other clientele.

'I have heard that when Osman Atalan laid the head of Gordon Pasha at the feet of the Divine Mahdi the angel Gabriel appeared at his side and made the sign of sanctification over the head of the Mahdi,' said one.

'I heard it was two angels,' countered another.

'I heard it was two angels and the Messenger of Allah, the first Muhammad,' said a third.

'May he live at Allah's right hand for ever,' said all three in unison.

So, Gordon is no more. Penrod sipped the viscous bitter coffee from the brass thimble, to cover his emotions. A brave man. He will be more at peace now than he ever was during his lifetime. A short while later, Yakub emerged from the back room looking pleased with himself. 'She was not beautiful,' he confided in Penrod, 'but she was friendly and industrious. She asked me to

155

commend her efforts to her owner or he would beat her.'

'Yakub, saviour of ugly maidens, you did what was expected of you, did you not?' Penrod asked, and Yakub rolled one eye knowingly while the other remained focused on his master.

'Apart from that, what else did she tell you that might be of value to us?' Penrod could not refrain from smiling.

'She told me that early this afternoon, just after the infidel steamers were driven in confusion and ignominy back downriver by the ever-victorious Ansar of the Mahdi, may Allah love him for ever, a dhow brought five women captives across the river from Khartoum. They were in the charge of Ali Wad, an aggagier of the Jaalin who is well known hereabouts for his ferocity and his foul temper. Immediately on landing Ali Wad conveyed the captives to the *zenana* of Muhammad, the Mahdi, may Allah love him through eternity. The women have not been seen again, nor are they likely to be. The Mahdi keeps firm control of his property.'

'Did your obliging young friend notice if one of those captives had yellow hair?' Penrod asked.

'My friend, who is not particularly young, was less certain of that. The heads and faces of all the women were covered.'

'Then we must keep a watch on the palace of the Mahdi until we are certain that these women are who we hope they are,' Penrod told him.

'The women of the *zenana* are never permitted to leave their quarters,' Yakub pointed out. 'Al-Jamal will never again be allowed to show herself beyond the gates.'

'Nevertheless you might learn something by

156

watching patiently.'

Early next morning Yakub joined the large group of worshippers and petitioners who were always gathered at the gates of the Mahdi's palace, ready to prostrate themselves before him when the Chosen One went to the mosque to lead the ritual prayers and deliver his sermons, which were not his words but the very words of Allah. This day, as was his custom, the Mahdi emerged punctually for the first prayers of the day, but so great was the press of humanity around him that Yakub caught only a glimpse of his embroidered *kufi* skullcap as he passed. Yakub followed him to the mosque, and after the prayers returned in his train to the palace. He followed this routine five times a day for the next three days, without receiving any confirmation of the existence or whereabouts of the women. On the third afternoon, as had become his habit, he settled down to wait again in the sparse shade of an oleander bush from where he could keep one eye on the palace gates. He was beginning to nod off in the somnolent heat when there was a light touch on his sleeve and a woman's voice entreated him, 'Noble and beloved warrior of God, I have clean sweet water to quench your thirst, and freshly roasted *asida* flavoured with chilli sauce as fiery as the flames of hell, all for the very reasonable price of five copper *pice*.'

'May you please God, sister, for your offer pleases me.' The woman poured from the waterskin into an enamelled tin mug, and spread sauce on a round of dhurra bread. As she handed these to him she said, in a low voice muffled by the headcloth that covered her face, 'O faithless one, you swore a mighty oath that you would remember me for ever but you have forgotten me already.'

'Nazeera!' He was amazed.

'Dimwitted one! For three days I have watched you flaunt yourself before the eyes of your enemies and now you compound your idiocy by shouting my name aloud for all to hear.'

'You are the light of my life,' he told her. 'I shall give thanks every day that you are well. What of your charges? Al-Jamal and her two little sisters, are they with you in the palace? My lord seeks to know these things.'

'They are alive, but their father is dead. We cannot talk here. After the afternoon prayers I shall be at the camel market. Look for me there.' Nazeera drifted away to offer her water and bread to others who waited at the gates.

As she had promised, he found her at the well in the centre of the camel market. She was drawing water in a large earthenware pitcher. Two other women lifted it and placed it on her head, Nazeera balanced it with one hand and set off across the marketplace. Yakub followed her closely enough to hear what she was saying, but not so close as to make it obvious that they were together.

'Tell your master that al-Jamal and al-Zahra are in the palace. They have been taken by the Mahdi as his concubines. Saffron escaped on the steamer of al-Sakhawi. I watched her go on board. Their father was beheaded by the Ansar. I saw it done.' Under the weight of the pitcher Nazeera moved with a straight back and rolling hips. Yakub watched the lively play of her buttocks with interest. 'What are your master's intentions?' she wanted to know.

'I think that his purpose is to rescue al-Jamal

158

and carry her off as his woman.'

'If he thinks to accomplish this alone, he is touched by the sun. They will be discovered and both of them will die. Come here again tomorrow at the same time. There is someone else you must meet,' she told him. 'Now, walk away and do not show yourself at the palace gates again.'

He turned aside to examine a string of camels that was being offered for sale, but from the corner of his eye he watched her go. She is a clever woman and skilled in the art of pleasing a man. 'Tis a pity she does not confine her affections to just one of us, he mused.

The following day Yakub was at the camel market again at the same hour. It took him some time to find Nazeera. She had changed her costume to that of a Bedouin woman, and she was cooking at a charcoal brazier. He might not have recognized her had she not called to him: 'Roasted locusts, lord, fresh from the desert. Sweet and juicy.' He took a seat on the stump of acacia wood that had been placed by the fire as a stool. Nazeera brought him a handful of locusts she had crisped on the brazier. 'The one I spoke of is here,' she said softly.

He had taken little notice of the man who sat on the opposite side of the fire. Although he was dressed in a *jibba* and carried a sword he was too plump and well fed to be an aggagier. In place of a man's beard his chin was adorned with only a few wisps of curly hair. Now Yakub looked at him with more attention, and then, with a thrill of jealous anger, he recognized him. 'Bacheet, why are you not cheating honest men with your shoddy goods, or prodding their wives with your inconsequential member?' he said coldly.

'Ah, Yakub of the quick knife! How many throats have you slit recently?' Bacheet's tone was every bit as chilled.

'From where I sit yours looks soft enough to tempt me.'

'Stop this childish squabbling,' said Nazeera sternly, although she found it more than a little flattering that she could still be at the centre of such rivalry for her waning charms. 'We have important things to discuss. Bacheet, tell him what you have already told me.'

'My master, al-Sakhawi, and I escaped from Khartoum on his steamer, the night that the Dervish attacked and captured the city. We found the girl-child, Filfil, and took her with us. Once we were clear of the city, we moored the steamer in the Lagoon of the Little Fish. My master sent me back here to seek out al-Jamal. However, he can tarry no longer at the lagoon. The Dervish are diligently searching both banks of the river for him, and within a short while they will surely find him. He is forced to flee further up the Blue Nile into the kingdom of the Emperor John of Abyssinia where he is known and respected as a trader. When he is secure there he will be able to make careful plans for the rescue of al-Jamal and al-Zahra. My master is not yet aware that you and your master are here in Omdurman, but when I bring him this news I know that he will wish to join his efforts with your master's to achieve the rescue of the two white women.'

'Your master is called al-Sakhawi for his generosity and liberality. It is rumoured that his courage surpasses that of a buffalo bull, although

160

no man has ever seen him fight. Now you tell me that this renowned warrior intends to run away and leave two helpless women to their fate. On the other hand, I know that Abadan Riji will remain here in Omdurman until he has procured their escape from the blood-drenched clutches of the Mahdi,' Yakub said scornfully.

'Ha, Yakub, how edifying to hear you talk of blood-drenched clutches,' said Bacheet smoothly. He stood up to his full height and sucked in his belly. 'The yapping of a puppy must not be mistaken for the baying of the hound,' he said mysteriously. 'If Abadan Riji wishes the assistance of al-Sakhawi in arranging the rescue of al-Jamal, he may desire to send a message to my master. He can do so through Ras Hailu, an Abyssinian grain trader from Gondar whose dhows trade regularly downriver to Omdurman. Ras Hailu is a trusted friend and partner of my master. I will not waste more breath and time in arguing with you. Stay with God.'

Bacheet turned his back on Yakub and stalked away.

'You are like a small boy, Yakub. Why do I allow you to waste *my* time and breath?' Nazeera asked the sky. 'Bacheet was speaking good sense. It will need more than reckless courage to lift my girls from the *zenana* of the Mahdi, and to carry them thousands of leagues across the desert to safety. You will need money to place as bribes within the palace, more money to buy camels and provisions, still more money to arrange relays along your escape road. Does your master have that much money? I think not. Al-Sakhawi does, and he also has the patience and brains that your master lacks.

161

Yet in your arrogance and conceit you turn away the offer of assistance that will certainly make the difference between success and failure in your master's enterprise.'

'If al-Sakhawi is a man of such merit and virtue, why do you not marry your beloved al-Jamal to him, rather than to my master, Abadan Riji?' Yakub demanded angrily.

'That is the first sensible thing you have said all day,' Nazeera agreed.

'Are you against us? Will you not help us to free these women? Knowing how much I love you, Nazeera, will you turn me away in favour of that beardless creature, Bacheet?' Yakub assumed a piteous expression.

'I am newly arrived in Omdurman. I know very few people in this city. I have no way to enter upon the pathways of power and influence. There is little in which I can help you. One thing only is certain. I will not risk the lives of the two girls I love to some wild and reckless scheme. If you want me to give you what help I can, you must work out a plan that has more chance of success than of failure. It must be a plan that above all, takes into account their safety.' Nazeera began to pack up her pots and dishes. 'It must be a plan in which I can place my trust. When you have made such a plan, you can find me here every sacred Friday morning.'

'Nazeera, will you tell al-Jamal that my master is here in Omdurman, and that soon he will rescue her?'

'Why would I kindle false hope in her heart, which has already been broken by her captivity, the death of her father, the loss of her little sister Fifil, and the sickness of her other sister al-Zahra?'

162

'But my master loves her and will lay down his own life for her, Nazeera.'

'As he also loves the woman Bakhita and fifty others like her. I do not care if he lays down his life for her, but I will not let her lay down her life for him. Have you never seen a woman stoned to death for adultery, Yakub? That is what will happen to al-Jamal if your plans fail. The Mahdi is a man without mercy.' She tied a cloth round her dishes and lifted it on to her head. 'Come to me again only when you have something sensible to discuss with me.' Nazeera walked away, balancing the parcel gracefully on her head.

*   *   *

'How much money do you have?' asked Yakub's putative uncle, Wad Hagma.

Penrod looked into his guileless eyes and replied with a question. 'How much will you need?'

Wad Hagma pursed his lips while he considered. 'I will have to bribe my friends in the Mahdi's palace to clear the way and they are important men whom I cannot insult with a paltry sum. Then I will have to find and pay for the extra camels to carry so many people. I must provide fodder and provisions along the road, pay the guards at the border. All this will cost a great deal, but of course I will take nothing for my own trouble. Yakub is like a son to me, and his friends are my friends also.'

*   *   *

'Of course, he does this willingly and without

163

thought of his own rewards.' Yakub endorsed his uncle's altruistic intentions. They were sitting together by the small fire in the soot-blackened lean-to kitchen of the caravanserai, and eating the stew of mutton, wild onions and chilli. Considering the insalubrious surroundings in which it had been cooked and the venerable age of the flyblown ingredients, the dish was tastier than Penrod had expected.

'I am grateful to Wad Hagma for his assistance, but my question was, how much does he need?' It was only as a last resort that Penrod had agreed to enlist the assistance of the uncle in his plans. Yakub had convinced him that Wad Hagma knew many of the Mahdi's entourage and members of his palace household. With his uncle to help them, Yakub had considered it unnecessary to bring to his master's attention the offer of assistance conveyed by Bacheet on behalf of his own master, al-Sakhawi. In any case, his animosity towards Bacheet was so deep that he could not bring himself to do anything that might redound to his rival's credit or profit. He had refrained from mentioning to Penrod his meeting with Bacheet.

'It will not be less than fifty English sovereigns,' Wad Hagma said, in a tone of deep regret, watching Penrod's reaction.

'That is a small fortune!' Penrod protested.

Wad Hagma was encouraged to be dealing with a man who considered fifty sovereigns only a small fortune, rather than an extremely large one, so he immediately raised the bidding. 'Alas, it could be a great deal more,' he said lugubriously. 'However, the fate of these poor females has touched my heart and Yakub is dearer to me than any son. You are a mighty man and famous. I will do my best for you. In God's Name I swear this!'

'In God's Name!' Yakub agreed automatically.

'I will give you ten pounds now,' said Penrod, 'and more when you show your intent in deeds rather than in fine words.'

'You will see that the promises of Wad Hagma are like the mountain of Great Ararat, on which the ark of Noah came to rest.'

'Yakub will bring the money to you tomorrow.' Penrod did not want to reveal where he kept his purse. They finished the meal and wiped the last drops of gravy from the bottom of the dishes with scraps of dhurra bread. Penrod thanked the uncle and wished him goodnight, then he signed to Yakub to follow him. They walked out into the desert.

'There are already too many people in Omdurman who know who we are. It will be unsafe to stay any longer in your uncle's house. From now onwards we will sleep every night at a different place. Nobody must be able to follow our movements. We must see but never be seen.'

*   *   *

It was some months after she had been confined in the *zenana* before the Mahdi took any further notice of Rebecca. Then he sent her and Amber new wardrobes of clothing. Amber received three simple cotton dresses and light sandals. Rebecca was sent apparel of a more elaborate but modest design, as befitted a concubine of Allah's prophet.

The clothes were a welcome distraction from the boredom of the harem. By this time Amber had

165

recovered sufficiently from her illness to take an active interest, and they tried on the dresses and showed them off to Nazeera and to each other.

The *zenana* was an enclosure the size of a small village. There was only one gate in the ten-foot-high wall of mud-brick that surrounded the hundreds of thatched huts that housed all the Mahdi's wives and concubines, the slaves and servants who attended them. The women were fed from the communal kitchen, but it was a monotonous diet of dhurra and river fish fried in ghee, clarified butter, and blindingly hot chilli. With so many mouths to feed, the Mahdi obviously believed that some economies were called for.

Those women who had a little money of their own could buy additional provisions and delicacies from the female vendors who were allowed within the walls of the *zenana* for a few hours each morning. From her hoard of coins Nazeera bought legs of mutton, thick cuts of beef, calabashes of soured milk, and onions, pumpkins, dates and cabbage. They cooked these in the small fenced yard behind the thatched hut that Ali Wad had had his men build for them. On this nourishing diet their bony bodies, the legacy of the long siege, filled out, the colour returned to their cheeks and the sparkle to their eyes. Twice during this time Nazeera had returned secretly at night to the ruins of the British consular palace across the river in the abandoned city of Khartoum. On the first visit she had brought back not only money but David Benbrook's journal.

Rebecca had spent days reading it. It was almost as though she was listening to his voice again, except that on these pages he was expressing ideas and feelings she had not heard before. Between the sheets she discovered her father's last will and testament, signed ten days before his death and witnessed by General Charles Gordon. His estate was to be divided in equal shares between his three daughters, but kept in trust by his lawyer in Lincolns Inn, a gentleman named Sebastian Hardy, until they reached the age of twenty-one. Newbury was as remote as the moon, and the chance of any of them returning there was so slim that she paid scant heed to the document and placed it back between the pages of the journal.

She read on through her father's closely written but elegant script, often smiling and nodding, sometimes laughing or weeping. When she reached the end she found that several hundred pages remained empty in the thick book. She determined to continue with his account of family joys and tragedies. When next Nazeera crossed the river Rebecca asked her to find her father's writing materials.

Nazeera returned with pens, spare nibs and five bottles of best-quality Indian ink. She brought also more money and some small luxuries that had been overlooked by the looters. Among these items was a large looking-glass in a tortoiseshell frame.

'See how beautiful you are, Becky.' Amber held up the mirror so they could both admire the long dress of silk and silver thread that the Mahdi had sent her. 'Will I ever look like you?'

'You are already far more beautiful than I am, and you will grow more so every day.'

Amber reversed the mirror and studied her own face. 'My ears are too big, and my nose too flat. My chest looks like a boy's.'

'That will change, believe me.' Rebecca hugged her. 'Oh, it's so good to have you well again.' With the resilience of the young, Amber had put most of the recent horrors behind her. Rebecca had allowed her to read their father's journal. This had helped her recovery, and alleviated the terrible mourning she had undergone for him and Saffron. Now she was able to reminisce about the happy times they had all spent together. She was also taking a more active interest in their alien surroundings and the circumstances in which they now found themselves. Using her natural charm and attractive personality she struck up acquaintances with some of the other women and children of the *zenana*. With the money that Nazeera brought home, there was enough for her to take small gifts to the most needy of the other women. She was soon a favourite in the *zenana* with many new friends and playmates.

Even Ali Wad softened under her warm, sunny influence. This forbidding warrior had renewed the intimate friendship with Nazeera that they had once enjoyed. On many occasions recently Nazeera had left their hut immediately after they had eaten the evening meal, and only returned at dawn. Amber explained her nocturnal absences to Rebecca. 'You see, poor Ali Wad has a bad back. He was unhorsed in battle. Now Nazeera has to straighten his back for him to stop the pain. She is the only one who knows how to do it.'

Rebecca alleviated her boredom by attempting to bring some order into the social and domestic chaos she found all around them. First, she concerned herself with the lack of hygiene that prevailed in the *zenana*. Most of the women were from the desert and had never been forced to live in such crowded conditions before. All rubbish was simply tossed outside the doors of the huts, to be scavenged by crows, rats, ants and stray dogs. There were no latrines and everybody answered the call of nature wherever they happened to be when they received it. To navigate the labyrinth of pathways between the huts required nimble footwork to dodge the odoriferous brown mounds that dotted open ground. For Rebecca the final provocation was coming upon two small naked boys competing to see which could urinate across the opening of the single well that supplied water to the entire *zenana*. Neither competitor was able to reach the far side and their puny streams tinkled into the depths of the well.

Rebecca, with the backing of Nazeera, prevailed on Ali Wad to set his men to dig communal earth latrines and deep pits in which the rubbish could be burned and buried, and to make sure that the women used them. Then she and Nazeera visited the mothers whose offspring were wasting away with dysentery and the occasional bout of cholera. Rebecca had remembered the name of the monastery from which Ryder had obtained the cholera powder, and Nazeera persuaded Ali Wad to send three of his men to Abyssinia to fetch fresh supplies of the medicine. Until they returned, the women used what remained of Ryder Courtney's gift sparingly and judiciously to save the lives of some infants. This earned them the reputation of infallibility as physicians. The women obeyed when they ordered them to boil the well water before they gave it to the children or drank it themselves. Their efforts were soon rewarded, and the epidemic of dysentery abated.

All of this kept Rebecca's mind from the threat that hung over them. They lived close to death. The smell of bloating human bodies wafted over the enclosure and their nostrils soon accepted this as commonplace. In the *zenana* Rebecca and Nazeera prevailed upon Ali Wad to enforce the Islamic custom: the bodies of the cholera victims and those who died of other illness were removed by his men and buried the same day. However, they had no control over the execution ground, which was separated from the *zenana* by only the boundary wall.

A line of eucalyptus trees grew along the back wall of the *zenana*. The children and even some of the women climbed into the branches whenever the braying of the *ombeya* horns announced another execution. From this viewpoint they overlooked the gallows and the beheading ground. One morning Rebecca even caught Amber in the branches, watching in white-faced and wide-eyed fascination as a young woman was stoned to death not more than fifty paces from where she was perched. She dragged Amber back to their hut, and threatened to thrash her if she ever found her climbing the trees again.

Yet her first thought when Rebecca awoke each morning was the dread that this day the summons from the Mahdi to attend him in his private quarters of the palace would be delivered. The arrival of the gift of clothing made the threat more poignant.

She did not have long to wait. Four days later Ali Wad came to inform her of her first private audience with the Chosen One. Nazeera delayed the inevitable by pleading that her charge was stricken by her moon sickness. This excuse could work only once, however, and Ali Wad returned a week later. He warned them that he would come back later to fetch Rebecca.

In the small screened yard at the back of their hut Nazeera undressed Rebecca, stood her naked on a reed mat and poured pitchers of heated water over her head. It was perfumed with myrrh and sandalwood that she had bought in the market. It was well known that the Mahdi detested unclean odours. Then she dried her and anointed her with attar of lotus flowers and dressed her in one of her new robes. At last Ali Wad came to escort her to the presence of the Chosen One.

Nothing was as Rebecca had expected. There was no grand furnishing or tapestries, no marble tiles upon the floor, no tinkling water fountains. Instead she found herself on an open roof terrace furnished only with a few quite ordinary *angarebs* and a scattering of Persian rugs and cushions. Instead of the mighty Mahdi alone, three men were reclining on the *angarebs*. She was taken aback and uncertain of what was expected of her, but the Mahdi beckoned to her. 'Come, al-Jamal. Sit here.' He indicated the pile of cushions at the foot of his bed. Then he went on talking to the other men. They were discussing the activities of the Dervish slavers along the upper reaches of the Nile, and how this trade could be increased tenfold now that Gordon Pasha and his strange Frankish aversion to the trade was no more.

Although she hung her head demurely, as Nazeera had cautioned her to do, Rebecca was able to study the other two men through her half

171

closed lashes. The Khalifa Abdullahi frightened her, though she could barely admit it to herself. He had the cold and implacable presence of a venomous snake; an image of the sleek, glittering mamba came to her mind. She shivered and looked to the third man.

This was the first opportunity she had had to study the Emir Osman Atalan closely. During their first meeting she had been too immersed in the game of survival for herself and Amber that she had played out with the Mahdi. Of course, since she had been in the *zenana* she had heard the other women discussing his reputation as a warrior. Since his final victory over Gordon Pasha, Osman was now the senior commander of the Dervish army. In power and influence with the Mahdi he ranked only below the Khalifa Abdullahi.

Now she was able to watch him from the corner of her eye and found him interesting. She had not realized that an Arab man could be so handsome. His skin did not have the usual dingy umber tone and his beard was lustrous and wavy. His eyes were dark, but sharp and alert with stars of light in their depths, like jewels of polished black coral. In contrast his teeth were very white and even. It seemed to Rebecca that he was in a jubilant mood, waiting for the first opportunity to deliver some important tidings to the others.

The Mahdi must also have sensed his eagerness, for at last he turned his smile upon him. 'We have spoken of the south, but tell me now what news you have from the north of my domains. What do you hear of the infidels who have invaded my borders?'

'Mighty Mahdi, the news is good. Within the last hour a carrier-pigeon has arrived from Metemma.

The last infidel crusaders who dared to march on your cities and attempt to rescue Gordon Pasha have fled from your sacred lands like a pack of mangy hyenas before the wrath of a great black-maned lion. They have abandoned the steamers that brought them to Khartoum, and which you and your ever-victorious army damaged and drove away. They have fled back past Wadi Halfa into Egypt. They have been vanquished, and will never again set foot upon your territories. All of Sudan is indisputably yours and, at your command, your ever-victorious army stands ready to bring more vast territory under your sway, and to spread your divine words and teachings to all the world. May Allah always love and cherish you.'

'All thanks is due to Allah, who promised me these things,' said the Mahdi. 'He has told me many times that Islam will flourish in Sudan for a thousand years, and all the monarchs and rulers of the world will relinquish their infidel ways and become my vassals, trusting in my benevolence and placing their faith in the one true God and his Prophet.'

'Praise be to God in his infinite power and wisdom,' said the others fervently.

The news of the withdrawal of the British army from the Sudan was devastating to Rebecca. Despite the fall of Khartoum and the repulse of the British river steamers, she had cherished a tiny flame of hope that one day soon British soldiers would march into Omdurman and they would be freed. That flame was cruelly snuffed out. She and Amber would never escape this smiling monster who now owned them, body and soul. She tried to fight back the dark despair that threatened to overwhelm her.

I must endure, she told herself, not only for my own sake but for Amber's. No matter the price I am forced to pay, no matter the obscene and unnatural practices forced upon me, I must survive.

With a start she realized that the Mahdi was speaking to her. Although she felt dizzy with grief she gathered her courage and gave him her full attention.

'I wish to send a letter to your ruler,' he told her. 'You will write it for me. What material do you need?' Rebecca was startled by this demand. She had expected to be roughly handled and treated as a harlot, not as a secretary. But she gathered her wits and told him her requirements. The Mahdi struck the brass gong beside the bed. A vizier scurried up the stairs and prostrated himself before his master. He listened to the orders he was given and backed away down the stairs, chanting the Mahdi's praises. In a short while he returned with three house slaves carrying a writing cabinet that had been looted from the Belgian consulate. They placed it front of Rebecca, and because the sun was setting and the daylight fading, they placed four oil lamps around her to light her work.

'Write in your own language the words I will tell you. What is your queen's name? I have heard that your country is ruled by a woman.'

'She is Queen Victoria.'

The Mahdi paused to compose his thoughts and then he dictated: ' "Victoria of England, know you that it is I, Muhammad, the Mahdi, the messenger of God who speaks to you. Foolishly you have sent your crusader armies against my might, for you did not know that I am under the divine protection of

174

Allah, and therefore must always triumph in battle. Your armies have been vanquished and scattered like chaff on the winds. Your powers in this world have been destroyed. Therefore I declare you to be my slave and my vassal."' He paused again, and told Rebecca, 'Be certain that you write only what I tell you. If you add anything else I will have you thrashed.'

'I understand your words. I am your creature, and I would never presume to disobey your lightest wish.'

'Then write this to your queen. "You have acted in ignorance. You did not know that my words and thoughts are the words of God Himself. You know nothing of the True Faith. You do not understand that Allah is one God alone, and that Muhammad, the Mahdi, is his true Prophet. Unless you make full recompense for your sins you will boil for ever in the waters of hell. Give thanks that Allah is compassionate, for he has told me that if you come immediately to Omdurman and prostrate yourself before me, if you place yourself and all your armies and all your peoples under my thrall, if you lay all your wealth and substance at my feet, if you renounce your false gods and bear witness that Allah is one and that I am his prophet, then you shall be forgiven. I will take you to wife, and you will give me many fine sons. I will spread my wings of protection over you. Allah will set aside a place for you in Paradise. If you defy this summons your nation will be cast down, and you will burn for all of eternity in the fires of hell. It is I, Muhammad, the Mahdi, who orders these things. They are not my words, but the words that God has placed in my mouth."'

The Mahdi sat back, pleased with his composition, and made the chopping sign with his right hand to show that he had finished.

'This is a masterpiece that you have created,' said Khalifa Abdullahi. 'It gives voice to the power and majesty of God. Your words should be embroidered on your banner for all the world to read, and to believe.'

'It is plain that these are the very words of Allah delivered through your mouth,' agreed Osman Atalan, gravely. 'I give thanks eternally that I have been privileged to hear them spoken aloud.'

If it ever becomes known that I wrote this traitorous nonsense, Rebecca thought, I will be locked in the Tower of London for the rest of my days. She did not look up from the page but, trusting that no other person in Omdurman could read English, she added a final sentence of her own: 'Written under extreme duress by Rebecca Benbrook, the daughter of the British Consul David Benbrook who was murdered along with General Gordon by the Dervish. God save the Queen.' It was worth the risk, not only to excuse herself but to send a message to the civilized world of her predicament.

She sanded the page and handed it to the Mahdi, with lowered eyes. 'Holy One, is this as you wished?' she whispered humbly. He took it from her and she watched his eyes move up the page from the lower right-hand corner to the top left, in the inverse direction. With a rush of relief she realized he was trying to read the Roman letters as though they were Arabic script. He would never be able to decipher what she had written. She was certain he would not admit this and show it to

176

another person for translation.

'It is as I wished.' He nodded, and she had to stifle an instinctive sigh of relief. He handed the sheet of paper to Kalifa Abdullahi. 'Seal this missive and make sure that it is delivered with all despatch to the Khedive in Cairo. He will send it onwards to this queen, whom I will take as my wife.' He made a gesture of dismissal. 'Now you may leave me, as I wish to disport myself with this woman.'

They rose, made obeisance and backed away to the staircase.

With a sharp surge of fear Rebecca found herself alone with God's prophet. She knew that her hands were trembling and she clenched them into fists to keep them still.

'Come closer!' he ordered, and she rose from her seat at the writing cabinet and went to kneel before him. He stroked her hair and his touch was surprisingly gentle. 'Are you an albino?' he asked. 'Or are there many women in your country with hair this colour, and eyes as blue as the cloudless sky?'

'In my country I am one of many,' she assured him. 'I am truly sorry if it does not please you.'

'It pleases me well.' In front of him as he sat on the *angareb* her eyes were at the same level as his waist. Beneath the brilliant white cloth of his *jibba* she saw his body stir: the extraordinary masculine tumescence that she still found incomprehensible—a distinct creature with a life of its own.

His tammy is waking up, she thought, and almost giggled at the absurdity of the prophet of God with a tammy between his legs, just like other men less divine. She realized how close she was to succumbing to hysteria and, with an effort, she controlled herself.

'I can see the lamplight through your flesh.' The Mahdi took her earlobe between his fingers and turned it to catch the beam of the lamp, admiring the pink luminosity of light that shone through. She blushed with embarrassment and he remarked the change immediately. 'You are like a little chameleon. Your skin changes colour in tune with your moods. That is remarkable, but enticing.' He took her earlobe between his teeth and bit it, hard enough to make her gasp but not enough to break the skin or draw blood. Then he sucked on the lobe, like an infant at the breast. She was unprepared for her body's reaction. Despite herself she felt the heightened sensitivity of her nipples rubbing against the silk of her bodice.

'Ah!' He noticed her inadvertent response, and smiled. 'All women are different, but also the same.' He cupped one of her breasts in his hand and pinched the engorging nipple. She gasped again. He sat back on his haunches and unfastened the front of her bodice. He seemed in no hurry. Like a skilled groom with a nervous filly, he moved with gentle deliberation so as not to startle her.

She realized he was highly skilled in the amorous arts. Well, he has had much practice, hundreds of concubines. She set herself to remain aloof and unmoved by his expertise. But when he lifted out one of her breasts from the opening of her bodice, and bit her nipple as he had her earlobe, with a tender sharpness that forced another gasp from her lips, she found her good resolution wavering. She tried to ignore the ripples of pleasure that radiated from her nipple through her body. When she started to pull away he held her with a light pressure of his teeth. The pleasant sensation was piqued by guilt and the conviction that what was happening was sinful. Not for the first time in her short life she realized that sin, as much as sanctity, held its own peculiar attraction. I do not want this to happen, she thought, but I am helpless to prevent it.

His mouth wandered over her breast, his lips kneading and plucking at her flesh, his tongue slithering and probing. She felt her sex melting, and the shame receded. She began to itch with a strange impatience. She needed something more to happen but she was not sure what.

'Stand up!' he said, and for a moment she did not understand the words. 'Stand up!' he ordered, more sharply. She rose slowly to her feet. Her bodice was still open and one breast bulged free. He smiled up at her as she stood over him, his smile sweet and almost saintly.

'Disrobe!' he ordered. She hesitated, and his smile faded. 'At once!' he said. 'Do as I tell you.'

She slipped the robe off her shoulders, and let it drop as far as her waist. He looked at her, and his eyes seemed to caress her skin. A light rash of goose pimples rose round her nipples. He reached out and drew the fingernail of his right forefinger over it, scratching the skin lightly. Her knees felt as though they might give way under her. Although she had known all along that this must happen, she felt her shame return powerfully. She was an English woman and a Christian. He was an Arab and a Muslim. It flew in the face of all her training and beliefs.

179

'Disrobe!' he repeated. Her dilemma was insoluble, until her father's words, which she had so recently read in his journal, returned to her: 'One must always bear in mind that this is a savage and pagan country. We should not seek to judge these peoples by the standards that apply at home. Behaviour that would be considered outlandish and even criminal in England is commonplace and normal here. We should never forget this, and make allowance for it.'

Daddy wrote that for me! she thought. She hung her head demurely. 'No man has ever laid eyes on what lies beneath this silk.' Shyly she touched the swelling of her own pudenda beneath the cloth. 'But if you will remove my covering I will know that it is the Hand of Allah and not of a common man that does so. Then will I rejoice.'

Unwittingly she had hit upon the perfect response. She had abrogated the responsibility to him. She had placed herself in his power, and she could see that in doing so she had pleased him inordinately.

He reached out again and slipped the dress down over the bulge of her hips. As it fell round her ankles, Rebecca cupped her hands over her Mount of Venus. He did not protest at this last demonstration of modesty. It was what he expected of a true virgin, but he said softly, 'Turn.' She revolved slowly and felt one of his fingers trace the curve of her buttock where it met the back of her thigh.

'So soft, so white, but touched with pink, like a cloud at dawn with the first ray of sunrise upon it.' With the touch and pressure of his finger he guided her, inducing her to lean over with straight legs

180

until her forehead almost touched her knees. She felt his warm breath on the back of her legs as he brought his face closer to examine her. Again his finger insisted and she moved her feet wider apart. She could feel his gaze, directed deeply into her most secret places. He was seeing things that no other person, nurse, parent, lover or herself, had ever laid eyes upon. In this respect she was truly a virgin. She knew she should resent this minute examination of her body, but she was too far gone, too deeply under his influence. He was possessing her with his dark, hypnotic gaze.

'Three things in this world are insatiable,' the Mahdi murmured. 'The desert, the grave and the quimmy of a beautiful woman.' He turned her back to face him again, and gently removed her hands, which still covered her mount. He touched her pubes. 'Surely this is not hair but spun thread of gold. It is silk and gossamer and soft morning sunlight.'

His admiration was so manifest and poetically expressed that she welcomed rather than resented his touch as he gently parted the outer lips of her sex. Of her own accord and without his further guidance she moved her feet apart.

'You must never pluck yourself here,' he said. 'I grant you special dispensation not to do so. This silk is too beautiful and precious to be discarded.'

The Mahdi took her hands, drew her down beside him on the *angareb* and laid her on her back. He lifted her knees and knelt between them. He lowered his face, and she was amazed as she realized what he was about to do to her. Nazeera had not warned her of this. She had believed that it would be the other way about.

181

What happened next exceeded her furthest imaginings. His skill was sure, his instinct faultless. She felt as though she were being devoured. As though she were dying and being reborn. In the end she cried out as if in mortal anguish and fell back on the *angareb*. She was bathed in perspiration and trembling. She was deprived of the powers of thought or movement. She seemed to have become merely a receptacle of overpowering bodily sensations. It seemed to last for an age, before at last the spasms and contractions deep within her stilled and she heard his whisper. Although his lips were at her ear, it seemed to come from far away. 'Like the desert and the grave.' He laughed softly. She lay for a long time, rousing herself only when she felt him begin to caress her again. When she opened her eyes she discovered to her mild surprise, that, like her, he was naked. She sat up and leant on one elbow looking down on him. He was lying on his back. After what he had done to her, all sense of modesty and shame had been expunged. She found herself examining him with almost as much attention as he had lavished on her. The first thing that struck her was that he was almost devoid of hair. His body was soft and almost feminine, not hard and muscled like Penrod's or Ryder's. Her eyes went down to his tammy. Although it stuck up stiffly, it was small, smooth and unmarred by ropes of blue veins. The circumcised head was bare and glossy. It looked childlike and innocent. It evoked an almost maternal feeling in her.

'It's so pretty!' she exclaimed, and was immediately frightened that he would find the description effeminate and derogatory, that he

182

might take it as an insult to his masculinity. She need not have worried. Once again her instinct had been correct. He smiled at her. Then she remembered Nazeera's advice: 'Master and Lord, would it give you offence if I presumed to do to you as you were gracious enough to do to me? For me it would be an undreamed-of honour.' He smiled until the gap between his front teeth was fully exposed.

At first she was clumsy and uncertain. He seemed to regard this as more evidence of her virginity. He started to direct her. When she was doing what pleased him, he encouraged her with murmurs and whispers and stroked her head. When she became over-enthusiastic, he restrained her with a light touch. She became absorbed in the task, and her reward was a gratifying sense of power and control over him, however fleeting it might be. Gradually he urged her to increase the tempo of her movements, until suddenly he gave her complete and undeniable proof that she had pleased him. For a moment she was at a loss as to what to do next. Then she remembered that Nazeera had advised her to swallow quickly and have done.

*　　　*　　　*

Like a barbellate catfish in the muddy waters of the Nile, Penrod Ballantyne allowed himself to be absorbed into the teeming byways, alleys and hovels of Omdurman. He became invisible. He changed his costume and appearance almost daily, becoming a camel herdsman, a humble beggar or a nodding, drooling idiot almost at will. Yet he knew that he could not remain in the town indefinitely without drawing attention to himself. So, for weeks on end he left the sprawling city. Once he found employment as a drover with a camel dealer taking his beasts downriver to trade them in the small villages along the banks. On another he joined the crew of a trading dhow, plying up the Blue Nile to the Abyssinian border.

When he returned to Omdurman he made it a rule never to sleep twice in the same place. On the warning of Yakub he did not attempt to make direct contact with Nazeera or anyone else who knew his true identity. He communicated with Wad Hagma only through Yakub.

The preparations for Rebecca's rescue were long drawn-out, seemingly interminable. Wad Hagma encountered many obstacles, all of which could only be surmounted with money and patience. Every time Yakub brought a message to Penrod it was for more cash to buy camels, hire guides or bribe guards and petty officials. Gradually the contents of Penrod's once-heavy money belt were whittled down. Weeks became months, and he fretted and fumed. Many times he considered making his own arrangements for a lightning raid to snatch the captives and run with them for the Egyptian border. But by now he knew just how futile that would be. The *zenana* of the Mahdi was impenetrable without inside help, and daily the Dervish were exerting more control and restrictions on strangers entering or leaving Omdurman. Alone Penrod was able to move around with relative freedom, but with a party of women it would be almost impossible unless the way had been carefully prepared.

At last he discovered a small cave in a limestone outcrop in the desert a few miles beyond the town. This had once been the haunt of a religious hermit. The old man had been dead for some years, but the spot had such an unhealthy reputation among the local people that Penrod felt reasonably secure in taking it over. There was a tiny water seep at the back of the cave, just sufficient for the needs of one or two persons, and for the small herd of goats he purchased from a shepherd he met on the road. Penrod used the animals to support his disguise as a desert herder. From the cave back to Omdurman was a journey on foot of a mere two or three hours. Thus he was always in contact with Yakub, who rode out at night to bring him a little food and the latest news from his uncle.

Often Yakub stayed in the cave for a few days, and Penrod was glad of his company. He was unable to carry openly the European sword that Ryder Hardinge had given him at Metemma. It would attract too much attention. He buried it in the desert from where he would be able to retrieve it, and perhaps one day return it to Major Hardinge's wife. He instructed Yakub to find him a Sudanese broadsword, then practised and exercised each day with it.

Whenever Yakub visited him they sparred in the wadi at the front of the cave where they were hidden from the eyes of a casual traveller or a wandering shepherd. Such was his skill that after half the day at practice Yakub disengaged their blades with the sweat dripping from his chin. 'Enough, Abadan Riji!' he cried. 'I swear, in the Name of God, that no man in this land can prevail against your blade. You have become a paragon of the long steel.'

They rested in the low mouth of the cave, and Penrod asked, 'What word from your uncle?' He knew the news could not be good: if it had been Yakub would have given it to him immediately on his arrival.

'There was a vizier of the Mahdi with whom my uncle had come to an understanding and everything was at last in readiness. Three days ago the vizier fell foul of his master on another matter. He had stolen money from the treasury. On the Mahdi's orders he was arrested and beheaded.' Yakub made a gesture of helplessness, then saw his master's face darken with rage. 'But do not despair. There is another man more reliable who is in direct charge of the *zenana*. He is willing.'

'Let me guess,' said Penrod. 'Your uncle needs only fifty pounds more.'

'Nay, my lord.' Yakub was hurt by the suggestion. 'He needs a mere thirty to seal the matter.'

'I will give him fifteen, and if all is not in readiness by this new moon at the latest, I will come to Omdurman to have further speech with him. When I arrive I will be carrying the long steel in my right hand.'

Yakub thought about this seriously for a while then replied, just as seriously, 'It comes to me that my uncle will probably agree to your offer.'

Yakub's instincts proved correct. Four days later he returned to the hermit's cave. When he was still some way off he waved cheerfully and as soon as he was within hail he shouted, 'Effendi, all is in readiness.'

As he came to where Penrod was waiting he slid

down from the saddle of his camel, and embraced his master. 'My uncle, so honest and trustworthy, has arranged everything as he promised. Al-Jamal, her little sister, and Nazeera will be waiting behind the old mosque at the river end of the execution ground three midnights hence. You should return to Omdurman earlier that day. It is best if you come alone and on foot, driving the goats before you in all innocence. I will meet you and the three women at the trysting place. I will bring six strong fresh camels all provisioned with waterskins, fodder and food. Then I, Yakub the intrepid, will guide you to the first meeting place with the next relay of camels. There will be five changes of animals along the road to the Egyptian border, so we will be able to ride like the wind. We will be gone before the Mahdi knows that his concubines are missing from the harem.'

They sat in the shade of the cave and went over every detail of the plans that Wad Hagma had laid out for Yakub. 'Thus you will see, Abadan Riji, that all your money has been spent wisely, and that there was no reason to distrust my beloved uncle, who is a saint and a prince among men.'

Three days later, Penrod gathered up his few meagre possessions, slipped the sword in its scabbard down the back of his robe, wrapped the turban round his head and face, whistled up his goats and ambled off towards the river and the city. Yakub had give him a flute carved from a bamboo shoot, and over the months Penrod had taught himself to play it. The goats had become accustomed to him and they followed him obediently, bleating appreciatively whenever he struck up a tune.

187

He wanted to arrive on the outskirts of Omdurman an hour or so before sunset, but he was a little premature. Half a mile short of the first buildings he turned the goats loose to graze on the dried-out thorn scrub and settled down to wait beside the track. Although he wrapped himself in his robe and pretended to doze, he was wide awake. An old man leading a string of six donkeys loaded with firewood passed him. Penrod continued to feign sleep, and after calling an uncertain greeting the old man walked on.

A short while later Penrod heard singing accompanied by the tapping of finger drums. He recognized the traditional country wedding songs, and then a large party of guests came along the road from the nearest village only a short distance to the south of the city. In their midst walked the bride. She was covered from head to foot with veils and the tinkling jewellery of gold and silver coins that formed part of her dowry. The guests and her male relatives were singing and clapping, and despite the Mahdi's restrictions on these ceremonies, they were dancing, laughing and shouting ribald advice to her. When they saw Penrod squatting on the roadside they called to him, 'Come on, old man. Leave your flea-bitten animals and join the fun.'

'There will be more food than you can eat, and perhaps even a sip of *arak*. Something you have not tasted for many years.' The man displayed a small waterskin with a conspiratorial smirk.

Penrod answered them in a quavering unsteady voice: 'I was married once myself, and I do not wish to see another innocent fellow take that same hard road.'

They roared with laughter.

'What a waggish old rascal you are.'

'You can give wise counsel to our doomed cousin in how best to appease a demanding woman.'

Then Penrod noticed that all the guests had the broad, over-developed shoulders of swordsmen, and despite their humble attire their swagger and strutting self-confidence was more that of aggagiers than cringing country oafs. He glanced down at the bare feet of the bride, all that was visible of her, and saw that they were broad and flat, not painted with henna, and that the toenails were ragged and broken.

Not the feet of a young virgin, Penrod thought. He reached over his shoulder and took a grip on the hilt of the sword concealed down the back of his robe. As his blade rasped from the scabbard he sprang to his feet, but the wedding guests had surrounded him. Penrod saw that they, too, had drawn weapons as they rushed at him from every direction. With surprise he realized that they were not edged blades but heavy clubs. He had little time to think about it before they were on him in a pack.

He killed the first with a straight thrust at the throat, but before he could disengage and recover, a blow from behind smashed into his shoulder and he felt the bone break. Still, he parried one-handed the next blow at his head. Then another hit him in the small of the back, aimed at his kidneys, and his legs started to give way. He stayed upright just long enough to send a deep thrust into the chest of the man who had broken his shoulder. Then a great iron door slammed shut in the centre of his skull and darkness descended upon him like an ocean wave driven by the storm.

*   *   *

When Penrod regained consciousness he was uncertain where he was and what had happened to him. Close by where he lay, he heard a woman moaning and groaning in labour.

Why does not the stupid bitch hold her mouth, and have her brat elsewhere? he wondered. She should show some respect for my aching head. It must have been cheap liquor I drank last night. Then, suddenly, the pain ripped through the roof of his skull and he realized that the groans were issuing from his own dried-out mouth. He forced his eyes open against the pain and saw that he was lying on a mud floor in an evil-smelling room. He tried to raise his hand to touch his damaged head, but his arm would not respond. Instead a new shaft of agony tore through his shoulder. He tried to use the other hand for the job, but there was a clink, and he found that his wrists were fastened together with chains. He rolled over painfully and cautiously on to his good side.

Good is a relative term, he thought groggily. Every muscle and sinew of his body throbbed with agony. Somehow he pushed himself into a sitting position. He had to wait a moment for the blinding agony in his head, caused by the movement, to clear. Then he was able to assess his situation.

The chains on his wrists and ankles were slaving irons, the ubiquitous utensils of the trade across the country. His leg shackles were anchored to an iron stake driven into the middle of the dirt floor. The chain was short enough to prevent him reaching either the door or the single high window. The cell reeked of excrement and vomit, of which traces were scattered around him in a circle at the limit of the chain.

He heard a soft rustle nearby and looked down. A large grey rat was feeding on the few rounds of dhurra bread that had been left on the filthy floor at his side. He flicked the chain at it, and it fled, squeaking. Next to the bread was an earthenware pitcher, which made him realize how thirsty he was. He tried to swallow but there was no saliva in his mouth and his throat was parched. He reached for the pitcher, which was gratifyingly heavy. Before he drank he sniffed the contents suspiciously. He decided it was filled with river water and he could smell the woodsmoke from the fire over which it had boiled. He drank and then drank again.

I think I might yet survive, he decided wryly, and blinked back the pain in his head. He heard more movement and glanced up at the window. Someone was watching him through the bars, but the head disappeared immediately. He drank again, and felt a little better.

The door to the cell opened behind him and two men stepped in. They wore *jibbas* and turbans, and their swords were unsheathed.

'Who are you?' Penrod demanded. 'Who is your master?'

'You will ask no questions,' said one. 'You will say nothing until ordered to do so.'

Another man followed them. He was older and grey-bearded, and he carried all the accoutrements of a traditional eastern doctor.

'Peace be upon you. May you please Allah,' Penrod greeted him. The doctor shook his head curtly, and made no reply. He set aside his bag, and came to stand over him. He palpated the large swelling on Penrod's head, obviously feeling for any fracture. He seemed satisfied and moved on. Almost at once he noticed that Penrod was favouring his left side. He took hold of the elbow and tried to lift the arm. The pain was excruciating. Penrod managed to prevent himself crying out. He did not want to give the two interested guards that satisfaction, but his features contorted and sweat broke out across his forehead. The Arab doctor lowered the arm, and ran a hand over his biceps. When he pressed hard fingers into the site of the broken bone, Penrod gasped despite his resolution. The doctor nodded. He cut away the sleeve of Penrod's *galabiyya* and strapped the shoulder with linen bandages. Then he folded and tied a sling to support the arm. The relief from pain was immediate.

'The blessing of Allah and his Prophet be upon you,' Penrod said, and the doctor smiled briefly.

From a small alabaster flask he poured a dark, treacly liquid into a horn cup, and gave it to Penrod. He drank it, and the taste was gall-bitter. Without having spoken a word the doctor repacked his bag and left. He returned the next day, and the four days that followed. On each visit the guards refilled the water pitcher and left a bowl of food: scraps of bread and sun-dried fish. During these visits neither the guards nor the doctor spoke; they did not acknowledge Penrod's greetings and blessings.

The bitter potions that the doctor gave him sedated Penrod, and reduced the pain and swelling in his head and shoulder. After he had completed his examination on the fifth day the doctor looked pleased with himself. He readjusted the sling, but when Penrod asked for another dose of the medicine, he shook his head emphatically. When he left the cell, Penrod heard him speaking in a low voice to the guards. He could not catch the words.

By the following morning the effects of the drug had worn off, and his mind was clear and sharp. The arm was tender only when he tried to lift it. He tested himself for any concussion he might have suffered from the head blow, closing first one eye and then the other while he focused on the bars of the window. There was no distortion or any double vision. Then he began to exercise the injured arm, starting first by simply clenching his fist and bending the elbow. Gradually he was able to raise the elbow to the horizontal.

The visits from the taciturn doctor ceased. He took this as a favourable sign. Only his guards made brief visits to leave water and a little food. This left him much time to consider his predicament. He examined the locks on his shackles. They were crude but functional. The mechanism had been developed and refined over the centuries. Without a key or a pick he wasted no more time upon them. Next he turned his mind to deducing where he was. Through the lop-sided window he could see only a tiny section of open sky. He was forced to draw his conclusions from sounds and smells. He knew he was still in Omdurman: not only could he smell the stink of the uncollected rubbish and the dungheaps but in the evenings he caught a softer sweeter whiff of the waters of the river, and could even hear the faint calls of the dhow captains as they tacked and altered sail. Five times a day he heard the wailing cries of the muezzin calling the faithful to prayer from the half-built tower of the new mosque, 'Hasten to your own good! Hasten to prayer! Allah is great! There is no God but Allah.'

From these clues he pinpointed his position with a certain precision. He was about three hundred yards from the mosque, and half that distance from the riverbank. He was due east of the execution ground and therefore approximately the same distance from the Mahdi's palace and harem. He could judge the direction of the prevailing wind from the occasional small high cloud that sailed past the window. When it was blowing the stench of rotting corpses from the execution ground was strong. This gave him a rough sense of triangulation. With a sinking sensation in his gut, he decided that he must be in the compound of the Beja tribesmen beside the Beit el Mal, the stronghold of his old enemy Osman Atalan. Next he had to consider how this had happened.

His first thought was that Yakub had betrayed him. He wrestled with this theory for days, but could not persuade himself to accept it. I have trusted my life too many times to that squint-eyed rascal to doubt him now, he thought. If Yakub has sold me to the Dervish, there is no God.

He used the shackle of his chain to scratch a crude calendar in the mud floor. With it he was able to keep track of the days. He had counted fifty-two days before they came to fetch him.

The two guards unlocked the chains from the iron stake. They left his legs and arms shackled. There was sufficient slack in this chain to enable him to shuffle along, but not to run.

194

They led him out into a small courtyard and through another door into a larger enclosure, around whose walls were seated a hundred or more Beja warriors. Their spears and lances rested against the wall behind them, and their sheathed swords were laid across their laps. They studied Penrod with avid interest. He recognized some of their faces from previous encounters. Then his eyes jumped to the familiar figure seated alone on a raised platform against the far wall. Even among this assembly of fighting men, Osman Atalan was the focus of attention.

The guards urged him forward and, with the chains hampering him, he shambled across the courtyard. When he stood before Osman a guard snarled in his ear, 'Down on your knees, infidel! Show respect to the emir of the Beja.'

Penrod drew himself to attention. 'Osman Atalan knows better than to order me to my knees,' he said softly, and held the emir's eyes coolly.

'Down!' repeated the guard, and drove the hilt of his spear into Penrod's kidney with such force that his legs collapsed under him and he fell in a heap of limbs and chains. With a supreme effort he kept his head up and his eyes locked on Osman's.

'Head down!' said the guard, and lifted the shaft of the spear to club him again.

'Enough!' said Osman, and the guard stepped back. 'Welcome to my home, Abadan Riji.' He touched his lips and then his heart. 'From our first encounter on the field of El Obeid I knew there was a bond between us that could not easily be sundered.'

'Only the death of one of us can do that,' Penrod agreed.

'Should I settle that immediately?' Osman mused aloud, and nodded at the man who sat immediately below his dais. 'What think you, al-Noor?'

Al-Noor gave full consideration to the question before he replied. 'Mighty lord, it would be prudent to scotch the cobra before he stings you again.'

'Will you do this favour for me?' Osman asked, and with one movement al-Noor rose to his feet and stood over the kneeling prisoner with the blade of his sword poised over Penrod's neck.

'It needs but the movement of your little finger, great Atalan, and I shall prune his godless head like a rotten fruit.'

Osman watched Penrod's face for any sign of fear, but his gaze never wavered. 'How say you, Abadan Riji? Shall we end it here?' Penrod tried to shrug, but his injured shoulder curtailed the gesture, 'I care not, Emir of the Beja. All men owe God a life. If it is not now, then it will be later.' He smiled easily. 'But have done with this childish game. We both know well that an emir of the Beja could never let his blood enemy die in chains without a sword in his hand.'

Osman laughed with genuine delight. 'We were minted from the same metal, you and I.' He motioned to al-Noor to go back to his seat. 'First we must find a more suitable name for you than Abadan Riji. I shall call you Abd, for slave you now are.'

'Perhaps not for much longer,' Penrod suggested.

'Perhaps,' Osman agreed. 'We shall see. But until that time you are Abd, my foot slave. You will sit at my feet, and you will run beside my horse when I ride abroad. Do you not wish to know who brought you to this low station? Shall I give you the name of your betrayer?' For a moment Penrod was too startled to think of a reply, and could only nod stiffly. Osman called to the men guarding the gate to the courtyard, 'Bring in the informer to collect the reward he was promised.'

They stood aside and a familiar figure sidled through the gate to stand gazing about him nervously. Then Wad Hagma recognized Osman Atalan. He threw himself upon the ground and crawled towards him, chanting his praises and protesting his allegiance, devotion and loyalty. It took him a while to traverse the yard for he stopped every few yards to beat his forehead painfully on the earth. The aggagiers guffawed and called encouragement to him.

'Let not your great belly drag in the dust.'

'Have faith! Your long pilgrimage is almost ended.'

At last Wad Hagma reached the foot of the dais, and prostrated himself full length with arms and legs splayed out flat against the dusty ground like a starfish.

'You have rendered me great service,' said Osman.

'My heart overflows with joy at these words, mighty Emir. I rejoice that I have been able to deliver your enemy to you.'

'How much was the fee on which we agreed?'

'Exalted lord, you were liberal enough to mention a price of five hundred Maria Theresa dollars.'

'You have earned it.' Osman tossed down a

purse so heavy it raised a small cloud of dust as it struck the ground.

Wad Hagma hugged it to his chest, and grinned like an idiot. 'All praise to you, invincible Emir. May Allah always smile upon you!' He stood up, head bowed in deep respect. 'May I be dismissed from your presence? Like the sun, your glory dazzles my eyes.'

'Nay, you must not leave us so soon.' Osman's tone changed. 'I wish to know what emotions you felt when you placed slavers' chains upon a brave warrior. Tell me, my fat little hosteller, how does the sly and treacherous baboon feel when it leads the great elephant bull into the pitfall?'

An expression of alarm crossed Wad Hagma's face. 'This is no elephant, mighty Emir.' He gestured at Penrod. 'This is a rabid dog. This is a cowardly infidel. This is a vessel of such ungodly shape that it deserves to be shattered.'

'In God's Name, Wad Hagma, I see that you are an orator and a poet. I ask only one more service of you. Kill this rabid dog for me! Shatter this misshapen pot so that the world of Islam will be a better place!' Wad Hagma stared at him with utter consternation. 'Al-Noor, give the courageous tavern-keeper your sword.'

Al-Noor placed the broadsword in Wad Hagma's hand and he looked hesitantly at Penrod. Carefully he placed the bag of Maria Theresa dollars on the ground, and straightened. He took a step forward, and Penrod came to his feet. Wad Hagma jumped back.

'Come now! He is chained and the bone in his arm is broken,' said Osman. 'The rabid dog has no teeth. He is harmless. Kill him.' Wad Hagma looked around the courtyard, as if for release, and the aggagiers called to him, 'Do you hear the emir's words, or are you deaf?'

'Do you understand his orders, or are you dull-witted?'

'Come, brave talker, let us see brave deeds to match your words.'

'Kill the infidel dog.'

Wad Hagma lowered the sword, and looked at the ground. Then, suddenly and unexpectedly, in the hope that he had lulled his victim, he let out a blood-chilling shriek and rushed straight at Penrod with the sword held high in both hands. Penrod stood unmoving as Wad Hagma slashed double-handed at his head. At the last moment he lifted his hands and caught the descending blade on his chain. Such was the shock as it hit the steel links that Wad Hagma's untrained hands and arms were numbed to the elbows. His grip opened involuntarily and the sword spun from his hands. He backed away, rubbing his wrists.

'In God's Holy Name!' Osman applauded him. 'What a fierce stroke! We have misjudged you. You are at heart a warrior. Now, pick up the sword and try again.'

'Mighty Emir! Great and noble Atalan! Have mercy on me. I shall return the reward.' He picked up the bag of coins and ran to place it at Osman's feet. 'There! It is yours. Please let me go! O mighty and compassionate lord, have mercy on me.'

'Pick up the sword and carry out my orders,' said Osman, and there was more menace in his tone than if he had shouted.

'Obey the Emir Atalan!' chanted the aggagiers. Wad Hagma whirled round and raced back to where the sword lay. He stooped to pick it up, but as his hand closed on the hilt Penrod stepped on the blade.

Wad Hagma tugged at it ineffectually. 'Get off!' he whined. 'Let me go! I meant nobody any harm.' Then he dropped his shoulder and lunged at Penrod with all his weight, trying to push him backwards off the sword. Penrod swung the loop of chain. It whipped across the side of Wad Hagma's jaw. He howled and sprang backwards, clutching the injury. With a loop of chain swinging threateningly Penrod followed him. He turned and scuttled across the yard towards the doorway, but when he reached it a pair of aggagiers blocked his way with crossed swords. Wad Hagma gave up, and turned back to face Penrod as he stalked after him, swinging the loop of chain.

'No!' Wad Hagma's voice was blurred, and the side of his face distorted. The chain had broken his jaw. 'I meant you no harm. I needed the money. I have wives and many children . . .' He tried to avoid Penrod by circling along the wall, but the seated aggagiers pricked him forward with the points of their swords and roared with laughter when he hopped like a rabbit at the sting. Suddenly he darted away again, back to where the sword lay. As he reached it and stooped to seize the hilt, Penrod stepped up behind him and dropped the loop of chain over his head. With a quick twist of his wrists he settled the links snugly under Wad Hagma's chin and round his throat. As Wad Hagma's fingertips touched the sword hilt Penrod applied pressure on the chain and pulled him up until he was dancing on tiptoe, pawing at the chain with both hands, mewing like a kitten.

'Pray!' Penrod whispered to him. 'Pray to Allah for forgiveness. This is your last chance before you stand before him.' He twisted the chain slowly and closed off Wad Hagma's windpipe, so that he could neither whimper nor whine.

'Farewell, Wad Hagma. Take comfort from the knowledge that for you nothing matters any longer. You are no longer of this world.'

The watching aggagiers drummed their sword blades on their leather shields in a mounting crescendo. Wad Hagma's dance became more agitated. His toes no longer touched the ground. He kicked at the air. His damaged face swelled and turned dark puce. Then there was a sharp crack, like the breaking of a dry twig. All the aggagiers shouted together as Wad Hagma's limbs stiffened, his entire body sagged and he hung from the chain round his throat. Penrod lowered him to the ground and walked back towards Osman Atalan. The aggagiers were in uproar, shouting and laughing, some mimicking Wad Hagma's death throes. Even Osman was smiling with amusement.

Penrod reached the spot where the sword lay, swept it up in a single movement and rushed straight at Osman, the long blade pointed at the emir's heart. Another shout went up, from every man in the yard, this time of wild surmise and alarm. Penrod had twenty paces to cover to reach the dais and the courtyard exploded into movement. A dozen of the aggagiers nearest to the dais leapt forward. Their swords were already unsheathed, and they had only to come on guard to present a glittering palisade of steel to prevent Penrod carrying his charge home. Al-Noor darted forward, not to oppose Penrod head on but cutting in behind him. He seized the dragging leg chain and hauled back on it, whipping Penrod's feet from under him. As he hit the ground the waiting aggagiers rushed forward.

'No!' shouted Osman. 'Do not kill him! Hold him fast, but do not kill him!' Al-Noor released his grip on the leg shackles and grabbed the loop of chain that held Penrod's wrists. He jerked this viciously against the half-healed shoulder. Penrod gritted his teeth to prevent himself crying out but the sword fell from his hands. Al-Noor snatched it away.

'In God's glorious Name!' Osman Atalan laughed. 'You give me great entertainment, Abd! I know now that you can fight, but tomorrow I shall see how well you run. By evening I doubt you will have the stomach for more of your games. Within a week you will be pleading for me to kill you.'

Then Osman Atalan looked down from the dais at al-Noor. 'You I can always trust. You are always ready to serve. You are my right hand. Take my Abd to his cell, but have him ready at dawn. We are going out to hunt the gazelle.'

*   *   *

News travelled swiftly in the *zenana*. Within hours it was known by all, including Ali Wad and the guards, that the Mahdi had expressed himself pleased with the infidel woman, al-Jamal. Rebecca's status was enhanced immeasurably. The guards treated her as though she was already a senior wife, not a low-ranking concubine. She was given three female house slaves to attend her. The other women of the Mahdi, both wives and concubines, called greetings and blessings to her as she passed, and they carried petitions and supplications to her hut, begging her to bring them to the notice of the Mahdi. The rations that were sent to her from the kitchens changed in character and quantity: large fresh fish straight from the river, calabashes of soured milk, bowls of wild desert honey still in the comb, the tenderest cuts of mutton, legs of venison, live chickens and eggs, all in such amounts that Rebecca was able to feed some of the sick children of the lowest-ranking concubines who were in real need of nourishment.

This new status was passed on to the others in her household. Nazeera was now greeted with the title Ammi, or Auntie. The guards saluted her when she passed through the gates. Because it was known that Amber was the sister of one of the Mahdi's favourites, she, too, was granted special privileges. She was a child and had not seen her first moon, so none of the guards raised any objection when she accompanied Nazeera on her forays beyond the gates of the *zenana*.

That particular morning, Nazeera and Amber left the *zenana* early to go down to the market on the riverbank to meet the farmers as they brought in their fresh crops from the country. Figs and pomegranates were in season, and Nazeera was determined to have the first selection of the day's offerings. As they passed the large edifice of the Beit el Mal there was a disturbance down the street ahead of them. A crowd had gathered, the war drums boomed and the ivory horns sounded.

'What is it, Nazeera?'

'I don't know everything,' Nazeera replied testily. 'Why do you always ask me?'

'Because you do know everything.' Amber jumped up to see over the heads of the crowd. 'Oh! Look! It is the banner of the Emir Atalan. Let's hurry or we shall miss him.' She ran ahead and Nazeera broke into a trot to keep up with her. Amber ducked between the legs of the crowd until she had reached the front rank. Nazeera forged her way in behind her, ignoring the protests of those she shoved aside.

'Here he comes,' the crowd chanted. 'Hail, mighty emir of the Beja! Hail, victor of Khartoum and slayer of Gordon Pasha!' With his banner-bearer riding ahead and four of his most trusted aggagiers flanking him, Osman Atalan was up on the great black stallion, al-Buq. As this entourage swept past Nazeera and Amber they saw that a man ran at the emir's stirrup. He wore a short sleeveless shift and a loincloth. On his head was a plain turban, but his legs and feet were bare.

'That's a white man!' exclaimed Nazeera, and around her the crowd laughed and applauded.

'He is the infidel spy, the henchman of Gordon Pasha.'

'He is the one they once called Abadan Riji, the One Who Never Turns Back.'

'He is the prisoner of the emir.'

'Osman Atalan will teach him new tricks. Not only will he learn to turn back, but he will be taught to turn in small circles.'

Amber shrieked with excitement, 'Nazeera! It is Captain Ballantyne!'

Even over the noise of the crowd Penrod heard Amber call his name. He turned his head and looked directly at her. She waved frantically at him but the cavalcade carried him away. Before he was gone Amber saw that there was a rope round his neck, the other end of which was tied to one of the emir's stirrups.

'Where are they taking him?' Amber wailed. 'Are they going to kill him?'

'No!' Nazeera placed an arm round her to calm her. 'He is far too valuable to them. But now we must go back and tell your sister what we have seen.' They hurried to the *zenana*, but when they reached the hut they found that Rebecca was gone.

Nazeera immediately taxed the house slaves. 'Where is your mistress?'

'Ali Wad came to fetch her. He has taken her to the quarters of the Mahdi.'

'It is too early in the day for the Mahdi to begin taking his manly pleasures,' Nazeera protested.

'He is sick. Wad Ali says he is sick unto death. He is struck down by the cholera. They know that al-Jamal saved her little sister al-Zahra and many others from the disease. He wishes her to do the same for the Holy One.'

As the news of the Mahdi's illness swept through the *zenana* a high tide of wailing, lamentation and prayer followed it.

*   *   *

As they reached the edge of the desert Osman reined in al-Buq lightly and at the same time urged him forward with his knees. It was the signal for the stallion to break into a triple gait, the smooth, flowing action so easy on both horse and rider. It is not a natural pace, and a horse has to be schooled to learn it. The emir's outriders followed his example and tripled away at a pace faster than a trot but not as fast as a canter.

At the end of the rope Penrod had to stretch out to keep up with them. They swung southwards, parallel to the river, and the heat of the day started to build up. They rode on as far as the village of Al Malaka, where the headman and the village elders all hastened out to greet the emir. They implored him to grant them the honour of providing him with refreshment. If Osman had been truly on the chase he would never have wasted time on such indulgences, but he knew that if the captive did not rest and drink he would die. His clothing was drenched with sweat and his feet were bloody from the prick of thorns and flint cuts.

While he sat under the tree in the centre of the village and discussed the possibility of finding game in the vicinity, Osman noted with satisfaction that al-Noor had understood his true purpose and was allowing Penrod to sit and drink from the waterskins. When Osman stood at last and ordered his party to mount up, Penrod seemed to have regained much of his strength. He had pulled his left arm out of the sling, although it was not yet completely healed: it unbalanced him, and hampered the swing of his shoulders as he ran.

They rode on and paused an hour later while Osman glassed the desert ahead for any sign of gazelle. In the meantime al-Noor let Penrod drink again, then allowed him to squat on his haunches, his head between his knees as he gasped for breath. Too soon Osman ordered the advance. For the rest of that day they described a wide circle through sand dunes, over gravelly plains and across ridges of limestone, pausing occasionally to drink from the waterskins.

An hour before sunset they returned to Omdurman. The horses had slowed to a walk and Penrod staggered along behind them at the end of his rope. More than once he was jerked off his feet and dragged in the dirt. When this happened al-Noor backed his horse until he was able to struggle up. When they rode through the gates and dismounted in the courtyard Penrod was swaying on his torn, bloody feet. He was dazed with exhaustion, and it required all his remaining strength merely to remain upright.

Osman called to him: 'You disappoint me, Abd. I looked for you to find the gazelle herds for us but you were more happy rolling in the dust and looking for dung beetles.'

The other hunters shouted with delight at the jest, and al-Noor suggested, 'Dung beetle is a better name for him than Abd.'

'So be it, then,' Osman agreed. 'From henceforth he shall be known as Jiz, the slave who became a dung beetle.'

As Osman turned towards his own quarters a slave prostrated himself in front of him. 'Mighty Emir, and beloved of Allah and his true Prophet, the Divine Mahdi has been taken gravely ill. He has sent word for you to go to him at once.'

Osman leapt back into al-Buq's saddle and galloped out through the gates of the compound.

The jailers came for Penrod and dragged him to his cell. As previously, they chained him to the iron stake. But before they locked the door and left him, one of the jailers grinned at him. 'Do you still have the strength to attack the great emir?'

'Nay,' Penrod whispered. 'But perhaps I could still twist off the head of one of his chickens.' He showed the jailer his hands. The man slammed the door hurriedly and locked it.

Standing within his reach were three large pitchers of water in place of the usual one, and a meal that in comparison to those he had previously been offered was a banquet. Rather than having been thrown on to the bare floor, the food had been placed in a dish. Penrod was so exhausted that he could hardly chew, but he knew that if he were to survive he must eat. There was half a shoulder of roasted lamb, a lump of hard cheese and a few figs and dates. As he munched he wondered who had provided this fare, and if Osman Atalan had ordered it. If that was the case, what game was he playing? They let him rest on the following day, but on the next his jailers woke him before sunrise.

'Up, Abd Jiz! The emir presents his apologies. He cannot join you in the gazelle hunt this day. He has urgent business at the palace of the Mahdi. However, al-Noor, the famous aggagier, invites you to hunt with him.' They placed the rope round his neck before they removed his chains.

Penrod's feet were so swollen and torn that standing on them was agony, but after the first few miles the pain receded and he ran on. They found not a single gazelle, although they scoured the desert for many leagues. By the time they returned the nails on three of Penrod's toes had turned blue.

They hunted again, day after day. Osman Atalan did not accompany them and they killed no gazelle, but al-Noor ran him hard. The nails fell off his injured toes. Many times over the next few weeks Penrod thought that the infected wounds and scratches on both feet might turn gangrenous and he would lose his legs.

By the onset of the new moon that signalled the beginning of Ramadan, both his feet had healed and the soles were toughened and calloused as though he wore sandals. Only the sharpest thorns could pierce them. He was as lean as a whippet. The fat had been stripped from his frame, replaced with rubbery muscle, and he could keep pace with al-Noor's horse.

Penrod had not seen Osman Atalan since the first unsuccessful gazelle hunt, but when he returned to Omdurman from the field on the third day of Ramadan, he was running strongly beside al-Noor's stirrup. He looked like a desert Arab now: he was lean and bearded, sun-darkened and hard.

As they reached the outskirts of the holy city, al-Noor reined in. 'There is something amiss,' he said. 'Listen!' They could hear the drums beating and the *ombeyas* blaring. The music was not a battle hymn or the sound of rejoicing. It was a dirge. Then they heard salvoes of rifle fire, and al-Noor said, 'It is bad news.'

A horseman galloped towards them, and they recognized another of Osman Atalan's aggagiers. 'Woe upon us!' he shouted. 'Our father has left us. He is dead. Oh, woe upon us all.'

'Is it the emir?' al-Noor yelled back. 'Is Osman Atalan dead?'

'Nay! It is the Holy One, the Beloved of God, the light of our existence. Muhammad, the Mahdi, has been taken from us! We are children without a father.'

*   *   *

209

For weeks they waited at the bedside of the Mahdi. Chief among them was Khalifa Abdullahi. Then there were the Ashraf, the Mahdi's brothers, uncles and cousins, and the emirs of the tribes: the Jaalin, the Hadendowa, the Beja and others. The Mahdi had no sons, so if he should die the succession was uncertain. There were only two women in his sickroom, both heavily veiled and sitting unobtrusively in a far corner. The first was his principal wife, Aisha. The second was the concubine al-Jamal. Not only was she his current favourite, but it was well known that she possessed great medical skills. Together these two women waited out the long and uncertain course of his disease.

Rebecca's Abyssinian cure seemed highly effective during the first stages of the illness. She mixed the powder with boiled water, and she and Aisha prevailed upon the Mahdi to drink copious draughts of it. As with Amber, his body was drained of fluids by the scouring of his bowels and the prolonged vomiting, but between them the two women were able to replace the liquid and mineral salts he had lost. It was fourteen days before the patient had started along the road to full recovery, and prayers of thanksgiving were held at every hour in the new mosque below his window.

When he could sit up and eat solid food, the city resounded to the beat of drums and volleys of rapturous rifle fire. The following day the Mahdi complained of insect bites. Like most of the other buildings in the city the palace was infested by fleas and lice, and his legs and arms were speckled with red swellings. They fumigated the room by burning branches of the turpentine bush in a brazier.

However, the Mahdi scratched the flea bites, and soon a number were infected with the faeces of the vermin that had inflicted them. The temperature of his body soared, and he suffered alternating bouts of fever and chill. He would not eat. He was prostrated by nausea. The doctors thought that these symptoms were a complication of the cholera.

Then, on the sixteenth day, the characteristic rash of typhus fever covered most of his body. By this time he was in such a weakened condition that he sank rapidly. Near the end he asked the two women to help him sit up and, in a faint, unsteady voice, he addressed all the important men crowded around his *angareb*. 'The Prophet Muhammad, who sits on the right hand of Allah, has come to me and he has told me that the Khalifa Abdullahi must be my successor on earth. Abdullahi is of me, and I am of him. As you have obeyed me and treated me, so must you obey and treat him. Allah is great and there is no other God but Allah.' He sagged back on the bed and never spoke again.

The men around the bed waited, but the tension in the crowded room was even more oppressive than the heat and the odour of fever and disease. The Ashraf whispered among themselves, and watched the Khalifa Abdullahi surreptitiously. They believed that their blood-tie to the Mahdi superseded all else: surely the right to take possession of the vacant seat of power belonged to one of their number. However, they knew that their claim was weakened by the last decree of the Mahdi, and by the sermon he had preached in the new mosque only weeks before he fell ill. Then he had reprimanded his relatives for their luxurious

211

living, their open pursuit of wealth and pleasure.

'I have not created the Mahdiya for your benefit. You must give up your weak and wicked ways. Return to the principles of virtue I have taught you which are pleasing to Allah,' he had ranted, and the people remembered his words.

Even though the claim of the Ashraf to the Mahdiya was flawed, if one or two powerful emirs of the fighting tribes declared for them, Abdullahi would be sent to the execution grounds behind the mosque to meet his God and follow his Mahdi into the fields of Paradise.

Sitting quietly beside Aisha at the end of the room Rebecca had learnt enough of Dervish politics to be aware of the nuances and undercurrents that agitated the men. She drew aside the folds of her veil to ask Aisha if she might take a dish of water to bathe the fevered face of the dying Mahdi.

'Leave him be,' Aisha replied softly, 'He is on his way to the arms of Allah who, even better than we can, will love and cherish him through all eternity.'

It was so hot and muggy in the room that Rebecca kept her veil open a little longer, making the most of a sluggish movement of air through the tiny windows across the room. She felt an alien gaze upon her, and flicked her eyes in its direction. The Emir Osman Atalan of the Beja was contemplating her bare face steadily, and though his dark eyes were implacable she knew he was looking at her as a woman, a young and beautiful woman who would soon be without a man. She could not look away: her eyes were held by a force beyond her control, as the compass needle is held by the lodestone.

Though it seemed an age, it was only a few moments before Abdullahi leant towards Osman Atalan and spoke to him so softly that his lips hardly moved. Osman turned his head to listen, and broke the spell that had existed between him and the young woman.

'How do you stand, noble Emir Atalan?' Abdullahi whispered, and his voice was so low that nobody else in the room could overhear.

'The east is mine,' Osman said.

'The east is yours,' Abdullahi agreed.

'The Hadendowa, the Jaalin and the Beja are my vassals.'

'They are your vassals,' Abdullahi acknowledged. 'And you are mine?'

'There is one other small matter.' Osman procrastinated a moment longer, but Abdullahi was ahead of him.

'The woman with yellow hair?'

So he had seen the exchange of glances between Osman and al-Jamal. Osman nodded. Like the rest of them, Abdullahi lusted after this exotic creature with her pale golden hair, blue eyes and ivory skin, but to him she was not worth the price of an empire.

'She is yours,' Abdullahi promised.

'Then I am the vassal of Abdullahi, the successor of the Mahdi, and I will be as the targe on his shoulder and the blade in his right hand.'

Suddenly the Mahdi opened his eyes and stared at the ceiling. He uttered a cry: 'Oh! Allah!' Then the air rushed from his lungs. They covered his face with a white sheet, and the opposing factions faced each other across the cooling body.

The Ashraf stated their case, which was based

on their holy blood. Against this the Khalifa Abdullahi's case was manifest: he did not have the blood but he had the word and blessing of the Mahdi. Still it hung in the balance. The newborn empire teetered on the verge of civil war.

'Who declares for me?' asked the Khalifa Abdullahi.

Osman Atalan rose to his feet and looked steadily into the faces of the emirs of the tribes that traditionally owed him allegiance. One after the other they nodded. 'I declare for the word and wish of the holy Mahdi, may Allah love him for ever!' said Osman. 'I declare for the Khalifat Abdullahi.'

Every man in the room shouted in homage to the new ruler, the Khalifat, of the Sudan, although the voices of the Ashraf were muted and lacked enthusiasm.

*   *   *

When Rebecca returned to the hut in the *zenana*, Amber greeted her ecstatically. They had been parted for all the long weeks of the Mahdi's last illness. They had never been separated for so long before. They lay together on one *angareb*, hugging each other and talking. There was so much to tell.

Rebecca described the death of the Mahdi and the ascendancy of Abdullahi. 'This is very dangerous for us, my darling. The Mahdi was hard and cruel, but we managed to inveigle ourselves into his favour.' Rebecca did not elaborate on how this had been achieved, but went on, 'Now he is gone, we are at the mercy of this wicked man.'

'He will want you,' Amber said. She had grown up far ahead of her years while they had been in

214

the clutches of the Dervish. She understood so much—Rebecca was amazed by it. 'You are so beautiful. He will want you just as the Mahdi did,' Amber repeated firmly. 'We can be sure he will send for you within the next few days.'

'Hush, my sweet sister. Let us not go ahead to search for trouble. If trouble is coming it will find us soon enough.'

'Perhaps Captain Ballantyne will rescue us,' Amber said.

'Captain Ballantyne is far away by now.' Rebecca laughed. 'He is probably at home in England, and has been these many months past.'

'No, he is not. He is here in Omdurman. Nazeera and I have seen him. All the town is talking about him. He was captured by that wicked man Osman Atalan. They keep him on a rope and make him run beside the emir's horse like a dog.'

In the lamplight Amber's eyes glistened with tears. 'Oh, it is so cruel. He is such a fine gentleman.'

Rebecca was astonished and dismayed. Her brief interlude with Penrod seemed like a dream. So much had happened since he had deserted her that her memory of him had faded and her feelings towards him had been soured by resentment. Now it all came flooding back.

'Oh, I wish he had not come to Omdurman,' she blurted. 'I wish he had stayed away, and that I never had to lay eyes on him again. If he is a prisoner of the Dervish, as we are, there is nothing he can do to help us. I don't even want to think about him.'

Rebecca spent most of the following day bringing up to date the journal she had inherited

215

from her father, describing in small, closely written script all that she had witnessed at the death bed of the Mahdi, then her own feelings at the news that Penrod Ballantyne had come back into her life.

From time to time her writing was disturbed by the shouts from the vast crowds in the mosque, which carried over the *zenana* wall. It seemed that the entire population of the country had gathered. Rebecca sent out Nazeera to investigate. Amber wanted to accompany her, but Rebecca forbade it. She would not let Amber out of her sight in these dangerous, uncertain times.

Nazeera returned in the middle of the afternoon. 'All is well. The Mahdi has been buried, and the Khalifat has declared that he has become a saint and that his tomb is a sacred site. A great new mosque will be built over it.'

'But what is all the noise in the mosque? It has been going on all day.' Rebecca demanded.

'The new Khalifat has demanded that the entire population take the Beia, the oath of allegiance to him. The emirs, sheikhs and important men were first to do so. Even the Ashraf have made the oath. There are so many of the common people clamouring to swear that the mosque is overflowing. They are administering the oath to five hundred men at a time. They say that the Khalifat weeps like a widow in mourning for his Mahdi, but still the populace crowds around him. Everywhere I walked in the streets I heard the crowds shouting the praises of the Khalifat and declaring their promises to obey him as the Mahdi decreed. They say the oath-taking will go on for many more days and even weeks before all can be satisfied.'

And when it is done, the Khalifat will send for me, Rebecca thought, and her heart raced with panic and dread.

She was wrong. It did not take that long. Two days later Ali Wad came to their hut. With him were six other men, all strangers to her. 'You are to pack everything you own, and go with these men,' Ali Wad told her. 'This is ordered by the Khalifat Abdullahi, who is the light of the world, may he always please Allah.'

'Who are these men?' Rebecca eyed the strangers anxiously. 'I do not know them.'

'They are aggagiers of the mighty Emir Osman Atalan. Nazeera and al-Zahra are to go with you.'

'But where are they taking us?'

'Into the harem. Now that the holy Mahdi is departed from us, he has become your new master.'

*   *   *

There was much work to be done. The Khalifat Abdullahi was a clever man. He understood that he had inherited a powerful, united empire, and that this had been built upon the religious and spiritual mysticism of the Mahdi and the political imperative of ridding the land of the Turk and the infidel. Now that the Mahdi was gone, the cement that held it together was dangerously weakened. The infidel would soon gather on his borders and the enemies within would emerge and gnaw away, like termites, the central pillars of his power. Not only was Abdullahi clever, he was also ruthless.

He called all the powerful men to him in a great conclave. Their numbers almost filled the new mosque. First he reminded them of the oath they had sworn only days before. Then he read to them the proclamation that the Mahdi had issued the previous year in which he had made abundantly clear the trust that he placed in Khalifa Abdullahi: 'He is of me, and I am of him,' the Mahdi had written in his own hand. 'Behave with all reverence to him, as you do to me. Submit to him as you submit to me. Believe in him as you believe in me. Rely on all he says, and never question his proceedings. All that he does is by the order or the permission of the Prophet Muhammad. If any man thinks evil or speaks evil of him, he will be destroyed. He has been given wisdom in all things. If he sentences a man to death, it is for the good of all of you.'

When they had listened earnestly to this proclamation he ordered the emirs and the Ashraf to write letters that were sent out with fast horsemen and camel-riders to the most remote corners of the empire to reassure and calm the population. He announced the creation of six new *khalifs*. In effect they would become his governors. His brothers were elevated to this rank, and so was Osman Atalan. The Khalif Osman was awarded a new green war-banner to go with the scarlet and black, and granted the honour of planting this at the gates of Abdallahi's palace whenever he was in Omdurman. All the eastern tribes were placed under his banner. Thus Osman now commanded almost thirty thousand élite fighting men.

It took several months for all this to be accomplished, and when it was achieved Abdullahi invited Osman Atalan to hunt with him. They rode out into the desert. There are no eavesdroppers in those great empty spaces, and the two mighty men

218

rode a mile ahead of their entourage. When they were alone Abdullahi disclosed his vision of the future.

'The Mahdiya was conceived in war and the flames of the *jihad*. In peace and complacency it will rust and disintegrate like a disused sword. Like spoilt children, the tribes will return to their old blood feuds, and the sheikhs will bicker among themselves like jealous women,' he told Osman. 'In the Name of God, we lack not real enemies. The pagan and the infidel surround us. They gather like locust swarms at our borders. These enemies will ensure the unity and strength of our empire, for their threat gives reason for the *jihad* to continue. My empire must continue to expand or it will collapse upon itself.'

'You wisdom astounds me, mighty Abdullahi. I am like an innocent child beside you. You are my father and the father of the nation.' Osman knew the man well: he fed on flattery and adulation. Yet the scope of his vision impressed Osman. He realized that Abdullahi dreamed of creating an empire to rival that of the Sublime Porte of the Ottoman Empire in Constantinople.

'Osman Atalan, if you are a child, and Allah knows that you are not, you are a warlike child.' Abdullahi smiled. 'I am sending Abdel Kerim with his *jihadia* northwards to attack the Egyptians on the border. If he is victorious, the entire country of Egypt from the first cataract to the delta will rise up behind our *jihad*.'

Osman was silent as he considered this extraordinary proposal. He thought that Abdullahi had wildly overestimated the appeal of the Mahdiya to the Egyptian population. It was true

219

that the majority were Islamic, but of a much milder persuasion than the Dervish. There was also a large Coptic Christian population in Egypt, which would oppose the Sudanese Mahdiya fanatically. Above all, there were the British. They had only recently taken over supreme power in that country, and would never relinquish it without a bitter fight. Osman knew the quality of these white men: he had fought them at Abu Klea where there had been a mere handful of them. He had heard that they were building up their armies in the north. Their battleships were anchored in Alexandria harbour. No army of the Khalifat could ever fight its way over those thousands of miles to reach the delta. Even if by some remote chance it did, then certain destruction awaited it there at the hands of the British. He was trying to find the diplomatic words to say this without incurring Abdullahi's ire, when he saw the sly glint in his eye.

Then he realized that the proposal was not what it seemed. At last he saw through it: Abdullahi was not intent on the conquest and occupation of Egypt; rather, he was setting a snare to catch his enemies. The Ashraf were the main threat to his sovereignty: Abdel Kerim was the cousin of the Mahdi and one of the leaders of the Ashraf. He had under his control a large army, including a regiment of Nubians who were superb soldiers. If Abdel Kerim failed against the Egyptians, Abdullahi could accuse him of treachery and have him executed, or at least strip him of his rank and take the Ashraf army under his own command.

'What an inspired battle plan, great Khalifat!' Osman was sincerely impressed. He realized now that Abdullahi, by virtue of his cunning and ruthlessness, was indeed fitted to become the one ruler of the Sudan.

'As for you, Osman Atalan, I have a task also.'

'Lord, you know that I am your hunting dog,' Osman replied. 'You have only to command me.'

'Then, my warlike child, my faithful hunting dog, you must win back for me the Disputed Lands.' This was the territory around Gondar, a huge tract of well-watered and fertile land that lay along the headwaters of the Atbara river, and stretched from Gallabat as far as the slopes of Mount Horrea. The Sudanese and the Abyssinian emperors had fought over this rich prize for a hundred years.

Osman considered the task. He looked for the pitfalls and snares that Abdullahi was setting for him, as he had done for Abdel Kerim, but found none. It would be a hard and difficult campaign, but not an impossible one. He had sufficient force to carry it out. The risks were acceptable. He knew he was a better general than the Abyssinian Emperor John. He would not be forced to campaign in the highlands where the advantage would pass to Emperor John. The prize was enormous, and the recaptured lands would become part of his own domain. The thought of moving his personal seat of government to Gondar, once he had captured the city, was attractive. Gondar had been the ancient capital of Abyssinia. There, he would be so far removed from Omdurman that he could establish virtual autonomy while paying lip service to Abdullahi.

'You do me great honour, exalted lord!' He accepted the command. 'Before the rise of the new moon I shall leave Omdurman and travel up the Atbara river to reconnoitre the border and lay my battle plans.' He thought for a moment, then went on, 'I shall need some pretence to travel along the border, and perhaps even visit Gondar. If great Abdullahi should write a letter of greetings and good wishes to the Emperor that he orders me to deliver to the Abyssinian governor at Gondar, I could secretly inspect the defences of the city and the deployment of the enemy troops along the border.'

'May Allah go with you,' said Abdullahi gently. 'You and I are as twin brothers, Osman Atalan. We think with one mind and strike with the same sword.'

*   *   *

In a flotilla of dhows, Osman Atalan and his entourage sailed up the Bahr El Azrek, the Blue Nile, as far as the small river town of Aligail. Here, one of the major tributaries joined the Nile. This was the Rahad river, but it was not navigable for more than a few leagues upstream. Osman offloaded his aggagiers, his women and slaves, almost three hundred souls. The horses had come up in the dhows from Omdurman. At Aligail he sent his aggagiers fifty miles in all directions to hire camels and camel-drivers from the local sheikhs. Once the caravan was assembled they moved eastward along the course of the Rahad. The caravan was strung out over several miles. Osman and a select band of his aggagiers rode well in advance of the main column. Penrod ran beside his horse with the rope round his neck.

The country became more wooded and pleasant as they moved slowly towards the mountains.

There were a few small villages along the river, but these were well separated and the land between was populated with wild game and birds. They came upon rhinoceros and giraffe, buffalo, zebra and antelope of all descriptions. Osman hunted as they travelled. Some days were passed entirely in the pursuit of a particular species of antelope that had caught his attention. Spurning firearms, he and his aggagiers used the lance from horseback to bring down the quarry. There were wild rides and Penrod was able to keep up only by grabbing hold of Osman's stirrup leather and letting himself be pulled along by al-Buq at full gallop, his feet touching the earth lightly every dozen paces or so. By this time he was in such superb physical condition that he delighted in the sport as much as any of the aggagiers. It was all that made his captivity bearable, for during the chase he felt free and vital once again.

Most nights Osman's party slept in the open under the starry sky wherever the day's hunting had taken them. They were usually far ahead of the main column. However, when they had killed some large animal, such as a giraffe or rhinoceros, they camped beside the carcass until the main body caught up with them. When the baggage train arrived, Osman's enormous leather tent was erected in the centre of a *zareba* of thorn bush. It was the size of a large house, furnished with Persian carpets and cushions. The smaller but no less luxurious tents of his wives and concubines were placed around it.

Unlike the Mahdi and the Khalifat Abdullahi, Osman had limited himself to four wives, as decreed in the Koran. The number of his concubines was also modest, and although it fluctuated, it did not exceed twenty or thirty. On this expedition he had brought with him only his latest wife: she had not yet borne him a child and he needed to impregnate her. He had also restricted himself to seven of his most attractive concubines. Among this small group was the recently acquired white girl, al-Jamal. Until now Osman had been so occupied with affairs of state and politics that he had not yet gathered and tasted her fruits. He was in no hurry to do so: the anticipation of this consummation added greatly to his pleasure.

Penrod knew that Rebecca was with the expedition. He had seen her going aboard one of the dhows when they embarked at Omdurman. He had also seen her from a distance on four different occasions since the land journey had begun. Each time she had avoided looking in his direction, but Amber, who was with her, had waved and given him a saucy grin. Of course, there was never an opportunity to exchange a word: Atalan's women were strictly guarded, while Penrod was kept on a leash during the day and locked in leg shackles each evening. At night he was confined to a guarded hut in the *zareba* of al-Noor and the other aggagiers.

Even though he was usually exhausted when he settled down on the sheepskin that served him as a mattress, he still had opportunity to think about Rebecca during the long nights. Once he had convinced himself that he loved her, that she was the main reason why he had defied Sir Charles Wilson's strict orders and returned to Khartoum after the battle of Abu Klea. Since then his feelings towards her had become ambivalent. Of course, she was still his fellow countrywoman. Added to that she had surrendered her virginity to him, and for those reasons he had a duty and responsibility towards her. However, her virtue, which had initially made her so attractive to him, was now indelibly tarnished. Although she had not done so of her own free will, she had become the whore of not one but at least two other men. His strict code of honour would never permit him to marry another man's whore, especially if that man was his blood enemy and of a dark, alien race.

Even if he were able to subdue these feelings and take her as his wife, what good could come of it? When they returned to England the full story of her defilement and degradation at the hands of the Dervish would not remain secret. English society was unforgiving. She would be branded for life as a scarlet woman. He could not present her to his friends and family. As a couple they would be ostracized. The regiment would never condone his choice of wife. He would be denied advancement, and forced to resign his commission. His reputation and standing would be destroyed. He knew that in time he would come to resent and, later, even hate her.

As an ambitious man with a well-developed instinct for self-preservation and survival, he knew what his course of action must be. First, he would do his duty and rescue her. Then, painful as it might be, they must part company and he would return to the world from which she would be for ever excluded.

If he were to carry through this determination, and rescue Rebecca and her little sister, his first

225

concern must be to find freedom himself. To achieve this he must gain the trust of Osman Atalan and his aggagiers, and lull any suspicions they harboured that the sole purpose of his miserable life was either to assassinate the Khalif or to escape from his clutches. Once he induced them to relax the conditions of his imprisonment he knew he would find his opportunity.

* * *

The closer they came to the Abyssinian border, the more wild and grand the land became. Magnificent savannahs gave way to forests of stately trees, interrupted by open glades of green grass. Twenty-five days after they had left the Nile they came upon the first herd of elephant. Closer to the towns and villages, these great animals had been ruthlessly pursued by ivory hunters and had been forced to withdraw deeper into the wilderness.

This herd was drinking and bathing at a pool in the Rahad river. The water was deep and broad, surrounded by fever trees with canary yellow trunks. They heard the squealing and splashing from a great distance, and manoeuvred downwind to climb the low kopje that overlooked the pool. From the summit they had a splendid view of the unsuspecting herd. It was made up of fifty or so cows with their offspring. There were three immature bulls with them, but they carried nondescript tusks.

One of Osman Atalan's young warriors had not yet killed an elephant in the classical manner, on foot and armed only with the sword. Osman described the technique to him. It was a masterly

226

dissertation.

Penrod listened with fascination. He had heard of this dangerous pastime in which the aggagiers earned their title, but had never seen its execution. Towards the end of his lecture, when Osman was pointing out the exact point on the back of the elephant's hind leg where the sword stroke must be aimed to sever the tendon, it occurred to Penrod that Osman was addressing him as much as the Arab novice. He dismissed this as an idle thought. The herd finished drinking and wandered away through the grove of fever trees. Osman let them go unmolested. They were not worthy of his steel. He ordered the aggagiers to mount up and they rode back to the encampment.

Three days later they came across more elephant tracks. The aggagiers dismounted to study them, and saw that they had been made by a pair of bulls. The pad marks were fresh and one set was enormous. With animation they speculated among themselves as to the size and weight of ivory that the larger bull carried. Osman ordered them to remount and led them forward at a smart walk, so that the sound of galloping hoofs would not alarm and stampede the quarry.

'They drank at the river early this morning and now they are returning to the hills to take cover in the thickets of kittar thorns where they feel secure,' Osman said. As they approached the hills they saw that the lower slopes were covered with the reptilian and venomous green thornbush, which contrasted with the brighter, fresher colour of the deciduous forest higher up the slope. They found the big bull standing alone on the edge of the thicket.

'The two bulls have parted company and gone their separate ways. This will make the hunt easier for us,' Osman said softly, and led them forward. The elephant was drowsing quietly, fanning his huge ears, rocking gently from one foot to the other. He was angled away from them and his head was lowered so that the thorn scrub reached to his lower lip and hid his tusks from view. The aggagiers reined in the horses to rest them before beginning the hunt. The breeze was steady and favourable and there was no reason to hurry. Penrod rested with the horses. He squatted on his haunches and drank from the waterskin that al-Noor unstrapped from the pommel of his saddle and dropped to the ground beside him.

Suddenly the bull shook his head so that his ears clapped loudly, then reached out with his trunk to pluck a bunch of kittar blossom. When he lifted his head to stuff the yellow flowers into the back of his throat, he revealed his tusks. They were perfectly matched, long and thick.

The hunters stirred and murmured in appreciation.

'This is a fine animal.'

'This is an honourable bull.'

They all looked to Osman Atalan to see whom he would choose for the honour, each hoping it would be himself.

'Al-Noor,' said Osman, and al-Noor pushed his mount forward eagerly, only to slump again in the saddle when his master went on, 'slip the leash off Abd Jiz.'

Penrod came to his feet with surprise and al-Noor removed the rope from round his neck.

'It is too great an honour for an infidel slave,'

Al-Noor whispered enviously.

Osman ignored his protest. He drew his sword and reversed it before he handed it to Penrod. 'Kill this bull for me,' he ordered.

Penrod tested the balance and weight of the blade, cutting with it forehanded, then backhanded. He spun it in the air and caught it with his left hand, then cut and thrust again. He turned back to Osman, on al-Buq. Penrod was balanced on the balls of his bare feet; he held the sword in the guard position. His expression was grim. The blade was steady as if fixed in the jaws of a steel vice, pointed at the Khalif's chest. Osman Atalan was unarmed and within the sweep of Penrod's sword arm. Their eyes locked. The aggagiers urged their mounts forward and their hands rested on their sword hilts.

Penrod brought the sword slowly to his lips and kissed the flat of the blade. 'It is a fine weapon,' he said.

'Use it wisely,' Osman advised him quietly.

Penrod turned away up the slope towards where the bull elephant stood. His bare feet made no sound on the stony earth and he stepped lightly. He felt the breeze chill the sweat on the back of his neck. He used its direction to guide him as he angled in behind the bull. It was an enormous creature: at the shoulder it stood over twice his own height.

Penrod had in mind every word of Osman's advice as he studied the hind legs. He could clearly make out the tendons beneath the grey and riven hide. They were thicker than his thumb, and as the beast rocked gently they tightened and relaxed. He fastened his gaze on them and moved in quickly.

Unexpectedly the bull humped his back and braced both back legs. From the pouch of loose skin between his back legs his penis dropped out and dangled until the tip almost touched the ground. It was longer than the span of Penrod's outstretched arms and as thick as his forearm. The bull began to urinate, a powerful yellow stream that hosed out a shallow trench in the hard earth. The smell was rank and strong in the noonday heat.

Penrod closed in to within three yards of the bull's haunches, and stood poised, the sword lifted. Then he ran forward and swung the blade, aiming two hand spans above the bull's right heel. It sliced down to the bone, and with a rubbery snap the tendon parted. In the same movement Penrod stepped across to the other leg, reversed his blade and cut again. He saw the recoil of the severed tendon under the thick hide, and jumped back. The crippled bull squealed and dropped heavily to his hindquarters in a sitting position with both back legs paralysed.

Behind him Penrod heard the aggagiers shout in acclamation. He watched the jets of blood squirting from the twin wounds. The bull's struggles to regain his feet aggravated the flow. It would not be long. The bull saw him and swung his head to face Penrod. He tried to drag himself forward, but his movements were awkward and ineffectual. Penrod retreated before him, watching until he was certain that the bull was mortally wounded, then turned and walked unhurriedly back towards the group of watching horsemen.

He had covered half the distance when another elephant squealed on his right flank. The sound was so unexpected that he wheeled to face it. All

230

this time the second, younger bull had been standing nearby, also asleep on its feet. The kittar bush had concealed it, but at the cries and struggles of its companion it burst out of the dense thornbush at full charge, pugnaciously seeking a focus for its alarm and anger. It saw Penrod immediately and swung towards him, rolling back the tips of its huge ears and coiling its trunk against its chest in a threatening attitude. It trumpeted wildly. As it began its charge the ground trembled under its weight.

Penrod glanced around swiftly for some avenue of retreat. There was no point in running towards the group of horsemen. They could offer him no help and would gallop away before he reached them. Even to climb into one of the tall trees that grew nearby would be of no avail. Standing on its back legs the bull could reach even to the top branches to pull him down, or it could knock over the whole tree almost effortlessly. He thought of the ravine they had crossed a short distance back. It was so narrow and deep that he might crawl down into it beyond the bull's reach. He whirled and ran. Faintly he heard the ribald shouts of the aggagiers.

'Run, Dung Beetle! Spread your wings and fly.'

'Pray to your Christian God, infidel!'

'Behold, the fields of Paradise lie before you.'

He heard the elephant crashing through the scrub behind him. Then he saw the opening of the ravine a hundred paces ahead. He was at the top of his own speed, his tempered, hardened legs driving so hard that the elephant was overhauling him only gradually. But he knew in his heart that it would catch him.

Then he heard pounding hoofs close behind

him. He could not help glancing back. The bull was towering over him like a dark cliff, already uncoiling its trunk to swipe him down. The blow would smash bone. Once he was on the ground the bull would kneel on him, crushing him against the hard earth until every bone in his body was smashed, then stabbing those long ivory shafts repeatedly through what remained of his body.

He tore away his gaze and looked ahead. Still the sound of hoofs crescendoed. Without slackening his run Penrod braced himself for the shattering blow that must surely come. Then the hoofs were alongside him, and he saw movement from the corner of his eye. The black bulk of al-Buq was overtaking him. Osman was leaning forward over his withers and pumping the reins. He had kicked his foot out of the nearside stirrup, and the empty iron bumped against al-Buq's flank.

'Come up, Abd Jiz!' Osman invited him. 'I have not finished with you yet.'

With his right hand Penrod snatched the stirrup leather and twisted it round his wrist. Instantly he was jerked off his feet, and he allowed himself to be carried away by the racing stallion. As he swung on the end of the leather he looked back. The bull was still at full charge behind them, but losing ground to the stallion. At last he abandoned the chase and, still squealing with rage, turned aside into the kittar thorn. As he ran off he ripped down branches from the trees in his path in frustration and hurled them high into the air. He vanished over the crest of the hill.

Osman reined in al-Buq, and Penrod released the stirrup leather. He still held the hilt of the sword in his left hand. Osman threw his leg over the stallion's neck and dropped to the ground, landing like a cat in front of him. The other aggagiers were widely scattered and for the moment the two were alone. Osman held out his right hand. 'You have no further need of that steel,' he said quietly.

Penrod glanced down at the sword. 'It grieves me to give it up.' He reversed the weapon and slapped the hilt into Osman's right hand.

'In God's Name, you are a brave man, and an even wiser one,' Osman said, and brought out his left hand from behind his back. In it he held a fully cocked pistol. He thumbed the hammer and let it drop to half-cock, just as al-Noor rode up.

Al-Noor also jumped down and spontaneously embraced Penrod. 'Two true strokes,' he applauded him. 'No man could have done it cleaner.'

They did not have time to wait for the tusks to rot free so they chopped them out. It took until noon the next day to remove the long cone-shaped nerve from the cavity in the base of each. It was painstaking work: a slip of the blade would mar the ivory and reduce drastically its monetary and aesthetic value.

They loaded them on to the packhorses, and when they rode into the main encampment the drummers beat loud and the horns blared. The women, even the Khalif's wife and his concubines, came out to watch. The men fired their rifles in the air, then crowded around the packhorse to marvel at the size of the tusks.

'This must have been the father and grandfather of many great bulls,' they told each other. Then they asked Osman Atalan, 'Tell us, we beg you, exalted Khalif, which hunter brought down this mighty beast?'

'The one who was once known as Abd Jiz, but who has now become the aggagier Abadan Riji.'

From then on no man ever called Penrod Abd Jiz again. That derogatory name was lost and forgotten.

'Command us, Supreme One. What must we do with these tusks?'

'I shall keep one in my tent to remind me of this day's sport. The other belongs to the aggagier who slew it.'

Early the following morning when Osman Atalan emerged from his tent he greeted his waiting aggagiers and discussed with them the usual business of the day, the route he intended to follow and the purpose and object of the day's ride. Penrod squatted nearby with the horses, taking no part until Osman called to him, 'Your style of dress brings your companions into disrepute.'

Penrod stood up in surprise and looked down at his shift. Although he had washed it whenever an opportunity presented itself, it was stained and worn. He had no needle or thread with which to mend it, and the cloth was ripped by thorn and branch, worn threadbare with hard use. 'I have become accustomed to this uniform. It suits me well enough, great Atalan.'

'It suits me not at all,' said Osman, and clapped his hands. One of the house slaves came scurrying forward. He carried a folded garment. 'Give it to Abadan Riji,' Osman ordered him, and he knelt before Penrod and proffered the bundle.

Penrod took it from him and shook it out. He saw that it was a clean, unworn *jibba* and with it were a pair of sandals of tanned camel hide.

'Put them on,' said Osman.

Penrod saw at once that the *jibba* was plain, not decorated with the ritual multi-coloured patches that had such powerful political and religious significance and constituted a Dervish uniform. He would not have donned the *jibba* if it had. He stripped off his rags and slipped it over his head. It fitted him remarkably well, as did the sandals. Somebody had observed his size shrewdly.

'That pleases me better,' said Osman, and swung up easily into al-Buq's saddle. Penrod moved up to his usual position at the stirrup, but Osman shook his head. 'An aggagier is a horseman.' He clapped again, and a groom led a saddled horse from behind the tent. It was a sturdy roan gelding that Penrod had noticed in the herd of spare horses.

'Mount up!' Osman ordered him, and he went into the saddle, then followed the group of riders into the forest. Penrod was conscious of his inferior rank in the band, so he kept well back.

Over the first few miles he assessed the roan under him. The horse had a comfortable gait and showed no vices. He would not be particularly fast. He could never outrun any of the other aggagiers. If Penrod ever tried to escape, they would run him down quickly enough.

No great beauty, but a hard pounder with good temperament, he decided. It felt good to have a horse between his knees again. They rode on towards the blue mountains and the Abyssinian border. They were heading now directly for Gallabat, the last Dervish stronghold before the border. Though the mountains seemed close, they were still ten days' ride ahead. Gradually they left the wilderness behind. There were no more signs of elephant or of the other great game animals. Soon they were passing through fields of dhurra and other cultivation and many small Sudanese villages. Then they started to climb through the foothills of the central massif.

When they off-saddled to recite the midday prayers, Osman Atalan always left the others and spread his carpet in a shaded place that overlooked the next green valley. After he had prayed he would usually eat alone, but that day he called Penrod, and indicated that he should sit facing him on the Persian carpet. 'Break bread with me,' he invited. Al-Noor set out between them a dish of unleavened dhurra cakes and *asida*, and another dish of cold smoked antelope meat. He had hastily cut the throats of the animals before they died from the lance wounds that had brought them down so the flesh was *halal*. There was a smaller dish filled with coarse salt. Osman gave thanks to Allah and asked for His blessing on the food. Then he selected a morsel of smoked meat and, with his right hand, dipped it in to the salt. He leant forward and held it to Penrod's lips.

Penrod hesitated. He was faced with a crucial decision. If he accepted food and salt from Osman's hand it would constitute a pact between them. In the tradition of the tribes it would be equivalent to a parole. If thereafter he tried to escape, or if he committed any warlike or aggressive act against Osman, he would break his word of honour.

Swiftly he made his decision. I am a Christian, not a Muslim. Also, I am not a Beja. For me this is not a binding oath. He accepted the offering,

236

chewed and swallowed, then picked out a scrap of venison, salted it and offered it to Osman. The Khalif ate it and nodded his thanks.

They ate slowly, savouring the meal, and their easy conversation concerned the affairs that absorbed them both: war, hunting and the pursuit of arms. At first it was wide-ranging, then became more specific as Osman asked how the British trained their troops and what qualities their commanders looked for in their officers.

'Like you we are a warlike people. Most of our kings were warriors,' Penrod explained.

'This I have heard.' Osman nodded. 'I have also seen with my own eyes how your people fight. Where do they learn these skills?'

'There are a people called the French, a neighbouring tribe. We have sport with them on occasion. There is always trouble in some part of the Empire that must be controlled. During periods of peace we have colleges, which have been established for many generations, to train our line and staff officers. Two are famous: the Royal Military Academy at Woolwich, and the Royal Military College at Camberley.'

'We also have a school for our warriors.' Osman nodded. 'We call it the desert.'

Penrod laughed, then agreed. 'The battlefield is the best training school, but we have found the academic study of the art of war invaluable too. You see, most of the great generals of all the ages from Alexander to Wellington have written of their campaigns. There is much in which they are able to instruct us.'

When they rode on eastwards, Osman summoned Penrod to ride at his side and they continued their discussion animatedly. At times they became heated. Penrod was describing how Bonaparte had been unable to break the British square at Waterloo, and Osman had mocked him lightly. 'We Arabs have not studied at any college, and yet unlike this Frenchman we broke your square at Abu Klea.'

Penrod rose to the bait, as Osman had intended he should. 'You never broke us. You penetrated locally, but the square held and healed itself, then became a trap for your emir al-Salida, his sons and a thousand of his men.' They argued with the freedom of blood-brothers, but when their voices rose the aggagiers looked at each other uneasily and pressed close to be ready to intervene if their *khalif* was threatened. Osman waved them back. He reined in on the skyline of another ridge in the series that climbed like a giant staircase towards the mountains.

'Before us lies the land of the Abyssinians, our enemies for many centuries past. If you were my general and I asked you to seize the territory as far as Gondar, then hold it against the rage of Emperor John, tell me how you, with your schoolroom studies, would accomplish this task.'

It was the kind of problem that Penrod had studied at the staff officer's college. He took up the challenge with enthusiasm. 'How many men will you give me?'

'Twenty-five thousand,' Osman replied.

'How many does the Emperor have to bring against me?'

'Maybe ten thousand at Gondar, but another three hundred thousand beyond the mountains at Aksum in the highlands.'

'They will have to descend through the high passes to bring me to battle, will they not? Then I must invest Gondar swiftly, and once the city is contained I will not pause to reduce it, but I will drive on hard to seal the mouths of the passes before the reinforcements can debouch into the open ground.'

They discussed this problem in detail, considering every possible response to the attack. Their discussion continued unflaggingly over the rest of the march to Gallabat. It was only when they came in sight of the town that it occurred to Penrod that it had not been an academic discussion, and that this journey was a prelude to the Dervish invasion of the kingdom of Abyssinia. Osman was calling on his training as a military adviser.

So the Mahdi's *jihad* did not end at Khartoum, Penrod realized. Abdullahi knows that he must fight or he will languish and perish. Then he considered how much damage he had unwittingly done by giving encouragement and expert advice to Osman.

Even if the Dervish triumphs here at Gondar, Abdullahi will not be satisfied. He will turn his eyes on Eritrea, and he won't stop there. He cannot stop. He will never stop until he is forcibly stopped. That will not happen until Abdullahi has aroused the wrath of the civilized world, he decided. In my own humble way I may have done something to help bring that about. He smiled coldly. There are exciting days ahead.

*   *   *

The Dervish governor of Gallabat was almost overcome by the honour of receiving the mighty Khalif Osman Atalan as a guest in his city. Immediately he vacated his own mud-brick palace and placed it at the disposal of the visitors. He moved into a much smaller, humbler building on the outskirts of the town.

Osman decided to rest in Gallabat until the cessation of the monsoon period, which would make travelling in the hilly country around Gondar almost impossible. This would entail a delay of several months, but there was much to keep him occupied. He wanted to gather every scrap of information that might be of importance during the coming campaign. He sent out word that the local guides who had taken caravans up to Gondar through the high passes, and those warlike sheikhs who had raided the Ethiopian territories for cattle and slaves must come to him in Gallabat. They hastened to his bidding. He questioned them at great length, and recorded all they had to tell him. This information would comprise the bulk of his report to the Khalifat Abdullahi when he returned to Omdurman.

Osman recalled that the Mahdi had used the white concubine, al-Jamal, as a scribe and letter-writer. She was skilled in many languages. He ordered her to be present at these interrogations to write down the facts as they were revealed by the witnesses. He had seen little of al-Jamal since the beginning of the expedition for he had had marital obligations elsewhere. But Osman had barely settled into the governor's palace before the older women slaves of the harem came to him with the news that his youngest wife had at last responded to his repeated attentions by missing her moon. They informed him that she had not flown her red banner for two months past.

Osman was pleased. His fourth wife was a niece of the Khalifat Abdullahi and therefore her pregnancy was of great political importance. Her name was Zamatta. Although she had a pretty face, she enjoyed her food and had thick thighs, a pudding-shaped belly and a pair of soft, cow-like udders. At this time in his life Osman Atalan demanded more from his favourites than a musical giggle and a willingness to lie back and open their legs. He had done what had to be done, and now he felt no inclination to spend more time in the company of the dull-witted Zamatta.

During the first few days of the interrogations al-Jamal had taken up an unobtrusive position behind the governor's dais in the audience hall. On the third day Osman ordered her to move to a seat below the front of the dais. Here she sat cross-legged with her writing tablet on her lap, directly in his line of vision. He liked the quick movements of her slim, pale hands, and the texture of the cheek that was turned towards him as she wrote. As was fitting, she never raised her eyes from the parchment or looked at him directly. Once or twice while he was watching her a mysterious smile touched her lips, and this intrigued him. Seldom before in his life had he been concerned with what his women were thinking, but this one seemed different.

'Read back to me what you have written,' he ordered.

She lifted those strangely pale blue eyes to look at him, and his breath caught. She recited the

241

evidence, without having to read it. When she finished she leant towards him and dropped her voice so that he alone could hear. 'Trust him not, Great Lord,' she said. 'He will give you little for your comfort.' They were the first words she had ever addressed to him.

Osman's expression remained impassive, but he was thinking quickly. He had let it be known that he was conducting these enquiries to facilitate trade with the Abyssinians and plan his state visit to Gondar. Had this woman guessed his true intentions, or had she been informed? What grounds did she have for the warning she had just given him? He went on with his enquiries, but now he studied the man before him more intently.

He was an elderly caravan master, prosperous from the cloth of his robes, intelligent judging by the depth of his knowledge. In all other respects he was unremarkable. He had stated that he was of the tribe of Hadendowa. Yet he did not affect the patched *jibba*, and there was something alien in his accent and the manner of his speech. Osman considered challenging his identity, but discarded the idea. He looked for the other signs that al-Jamal must have noticed. The man leant forward to take the small brass cup of coffee from the tray that had been placed before him, and the neck opening of his robe gaped to show a flash of silver. It was a fleeting glimpse, but Osman recognized the ornately engraved Coptic Christian cross that hung on a chain round his neck.

He is Abyssinian, Osman realized. Why would he dissemble? Are they spying on us as we are on them? He smiled at the man. 'What you have told me has been of great value. For this I thank you.

When do you begin your next journey?'

'Great Khalif, three days hence I leave with two hundred camels laden with rock salt from the pans at al-Glosh.'

'What is your destination?'

'I travel to the new city of Addis Ababa in the hills, where I purpose to barter my salt for ingots of copper.'

'Go with God, good merchant.'

'Stay with God, mighty Atalan, and may angels guard your sleep.'

When the caravan owner left the audience hall, Osman gestured al-Noor to his side. When the aggagier knelt beside him he whispered, 'The merchant is a spy. Kill him. Do it secretly and with cunning. None must learn who delivered the blow.'

'As you order, so shall it be done.'

The staff left the hall, each making an obeisance to the Khalif as he passed, but when al-Jamal rose to follow them Osman said curtly, 'Sit by me. We shall talk a while.'

By this time Rebecca could act the part of a concubine. The Mahdi had taught her how to please an Arab master. Flattery was the one sure way to achieve it. She was always astonished at how they would accept the most extravagant hyperbole as nothing more than their due. While she spouted this nonsense she could efface herself and keep her true feelings hidden. She sat as he had ordered and, with her face veiled, waited for him to speak.

'Remove your veil,' he said. 'I wish to see your face while we discourse.' She obeyed. He studied her features in silence for a while, then asked, 'Why do you smile?'

'Because, my lord, I am happy to be in your

243

presence. It gives me great pleasure to serve you.'

'Are all the women in your country like you?'

'We speak the same language, but none of us is like the others. Great Khalif, I am sure your women are no different.'

'Our women are all the same. The reason for their existence is to please their husbands.'

'Then they are fortunate, great Atalan, especially those who have the honour to belong to you.'

'How did you learn to read and write?'

'My lord, I was taught to do so from an early age.'

'Your father did not forbid this?'

'Nay, sweet master, he encouraged it.'

Osman shook his head with disapproval. 'What of his wives? Did he allow them to indulge in such dangerous practice?'

'My father had one wife, and she was my mother. When she died he never remarried.'

'How many concubines?'

'None, exalted Khalif.'

'Then he must have been very poor, and of little standing in this world.'

'My father was the representative of our queen, and well beloved by her. I have a letter from Her Majesty that says so.'

'If the Queen truly loved him, she should have sent him a dozen wives to replace the old one.' Osman was fascinated by her replies, each of which led him immediately to another question. He found it difficult to imagine a land where it rained almost every day and was so cold that the raindrops turned to white salt before they hit the ground.

'What do the people drink? Why do they not die

of thirst if the water turns to *salt*?'

'My master, before very long the snow turns back to water.'

Osman looked up to the spade-shaped windows. 'The sun has set. You must follow me to my quarters. I wish to hear more of these wonders.'

Rebecca's spirits quailed. Since she had been taken into his *zenana*, she had been able to avoid this confrontation. She smiled prettily, and covered her mouth with one hand as she had seen the other women do when overcome with shyness. 'Again you fill my heart with joy, noble lord. To be with you is all in this life that gives me pleasure.'

The cooks brought up the evening meal to his quarters while Osman prayed alone on the terrace, which commanded a grand vista of distant mountains. As soon as he had completed the complicated ritual he dismissed the cooks, and ordered Rebecca to serve his food, but showed little interest in it. He took a few mouthfuls, then made her sit at his feet and eat from his leavings.

He continued to ply her with questions, and listened intently to her replies, hardly allowing her a chance to swallow before he asked the next question. Some time in the early hours of the morning she slumped over and fell into a deep sleep on the cushions from sheer exhaustion. When she awoke it was dawn and she was stretched out still fully dressed on his *angareb*. She wondered how she had got there, then remembered her dream of being a small girl again and her father carrying her up the stairs to bed. Had the Khalif carried her to bed? she wondered. If he had, that was some small miracle of condescension.

She heard excited shouts and galloping hoofs

245

from below the terrace and rose from the bed, went to the window and looked down. In the courtyard Osman Atalan and some of his aggagiers were trying out a string of unbroken three-year-old horses that had been the gift of the governor of Gallabat. Penrod Ballantyne, almost indistinguishable from the Arabs, was up on a frisky bay colt that was bucking furiously around the yard with arched back and stiff legs. Osman and his other aggagiers shouted with laughter and offered ribald advice.

These days, whenever Rebecca laid eyes on Penrod her emotions were thrown into uproar. He was a heartbreaking reminder of that long-ago existence from which she had been snatched so untimely. Did she still love him, as she had once thought she did? She was not sure. Nothing was certain any longer. Except that the man who stood at the opposite end of the yard now ruled her destiny. She stared at Osman Atalan, and the despair she thought she had subdued returned in full force to overwhelm her like a dark wave.

She turned from the window and stared at the Webley revolver that lay on a side table across the room. She had seen the Khalif place it there before he went to his prayers the previous night. It had probably been taken from a dead British officer at Abu Klea or perhaps even looted at the sack of Khartoum.

She crossed the room and picked it up. She opened the action and saw that every chamber was fully loaded. She snapped it shut and turned to the mirror on the facing wall. She stared at her image as she cocked and lifted the pistol to point at her own temple. She stood like that trying to summon that last grain of determination to press the trigger.

Then she noticed in the mirror the initials engraved discreetly in the butt plate of the weapon. She lowered it and examined the inscription. 'D. W. B. From S. I. B. With love,' she read. 'David Wellington Benbrook from Sarah Isabel Benbrook.'

This had been her mother's gift to her father. She hurled it from her and ran from the room, back to the *zenana* to find Nazeera, the only person in the world to whom she could turn.

* * *

Penrod sat the colt easily and let him work himself into a lather as he whipped from side to side with long elastic jumps, then stood on his hind legs and pawed at the sky. When the colt lost his balance and toppled backwards, the watching aggagiers shouted and al-Noor beat on his leather shield with his scabbard. But Penrod jumped clear, still holding the long rein. With a convulsive heave the colt came up again on all four legs, and before he could break away, Penrod sprang lightly on to his bare back. The colt stood on planted hoofs and shivered with outrage and frustration at being unable to rid himself of the unfamiliar weight.

'Open the gates!' Penrod shouted, to the captain of the city guard, then lashed the colt across the shoulder with the end of the reins. He sprang into startled flight, and Penrod turned him towards the open gates. They flew through and out into the lane, scattering chickens, dogs and children, skirted the souk, then ran out into the open country, still at full gallop. Almost an hour later horse and rider returned. Penrod walked the colt round the courtyard, turning him left and right, halting him, making him back up and stand at last. He threw one leg over his neck and dropped to the ground, stood at the colt's head and stroked his sweat-drenched neck.

'What think you, Abadan Riji?' Osman Atalan called down from the terrace. 'Is this a horse fit for an aggagier?'

'He is strong and swift, and he learns quickly,' Penrod responded.

'Then he is my gift to you,' said the Khalif.

Penrod was astonished at this mark of approval. It enhanced his status yet again. He lacked only a sword to be counted a full warrior of the Beja. He clenched his right fist and held it to his heart in a gesture of respect and gratitude. 'I am not worthy of such liberality. I shall name him Ata min Khalif, the Gift of the Khalif.'

The following day Penrod loaded his ivory tusk on to one of the packhorses and carried it down to the souk. For an hour he sat drinking coffee and haggling with a trader from Suakin. In the end he sold the tusk for two hundred and fifty Maria Theresa dollars.

When he had entered the souk he had passed the stall of a fat Persian. In pride of place among the merchant's wares a sword was laid out on a sheepskin fleece. Now Penrod came back to him. He examined all his other stock, showing particular interest in a matched necklace and earrings of polished amber, and avoided glancing at the sword. He haggled the price of the amber jewellery, and drank so many more cups of coffee that his bladder ached. In the end he struck a bargain at three

Maria Theresas for the necklace. He bid the Persian farewell, and was leaving his stall when his eye fell at last upon the sword. The Persian smiled: he had known all along where Penrod's true interest lay.

The slim curved blade was of the finest Damascus steel, unembellished by gold engravings and inscriptions for the graceful wavy patterns in the metal, caused by the strip forgings, were sufficient ornamentation. This was not a pretty bauble but a true killing blade. With the bright edge Penrod shaved a patch of hair off his forearm, then flicked his wrist. The steel sang like a crystal glass. It cost him seventy-five Maria Theresas, the equivalent price of two pretty Galla slave girls.

Three days later Osman Atalan held an audience in the great tent that had been set up at the edge of the city. Penrod waited his turn among the supplicants, then knelt before the Khalif. 'What more do you require of me, Abadan Riji?' Osman asked, and his tone was sharp and brittle as flint.

'I beg the mighty and noble Atalan to accept the gift of one he has honoured with his benevolence.' He placed the roll of sheepskin at Osman's feet.

Osman unwrapped it and smiled when he saw the lovely weapon. 'This is a fine gift and one that I accept with pleasure.' He handed the sword back to Penrod. 'Carry it for me. If you must use it, use it wisely.'

Between them they had reached a compromise. The slave was still a slave, but accoutred like a warrior.

*   *   *

Rebecca sat at the Khalif's feet each day, recording the proceeds in the audience hall. Every evening she was sent back to the *zenana* in the governor's palace. At first his indifference was a relief to her, but after three days it irked her. Had she given him offence by falling asleep in his presence, or bored and annoyed him with garrulousness, she wondered. Or am I just unattractive to him? It really does not matter what he feels. Only what happens to Amber and Nazeera, and of course to me also. Endlessly she and Nazeera discussed this predicament, which involved them all so intricately and intimately. Their well-being and even their lives were in the Khalif's hands. From hating the thought of allowing Osman Atalan to touch her, Rebecca began to fear that he would not do so.

Nazeera held up to her the example of his fourth wife Zamatta. 'She was unable to hold his interest. And so, even though she is a relative of the Khalifat Abdullahi, he sent her back to Omdurman as soon as she had a babe in her belly. She may never see him again, and will probably pass the entire remainder of her life locked in the *zenana*. Beware, al-Jamal. If he rejects you, you may not be so fortunate as Zamatta. He might sell you, or give you to some old emir or sheikh who smells like a goat. And Amber—what will he do with her? The Khalifat likes children, young children. He would welcome her into his own harem, if Osman Atalan offered her to him. You must strive to please him. I shall teach you how, for I have some small experience in these matters.'

With these threats as an incentive Rebecca determined to pay full attention to Nazeera's advice and instruction.

The following afternoon Nazeera returned from a visit to the souk, and displayed her purchase: the tusk from the lower jaw of a hippopotamus. 'We shall use this as a tool of instruction,' she informed Rebecca. 'There is much demand for toys such as this among the women of the harem and *zenana* who do not see their husbands from one feast of Ramadan to the next. They call them the jinn of the *angareb*. The Khalif Atalan has different tastes from those of the Divine Mahdi. Your mouth and sweet lips alone will not suffice. He will require more of you than the Mahdi ever did.' She held up the tusk. 'The Khalif will be this shape, but if he is so large you will be blessed indeed.' Nazeera went on to demonstrate her artistry.

Rebecca would never have dreamt that some of the behaviour Nazeera described between man and woman was possible, and she found herself becoming more interested in the subject than the cold contemplation of survival required. She thought about it a great deal at night before she slept, and if Amber had not been lying beside her on the same *angareb* she might have indulged in some preliminary experimentation with the ivory toy.

However, it seemed that Osman Atalan had lost interest in her even before he had pursued their relationship to its full potential. Eventually he finished questioning the last of the witnesses. He was about to leave the audience hall without having acknowledged her, when unexpectedly he turned to one of his viziers. 'This evening the concubine al-Jamal will serve my evening meal. See to it.'

Although she kept her eyes downcast Rebecca felt a lift of intense relief, tempered by a stirring of

251

trepidation. I must play the game that Nazeera has taught me to arouse his carnal passions, and make our lives secure, she thought, then tried to suppress the flutter of excitement in the pit of her stomach. It seemed, however, that this particular evening the Khalif's passions were more conversational than concupiscent. He gave her little opportunity to try out her freshly acquired knowledge.

'I know that in your country the ruler is a woman,' he said, before he had finished eating.

'Yes. Victoria is our queen.'

'Does she rule firmly and are her laws strong?'

'She does not make the laws. The laws are made by Parliament.'

'Ah!' said the Khalif knowingly. 'So Parliament is her husband, and he makes the laws. That is clever of him. He must be cunning and wise. I knew that a man must be behind it all. I should like to write a letter to Lord Parliament.'

'Parliament is not a single man. It is an assembly of the people.'

'The common people make the laws? Do you mean the cooks and grooms, the carpenters and masons, the beggars, *fellahin* and gravediggers? Anyone of this riff-raff can make a law? Surely this is not possible.'

Rebecca struggled for half of the rest of the night to explain an electoral system of government and the democratic process. When finally she succeeded Osman was appalled. 'How can warriors like those Englishmen I have fought allow this obscenity to exist?' He was silent for a while as he paced the floor. Then he stopped in front of her, and his tone was diffident, as though he feared her answer. 'Women also have this thing you call a

252

vote?'

'Women do not have a voice. No woman may cast a vote,' she replied.

Osman placed his fists on his hips and laughed triumphantly. 'Ha! Now at least I can still respect my enemies. At least your men keep control of their wives. But tell me, please. You say your ruler is a woman. Does she not have a voice, a vote?'

'I—I don't know. I don't think so.'

'You Franks!' He clutched his head theatrically. 'Are you mad? Or is it me alone?'

Rebecca found that she was beginning to enjoy herself. Like a pack of hunting dogs, their discussion ranged over wide territory and started some extraordinary game. This was like the unrestricted and open-ended discussions in which her father had indulged her. Beyond the open windows the cocks crowed at dawn while she was still trying to explain to him that the Atlantic Ocean was wider than the Nile or even, in God's Name, Lake Tana. When he sent her back to the harem unmolested, her relief was tempered by a strange feeling of inadequacy.

Before she joined Amber on the mattress she held up the oil lamp and studied herself in the small mirror. Most men find me appealing, she reminded herself, and thought of Ryder Courtney and Penrod Ballantyne. So why does this savage treat me like another man? she wondered.

The next morning she watched with Amber and the rest of the women from the terrace of the harem as Osman Atalan rode out at the head of a band of his aggagiers on a hawking expedition along the eastern border.

'Look!' cried Amber. 'There is Captain

Ballantyne. They say that the Khalif gave him that horse. On him the *jibba* looks as dashing as a cavalry dolman. He is so handsome, would you not agree, Becky?'

Rebecca had barely noticed Penrod but she made a non-committal sound while she followed with her eyes the elegant, exotic figure at the head of the cavalcade of horsemen. He is as fierce and dangerous as the falcon on his wrist, she thought.

Osman Atalan was gone from the city for almost ten days. When he returned he sent for Rebecca. He stood behind her shoulder as he directed her to draw a detailed map of the ground he had covered in his foray across the Abyssinian border. When she had completed it to his satisfaction, he dismissed her. Then he called her back from the door, 'You will attend me after evening prayers. I want to discuss with you certain matters that interest me.'

When she found Nazeera in the harem, she whispered the news to her. 'He wants me to go to him again this evening, Nazeera. What shall I do?'

Nazeera saw the colour in her cheeks. 'I am sure you will think of something,' she said. 'Now I will prepare your bath.' She poured a liberal measure of attar of roses and sandalwood essence into the pitchers of hot water, then rummaged through the chests to choose a robe fitting to the occasion from the wardrobe that the Mahdi had provided for Rebecca.

'You can see through it,' Amber protested, when Rebecca put it on. 'With the lamp behind you it makes you seem *naked*!' She placed a powerful pejorative emphasis on the last word. 'You will look like a belly-dancer!'

'I shall wear my woollen shawl over it, and keep myself covered throughout the dinner,' Rebecca reassured her.

As soon as they were alone in his quarters, the Khalif picked up the subject of their conversation of ten days previously, as though it had not been interrupted. 'So this large water you call the ocean is alive. It moves backwards and forwards, and leaps up and down. Is that not what you told me?'

'Indeed, mighty Atalan, at times it is like a ravening beast with the strength of a thousand elephants. It can overwhelm ships fifty times larger than any that voyage on the Nile as though they were dried leaves.'

He looked into her eyes to discover if there was any truth at all in these improbable statements. All he found were points of light, like those in the depths of a sapphire. This diverted his train of thought and he took her chin and lifted it to gaze deeply into her eyes. His hands were strong and his fingers hard as bone from sword-play and from handling his hawks and horses.

He made her feel helpless and vulnerable. I must remember everything Nazeera has taught me. She felt her loins melt lubriciously. This might be the only opportunity he will ever give me.

'I shall send an expedition of a thousand of my most intrepid men to find this wild water and bring it back in large skins,' Osman announced. 'I will pour it into the Nile to overwhelm the British steamers when next they sail upriver to attack us.'

She was touched by his naïvety. Sometimes it was like talking to a small child. Not for the first time she felt an extraordinary tenderness towards him, which she had forcibly to suppress. This is no

255

child. This is a shrewd, ruthless, arrogant tyrant. I am completely at his mercy. Why did that thought excite her, she wondered. But before she could decide the answer he made another disconcerting change of subject.

'But I have heard that their steamers are able to voyage on the land further and faster than the bravest horse. Is this true?'

'It is true, mighty Khalif. These carriages are different from the river steamers and are called steam locomotives.' It took her a few moments to rally her thoughts, and she described how she had journeyed from London to Portsmouth in a single day, including a stop for refreshment. 'That is a distance greater than from Metemma to Khartoum.' Her voice was husky and disturbed. He still held her chin, but now he stroked her cheek and touched a lock of her hair. She was surprised at the gentleness of his hard fingers, this savage warrior from the primal deserts.

'What unguent do you use to keep your skin and hair so soft?' he asked.

'This is how I was born.'

'It grows dark. Light the lamps so that I may see you more clearly.'

She remembered how Amber had disapproved of the transparency of the silk she wore. She slipped the light woollen shawl off her shoulder as she stood up, and tossed it over the table as she went to take a taper from the fire pot. She cupped the flame in her hands and carried it across to the lamp. It caught, then burnt brightly; the warm yellow light chased the shadows along the walls. She lingered there a little longer, trimming the wick until the flame was burning evenly. Her back was turned to him, but she was aware of the picture she made. I am acting like a harlot, she thought, then seemed to hear her father's voice: 'It's an honourable profession. The oldest in the world.' She smiled in confusion as the ghost voice went on, delivering his often repeated advice to her: 'Whatever you do, do it to the very best of your ability.' It was a blessing.

'I shall try, Daddy,' she replied inwardly, and at that she felt a touch. She had not heard Osman Atalan cross the room behind her. His hands on her shoulders were strong and steady. She smelt him. It was a good smell like a well-groomed horse or a cat. Muslim men of his rank bathed as many times in a day as an Englishman did in a month.

She stood submissively as his hands ran down from her shoulders, under her armpits, then reached in front of her to take her breasts. They filled each of his hands. He took her nipples and rolled them between his fingers, then pinched them until she gasped. The pressure was skilfully applied, just sufficient to startle and arouse her without inflicting pain. Then he pulled her back against him. It was some moments before she realized that he had shed his *jibba* and was now naked. Through the silk of her robe she could feel the hard muscular length of his body pressing against her back. Tentatively she pushed back with her buttocks, and found conclusive proof that he did not find her repellent. With Nazeera's advice and instruction still sharp in her mind, Rebecca stood without moving as she appraised that which the Khalif was pressing against her. It seemed to be of similar shape to Nazeera's hippo tusk, and it was certainly every bit as hard.

She turned slowly in his arms and looked down. It seems that I am to be blessed indeed, she thought. Like the ivory tusk, he was smooth and slightly curved. She touched him, then encompassed him with her hand. Her fingers were barely able to meet round his girth. She made the movements of her hand that Nazeera had demonstrated and felt him throb and leap in her grip.

'Great Khalif, in your manly attributes you are peerless and imperial.'

He took the word 'imperial' as a comparison to the Light of the World, Muhammad el Mahdi, who now sat at the right hand of Allah, and he was well pleased. 'I am your stallion,' he said.

'And I am your filly, in awe of your strength and majesty. Treat me gently, I beg you, sweet lord.'

She continued to hold him. She expected him to pounce upon her as Ryder Courtney had done, but his restraint surprised, then titillated her. She kept her grip on him as he undressed her, and was still holding him as she fell back on his mattress. She attempted to direct him to her source, using both hands and coming up on her elbows so she could watch him disappear inside her. But he resisted her urging, and began to examine her as though she were indeed a thoroughbred filly, turning her this way and that, lifting each limb in turn, admiring and caressing them. It was at first flattering to be at the centre of his attention, but he was so unhurried and deliberate that she became impatient. She longed for the delicious sensation of being deeply invaded that she had last known with Ryder Courtney.

Still he lingered over her, taking his time so

deliberately that she felt she must scream in her desperation. She had once owned a tabby cat named Butter. In her season Butter would yowl and sob to attract feline admirers. Rebecca understood that imperative now. How many thousand women has he known? she wondered. For him there is no urgency. He cares not at all that he is causing me such distress.

She tugged at him again with both hands. 'I beg of you, great Atalan, lack of you is torture beyond my ability to endure. Please be merciful and end it now.'

'You asked me to treat you gently,' he reminded her, with a smile.

'I am a silly creature who does not know her own mind or nature. Forget what I have said, my lord. You know much better than I ever will what must be done. Make haste, I entreat you. I can wait no longer.' He did as she asked, and this time she could not forbear from screaming, louder and longer than Butter ever had. None of Osman Atalan's other women had ever acknowledged his mastery in such a comprehensive vocal fashion. He was flattered and amused.

He did not dismiss her on rising, as was his habit, but kept her beside him as he ate his breakfast. Soon none of the other concubines he had brought with him from Omdurman were honoured by a summons to his private quarters. Rebecca took up almost permanent abode in them. She did not bore him, as the others were wont to do.

*   *   *

Once Osman Atalan had assembled all the expert

259

first-hand information of the local guides and hunters and traders, he employed Rebecca's artistic skills and penmanship to incorporate it into a large-scale map of the border and the disputed country immediately beyond, where he expected one day soon to do battle with the Ethiopians. He gave a tracing of this map to Penrod and sent him out on a scouting mission to check it against the terrain. He could not entrust this task to any of his aggagiers: for all their loyalty and dedication to him, none was more than barely literate and none possessed more than a vestige of map-reading skills. However, to exclude any from such an important expedition would be to afford them deep insult.

On the other hand he was still not certain how far out of his sight he could trust the slave Abadan Riji. He solved this delicate problem by selecting al-Noor and six other aggagiers to accompany him, ostensibly as his jailers but in reality as his bodyguard. Osman left them in no doubt that they should accede to the reasonable orders and directions of Abadan Riji in the accomplishment of the objects of the expedition. On the other hand if they returned to Gallabat without their charge, he would decapitate them.

After his scouts had left, Osman Atalan remained at Gallabat to review with the Dervish governor the state of his province, also to receive the Abyssinian emissaries from Aksum. Emperor John was anxious to discern the true reason for the presence of such an important Dervish on his borders. His ambassadors brought valuable gifts, and assurances of mutual peace and goodwill. Osman sent back a message that as soon as the season of the big rains ended he would travel to Gondar to meet the emperor.

Meanwhile the thunderstorms raged daily over the mountains, affording him ample opportunity for prolonged discourse with his new favourite.

*　　　*　　　*

Penrod's expedition left Gallabat in the middle of the morning, just as soon as the rain of the previous night had blown over and the sun broken out between the high cumulus-nimbus cloud mountains. They were as lightly equipped as a tribal raiding party. Each man carried his own weapons and bedroll on the pommel of his saddle, while three pack mules brought up the rear with leather bags of provisions and cooking pots bouncing on their backs. Half a mile beyond the last buildings of the town they came upon a group of five women sitting beside the track. They were engaged in the endless feminine pastime of hairdressing. This was the equivalent of the aggagiers' sword-honing, and filled their idle hours, of which there were many.

It was not possible for an Arab woman to arrange her hair alone: it was a social enterprise that involved all her close companions. The styling was elaborate and might take two or three days of patient, skilled creation. In the year that Amber had lived in the harem she had learnt the art so well that, with her nimble fingers and eye for detail, her skills were much in demand among the other women of Osman Atalan's *zenana*; so much so that she was able to charge a fee of two or three Maria Theresas, depending on the labour required.

261

First, the hair had to be combed out. It was usually wiry, matted with congealed cosmetics and twisted into tight curls from its previous dressing. Amber used a long skewer to separate the strands. After that she employed a coarse wooden comb to bring about some order to the dense tresses. All these preliminaries might occupy a full day, which was enlivened by laughter and the exchange of juicy morsels of scandal and gossip.

Once it was possible to burrow down as far as the scalp, a hunt for trespassers was conducted in which everyone participated. The sport was accompanied by cries of triumph and shrieks of delight as the scurrying vermin were hunted down and crushed between the fingernails. Once the field had been cleared, Amber dressed the locks with a concoction of oil of roses, myrrh, dust of sandalwood, and powder of cloves and cassia mixed with mutton fat. Then the most delicate part of the operation took place. The hair was twisted into hundreds of tiny tight plaits and set with a liberal application of sticky gum arabic and dhurra paste. This was allowed to dry until it was stiff as toffee. On the final day each tiny plait was carefully unpicked with the long tortoiseshell skewer, and allowed to stand on its own, free and proud, so the woman's head appeared twice its normal size. The finished work was usually greeted with squeals of admiration and approbation. After ten days the entire process was repeated, affording Amber a steady income.

This morning Amber was so intent on her work that she was not aware of the approaching band of aggagiers until they were less than a hundred paces off. All present were now placed in an invidious situation. Here were five of the Khalif Osman Atalan's women, unveiled and unchaperoned, except by each other, about to be confronted by a war party of the same Khalif's trusted warriors. The correct and diplomatic behaviour would have been for both sides to ignore the presence of the other, and for the aggagiers to pass by as though they were as invisible as the breeze.

'Captain Ballantyne!' screamed Amber, and jumped to her feet, leaving the skewer sticking from her customer's bushy curls. She flew down the road to meet him. None of the women knew quite what to do. So they giggled and did nothing. Al-Noor, at the head of the band of horsemen, was in a similar predicament. He scowled ferociously and glanced at Penrod. Penrod ignored both him and Amber and rode on expressionlessly. Al-Noor could think of no rules to cover this situation. Al-Zahra was still a child, not a woman. She was in sight of four other women, and six warriors. By no stretch of the imagination could she be in any danger of violation. In the event of any repercussions all the others present were in equal guilt. In the last resort, he could plead with the Khalif that Abadan Riji was the leader of the band and therefore responsible for any breach of etiquette or custom. He stared straight ahead and pretended that this was not happening.

'Penrod Ballantyne, this is the first opportunity I have had to speak to you since Khartoum.' Amber danced along beside Ata.

'And you know very well why.' Penrod spoke from the corner of his mouth. 'You must go back to the other women or we shall both be in serious trouble.'

263

'The women think you very dashing. They would never tell on us.' They were speaking English, and Penrod was sure that none of the aggagiers understood a word of it.

'Then take a message to your sister. Tell Rebecca that I will seize the first opportunity to arrange your escape, and bring both of you to safety.'

'We know that you will never let us down.'

His expression softened: she was so pretty and winsome. 'How are you, Amber? Are you bearing up?'

'I was very sick, but Rebecca and Nazeera saved me. I am well now.'

'I can see that. How is your sister?'

'She is also well.' Amber wished he would not keep harking back to Rebecca.

'I have a little gift for you,' said Penrod. Surreptitiously he slipped his hand into the saddlebag and found the amber necklace and earrings he had bought in the souk. He had wrapped them in a scrap of tanned sheepskin. He did not hand them to her directly but dropped them into the road, using his horse to conceal the move from the other aggagiers.

'Wait until we have gone before you pick it up,' he instructed her, 'and don't let the other women see you do it.' He pressed his heels into Ata's flanks and rode on. Amber watched him out of sight. The eyes of the other women also followed the band of horsemen. Amber scooped up the small roll of sheepskin. She could barely contain herself until she was alone in the *zenana* before she opened it. When she did she was almost overcome with delight.

'It is the most beautiful gift I have ever had.' She showed it to Rebecca and Nazeera. 'Do you think he really likes me, Becky?'

'It is a very handsome gift, darling,' Rebecca agreed, 'and I am sure he likes you very much.' She chose her words carefully. 'As does everyone who knows you.'

'I wish I could grow up soon. Then he would no longer treat me as a child,' said Amber wistfully.

Rebecca hugged her hard and felt her tears just below the surface. At times like this the peril of their situation and her sense of responsibility towards Amber was a burden almost too heavy for her to bear. If you do to this beautiful child what you did to me, Penrod Ballantyne, she vowed silently, I shall kill you with my bare hands and dance on your grave.

*   *   *

The principal object of the expedition into Abyssinian territory was to scout the three main mountain passes through which any army coming down from the highlands to the relief of Gondar would have to march.

The major combe in the mountain chain was the gorge of the Atbara river. Although the ground on the north bank of this river was precipitous and guarded by sheer rock cliffs, the slope of the south bank was less demanding. The ancient trade route ran along this side of the river. It took Penrod's party almost three weeks to reach the mouth of the pass. It rained heavily almost every night, and during the day the rivers and streams were swollen, the ground sodden and swampy. The going was so

265

heavy that on some days they covered less than ten miles. The aggagiers suffered cruelly from the wet and cold, to which they were unaccustomed.

Once they reached the Atbara gorge they climbed the slope of the south bank and about three hundred feet above the level of the river they came upon a saucer of ground that was hidden from any traveller on the caravan road below. A tiny stream ran down the middle of this hollow. Fresh green grass grew along both banks of the stream. They had driven the horses and mules hard, and Penrod decided to rest them for a few days while he observed any traffic coming down through the pass.

Each morning Penrod and al-Noor climbed to the lip of the saucer and took up a position in a patch of dense scrub just below the skyline. On the first two days they saw no sign of any human activity. The only living creatures were a pair of black eagles who had their eyrie in the cliffs above the north bank of the river: they were curious about the two men and came sailing along the hills on their immense wings to pass close over their heads as they crouched in the scrub. During the rest of the day they were often in sight, carrying hare and small antelope in their talons to their young in the shaggy pile of their nest.

Apart from these birds, the mountains seemed barren and deserted, the silence so complete that the mournful cry of the eagles carried clearly to them, although the birds were mere specks in the blue vault of cloud and sky.

Towards evening on the third day Penrod was roused from a drowsy reverie by another alien sound. At first he thought it might be a fall of rock rattling down the hillside. Then he was startled to hear the faint sound of human voices. He reached for his telescope and scanned the caravan road as far as the first bend of the pass. He saw nothing, but over the next half-hour the sounds grew louder, and when the echoes picked them up and accentuated them he was no longer in any doubt that a large caravan was threading its way down the pass. He lay on his belly and focused the spyglass on the head of the pass. Suddenly a pair of mules appeared in the field of his lens. They were heavily laden, followed immediately by another pair, then a third, until finally he counted a hundred and twenty beasts of burden and their drovers descending along the riverbank towards the vale of Gondar.

'A rich prize.' The sight had woken the bandit instincts in al-Noor and he watched the caravan hungrily. 'Who can say what is in those sacks? Silver Maria Theresas? Gold sovereigns? Enough for each of us to afford a hundred camels and a dozen beautiful slave girls. Paradise enow!'

'Paradise indeed! Who could ask for more?' Penrod agreed, grim-faced. 'If we lifted a finger to these good merchants, Abyssinia would be thrown into uproar. The plans of the exalted Khalif Atalan would be frustrated, and you and I would be sent to Paradise without our testicles with which to enjoy its pleasures. All things in their season, al-Noor.'

Slowly the leading mules of the column came closer until they were passing directly below Penrod's lookout. Three men were bringing up the rear. Penrod studied them. One was a young lad, the second was short and pudgy and the third was a powerfully built rascal, who looked as if he could

267

give good account of himself in a fracas. As they rode closer still, their features became more distinct, and Penrod almost let out an exclamation of surprise. He checked the outburst before it passed his lips. He did not want to arouse curiosity in al-Noor. He looked again more carefully and this time there could be no doubt. Ryder Courtney! His mind had difficulty accepting what his eyes had seen.

He moved the lens to the plump figure who rode at Ryder's left side. Bacheet, the fat rogue!

Then he turned his lens to the third person, a stripling dressed in baggy crimson trousers, a bright green coat with long skirts and a wide-brimmed yellow hat that seemed to have been designed in anger or in a state of mental confusion. The boy was laughing at something Courtney had said. But the laughter had a decidedly feminine lilt, and Penrod started, then controlled himself. Saffron! Saffron Benbrook! It seemed impossible. He had believed she must have perished with her father in Khartoum. The thought had been too painful to contemplate squarely, and he had pushed it to the back of his mind. Now here she was, as lively as a grasshopper and pretty as a butterfly despite her outlandish garb.

'They are on their way down to Gondar from either Aksum or Addis Ababa.' Al-Noor gave his opinion morosely, still mourning the fortune in camels and nubile wenches that he was being forced to pass by.

'They are going into camp,' said Penrod, as the head of the long column turned aside from the route and drew up on a clear, level stretch of ground above the bank of the Atbara. He looked at the height of the sun. There would be at least another two hours of light by which to travel, but Ryder was setting up his camp. While the herders cut fodder from the riverbank and carried it back in bundles to feed the mules, the servants erected a large dining and sitting tent and two smaller sleeping tents. They set out a pair of folding chairs in front of the fire. Ryder Courtney travelled in comfort and style.

Just as the sun set and the light began to fade Penrod saw Ryder, accompanied by Saffron, who had divested herself of the yellow hat, making his rounds of the camp and posting his sentries. Penrod made a careful note of the position of each guard. He had seen that they were armed with muzzle-loaders, and he could be certain these were filled with a mixture of pot-legs, rusted nails and assorted musket balls, all of which would be unpleasant missiles to receive in the belly at close range.

Penrod and al-Noor kept watch on Ryder's camp until darkness obscured it, except for the area in front of the main tent, which was dimly lit by an oil lamp. Penrod observed that Saffron retired early to her small tent. Ryder remained by the fire smoking a cheroot, for which Penrod envied him. At last he threw the stub in to the embers, and went to his own bed. Penrod waited until the lamplight had been extinguished in both tents, then led al-Noor back to their own camp beside the stream. They built no fire and ate cold *asida* and roast mutton. Firelight and the smell of smoke might warn unfriendly strangers of their presence.

Al-Noor had been quiet since they left the ridge, but now he spoke through a mouthful of cold food.

269

'I have devised a plan,' he announced. 'A plan that will make all of us rich.'

'Your wisdom will be received as cool rain by the desert. I wait in awe for you to impart it to me,' Penrod replied, with elaborate courtesy.

'There are twenty-two Abyssinians with the caravan. I have counted them, but they are fat traders and merchants. We are six, but we are the fiercest warriors in all of Sudan. We will go down in the night and kill them all. We will allow none to escape. Then we will bury their bodies and drive their mules back to Gallabat, and the Abyssinians will believe that they were devoured by the djinni of the mountains. We will hand all the treasure to our exalted lord Atalan, and from him we will win great preferment and riches.' Penrod was silent, until al-Noor insisted, 'What think you of my plan?'

'I can see no vice in it. I think that you are a great and noble *shufta*,' Penrod replied.

Al-Noor was surprised but pleased to be called a bandit. To an aggagier of the Beja, the epithet was a compliment. 'Then this very night in the time when all of them are asleep, we will go down to the camp and do this business. Are we agreed, Abadan Riji?'

'Once we have been given permission by the Emir Osman Atalan, may Allah love him for ever, we will murder these fat merchants and steal their wares.' Penrod nodded, and another long silence ensued.

Then al-Noor spoke again: 'The mighty Emir Atalan, may Allah look upon him with the utmost favour, is in Gallabat two hundred leagues to the north. How will it be possible to solicit his permission?'

'That is indeed a difficulty.' Penrod agreed. 'When you have found an answer to that question, we shall discuss your plan further. In the meantime, Mooman Digna will take the first watch. I shall take the midnight shift. You, Noor, will take the dawn watch. Perhaps then you will have time to consider a solution to our dilemma.' Al-Noor moved away in dignified silence, rolled himself in his sheepskin and, within a short while, emitted his first snore.

Penrod slept fitfully and was fully awake at Mooman Digna's first touch on his shoulder, and his whisper, 'It is time.'

Penrod allowed almost an hour for the aggagiers to settle again. He knew from experience that once they were cocooned in their sheepskins, they could not be easily roused to face the bitter mountain cold. He rose from his seat on the rock that overlooked the camp and, barefooted, moved silently up over the lip of the ridge. He approached Ryder's camp with great caution. By this time there was a slice of crescent moon above the horizon, and the stars were bright enough for him to pick out the sentries. He avoided them without difficulty. As al-Noor had pointed out, they were not warriors. He crept up behind the rear wall of Ryder's tent, and squatted beside it. He could hear Ryder breathing heavily on the other side of the canvas, only inches from his ear. He scratched on the canvas with his fingernails, and the sound of breathing was cut off immediately.

'Ryder,' Penrod whispered, 'Ryder Courtney!'

He heard him stir, and ask in a sleepy whisper, 'Who is that?'

'Ballantyne—Penrod Ballantyne.'

271

'Good God, man! What on earth are you doing here?' A wax vesta flared, then lamplight glowed and cast a shadow on the canvas. 'Come inside!' Ryder urged him.

When Penrod stooped through the doorway, he was astounded. 'Is it really you, Ballantyne? You look like a wild tribesman. How did you get here?'

'I don't have long to talk to you. I am a prisoner of the Dervish and under restraint. I would appreciate it if you waste no more time on fatuous questions.'

'I stand corrected.' Ryder's friendly smile faded. 'I shall listen to what you have to tell me.'

'I was captured after the fall of Khartoum. I had returned there in an attempt to discover the fate of those who had been unable to escape, especially David Benbrook and his family.'

'I can reassure you that Saffron is with me. We managed to get out of Khartoum on my steamer at the last minute. I have been trying to contact her family in England, to send her back to them, but these things take a great deal of time.'

'I know she is with you. I have been keeping watch on your camp. I saw her this evening.'

'I have been waiting to receive a message from you,' Ryder said. 'Bacheet met your man, Yakub, in Omdurman. He told Yakub that Ras Hailu could carry messages between us.'

'I have not seen Yakub since the day I was captured in Omdurman. He did not tell me anything about a meeting with Bacheet, or about this man Ras Hailu,' Penrod said grimly, 'Yakub has disappeared. I think that he and his uncle, a rogue named Wad Hagma, betrayed me to the Dervish. I was able to deal with his uncle, and

272

Yakub is next on my list of unfinished business.'

'You cannot trust any of these people,' Ryder agreed, 'no matter how long you have known them and how well you have treated them.'

'So you know, then, that David Benbrook was killed in the sack of Khartoum, and that Rebecca and Amber were captured by the Dervish and handed over to the Mahdi?'

'Yes. Bacheet heard all this terrible news from Nazeera when he was looking for you in Omdurman. It is hard to imagine those two lovely young Englishwomen in the clutches of that dissipated maniac. I hope and pray that Amber is young enough to have been spared the worst, but Rebecca! The good Lord alone knows what she has suffered.'

'The Mahdi is dead. He died of cholera or some other disease. Nobody can be certain what carried him off.'

'I had not heard. I don't suppose that will change anything. But what has become of Rebecca now?' Ryder's concern was apparent. He made little effort to hide his feelings for Rebecca.

So Courtney has also had the benefit of Rebecca Benbrook's liberal nature, Penrod thought cynically. She has had so much experience now that when she returns to London she can turn professional and ply her trade in Charing Cross Road. Although his pride was stung, it did not detract from the responsibility he felt for her safety, or for that of her little sister. Aloud he said, 'When the Mahdi died the two sisters, Rebecca and Amber, were taken into the harem of the new Khalif Osman Atalan.' As he said it, there was a gasp behind him, and he turned quickly with his

273

hand on the hilt of his dagger.

Saffron stood in the tent doorway. She was dressed in a man's shirt, which was many times too large for her and hung well below her knees. She must been awakened by their voices, and had come from her own tent just in time to overhear his last words. The thin cloth of the shirt was artlessly revealing, so that Penrod could not help but notice her figure under it. She had changed a great deal from when he had last seen her. Her hips and bosom were swelling and her face had lost its childish roundness. She was already too mature to be sharing a camp in the remote African wilderness with a man.

'My sisters!' Her eyes were huge with sleep and shock. 'First my father, and now my sisters. Ryder, you never told me that they were in the harem. You said they were safe. Is there never to be an end to this nightmare?'

'But, Saffron, they are safe. They have not been harmed.'

'How do you know that?' she demanded. 'How can they be safe in the den of the pagan and the barbarian?'

'I spoke to Amber not two weeks ago,' Penrod intervened, to comfort her. 'She and Rebecca are brave and are making the best of the hard blows that Fate has dealt them. It may seem impossible, but they are being treated . . . if not kindly then gently enough. The Dervish see them as valuable chattels, and they will want to preserve their worth.'

'But for how long? We have to do something. Especially for Amber. She is so sweet and sensitive. She is not strong like Rebecca and me. We have to

274

rescue her.'

'That is why I am here,' Penrod told her. 'It is the most incredible good fortune that I stumbled across your path. It must be one chance in a million. But now that we have met we can plan the rescue of your sisters.'

'Is that possible? Abyssinia, where we are now, is primitive and backward, but at least the people are Christians. The Sudan is hell on earth, ruled by demons. No white man or woman can remain there long with any chance of survival.'

'I will be going back,' said Penrod. 'I can stay with you only a few minutes more, and then I am going to do what I can for your sisters. But if I am to get them out of the Sudan, I will need all your help.' Penrod turned back to Ryder. 'Can I count on you?'

'I feel insulted that you need to ask,' said Ryder, stiffly.

It was amazing how quickly the two of them could give and take offence, Saffron thought angrily. In these dreadful circumstances why did they have to bicker and posture? Why were men always so pigheaded and arrogant? 'Captain Ballantyne, we will help you,' she promised, 'in every way within our power.'

Penrod noticed that she used the plural 'we' with the proprietary air of a wife. Penrod wondered if she had good reason to do so. The idea was repugnant: despite appearances Saffron was still a child. And a man like Ryder Courtney would never molest her.

'I can waste no more time,' he said. 'I must return to my keepers, if my delicate position of trust with the Dervish is not to be compromised.

275

We have much to plan. First, we must be able to contact each other and exchange news and plans. Tell me about Ras Hailu.'

'He was my friend and trading partner,' Ryder explained. 'He used to travel to Omdurman in his dhow two or three times a year to trade with the Dervish. Tragically he fell foul of the Mahdi, who accused him of spying for Emperor John. He was executed in Omdurman. I have no other agents in the Sudan.'

'Well, we shall have to set up some new line of communication. Do not to try to contact me directly, for I am carefully watched at all times. You must try to get any message to Nazeera. She is allowed much freedom of movement. I shall try to arrange for a messenger of my own. There are other European captives in Omdurman. One of them is Rudolf Slatin, who was the Egyptian governor of Dongola. He is a resourceful fellow, and I suspect that he has ways of communicating with the outside world. If I am successful in finding a messenger, where will he be able to contact you?'

Quickly Ryder gave Penrod a list of his trading posts closest to the Sudanese border, and the names of his trusted agents there. 'Any message they receive will be passed on to me but, as you can see, I am forced to travel great distances in pursuit of my business affairs. It may take an inordinate length of time to reach me.'

'Nothing happens swiftly in Africa,' Penrod agreed. 'What I will ask from you, when the time comes, is that you make the travel arrangements to get us to the Abyssinian border as swiftly as possible. As soon as we leave Omdurman the entire Dervish army will be alerted, and will pursue us relentlessly.'

'The safety of Saffron's sisters takes priority over everything else,' Ryder assured him.

'Where is the *Intrepid Ibis*?' Penrod asked. 'A steamer would be the fastest and surest method of getting us to the border. I should not like to attempt a flight on camels across the desert. The distances are enormous and the going is killing hard on the women.'

'Unfortunately I was obliged to sell the little steamer. Now that the upper reaches of both Niles have been closed to me by the Dervish, I have been forced to restrict my business activities to Abyssinia and Equatoria. The *Ibis* was of no further use to me.'

'That is a great pity, but I shall devise another route.' Penrod stood up. 'I can spend no more time with you. Before I go, there is one other important matter. The reason I am here is that Abdullahi is planning to attack Abyssinia, and seize all the disputed territories from Gondar to Mount Horea. He is going through all the diplomatic motions of lulling Emperor John with overtures of friendship and peace. But he will attack, probably after the big rains of next year. Osman Atalan will command the Dervish army of about thirty thousand. His first and main objective will be the passes here at Atbara gorge and Minkti. His purpose will be to prevent the Emperor coming down from the plateau with his main forces to intervene. I have been sent here by Atalan, may he rot in hell, to scout the terrain over which he will attack.'

'My God!' Ryder looked aghast. 'The Emperor has no inkling of this.'

'Do you have access to him?' Penrod demanded.

277

'I do, yes. I know him well. I shall be seeing him immediately on my return to Entoto in three or four months' time.'

'Then give him this warning.'

'I will—depend on it. He will be grateful. I am sure he will offer his assistance in the rescue of Rebecca and Amber,' Ryder assured him. 'But tell me, Ballantyne, why do you offer him this warning? What is it to you if the Dervish invade this country?'

'Need you ask? Your enemy is my enemy. The evil that is abroad can only be appreciated by those who have witnessed the sack of a city by the Dervish. You were at Khartoum?' Ryder nodded. 'Emperor John is a Christian monarch. Abdullahi and his bloodthirsty maniacs must be stopped. Perhaps he will be able to put an end to these horrors.' Penrod turned to Saffron. 'What message can I take back to Omdurman for your sisters?' he asked.

Her eyes glistened with tears in the lamplight as she struggled with her reply. 'Tell them that I love them both with all my heart, and always shall. Tell them to be brave. We will help them. We shall all be together again soon. But whatever happens I still love them.'

'I will give them that message,' Penrod promised. 'I am certain it will be of great comfort to them.' He turned back to Ryder, and held out his hand. 'I think we would be wise to forget our personal differences and work together towards our common goal.'

'I agree with all my heart,' said Ryder, and shook the proffered hand.

Penrod stooped over the lamp and blew out the

flame, then disappeared out into the night.

*　　　*　　　*

It was almost Christmas before Ryder Courtney returned to Entoto, the capital of Abyssinia and the city where he had his main trading compound.

'This must be the bleakest place in the world,' said Saffron, as they rode in through the city gates at the head of the caravan of mules, 'even worse than Khartoum. Why can't we live in Gondar, Ryder?'

'Because, Miss Saffron Benbrook, in the near future you will be living in the village of Bishop's Sutton in Hampshire with your uncle Thomas and aunt Jane.'

'You are being tiresome again, Ryder,' she warned him. 'I don't want to live in England. I want to stay here with you.'

'I am flattered.' He touched the brim of his hat. 'But, most unfortunately for all concerned, you cannot spend the rest of your life traipsing through the African bush like a gypsy. You have to go back to civilization and learn to be a lady. Besides, people are beginning to talk. You are a child no longer—indeed, you are a big girl now.'

Ah, so you have noticed! Saffron thought complacently. I was beginning to think you, Ryder Courtney, were blind. Then, aloud, she reiterated the promise that was usually enough to satisfy him: 'I will go back to England without any fuss when Rebecca and Amber have been rescued,' she spoke with a straight face and total insincerity, 'and when my uncle Thomas promises to take care of us. He has not replied to your letters yet, and it's over a

279

year since you first wrote,' she reminded him smugly. 'Now, let us speak of more interesting matters. How long will we stay in Entoto, and where will we travel to next?'

'I have business here that will take some time.'

'It's so cold and windy in the mountains after the warmth of the lowlands, and there is no firewood for miles. All the trees have been cut down.'

'You must have been talking to Empress Miriam. She shares your opinion of Entoto. That's why the Emperor is moving the capital to the hot springs at Addis Ababa. She is a nag, just like somebody else I know.'

'I am not a nag, but sometimes I know best,' said Saffron sweetly. 'Even though you treat me like a baby.'

Despite her protests, the Courtney compound at Entoto was really very comfortable and welcoming, and she had managed, with the help of Bacheet, to make it even more so. She had even prevailed on Ryder to convert one of the old disused storerooms into a bedroom and studio for her exclusive use. It had not been easy. Ryder was reluctant to do anything that might give her reason to believe that her stay with him was permanent.

In order to procure a studio Saffron had enlisted the help of Lady Alice Packer, wife of the British ambassador to the court of the Emperor, who had taken her under her wing. Of course, her husband had known David Benbrook when they had both worked under Sir Evelyn Baring in the diplomatic agency in Cairo so she felt some responsibility for his orphaned daughter.

Alice was an amateur artist, and when she recognized Saffron's natural talent in the same

280

field she had assumed the role of teacher. She provided Saffron with paints, brushes and art paper brought in from Cairo in the diplomatic pouch, and taught her how to make her own canvas stretchers and charcoal sticks.

Within the time that they had known each other Saffron had almost outstripped her teacher. Her portfolio contained at least fifty lovingly wrought portraits of Ryder Courtney, most of which had been drawn without the subject's knowledge, and she had completed numerous African landscapes and animal sketches, which astonished both Alice and Ryder with their maturity and virtuosity. Recently she had commenced a series of drawings and paintings from her memories of Khartoum and the horrors of the siege. They were beautiful but harrowing. Ryder realized that they were a form of catharsis for her, so he encouraged her to continue with them.

Two days after their return to Entoto, Saffron made her way up to the embassy to take tea with Alice. She showed her tutor all the Khartoum sketches, which they discussed at some length. Alice wept as she looked at them. 'These are magnificent, my dear. I stand in awe of your skill.'

Saffron stopped repacking them and turned to Alice, her eyes full of tears.

'What is it, Saffron?' Alice asked kindly. Although she had been sworn to secrecy by Ryder, Saffron blurted out a full account of the nocturnal meeting with Penrod Ballantyne in the Atbara gorge. Alice promised her husband would inform Sir Evelyn Baring at once of the predicament of her sisters and also of Captain Ballantyne. Saffron was much cheered by this. Then, as she was leaving, she asked innocently, 'If any mail for Mr Courtney has arrived, I would be pleased to deliver it to him, and perhaps save one of your staff the trouble.'

Alice sent down to the chancery and a secretary returned with a stack of envelopes addressed to 'Ryder Courtney Esq,' care of the British ambassador at Entoto, Abyssinia.

Saffron examined them as she walked through the town to the market. She recognized the handwriting on the first envelope. It was from Ryder's nephew, Sean Courtney, at the newly discovered goldfields in the Transvaal Republic of South Africa. Saffron knew that Sean was importuning his uncle to invest several thousand pounds in a new mine. The next was a bill for goods supplied by the Army and Navy stores in London. The third envelope bore the seal of 'The Office of the Government Assayer of the Cape of Good Hope', and the fourth was the one that Saffron had been dreading. On the reverse was the inscription:

> Sender:
> The Reverend Thomas Benbrook
> The Vicarage
> Bishop's Sutton
> Hampshire. England

She placed the other letters in her pocket, but this one she hid down the front of her bodice. Saffron spent less time than usual in the market. She bought a large bunch of wild mountain gladioli from her favourite flower-seller. Then she came across a handsome silver hip-flask, which she decided might do for Ryder's birthday. The price was beyond her meagre resources and she was in too much of a hurry to bargain with the merchant, so she promised to return the following day.

She hurried back to the compound and placed the flowers in the tub beside the kitchen door. Then she retired to the earth closet, which was discreetly tucked away in a corner behind the living quarters. She bolted the door, perched on the high seat and carefully split the seal on the fourth envelope. The single sheet was covered with writing on both sides, and dated seven months earlier. She read it avidly;

Dear Mr Courtney,

My wife and I were saddened to receive your letter and to hear of the tragic murder of my brother David in Khartoum, and of the plight of his daughters. I understand your predicament and agree that it is beyond common decency for poor little Saffron to continue in your care, as you are a bachelor and there is no woman with you to see to her upbringing.

I have addressed enquiries to Sebastian Hardy Esquire, my dear brother's solicitor, as you suggested I might. It pains me to have to inform you that the value of my brother's few remaining assets are far exceeded by his substantial debts. Sarah, his deceased wife, was a lady of profligate disposition. None of my brother's daughters will be due any inheritance from his estate.

My wife and I have discussed the possibility of taking Saffron into our home. However, we have nine children of our own to support on my stipend as a country vicar. Alas, we would not be able to feed and clothe the poor orphan. Fortunately I have been able to make adequate arrangements for her to be taken into a suitable institution where she will receive strict Christian instruction and an education that will be adequate for her later entry into respectable employment as governess to a child of the nobility.

If, in your Christian charity, you would be kind enough to provide her with passage to England and the train fare from the port of her arrival to the Bishop's Sutton railway station, I would meet the poor child there and convey her to the institution. Unfortunately I am not able to contribute to her subsequent upkeep and maintenance.

I wait to hear from you.
Your brother in Christ,
Thomas Benbrook

Slowly, and with relish, Saffron tore the letter into shreds, and dropped each scrap separately into the malodorous pit beneath her. Then she pulled up her skirts and urinated vigorously on the remains of the offending document.

'A fitting end for such a nasty piece of rubbish,' she said to herself. 'So much for an institution, Christian instruction and employment as a governess. I would prefer to walk back to Khartoum on my own bare feet.' She stood up and smoothed down her skirts. 'Now I must hurry to see that Ryder's dinner is ready, and to prepare his whisky peg for him.'

For Saffron, dinner-time was the highlight of her busy day. After she had discussed the roasting of the chicken and yams with the cook, she made certain there was hot water, soap and a clean towel on the washstand in Ryder's bedroom, and a freshly ironed shirt folded on the bed. Next she laid the table, and arranged the flowers and candles. She would not trust one of the servants, even Bacheet, with such an important task. Then she unlocked the strongroom with the key that Ryder had entrusted to her and brought out the bottle of whisky, the crystal glass and the cedarwood cigar box. She set them on the table at the end of the veranda from where there would be a fine view of the sunset over the mountains.

She hurried to her own room and changed the clothes she had worn all day for a dress of her own design and creation. With the help of two Amharic women from the town, who were expert seamstresses, she had assembled her own abundant and unusual wardrobe. Lady Alice Packer and even Empress Miriam had complimented her on her style.

While she was still combing her hair she heard the clatter of hoofs in the courtyard as Ryder returned from the palace, where he had been in day-long discussions with the Emperor and various royal functionaries. She was waiting for him on the veranda when he emerged from his private quarters in the fresh shirt, his face glowing from the hot water and his wet hair combed back neatly. He is the most handsome man in the world, but his hair needs cutting again. I shall see to it tomorrow, she thought, as she held the whisky bottle over the glass. 'Say when,' she invited.

'"When" is a four-letter word that should be uttered only with great deliberation after long reflection,' he replied. It was their private joke, and she poured him a liberal quantity. He tasted it and sighed. 'Too good for human consumption! Such nectar should be drunk only by angels in their flight!' That completed the ritual. He sank down comfortably on to the leather cushions of his favourite chair. She sat opposite him and they watched the sun set in crimson splendour over the mountains.

'Now tell me what you did today,' Ryder said.

'You first,' she replied.

'I spent the morning in council with the Emperor and two of the generals of his army. I told them what Penrod Ballantyne had reported about the intentions of the Dervish to attack his country. Emperor John was grateful for this warning, and I think he has taken it seriously. I did not tell him of our plans to rescue your sisters. I thought it premature to do so. However, I believe that he will be helpful when we are in a position to act.'

Saffron sighed. 'I do wish Captain Ballantyne would be in touch. It seems ages since he was.'

'He and your sisters have probably been travelling in the entourage of Osman Atalan. Penrod is so closely guarded that he might not have been able to find a reliable messenger. We must be patient.'

'So easy to say, so hard to do,' she said.

To distract her he went on with a recital of his day. 'After I left the Emperor, I spent the rest of the day with his treasurer. He finally agreed to renew my licence to trade throughout the country for another year. The bribe he demanded was extortionate, but in all other respects quite reasonable.' He made her laugh—he always made

286

her laugh. 'By the way, I forgot to mention that we are invited to the royal audience next Friday. Emperor John is to award me the Star of the Order of Solomon and Judea, in recognition of my services to the state. I think that the truth of the matter is that Empress Miriam wants to admire your latest high-fashion creation and persuaded her husband to invite us. Either that or she wants you to paint another portrait of her.'

'How exciting. Will the Star of Solomon be enormous and covered with lots of diamonds?'

'I am sure it will be gigantic, and perhaps not diamonds, but at least good-quality cut glass,' he said, and reached across the table to the small stack of mail that Saffron had brought down from the embassy. First he opened the bill from the Army and Navy Stores. 'Good!' he exclaimed with pleasure. 'They have my pair of number-ten rifles ready to ship out to me. I shall arrange payment tomorrow. They should arrive before our next journey to Equatoria where they will be most useful.' He set aside the bill and opened the letter from his nephew. 'Sean is insistent that this new gold reef they have opened will persist to great depth. I do not have the same hopes for it. I believe that the reef will pinch out before long and leave him much poorer in pocket, if richer in experience. I am afraid I shall have to disabuse him of his hopes that I might provide any capital for his venture.' He picked up the letter with the Cape Colony postage stamp, and examined it. 'I have been waiting for this!'

He opened the envelope, took out the assay report, scanned it anxiously, then smiled comfortably. 'Excellent! Oh, so very good indeed.'

'Can you tell me?' Saffron asked.

'Certainly! Before we left for Gondar I sent a bag of rock samples to the assay office of the Cape Colony. The year before I was caught up in the siege of Khartoum I gathered them from the mountains a hundred miles east of Aksum while I was hunting mountain nyala. This is the report on those samples. Over thirty per cent copper, and just on twelve per cent silver. Even taking into account how remote the area is, and the difficulty of reaching it, it should be a highly profitable deposit. The only trouble is that I will have to go back to the royal treasurer to ask for a mining licence. He had my skin today, so tomorrow he will want my scalp and my teeth.'

'*Sans* teeth and *sans* hair, you might set a new fashion,' Saffron suggested, and he laughed.

As usual they sat late after dinner, talking endlessly. When Ryder climbed into his own bed he was still chuckling at her saucy Parthian shot. He blew out the lamp, and as he composed himself for sleep he realized he had not once thought of Rebecca that day.

*   *   *

When they entered the audience hall at the palace, Alice Packer summoned Saffron with a peremptory wave of her fan.

'Will you forgive me, please, Ryder?'

'Off you go and do your duty.' Ryder watched her cross the room, as did almost everybody else. It was not only the yellow dress that was so striking. Youth has beauty inherent in its very nature. He realized he was staring and looked away quickly, hoping no one had noticed.

The rest of the company was made up of a number of Abyssinian princes and princesses, for the Emperor and the other members of the house of Memelik were prolific breeders. There were also generals and bishops, prosperous merchants and landowners, the entire corps of foreign diplomats, with a few foreign travellers and adventurers. The uniforms and costumes were so exotic and colourful that Saffron's dress seemed restrained and understated by comparison.

Suddenly Ryder became aware that somebody in the throng was watching him. He looked about quickly, then started with surprise. The person who had purchased the *Intrepid Ibis* from him was standing at the far corner of the room, but even at that range her Egyptian eyes above the veil had a hypnotic quality that could not be ignored. As soon as she had his attention she resumed her conversation with the elderly general beside her who was resplendent in an array of medals, jewelled orders and a cloak of leopardskins.

'Peace and the blessing of Allah be upon you, Sitt Bakhita al-Masur,' Ryder greeted her in Arabic, as he came to her side.

'And upon you in equal measure, Effendi.' She made a graceful gesture in reply, touching her lips, then her heart with her fingertips.

'You are a long way from your home,' he remarked. Her eyes slanted upwards at the outer corners, and her dark gaze was direct, unusual in an Egyptian lady even of the highest rank, yet also mysterious. Some men would find her irresistible, but she was not to Ryder's taste.

'I came by the river. In my fine new steamer it

was not such a long journey from the first cataract.' Her voice was soft and musical.

'You encountered no let or hindrance along the way, I hope? These are troubled times and the *Ibis* is well known.'

'She is the *Ibis* no longer but the *Durkhan Sama*, the Wisdom of the Skies. Her appearance is much altered. No one would recognize her for what she once was. My boat-builders at Aswan have lavished much attention on her. I paid my dues to the men of God in Omdurman when I passed that pestilential if holy city.'

'Where is she moored now?' Ryder demanded eagerly.

Bakhita looked at him quizzically. 'She is at Roseires.' That was the small port at the uppermost limit of navigation on the Blue Nile. It was still within the Sudan, but less than fifty miles from the Abyssinian border.

Ryder was pleased. 'Is Jock McCrump still the engineer?' he asked.

Bakhita smiled. 'He is captain also. I think it would be difficult to dislodge him from his berth.'

Ryder was even better pleased. Jock would be a useful man to have aboard if they were to use the steamer in any rescue attempt. 'You seem interested in your old steamer, Effendi. Do I imagine it, or is it indeed so?'

Immediately Ryder was wary. He knew little about this woman, except that she was wealthy and had influence in high places in many countries. He had heard it said that even though she was a Muslim she was favourably inclined towards British interests in the Orient, and opposed to those of France and Germany. It was even rumoured that she was an agent of Sir Evelyn Baring in Cairo. If this was true she would not support the Dervish *jihad* in Omdurman, but it was best not to trust her.

'Indeed, Sitt Bakhita, I did have some idea of chartering the steamer from you for a short period but I am not sure that you would be agreeable to the proposition,' he said.

She dropped her voice when she spoke next: 'General Ras Mengetti speaks only Amharic. Nevertheless we should continue this conversation in private. I know the whereabouts of your compound. May I call upon you there? Say, tomorrow an hour before noon?'

'I will be at your disposal.'

'I will have matters of mutual interest to relate to you,' she promised. Ryder bowed and moved away.

Saffron was still with Alice, but the moment Ryder was free she came across to join him. 'Who was the fat Arab lady?' she asked tartly. 'She was making huge cow eyes at you.'

'She may be useful to us in uniting us with friends and family.'

Saffron considered this, then nodded. 'In that case I forgive her.'

Ryder was uncertain as to how Bakhita had transgressed, but before he made the mistake of pursuing the subject, a flourish of trumpets announced the entrance of the Emperor and his wife.

*   *   *

Much later that evening when they returned to the compound, Saffron brought Ryder his slippers and poured him a nightcap. Then she unpinned the Star of Solomon from his lapel and examined it in the lamplight. 'I am certain they are real diamonds,' she said.

'If you are correct then we are probably millionaires.' He chuckled, and noted that he had picked up the habit from her of using the plural pronoun. It seemed somehow to constitute a formal link between them. He wondered if that was wise, and concluded that perhaps it was not. In future I shall be more circumspect, he promised himself.

* * *

The following day Bakhita arrived at the compound in a closed coach drawn by four mules. Ryder recognized the coach and driver and knew that they had probably been put at her disposal by the Emperor. This was further proof, if any were needed, of Bakhita al-Masur's influence and importance. Behind the coach half a dozen armed bodyguards followed closely. They waited in the courtyard while Ryder ushered Bakhita into the main room, where Saffron served coffee and little honey cakes.

When she stood up and excused herself, Bakhita held up her hand. 'Please do not go, Sitt Benbrook. What I have to say concerns you above all others.' Saffron sank back on the sofa, and Bakhita went on, 'I have come to Entoto for the main purpose of meeting you and Mr Courtney. The three of us have affairs of great concern that are all linked in Omdurman. I have a friend to whom I owe complete loyalty, and close members of your family are held in captivity by the Dervish. I am certain that you are as anxious to procure their release as I am. To this end I wanted to pledge to you all the assistance and support of which I am capable.' Ryder and Saffron stared at her in silent astonishment. 'Yes, I know that your elder sister and your twin are in the harem of the Emir Osman Atalan. My friend is the slave of the same man.'

'May we know the name of your friend?' Ryder asked cautiously.

Bakhita did not answer at once then said, 'My English is not good, but I think we must use your language for very few people in Abyssinia understand it.'

'Your English is very good, Sitt Bakhita,' said Saffron. Her latent antagonism towards the other woman had undergone a sea-change.

'You are kind, but it is not so.' She smiled at Saffron, then turned back to Ryder. 'I could refuse to answer your question, but I want us to be honest with each other. I am sure that my friend is well known to both of you. He is Captain Penrod Ballantyne of the 10th Hussars.'

'He is a valiant officer and a fine gentleman,' Saffron exclaimed. 'We last met him at the Atbara gorge not more than five months ago.'

'Oh, please tell me how he was!' Bakhita exclaimed.

'He was well, although indistinguishable in dress and deportment from his captors,' said Saffron.

'I knew he had been captured by the Dervish, but I heard he had been terribly abused and tortured. Your assurances are of much comfort to me.'

While they discussed Penrod, Ryder was

293

thinking swiftly. From Bacheet he had heard a rumour, which Nazeera had told him, that Penrod had an intimate Egyptian friend. From the depth of her concern for him there was little doubt that Bakhita must be the lady in question. Ryder was shocked. Penrod was a highly decorated officer in a first-rate regiment. A liaison of this nature, if it came to light, might easily cost him his commission and his reputation.

'From all that you have told us, Sitt Bakhita, it is clear that we must pool all our intelligence and resources,' he said. 'Our first concern, which has been troubling me deeply, is how to get messages to and from our friends in Omdurman.'

'I believe I am able to offer a means of communication.' Bakhita stood up and went to the door that led into the courtyard. She clapped her hands, and one of her bodyguard appeared before her. 'I think you know this man,' said Bakhita, as he removed his headcloth and made a deep *salaam* towards Ryder.

'May God always protect you, Effendi.'

'Yakub!' Ryder was truly astonished. 'I heard bad things about you. I heard that you had betrayed your master, Abadan Riji.'

'Effendi, sooner would I betray my father and mother, and may Allah hear my words and strike me down into hell if I lie,' said Yakub. 'The only remaining purpose in my life is to bring my master safely out of the clutches of the Dervish into which my uncle so treacherously led him. I will do anything . . .' Yakub hesitated, then qualified his statement: 'I will do anything except have any truck with the despicable Bacheet to save my master from the Dervish. If there is no other way, I may

294

even abide with, for some brief time, the company of the nefarious Bacheet. However, I shall probably kill him afterwards.'

'On the matter of killing,' Ryder told him grimly, 'Abadan Riji believes that you were as much the traitor as your uncle. He slew your uncle, and he means to do the same to you.'

'Then I must go to him and place my life and loyalty in his hands.'

'While you are about it,' said Ryder, drily, 'you may as well take your master a message and return to us with his reply.'

It took five more days for Ryder and Bakhita to evolve an escape plan for the prisoners in Omdurman that had a reasonable chance of success.

On the following day Yakub left alone for the Sudan.

*   *   *

Osman Atalan was well pleased with the report that Penrod brought him back from the passes of the Abyssinian highlands. He listened with great attention to his suggestions concerning the conduct of the campaign against Emperor John, and they discussed all these in exhaustive detail during the course of the long return journey to Omdurman.

Once they reached that city, Penrod found that the conditions of his imprisonment were much relaxed. He had achieved a position of conditional trust, which had been his objective from the first day of his capture. It was what he had set out to achieve by indulging Osman Atalan, and pretending to submit to his will. However, he was still accompanied at all times by selected aggagiers of Osman's personal bodyguard. During the months after their return to Omdurman Osman spent much time with the Khalifat Abdullahi. Al-Noor told Penrod that he was trying to persuade Abdullahi to allow him to return to his tribal domain in the desert. However, Abdullahi was too foxy and devious to allow a man of such power and influence as Osman Atalan to escape his direct supervision and control. Osman was allowed out of Omdurman only for brief punitive raids and reprisals on those persons and tribes who had incurred Abdullahi's displeasure, or for hunting and hawking excursions into the desert.

When he returned to the city, Osman found himself with much time on his hands. One day he sent for Penrod. 'I have watched the way you wield a blade. It is contrary to usage and custom, and lacks even the semblance of grace.'

Penrod lowered his gaze to hide his anger at the insult, and with an effort refrained from reminding him of their first meeting at El Obeid in which the mighty Khalif Atalan had countered Penrod's feint by raising his targe and blocking his own view of the thrust that followed, a riposte that passed close to his heart.

'However,' said Osman, 'it holds some interest.'

Penrod looked up at him and saw the glimmer of mockery in his eyes. 'Exalted Khalif, from such a master swordsman as you are, this is praise that warms my soul,' he mocked in return.

'It will amuse me to practise at arms against you, and to demonstrate the true and noble usage of the long blade,' said Osman. 'We will begin tomorrow after the morning prayers.'

The next morning as they faced each other with naked blades, Osman set out the rules of engagement, 'I shall try to kill you. You will try to kill me. If I succeed I will hold your memory in contempt. If you succeed, my aggagiers,' he indicated the fifteen men that formed a circle around him, 'will immediately kill you, but you will be buried with much honour. I shall commission a special prayer to be recited in the mosque in your memory. Am I not a benevolent master?'

'The mighty Atalan is fair and just,' Penrod agreed, and they went to it. Twenty minutes later, when Osman was slow on the recovery, Penrod nicked his forearm in warning.

Osman's gaze was murderous. 'Enough for now. We shall fight again in two days' time.'

After that they fought for an hour every second day, and Osman learnt to recover swiftly and riposte like a hussar. Gradually Penrod found himself more seriously taxed, and was forced to exert all his own skill to restrain his opponent. At the end of Ramadan Osman told him, 'I have a gift for you.'

Her name was Lalla. She was a frightened and abused little thing, a child of war, pestilence and famine. She did not remember her father or mother, and in all her short life nobody had ever shown her kindness.

Penrod was kind to her. He paid one of al-Noor's concubines to wash her as though she were a stray puppy, and to dress her tangled hair. He provided her with fresh clothing to replace her rags. He allowed her to cook his meals, launder his clothes, and sweep the floor of the small cell off the courtyard of the aggagiers, which was his lodging.

He let her sleep outside his door. He treated her as though she was human, not an animal.

For the first time in her life Lalla had sufficient food. Hunger had been part of her life from as far back as she could remember. She did not grow fat, but her bones were gradually covered with a little flesh. Sometimes he heard her crooning softly over the fire as she cooked his meal. Whenever he returned to the courtyard of the aggagiers she smiled. Once when Osman had succeeded in touching his right shoulder with the long blade, Lalla dressed the wound under his instruction. It was a flesh wound and healed swiftly. Penrod told her she was an angel of mercy, and he bought her a cheap silver bracelet in the souk as a reward. She crept away with it to a corner of the yard and wept with happiness. It was the first gift she had ever received.

That night she crept shyly on to Penrod's *angareb*, and he did not have the heart to send her away. When she whimpered with her nightmares, he stroked her head. She woke and cuddled closer to him. When he made love to her it was without lust or passion, but with pity. The following evening while she was cooking his dinner he spoke to her quietly: 'If I asked you to do something dangerous and difficult for me, would you do it, Lalla?'

'My lord, I would do whatever you ask.'

'If I asked you to put your hand in the fire and bring out a burning brand for me, would you do it?' Without hesitation she reached towards the flames and he had to seize her wrist to prevent her thrusting her hand into them. 'No, not that! I want you to carry a message for me. Do you know the woman Nazeera, whom they call Ammi? She works in the harem as a servant of the white concubines.'

'I know her, my lord.'

'Tell her that Filfil is safe with al-Sakhawi in Abyssinia.' Filfil, or Pepper, was Saffron's Arabic name.

Lalla waited her chance to accost Nazeera discreetly at the well, which was a gathering place for all the women, and delivered the message faithfully. Nazeera hurried back to give the news to Rebecca and Amber.

Within days Nazeera had met Lalla again at the well. She had a message for her to take to Penrod. 'Yakub is here in Omdurman,' Lalla reported faithfully.

Penrod was amazed. 'It cannot be the Yakub I know. That rascal disappeared a long time ago.'

'He wants me to meet him,' Lalla said. 'What will you have me do?'

'Where will you meet?'

'I will be with Nazeera in the souk, at the camel market.'

'Will it be safe for you?' Penrod asked.

Lalla shrugged. 'That is of no account. If you ask it, I will do it.'

When she returned he asked, 'How was this Yakub?'

'He has two eyes, but they do not follow each other. One looks east and the other north.'

'That is the Yakub I know.' How could he ever have doubted him, Penrod asked himself.

'He said to tell you that the peerless Yakub is still your servant. He has languished a year and three months in an Egyptian prison, unjustly accused of trading in slaves. Only when he was released was he able to go to the lady of Aswan.

Now she has sent him back to you with tidings that are much to your benefit.'

Penrod knew instantly who was the lady of Aswan, and his heart leapt. He had not thought of Bakhita recently, but she was still there, as constant as she had ever been. With her and Yakub he was no longer alone. 'You have done well, Lalla. No one could have done better,' he said, and her face glowed.

He had now established a line of communication to the outside world, but Lalla was a simple child, incapable of remembering more than a few sentences at a time, and the meetings with Nazeera and Yakub could be risked only at intervals of several days: Abdullahi and Osman had spies everywhere.

Planning the escape was a long-drawn-out and complicated business. Twice Yakub had to leave Omdurman and make the hazardous journey to Abyssinia to consult Ryder Courtney and Bakhita. But, very slowly, the plan took shape.

The attempt would be made on the first Friday of Ramadan, five months hence. Yakub would have camels waiting on the far bank of the Nile, hidden among the ruins of Khartoum. By some ruse or subterfuge, Penrod would find his own way out of the courtyard of the aggagiers. Nazeera would spirit Rebecca and Amber out of the harem to a waiting felucca that she would arrange. Penrod would meet them there, and the felucca would ferry them across the Nile. Then, on Yakub's camels, they would dash up the south bank of the Blue Nile to where Jock McCrump would have the old *Ibis* hidden in the Lagoon of the Little Fish. He would take them up to Roseires, where horses

300

would be waiting for the final dash to the Abyssinian border.

'Will you take me with you, my lord?' Lalla asked wistfully.

What on earth would I do with her? Penrod wondered. She was not pretty, but had an endearing monkey face, and she looked at him with worshipful adoration. 'I will take you with me wherever I go,' he promised, and thought, Perhaps I can marry her to Yakub. She would make him a perfect little wife.

Only four weeks later, when everything was at last in place, Lalla brought Penrod another message, which struck him like the broadside of heavy cannon.

'Ammi Nazeera says that al-Zahra has seen her first moon and become a woman. She can hide this from the exalted Osman Atalan, but in one month's time her moon will rise again. She will not be able to conceal it longer from him. The mighty Atalan has already ordered Nazeera to watch for and report to him the first show of her woman's blood. He has announced that, as soon as she is marriageable, he will offer al-Zahra as a gift to the Khalifat Abdullahi, who hungers for her.'

Even if he had to risk all of them, Penrod could not possibly allow Amber to go to Abdullahi. It would be worse than feeding her alive to some obscene carnivorous monster. The entire plan had to be brought forward. They had a month's grace in which to change the arrangements. It would be a near-run thing. He sent the willing Lalla almost daily to carry messages to Yakub.

Two weeks before the new date of the escape attempt, the Khalif Osman Atalan announced a feast and entertainment for all his relatives and his most loyal followers. The main compound was decorated with palm fronds and two dozen prime sheep were roasted on spits. The low tables at which the company sat on soft cushions were piled with dishes of fruit and sweetmeats. Penrod found himself placed in a position of preference, close to the Khalif, with al-Noor at one hand and Mooman Digna on the other.

When all had eaten their fill and the mood was as warm as the sunshine, with laughter rippling like the waters of the Nile, Osman rose, made a short speech of welcome and commended them on their loyalty and duty. 'Now let the entertainment begin!' he ordered, and clapped his hands.

A finger drum began to tap a staccato rhythm and then a murmur of surprise went up. Every head craned towards the side gate of the courtyard. Two men led in a creature on a leash. It was impossible at first to guess the nature of the animal. It moved slowly and painfully on all fours, forced by its handlers to make a torturous circuit of the yard. It was only gradually that they realized it was a human female. Her hands and feet had been crudely amputated at wrists and ankles. The stumps had been dipped in hot pitch to staunch the bleeding. She crawled on elbows and knees. The rest of her naked body had been whipped with thorn branches. The thorns had lacerated her skin. The mutilations were so horrible that even the hardened aggagiers were silenced. Slowly she crawled to where Penrod sat. The handlers tightened the leash and forced her to lift her head.

Cold with horror Penrod stared into Lalla's little monkey face. Blood was trickling from her torn scalp into her empty eye-sockets. They had burned out her eyeballs with hot irons. 'Lalla!' he said softly. 'What have they done to you?'

She recognized his voice, and turned towards him. Blood was still oozing down her cheeks. 'My lord,' she whispered, 'I told them nothing.' Then she collapsed with her face in the dust, and though they yanked on the leash they could not rouse her.

'Abadan Riji!' Osman Atalan called. 'My trusted aggagier of the famous sword arm, put this sorry creature out of her agony.' A terrible silence hung over the gathering. Every man looked at Penrod, not understanding but enthralled by the drama of the moment.

'Kill her for me, Abadan Riji,' Osman repeated.

'Lalla!' Penrod's voice trembled with pity.

She heard him and rolled her head towards him, blindly seeking his face. 'My lord,' she whispered, 'for the love I bear you, do this thing. Give me release, for I can go on no longer.'

Penrod hesitated only a moment. Then he rose and drew his sword from its sheath. As he stood over her she spoke again: 'I will always love you.' And with a single blow he struck her head off the maimed body. Then he placed his foot on the blade and, with a sharp tug at the hilt, snapped it in two.

'Tell me, Abadan Riji,' said Osman Atalan, 'are those tears I see in your eyes? Why do you weep like a woman?'

'They are tears indeed, mighty Atalan, and I weep for the manner of your death, which will be terrible.'

'With the help of this creature, Abadan Riji was planning to escape from Omdurman,' Osman explained to his aggagiers. 'Bring in the *shebba*, and place it round his neck.'

*   *   *

The *shebba* was a device designed to restrain and punish recalcitrant slaves, and to prevent them escaping. It was a heavy Y-shaped yoke cut from the fork of an acacia tree. The prisoner was stripped naked, to add to his humiliation, then the crotch of the *shebba* was fitted against his throat. The thick trunk extended in front of him. They lifted it to shoulder height, and bound the fork in place behind his neck with twisted rawhide ropes. Finally Penrod's bare arms were lashed to the long pole in front of him. With both arms pinioned, he was unable to feed himself or lift a bowl of water to his lips. He could not clean himself of his bodily waste. If he allowed the pole to sink from horizontal the fork would crush his windpipe and choke him. To move he had first to raise the whole massive contraption and keep it balanced. He could not lie on his side or back, nor was he able to sit. If he wished to rest or sleep he must do so on his knees, with the end of the pole resting on the earth in front of him. At best he could only totter a few paces before the weight of the unbalanced pole forced him to his knees again.

The feast continued while Penrod knelt in the centre of the courtyard. Afterwards he was driven back to the courtyard of the aggagiers. Mooman Digna whipped him along like a beast of burden. He was unable to eat or drink, and nobody would help him. He could not sleep for the pain of the *shebba* goaded him awake. It was too large and cumbersome to allow him to enter his cell so he knelt in the open courtyard, with an aggagier assigned to guard him day and night. By the third day he had lost all feeling in his arms, and his hands were blue and swollen. Although he staggered around the wall of the courtyard to keep in the shadow, the sun's rays reflected from the limewashed walls and his naked body reddened and blistered. His tongue was like a dry sponge in his parched mouth for the heat in the noonday was intense.

By the morning of the fourth day he was becoming weak and disoriented, hovering on the verge of unconsciousness. Even his eyeballs were drying out, and still no one would help him. As he knelt in a corner of the courtyard he heard the voices of the aggagiers arguing nearby. They were discussing how much longer he would be able to hold out. Then there was silence and he forced open his swollen eyelids. For a moment he thought he was hallucinating.

Amber was coming towards him across the yard. She carried a large pitcher balanced on her head in the manner of an Arab woman. The aggagiers were watching her, but none tried to intervene. She took the pitcher off her head and placed it on the ground. Then she dipped a sponge into it and held it to his lips. He was unable to speak, but he sucked it gratefully. When she had given him as much as he could drink, she replaced the empty pitcher on her head and said softly, 'I will come again tomorrow.'

At the same time the following day Osman Atalan entered the yard and stood in the shade of the cloister with al-Noor and Mooman Digna. Amber came in shortly after his arrival. She saw him at once and stopped, balancing the pitcher with one hand, slim and graceful as a gazelle on the point of flight. She stared at Osman, then she lifted her chin defiantly and came to where Penrod knelt. She dipped the sponge and gave him drink. Osman did not stop her. When she had finished and was ready to leave, she whispered, without moving her lips, 'Yakub will come for you. Be ready.' She walked past Osman on her way to the gate. He watched her go impassively.

Amber came again the next day. Osman was not there and most of the aggagiers seemed to have lost interest. She gave Penrod water, then fed him *asida* and dhurra porridge, spooning it into his mouth as though he were an infant, wiping the spillage off his chin. Then she used another sponge to wash his filth from the back of his legs and his buttocks. 'I wish you did not have to do that,' he said.

She gave him a particular look and replied, 'You still do not understand, do you?' He was too bemused and weak to try to fathom her meaning. She went on, with barely a pause, 'Yakub will come for you tonight.'

*   *   *

Darkness fell and Penrod knelt in his corner of the courtyard. The aggagier Kabel al-Din was his guard that night. He sat nearby, with his back against the wall and his sheathed sword across his lap.

The muscles in Penrod's arms were cramping so violently that he had to bite his lip to stop himself screaming. The blood in his mouth tasted bitter and metallic. Eventually he slipped into a dark, numb sleep. When he woke he heard a woman's soft laughter nearby. It was a vaguely familiar sound. Then the woman whispered salaciously, 'The enormity of your manhood terrifies me, but I am brave enough to endure it.' Incredibly Penrod realized that it was Nazeera. What was she doing here, he wondered. He opened his eyes. She was lying on her back in the moonlight with her skirts drawn up to her armpits. Kabel al-Din was kneeling between her parted thighs, about to mount her, oblivious to everything about him.

Yakub came over the wall as silently as a moth. As Kabel al-Din humped his back over Nazeera, Yakub sank the point of his dagger into the nape of the man's neck. With the expertise of long practice he found the juncture of the third and fourth vertebrae and severed the spinal column. Al-Din stiffened, then collapsed soundlessly on Nazeera. She pushed aside his limp body and rolled out from beneath him. Then she scrambled to her feet, pulling down her skirts as she came to help Yakub, who was stooped over Penrod. With the blood-smeared dagger Yakub cut the thongs that pinioned his arms and Penrod almost screamed as the blood coursed back into his starved arteries and veins. While Nazeera took the weight of the yoke to prevent it crushing Penrod's larynx, Yakub cut the thongs at the back of his neck. Between them they lifted it off.

'Drink.' Nazeera held a small glass flask to his lips. 'It will deaden the pain.' With three gulps Penrod swallowed the contents. The bitter taste of laudanum was unmistakable. They helped him to his feet and half carried him to the wall. Yakub had left a rope in place. While Nazeera propped him

307

up, Yakub settled the loop on the end of the rope under Penrod's armpits. As he straddled the top of the wall and heaved on the rope Nazeera pushed from below and they hoisted Penrod over. He fell in a heap on the far side. Nazeera slipped quietly away in the direction of the harem. Yakub dropped down beside Penrod and hauled him on to his numb feet.

At first their progress towards the riverbank was torturously slow, but then the laudanum took effect and Penrod pushed away Yakub's hands. 'In future, do not stay away so long, tardy Yakub,' he mumbled, and Yakub giggled at the jest. Penrod broke into a shambling run towards the river, where he knew the felucca was waiting to take them across.

*   *   *

As the favourite of Osman Atalan, Rebecca had her own quarters and Amber was allowed to share them with her. The two waited by the small grilled window through which they had a glimpse of the silver moonlight reflected from the wide river. Rebecca had turned the wick of the oil lamp low, so they could just make out each other's faces. Amber was wearing a light woollen robe and sandals, ready to travel, and she was quivering with excitement.

'It is almost time. You must make ready, Becky,' she entreated. 'Nazeera will be back at any moment to fetch us.'

'Listen to me, my darling Amber.' Rebecca placed her hands on her sister's shoulders. 'You must be brave now. I am not coming with you. You are going alone with Penrod Ballantyne.'

Amber went as still as stone, and stared into her sister's eyes, but they were unfathomable in the gloom. When she spoke at last her voice shook. 'I don't understand.'

'I cannot go with you. I must stay here.'

'But why, Becky? Why, oh, why?'

In reply Rebecca took her sister's hands and guided them under her shift. She placed them on her own naked belly. 'Do you feel that?'

'It's just a little fat,' Amber protested. 'That won't stop you. You must come.'

'There is a baby inside me, Amber.'

'I don't believe it. It cannot be. I still love you and need you.'

'It's a baby,' Rebecca assured her. 'It's Osman Atalan's bastard. Do you know what a bastard is, Amber?'

'Yes.' Amber could not bring herself to say more.

'Do you know what will happen if I go home to England with an Arab bastard inside me?'

'Yes.' Amber's voice was almost inaudible. 'But the midwives could take it away, couldn't they?'

'You mean kill my baby?' Rebecca asked. 'Would you kill your own baby, Amber darling?' Amber shook her head. 'Then you cannot ask me to do it.'

'I will stay with you,' said Amber.

'You saw what a sorry condition Penrod is in.' Rebecca knew it was the strongest lever she had to move Amber. 'You have saved his life already. You fed him and gave him water when he was dying. If you desert him now, he will not survive. You must do your duty.'

'But what about you?' Amber was cruelly torn.

'I will be safe, I promise.' Rebecca hugged her

hard, and then her tone became firm and brisk. 'Now, you must take this with you. It's Daddy's journal, which I have added to. When you reach England, take it to his lawyer. His name is Sebastian Hardy. I have written his name and address on the first page. He will know what to do with it.' She handed the book to Amber. She had packed it into a bag of woven palm leaves and bound it up carefully. It was heavy and bulky, but Rebecca had plaited a rope handle to make it easier to carry.

'I don't want to leave you,' Amber blurted.

'I know, darling. Duty can be hard. But you must do it.'

'I will love you for ever and always.'

'I know you will, and I will love you just as hard and just as long.' They clung to each other until Nazeera appeared quietly beside them.

'Come, Zahra. It is time to go. Yakub and Abadan Riji are waiting for you by the riverside.'

There was nothing left to say. They embraced for the last time, then Nazeera took Amber's hand and led her away, with the bag that contained her legacy. Only once she was alone did Rebecca allow her grief to burst out. She threw herself on to their *angareb* below the window and wept. Every sob came up painfully from deep inside her.

Then something inside her was awakened by the strength of her sorrow, and for the first time she felt the infant kick in her womb. It startled her into stillness, and filled her with such bitter joy that she clasped her arms round her belly and whispered, 'You are all I have left now.' She rocked herself and the infant to sleep.

*　　　*　　　*

The felucca was anchored close to the muddy strip of beach below the old mosque. It was a battered, neglected craft that stank of river mud and old fish. The owner hoped to replace it with a new vessel paid for out of the exorbitant fee he had been promised for a single crossing of the river. Its amount warned him that he was at great risk, and he was edgy and fidgety as he waited.

The laudanum made Penrod Ballantyne feel muzzy-headed and divorced from reality, but at least he was without pain in his limbs. He and Yakub were lying on the floorboards where they would be concealed from casual inspection. In a whisper Yakub was trying to tell him something that he seemed to think was of prime importance. However, Penrod's mind kept floating off on the wings of opium, and Yakub's words made no sense to him.

Then, vaguely, he was aware that somebody was wading out to the vessel. He lifted himself on one elbow and looked groggily over the side. Nazeera was standing on the beach, and the lithe figure of Amber Benbrook, with a large bag on her head, was moving towards the felucca. 'Where is Rebecca?' he asked, and blinked to make certain he was seeing straight.

Amber pulled herself aboard the felucca, then Nazeera turned away from the water and ran off.

'Where is Nazeera going?' he wondered vaguely.

Amber dropped her bag on the deck and stooped over him. 'Penrod! Thank goodness! How are you feeling? Let me see your arms. I have some ointment for your bruises.'

'Wait until we get to the other side,' he demurred. 'Where is Nazeera going? Where is Rebecca?' Neither Amber nor Yakub answered him. Instead Yakub gave a sharp order to the boat-owner and scrambled to help him hoist the lateen sail. It filled to the night breeze and they bore away.

The felucca sailed closer to the wind than her age would suggest, and she kicked up such a bow wave that the spray splattered over them. On the Khartoum side they went aground with such force that the rotten keel was almost torn off her. Amber and Yakub helped Penrod ashore, and Yakub propped his shoulder under his armpit to steady him as they hurried through the deserted streets of the ruined city. They met not a living soul until they reached Ryder Courtney's abandoned compound. There, a Bedouin boy was waiting for them with a string of camels. As soon as he had handed the lead reins to Yakub, he fled into the shadows.

The riding camels were fully saddled and equipped. They mounted at once, but Yakub had to help Penrod into the saddle and he was almost unseated as the animal lurched to its feet. Yakub took him on the lead rein and led the little caravan through the mud of the almost dry canal and into the desert beyond. There he goaded the camels onwards and they paced away, keeping the river in sight on their left-hand side. Within the first mile, Penrod lost his balance and slipped sideways out of the saddle. He hit the ground heavily and lay for a while like a dead man. They dismounted and helped him back into the saddle.

'I will hold him,' Amber told Yakub. She climbed

up, sat behind Penrod and placed both arms round his waist to steady him. They went on for hours without a halt, until in the first light of dawn they picked out the shape of the lagoon ahead in the river mist. There was no sign of the steamer out on the open water.

On the edge of the reed bed Yakub reined in his camel and stood upright on his saddle. He sang out over the lagoon in a high wail that would carry for a mile. 'In God's Name, is there no man or jinnee who hears me?'

Almost immediately, from close by in the reeds, a jinnee replied in a broad Scots burr: 'Och, aye, laddie! I hear you.' Jock McCrump had camouflaged his steamer with cut reeds so that it was almost invisible from the bank of the lagoon. As soon as they had turned the camels loose and were safely aboard he reversed the old *Ibis*, now the *Wisdom of the Skies*, out into the open water and turned her bows eastwards for Roseires, almost two hundred miles upstream. Then he came down to the cabin where Penrod was stretched out on the bunk with Amber anointing his blisters and bruises with the lotion that Nazeera had provided. 'And now you'll be expecting me to make you a cuppa tea, I hae nae doot,' said Jock, morosely. It was Darjeeling Orange Pekoe, with condensed milk, and Penrod had never tasted anything so heavenly. He fell asleep immediately after he had downed a third mug, and did not wake again until they were a hundred miles upriver from Khartoum, and beyond the pursuit of even the swiftest camels of Osman Atalan's aggagiers.

When he opened his eyes Amber was still sitting at the end of his bunk, but she was so engrossed in

313

reading her father's bulky journal that for some time she did not realize he was awake. Penrod studied her countenance as the emotions that her father's writing evoked flitted across it. He saw now that she had become far and away the beauty of the trio of Benbrook girls.

Suddenly she looked at him, smiled and closed the journal. 'How are you feeling now? You have slept for ten hours without moving.'

'I'm a great deal better, thanks to you and Yakub.' He paused. 'Rebecca?'

Amber's smile faded, and she looked bereft. 'She will stay in Omdurman. It was her choice.'

'Why?' he asked, and she told him. They were both silent for a while and then Penrod said, 'If I had had my wits about me, I would have gone back to fetch her.'

'She did the right thing,' Amber said softly. 'Rebecca always does the right thing. She made that sacrifice for love of me. I will never forget it.'

Over the rest of the river voyage, as they talked, Penrod discovered that she was no longer a child in either body or mind, but that she had become a courageous, mature young woman, her character tempered in the forge of suffering.

*   *   *

The horses were waiting at Roseires, and they picked up relays of mules as they journeyed through the foothills of the Abyssinian highlands. They reached Entoto after eleven days of hard going, and as they rode into the courtyard of Ryder Courtney's compound Saffron rushed out to greet her twin. Amber tumbled off her mule and they fell into each other's arms, too overcome to speak. Ryder watched them from the veranda with a benign smile.

Once they had recovered their tongues, the twins could barely pause to draw breath. They sat up all night in Saffron's studio, talking. They wandered hand in hand through the souks and lanes of Entoto, talking. They rode out into the mountains and came back with armfuls of flowers, still talking. Then they read their father's journal aloud to each other, and Rebecca's additions to it, and they hugged each other as they wept for their father and elder sister, both of whom they had lost for ever.

Amber studied Saffron's portfolio of Khartoum sketches. She pronounced them wonderfully accurate and evocative, then suggested a few small changes and improvements, which Saffron, anxious to please her, adopted immediately. Saffron designed and made a complete wardrobe of new clothes for Amber, and took her to have tea with Lady Alice Packer and Empress Miriam. The queen thought Amber's new outfit stylish and fetching, and asked Saffron to design her a dress for the next state dinner.

Amber continued David Benbrook's journal from the point where Rebecca had left off. In it she described her escape from Omdurman and the flight up the Blue Nile to the Abyssinian border. In the process she discovered she had a natural talent with the written word.

Only Ryder was not completely enchanted by Amber's arrival in Entoto. He had become accustomed to having Saffron's undivided attention. Now that it had been diverted to her twin, he realized, with something of a shock, how much he missed it.

Penrod recovered swiftly from the injuries he had suffered in Osman Atalan's *shebba*. He exercised his sword arm in practice with Yakub, and his legs in long, solitary walks in the mountains. His first urgent duty was to report his actions and whereabouts to his superiors in Cairo, but the telegraph line ran only as far as Djibouti on the Gulf of Aden. He wrote letters to Sir Evelyn Baring and Viscount Wolseley, and to his elder brother in England. The British ambassador sent these out in the diplomatic pouch, but they all knew how long it would be before he could expect a reply.

Ryder Courtney had a sealed blank envelope for Penrod. When Penrod weighed it in his hand he realized that it contained more than paper. 'Who is it from?' he asked. 'Regrettably I have been sworn to silence,' Ryder replied, 'but I am sure the answer is contained in it. You must ask nothing more from me concerning the matter, for I am unable to discuss it.'

Penrod took it to the bedroom that Ryder had set aside for him and bolted the door. As he slit open the envelope, a weighty object fell out, but he caught it before it struck the tiles. It lay in his palm, shimmering gold and magnificent, its beauty undiminished by the ages. On the obverse side was the crowned portrait of Cleopatra Thea Philopator and on the reverse the head of Marcus Antonius. In the envelope with the coin was a single line of Arabic written on parchment. 'When my lord needs me, he knows where I shall be.' The coin was her signature.

'Bakhita!' He rubbed the portrait of the woman

316

with his thumb. How did she fit into the scheme of things now? Then he remembered Yakub trying to tell him something important while he was drugged with laudanum on the first night of the escape from Omdurman.

The next day he and Yakub rode up into the mountains where they could be alone. Yakub related in detail how, after Penrod had been captured by Osman Atalan, he had set out for Aswan to enlist the aid of the only person who could and would help them. He explained how he had been arrested on the Egyptian border while travelling with a dealer in slaves, and how he had been imprisoned for over a year before he could go on to Aswan.

'As soon as I found Bakhita al-Masur she travelled with me here to Entoto, and arranged your escape with al-Sakhawi.'

Penrod considered ignoring Ryder Courtney's warning and taxing him with Bakhita's role in their rescue, but in the end he shied away from doing so. He and Bakhita had always maintained the greatest secrecy and discretion in their relationship. It even surprised him that Yakub had known of it. By this time I should have learnt not to be surprised by anything that the intrepid Yakub comes up with. He smiled to himself. Then he considered writing to Bakhita, but this would be equally unwise. Even if the letter went through diplomatic channels, there was no telling which of the embassy staff was in the pay of the ubiquitous Evelyn Baring. There was another reason not to contact Bakhita. This was less clear-cut in his mind but it had to do with Amber Benbrook. He did not want to do anything that might later hurt the child.

317

Child? He questioned his choice of word as he watched her cross the yard in deep conversation with her twin sister. You deceive yourself, Penrod Ballantyne.

It was five months before Penrod received a reply to the letter he had written to his elder brother Sir Peter Ballantyne, at the family estate on the Scottish Borders. In his reply Sir Peter agreed that the Benbrook sisters might make their home at Clercastle until such time as their future had been decided. Penrod would sail back to England with Amber and Saffron and take care of them until they reached Clercastle. Once they arrived Sir Peter's wife, Jane, would take over the responsibility from him.

As soon as Penrod received his brother's letter he went up to the British Embassy and telegraphed to the office of the Peninsular and Orient Steamship line in Djibouti. He booked passage for himself and the twins on board the SS *Singapore*, sailing via Suez and Alexandria for Southampton in six weeks' time. When Amber learnt that she would be sailing home in company with Penrod Ballantyne, then staying at Clercastle with the Ballantyne family she made no objection. On the contrary she seemed well pleased with the arrangement.

It did not go so easily with the other twin. There followed long and difficult discussions with Saffron, who announced with passion that she could see no reason why she should return to England 'where it rains all the time, and I shall probably expire with double pneumonia on the same day I arrive'. It was necessary to appeal to Alice Packer for a ruling.

'My dear Saffron, you are only fourteen.'

318

'Fifteen in a month's time,' Saffron corrected her grimly.

'Your education has been somewhat neglected,' Alice went on imperturbably. 'I am sure Sir Peter will provide a governess for you and Amber. After all, he has daughters of very much the same age as you two darling girls.'

'I don't need geography and mathematics,' said Saffron, stubbornly. 'I know all about Africa and I can paint.'

'Ah!' said Alice. 'Sir John Millais is a dear friend of mine. How would you like to study art under him? I'm sure I can arrange it.'

Saffron wavered: Millais was a founder of the Pre-Raphaelite Brotherhood, the most celebrated painter of the day. David Benbrook had kept a book of his paintings in his study at Khartoum. Saffron had spent hours dreaming over them. Then Alice played her trump: 'And, of course, as soon as you are sixteen you will always be welcome to return to Entoto as my guest, whenever and as often as you wish.'

As the day of their departure for Djibouti drew nearer, Saffron spent less time with her twin and more in helping Bacheet look after Ryder. He agreed to pose for an hour or two each evening for one last portrait. Since the twins' future had been agreed upon, his mood had been subdued, but it lightened perceptibly during these daily painting sessions. Saffron was an amusing girl and made him laugh.

Two days before Penrod and the twins were due to leave Entoto for Djibouti, Ryder announced his intention of joining their little caravan, as he was expecting a shipment of trade goods to arrive on board the SS *Singapore* from Calcutta. During the journey down to the coast Ryder and Saffron spent much time riding side by side at the rear of the convoy. The closer they came to Djibouti, the more serious their expressions became. The day before they came in sight of the town and harbour a flaming row broke out between them. Saffron left Ryder and galloped to the head of the column to ride beside Amber.

That night, as was the custom, the four of them ate supper beside the fire. When Ryder addressed a polite remark to her, Saffron pulled a face and deliberately moved her chair so that her back was turned to him. She did not bid him goodnight when she and Amber went to their tent.

The next day as they came in sight of Djibouti harbour the SS *Singapore* was lying in the roads and discharging cargo into the lighters clustered around her. While Ryder and Bacheet set up camp on the outskirts of the town, Penrod and the twins rode down to the shipping office at the wharf to pay for and receive their tickets for the voyage to Southampton. The shipping clerk assured them that the *Singapore* would sail on schedule at noon the following day. Penrod managed to buy a bottle of Glenlivet whisky from the purser. He and Ryder made short work of it that evening, when the twins had retired to their tent not long after nightfall.

Due to the exigencies of the previous evening's consumption of liquor the two men were late in rising. In the roads the *Singapore* was already making steam in preparation for her sailing in three hours' time. Penrod took the luggage down to the wharf and sent it on board, then rode back to the camp and found it in a state of uproar.

'She has gone!' Bacheet lamented, and wrung his plump hands. 'Filfil has gone!'

'What do you mean, Bacheet? Where has she gone?'

'We do not know, Effendi. During the night she took her mule and rode away. Al-Sakhawi has gone after her, but I think Filfil has six hours' start on him. He won't be able to catch her before nightfall.'

'By that time the *Singapore* will have sailed,' Penrod fumed, and went to find Amber.

'After Saffron and I climbed into bed, I went to sleep directly. When I woke it was already light and Saffy had gone, just like that, without even a goodbye.'

Penrod studied her face for some hint of the truth. He was sure he had heard the twins whispering when he had passed their tent on the way to his own bed. He knew for certain it had been after midnight, because he had wound his pocket watch before he blew out the lamp. 'We will have to go on board. We cannot miss this sailing. There will not be another for months. I will try to persuade the captain to delay until Saffron is on board,' he said, and Amber agreed with an angelic expression.

While Penrod and Amber stood at the starboard rail of the *Singapore*, Penrod was staring anxiously through a pair of borrowed binoculars as the last boat from the shore approached the ship's side.

'Blue bloody blazes!' he muttered furiously. 'She isn't on board.'

As he lowered the binoculars, the ship's third officer hurried down the ladder from the bridge and came to them. 'The captain's compliments,

321

Captain Ballantyne, but he very much regrets that he is not able to delay the sailing until the arrival of Miss Benbrook. If he does he will be unable to make his reservation for the transit of the Suez Canal.' Just then the ship's siren wailed and cut off the rest of his apology. The capstan in the bows began to clatter and the anchor broke free.

'Now, Miss Amber Benbrook,' Penrod said grimly, 'I think it's time you delivered the truth. Just what is your sister playing at?'

'I should think that is perfectly obvious, Captain Ballantyne, except to a blind man or an imbecile.'

'Nevertheless, I would be most obliged if you could explain it to me.'

'My sister is in love with Mr Ryder Courtney. She has not the slightest intention of leaving him. I am afraid we are to be deprived of her company on this voyage. You will have to make do with mine.'

A prospect that I do not find particularly distressing, he thought, but tried to disguise his pleasure.

*   *   *

The tracks of Saffron's mule headed straight back along the main route towards the Abyssinia border. Except where they had been overridden by other travellers they were easy to follow. Saffron had made no attempt to cover them or to throw off any pursuit. Soon Ryder knew that he was overhauling her, but it was the middle of the afternoon before he made out her mule in the distance. He urged his own mount into a gallop. As he came within hail he let out an angry shout. She stopped and turned back towards him. Then he saw that it was not her

322

at all, but one of the camp servants: a dim-witted lad whose sole employment was chopping firewood for the camp. Anything more demanding was beyond his limited capabilities.

'What in the name of God are you up to, Solomon? Where do you think you are going on Filfil's mule?'

'Filfil gave me a Maria Theresa to ride back to Entoto and fetch a box she had forgotten,' he announced importantly, proud of the task with which he had been entrusted.

'Where is Filfil now?'

'Why, Effendi, I know not.' Solomon picked his nose with embarrassment at the complexity of the question. 'Is she not still in Djibouti?'

When Ryder came in sight of the harbour again, the *Singapore*'s anchorage was empty, and the smoke from her funnels was merely a dark smear on the watery horizon. Ryder stormed into his camp and shouted at Bacheet: 'Where is Filfil?' Bacheet remained silent but rolled his eyes in the direction of her tent.

Ryder strode to the tent and stooped through the opening of the fly. 'There you are, you scamp.'

Saffron was sitting cross-legged on her camp-bed. She was bare-footed and her most extravagant hat was perched on her head. She was looking extremely pleased with herself.

'What have you to say for yourself?' he demanded.

'All I have to say is that you are my dog and I am your flea. You can scratch and scratch as much as you will, but you'll not get rid of me, Ryder Courtney.'

They were half-way back to Entoto before he

had recovered from the shock, and had come to realize how happy he was that she had not sailed with the *Singapore*. 'I still don't know what we should do now,' he said. 'I shall probably be arrested for child abduction. I have no idea of the legal age for marriage in Abyssinia.'

'It's fourteen,' said Saffron. 'I asked the Empress before we left Entoto. Anyway, that is merely a guideline. Nobody pays much attention to it. She was thirteen when the Emperor married her.'

'Have you any other gems of information?' he asked tartly.

'I have. The Empress has expressed her willingness to sponsor our union, should you care to marry me. What do you think of that?'

'I had not thought about it at all,' he exclaimed, 'but, by God, now that you raise the subject it is not the worst notion I have ever heard of.' He reached across, lifted her off the back of her mule, seated her on the pommel of his own saddle and kissed her.

She clamped her hat onto her head with one hand and flung her other arm round his neck. Then she kissed him back with a great deal more vigour than finesse. After a while she broke away to breathe. 'Oh, you wonderful man!' she gasped. 'You cannot imagine how long I have wanted to do that. It feels even nicer than I hoped it might. Let's do it again.'

'An excellent idea,' he agreed.

The Empress was as good as her word. She sat in the front pew of the Entoto cathedral with the Emperor at her side, beaming on the ceremony like the rising sun. She was dressed in a Saffron Benbrook creation, which made her look rather

324

like a large sugar-iced chocolate cake.

Lady Packer had prevailed on her husband, Sir Harold White Packer, Knight Commander of Michael and George, Her Britannic Majesty's ambassador, to give Saffron away. He was in full fig, including his bicorne hat with gold lace and white cockerel feathers. The groom was handsome and nervous in his black frock-coat, with the dazzling Star of the Order of Solomon and Judea on his breast. The Bishop of Abyssinia performed the service.

Saffron had designed her own wedding dress. When she came down the aisle on Sir Harold's arm, Ryder was mildly relieved to see that it was in pure virginal white. Saffron's taste usually ran to brighter hues. When they left the church as man and wife, a troop of the Royal Abyssinian Artillery fired a nine-gun salute. In the fever of the moment, one of the ancient cannon had been double charged and it burst in spectacular fashion on the first discharge. Fortunately nobody was injured, and the bishop declared it a propitious omen. The Emperor provided vast quantities of fiery Tej to the populace, and toasts were drunk to bride and groom for as long as the liquor held out and their well-wishers remained upright and conscious.

For the honeymoon Ryder took his bride into the southern Abyssinian highlands on an expedition to capture the rare mountain nyala. They returned some months later without having caught even a glimpse of the elusive beast. Saffron painted a picture to commemorate the expedition: on a mountain peak in the background stood a creature that bore more than a passing resemblance to a unicorn, and in the foreground a

325

man and woman whose identities were in no doubt. The woman wore a huge yellow hat decorated with seashells and roses. They were not looking at the unicorn, but clasped between them was a large and magnificent bird, half ostrich and half peacock. The legend beneath the painting read, 'We went to find the elusive nyala, but found instead the elusive bird of happiness.'

Ryder was so enchanted by it that he had the picture mounted in an ivory frame, and hung it on the wall above their bed.

* * *

The voyage up the Red Sea was calm and peaceful. There were only four passenger cabins on board the SS *Singapore*, two of which were unoccupied. Amber and Penrod dined each evening with the captain, and after dinner they strolled around the deck or danced to the music of the violin played by the Italian chef, who thought Amber was the most lovely creature in all creation.

During the day Amber and Penrod worked together in the card room, editing David Benbrook's journal. Amber exercised her new-found writing talent, and Penrod provided military and historical background. Amber suggested he write his own account of the battle of Abu Klea, his subsequent capture by Osman Atalan and their escape from the captivity of the Dervish. They would combine this with the writings of David and Rebecca. The further they advanced into the project, the greater their enthusiasm for it became. By the time the *Singapore* anchored in Alexandria harbour they had made great progress in expanding and correcting the text. It could now be published as an inspiring true adventure, and they had the remainder of the voyage home to complete it.

Penrod went ashore in Alexandria, and hired a horse. He rode the thirty miles to Cairo, and went directly to the British agency. Sir Evelyn Baring kept him waiting only twenty minutes before he sent his secretary to summon him into his office. He had the thirty-page letter that Penrod had sent from Entoto spread like a fan on the desk in front of him. On it were many cryptic notations written in red ink in the margins. Baring maintained his usual cold, enigmatic manner and expression during the interview, which lasted almost two hours. At the end he rose to dismiss Penrod without making any comment, expressing any opinion, or offering either censure or approval. 'Colonel Samuel Adams at Army headquarters in Giza is anxious to speak to you,' he told Penrod, at the door.

'Colonel?' Penrod asked.

'Promotion,' Baring replied. 'He will explain everything to you.'

*　　　*　　　*

Sam Adams limped only slightly and he no longer used a cane as he came round his desk to greet Penrod warmly. He looked fit and suntanned, although there were a few grey hairs in his moustache.

'Congratulations on the colonel's pips, sir.' Penrod saluted.

Adams was without a cap so he could not return the salute, but he seized Penrod's hand and shook it warmly. 'Delighted to have you back, Ballantyne. Much has happened while you have been away. There is a great deal we must talk about. Shall we go for lunch at the club?'

He had reserved a table in the corner of the dining room at the Gheziera Club. He ordered a bottle of Krug, then waited until the glasses were filled and they had placed their order with the waiter, in red fez and white *galabiyya*, before he got down to business. 'After the disaster of Khartoum, and the murder of that idiot Gordon, there were many unpleasant repercussions. The press at home were looking for scapegoats and fastened on Sir Charles Wilson's delay in pressing on to the relief of Gordon after the victory at Abu Klea. Wilson sought to defend himself by placing the blame on his subordinates. Unfortunately you were one of those to suffer, Ballantyne. He has brought charges of subordination and desertion against you. Now that you have come back from limbo, you will almost certainly be court-martialled. Capital offence, if you're found guilty. Firing squad, don't you know?'

Penrod blanched under his suntan and stared at Adams in horror.

He went on hurriedly: 'You have friends here. Everyone knows your worth. Victoria Cross, derring-do, heroic escapes and all that. However, you will have to resign your commission in the Hussars.'

'Resign my commission?' Penrod exclaimed. 'I will let them shoot me first.'

'It might come to that. But hear me out.' Adams reached across the table and laid his hand on Penrod's arm to prevent him leaping to his feet.

328

'Drink your champagne and listen to me. Damn fine vintage, by the way. Don't waste it.' Penrod subsided, and Adams went on,

'First, I must give you some other background information. Egypt now belongs to us in all but name. Baring calls it the Veiled Protectorate, but it's a bloody colony for all the pretty words. The decision has been taken by London to rebuild the Egyptian army from a disorganized rabble into a first-rate fighting corps. The new sirdar is Horatio Herbert Kitchener. Do you know him?'

'I cannot say that I do,' Penrod said. The sirdar was the commander-in-chief of the Egyptian army.

'Cross between a tiger and a dragon. Absolute bloody fire-eater. He desperately needs first-class officers for the new army, men who know the desert and the lingo. I mentioned your name. He knows of you. He wants you. If you join him he'll quash all Wilson's charges against you. Kitchener is going up the ladder to the top and will take his people with him. You will start at your equivalent rank of captain, but I can almost guarantee you a battalion within a year, your own regiment within five. For you the choice is between ruin and high rank. What do you say?'

Penrod smoothed his whiskers thoughtfully—on board ship Amber had trimmed his sideburns and moustache for him and once again they were luxuriant. He had learnt never to jump at the first offer.

'Camel Corps.' Adams tossed in another plum. 'Plenty of desert fighting.'

'When can I meet the gentleman?'

'Tomorrow. Nine hundred hours sharp at the new army headquarters. If you love life, don't be late.'

*   *   *

Kitchener was a muscular man of middling height and moved like a gladiator. He had a full head of hair and a cast in one eye, not unlike Yakub's. This made Penrod incline towards him. His jaw had been shot half away in a fight with the Dervish at Suakin when he had been governor of that insalubrious and dangerous corner of Africa. The bone was distorted and the keloid scar was pale pink against his darkly tanned skin. His handshake was iron hard and his manner harsh and unyielding.

'You speak Arabic?' he asked, in that language. He spoke it well, but with an accent that would never allow him to pass him as a native.

'Sirdar effendi! May all your days be perfumed with jasmine.' Penrod made the gesture of respect. 'In truth, I speak the language of the One True God and His Prophet.'

Kitchener blinked. It was perfect. 'When can you come on strength?'

'I need to be in England until Christmas. I have been out of contact with civilization for some time. I must settle my personal affairs, and I shall have to resign my commission with my present regiment.'

'You have until the middle of January next year and then I want you here in Cairo. Adams will go over the details with you. You are dismissed.' His uneven gaze dropped back to the papers on the desk in front of him.

As he and Adams went down the steps of the headquarters building to where the grooms were holding their horses, Penrod said, 'He wastes little time.'

'Not a second,' Adams agreed. 'Not a single bloody second.'

*   *   *

Before he rode back to Alexandria to rejoin the *Singapore*, Penrod went to the telegraph office and sent a wire to Sebastian Hardy, David Benbrook's lawyer, at his chambers in Lincolns Inn Fields. It was a lengthy message and cost Penrod two pounds, nine shillings and fourpence.

*   *   *

Hardy came from London by train to meet the ship when she docked at Southampton. In appearance he reminded Penrod and Amber of Charles Dickens's Mr Pickwick. However, behind his *pince-nez* he had a shrewd and calculating eye. He travelled back to London with them.

'The press has got wind of your escape from Omdurman, and your arrival in this country,' he told them. 'They are agog. I have no doubt they will be waiting at Waterloo station to pounce upon you.'

'How can they know what train we will arrive on?' Amber asked.

'I dropped a little hint,' Hardy admitted. 'What I would refer to as pre-baiting the waters. Now, may I read this manuscript?'

Amber looked to Penrod for guidance, and he nodded. 'I think you should trust Mr Hardy. Your father did.'

Hardy skimmed through the thick sheaf of papers so rapidly that Amber doubted he was reading it. She voiced her concern, and Hardy answered, without looking up, 'Trained eye, my dear young lady.'

As the carriage ran in through the suburbs he shuffled the papers together. 'I think we have something here. Will you allow me to keep this for a week? I know a man in Bloomsbury who would like to read it.'

Five journalists were waiting on the platform, including one from *The Times* and another from the *Telegraph*. When they saw the handsome, highly decorated hero of El Obeid and Abu Klea, with the young beauty on his arm, they knew they had a story that would electrify the whole country. They barked hysterically as a pack of mongrels who had chased a squirrel up a tree. Hardy gave them a tantalizing statement about the horrifying ordeal the couple had survived, mentioning Gordon, the Mahdi and Khartoum more than once, all evocative names. Then he sent the press away and led the couple out to a cab he had waiting at the station entrance.

The cabbie whipped up his horse and they clattered through the foggy city to the hotel in Charles Street where Hardy had booked a room for Amber. Once she was installed they went on to the hotel in Dover Street where Penrod would stay.

'Never do for the two of you to frequent the same lodging. From now on you will be under a magnifying lens.'

Four days later Sebastian Hardy summoned them to his office. He was beaming pinkly through his *pince-nez*. 'Macmillan and Company want to publish. You know they did Sir Samuel White Baker's book on the Nile tributaries of Abyssinia? Your book is caviar and champagne to them.'

'What can the Benbrook sisters expect to receive? You know that Miss Amber wishes any proceeds to be shared equally between them, following the example their father set in his will?'

Hardy sobered and looked apologetic. He removed his reading glasses and polished them with the tail of his shirt. 'I pressed them as hard as I could, but they would not budge beyond ten thousand pounds.'

'Ten thousand pounds!' Amber shrieked. 'I did not know there was that much money outside the Bank of England.'

'You will also receive twelve and a half per cent of the profits. I doubt this will amount to much more than seventy-five thousand pounds.'

They gaped at him in silence. Placed in consols, irredeemable government treasury bonds, that sum would bring in almost three and a half thousand pounds per annum in perpetuity. They would never have to worry about money.

In the event, Hardy's estimate erred on the side of caution. Months before Christmas *Slaves of the Mahdi* was all the rage. Hatchard's in Piccadilly was unable to keep copies on its shelves for more than an hour. Irate customers vied with each other to snatch them and carry them triumphantly to the till.

In the House of Commons the opposition seized on the book as a weapon with which to belabour the government. The whole sorry business of Mr Gladstone abandoning Chinese Gordon to his fate was resuscitated. Saffron Benbrook's harrowing painting depicting the death of the general, to which she had been an eye-witness, formed the book's frontispiece. It was reported in a leading article in *The Times* that women wept and strong men raged as they looked at it. The British people had tried to forget the humiliation and loss of prestige they had suffered at the hands of the Mad Mahdi, but now the half-healed wound was ripped wide open. A popular campaign for the reoccupation of the Sudan swept the country. The book sold and sold.

Amber and Penrod were invited to all the great houses, and were surrounded by admirers wherever they went. London cabbies greeted them by name, and strangers accosted them in Piccadilly and Hyde Park. Hundreds of letters from readers were forwarded to them by the publishers. There was even a short note of congratulation from the sirdar, Kitchener, in Cairo.

'That will do my new career no harm at all,' Penrod told Amber, as they rode together down Rotten Row, acknowledging waves.

The book sold a quarter of a million copies in the first six weeks, and the printing presses roared night and day churning out fresh copies. They were unable to keep up with the demand. Putnam's of 70 Fifth Avenue, New York, brought out an American edition, which piqued the interest of readers who had never heard of the Sudan. *Slaves of the Mahdi* outsold Mr Stanley's account of his search for Dr Livingstone by three to one.

The French, true to the national character, added their own fanciful illustrations to the Paris edition. Rebecca Benbrook was depicted with her bodice torn open by the evil Mahdi as he prepared to ravish her as she courageously sheltered her beautiful, terrified little sister Amber. The indomitable thrust of her bare bosom declared her defiance in the face of a fate worse than death. Copies were smuggled across the Channel and sold at a premium on stalls in the streets of Soho. Even after the payment of income tax at sixpence in the pound, by Christmas the book had earned royalties little short of two hundred thousand pounds. Amber, at the suggestion of Penrod Ballantyne, instructed Mr Hardy to place this in a trust fund for the three sisters.

Amber and Penrod celebrated Christmas at Clercastle. They walked and rode together every day. When the house-party went out to shoot Sir Peter's high-flying pheasant, Amber stood in the line of guns beside Penrod and, thanks to her father's training, acquitted herself so gracefully and skilfully that the head keeper came to her after the last drive, tugged at the peak of his cap and mumbled, 'It was a joy to watch you shoot, Miss Amber.'

January came too soon. Penrod had to take up his post in Cairo. Amber, chaperoned by Penrod's sister-in-law Jane, went to see him off from Waterloo station on the boat train. With Jane's assistance, Amber had spent the previous week shopping for the correct attire at such a momentous parting. Of course, price was now of little consequence.

She settled on a dove-grey jacket, trimmed with sable fur, worn over ankle-length skirts and a fashionable bustle. Her high-heeled boots buckled up the sides and peeped out from under the sweeping skirts. The artful cut of the material

335

emphasized her tiny waist. Her wide-brimmed hat was crowned with a wave of ostrich feathers. She wore the amber necklace and earrings that he had given her on the road outside Gallabat.

'When will we see each other again?' Amber was trying desperately but unsuccessfully to hold back her tears until after the train had departed.

'That I cannot say.' Penrod had determined never to lie to her, unless it was absolutely necessary. The tears broke over Amber's lower lids. She tried to sniff them back, and Penrod hurried on: 'Perhaps you and Jane could come out to Cairo to spend your sixteenth birthday at Shepheard's Hotel. Jane has never been there and you might show her the pyramids.'

'Oh, can we do that, Jane? Please?'

'I will speak to my husband,' Jane promised. She was about the same age as Rebecca, and in the few weeks that Amber had lived at Clercastle they had become as close as sisters. 'I can see no possible reason why Peter should object. It will be the height of the grouse-shooting season and he will be much occupied elsewhere. He will hardly miss us.'

*   *   *

Sam Adams came down from Cairo to meet Penrod when his ship docked in Alexandria. Almost his first words were 'We have all read the book. The sirdar is as pleased as a cat with a saucer of cream. London was starting to have second thoughts about rebuilding the army. Gladstone and those other idiots were dithering with the idea of using the money to build a bloody great dam on the Nile instead of giving it to us. Miss Benbrook's

336

book created such a rumpus in the House that they changed their dim minds sharpish. Kitchener has another million pounds, and to the devil with the dam. Now we will certainly have new Maxim guns. As for myself, well, we desperately need a good number two if we're to have any chance of retaining the Nile Cup this year.'

'After my brief meeting with the sirdar, I estimate that he is not likely to set aside much time for polo.'

Adams's wife had found and rented a comfortable house for Penrod on the bank of the river, close to army headquarters and the Gheziera Club. When Penrod climbed the steps to the shady veranda, a figure in a plain white *jibba* and turban rose from his seat beside the front door and made a deep salaam.

'Effendi, the heart of the faithful Yakub has pined for you as the night awaits the dawn.'

The next morning Penrod found out what Kitchener and Adams had in store for him. He was to recruit and train three companies of camel cavalry to travel far and fast, and fight hard. 'I want men from the desert tribes,' he told Adams. 'They make the best soldiers. Abdullahi has driven many of the Ashraf out of Sudan, emirs of the Jaalin and the Hadendowa. I want to go after them. Hatred makes a man fight harder. I believe I shall be able to turn them against their former masters.'

'Find them,' Adams ordered.

Penrod and Yakub took the steamer to Aswan. Here they waited thirty-six hours for the sailing of another boat that would carry them up beyond the first cataract, as far as Wadi Halfa. Penrod left Yakub at the dock to guard the baggage, and went alone to the gate at the end of the narrow, winding alley. When old Liala heard his voice she flung open the gate and collapsed in a heap of faded robes and veils, wailing pitifully. 'Effendi, why have you come back? You should have spared my mistress. You should never have returned here.'

Penrod lifted her to her feet. 'Take me to her.'

'She will not see you, Effendi.'

'She must tell me that herself. Go to her, Liala. Tell her I am here.' Sobbing pitifully, the old woman left him beside the fountain in the courtyard and tottered into the back quarters. She was gone a long time. Penrod picked tiny green flies from the flowering fuchsias and dropped them into the pool. The perch rose to the surface and gulped them down.

Liala returned at last. She had stopped weeping. 'She will see you.' She led him to the bead screen. 'Go in.'

Bakhita sat on a silk rug on the far side of the well-remembered room. He knew it was her by her perfume. She was heavily veiled. 'My heart fills with joy to see you safe and well, my lord.'

Her soft, sweet voice tugged at his heart. 'Without you, Bakhita, that would not have been possible. Yakub has told me of the part you played in bringing me to safety. I have come to thank you.'

'And the English girl's Arabic name is al-Zahra. I am told that she is young and very beautiful. Is that so, my lord?'

'It is so, Bakhita.' He was not surprised that she knew. Bakhita knew everything.

'Then she is the one we spoke of. The girl of your own people who will be your wife. I am happy for you.'

'We will still be friends, you and I.'

'Friends and more than that,' she said softly. 'Whenever there is something that you should know I will write to you.'

'I will come to see you.'

'Perhaps.'

'May I see your face once more before I go, Bakhita?'

'It would not be wise.'

He went to her and knelt in front of her. 'I want to see your lovely face again, to look into your eyes and to kiss your lips one last time.'

'I beg of you, lord of my heart, spare me this thing.'

He reached out and touched her veil. 'May I lift it?'

She was silent for a while. Then she sighed. 'Perhaps, after all, it would be easier this way,' she said.

He lifted the veil and stared at her. Slowly she watched the horror dawn in his eyes.

'Bakhita, oh, my dear heart, what has happened to you?' His voice trembled with pity.

'It was the smallpox. Allah has punished me for loving you.' The pockmarks were still fresh and livid. Her luminous eyes shone in the ruins of the face that had once been so lovely. 'Remember me as I once was,' she pleaded.

'I will remember only your courage and your kindness, and that you are my friend,' he whispered, and bent forward to kiss her lips.

'It is you who are kind,' she replied. Then she reached up and covered her face with the veil. 'Now you must leave me.'

He stood up. 'I shall return.'

'Perhaps you will, Effendi.'
But they both knew he never would.

*   *   *

The aggagiers found the corpse of Kabel al-Din lying in the courtyard beside the abandoned yoke of the *shebba*. Osman Atalan called all his men to horse and for many days they scoured both banks of the river. Osman was in a murderous mood when at last he returned to Omdurman without having found any trace of the fugitive. This was a bad time for the women to come to him and tell him that al-Zahra was also missing.

'How long has she been gone?' he demanded.

'Eight days, exalted Khalif.'

'The same time as Abadan Riji,' he exclaimed. 'What of the woman al-Jamal?'

'She is still in the *zenana*, mighty Atalan.'

'Bring her to me, and her servant also.'

They dragged in the two women and flung them at his feet.

'Where is your sister?'

'Lord, I do not know,' Rebecca replied.

Osman looked at al-Noor. 'Beat her,' he ordered. 'Beat her until she answers truthfully.'

'Mighty Khalif!' Nazeera cried. 'If you beat her she will lose your child. It may be a son. A son with golden hair like his mother and the lionheart of his sire.' Osman looked startled. He hesitated, staring at Rebecca's belly. Then he snarled at his aggagiers, 'Leave us. Do not return until I call you.'

They hurried out of the room, relieved to be sent away, for when a *khalif* and emir of the Beja is angry all men around him are in jeopardy.

340

'Disrobe,' he ordered. Rebecca rose to her feet and let her robe drop to her feet. Osman stared at her white, protruding belly. Then he went to her and placed his hand upon it.

Move! Please, my darling, move! Rebecca begged silently, and the foetus kicked.

Osman jerked away his hand and jumped back.

'In God's Name, it is alive.' He stared in awe at the bulge. 'Cover yourself!'

While Nazeera helped her to dress, Osman tugged furiously in his beard as he considered his dilemma. Suddenly he let out another angry shout and his aggagiers trooped back into the room. 'This woman.' He pointed at Nazeera. 'Beat her until al-Jamal tells us the whereabouts of her sister.'

Two of them held Nazeera's arms and Mooman Digna grabbed the cloth at the back of her neck and ripped it open to the knees. Al-Noor hefted the kurbash in his right hand. The first blow raised a red stripe across her shoulder-blades.

'Yi! Yi!' screeched Nazeera, and tried to throw herself flat, but the aggagiers held her.

'Yi!' she howled.

'Wait, Lord. I will tell you everything.' Rebecca could bear it no longer.

'Stop!' Osman ordered. 'Tell me.'

'A stranger came and led al-Zahra away,' Rebecca gabbled. 'I think they went north towards Metemma and Egypt, but I cannot be certain of it. Nazeera had nothing to do with this.'

'Why did you not go with them?'

'You are my master, and the father of my son,' Rebecca replied. 'I will leave you only when you kill me or send me away.'

'Beat the old whore again.' Osman waved to

assuage his fury without endangering the well-being of the son who might have blue eyes and golden hair.

Rebecca clutched her belly with both hands and cried, 'I can feel the distress of my son within me. If you beat this woman, who is as my own mother, I shall not be able to hold the boy longer in my womb.'

'Hold!' Osman shouted. He was torn. He wanted to see blood. He drew his sword and Nazeera quailed under his gaze. Then he rushed at the stone column in the centre of the room and struck it with such force that sparks showered from the steel.

'Take these two women to the mosque at the oasis of Gedda.' It was a lonely place run by a few old mullahs fifty leagues out in the desert, a religious retreat for the devout, and for students of the Noble Koran. 'If the child that al-Jamal brings forth is a female, kill all three of them. If it is a son, bring them back to me and make certain they remain alive, especially my son.'

*   *   *

Five months later, lying on a rug spread on the floor of her cell at Gedda, while Nazeera attended her and the mullahs waited at the door, Rebecca gave birth to her first child. As soon as she felt the slippery burden she had carried for so long rush out of her, she struggled up on her elbows. Nazeera held the infant in her arms, all shiny with blood and mucus, still bound to Rebecca by the thick cord.

'What is it?' Rebecca gasped. 'Is it a boy? Sweet God, let it be a boy.'

Nazeera cackled like a broody hen and presented the child for her inspection. 'This one is a little stallion.' With her forefinger she tickled the baby's tiny penis. 'See how hard he stands already. You could crack an egg on the end of it. Beware anyone in skirts who stands in this one's way.'

The mullahs of Gedda sent word to Omdurman, and within days twenty aggagiers headed by al-Noor came to escort them back to the Holy City. When they reached the gates of Osman Atalan's palace, he was waiting to meet them. During the past five months his fury had had time to abate. However, he was trying not to appear too benign, and stood with one hand on the hilt of his sword, scowling hideously.

Al-Noor dismounted and took the child from Rebecca's arms. He was wrapped in cotton swaddling clothes and his face was covered to protect him from the sunlight and the dust. 'Mighty Atalan, behold your son!'

Osman glared at al-Noor. 'This I must see for myself.'

He took the bundle and placed it in the crook of his left arm. With his right hand he unwrapped it. He stared at the tiny creature. His head was bald, except for a single copper-tinted quiff. His skin was the colour of goat's milk with a splash of coffee added to it. His eyes were the colour of the waters of the Bahr al-Azrek, the Blue Nile. Osman opened the lower folds of his covering, and his scowl slipped, hovered on the verge of a smile.

The infant felt the cool river breeze fan his genitals, and let fly a yellow stream that splashed down his father's brightly patched *jibba*.

Osman let forth a startled roar of laughter.

343

'Behold! This is my son. As he pisses on me, so he shall piss on my enemies.' He held the child high, and he said, 'This is my son, Ahmed Habib abd Atalan. Approach and show him respect.' One after another his aggagiers came forward and, with a full salaam, greeted Ahmed, who kicked and gurgled with amusement. Osman had not glanced in the direction of the two waiting women, but now he handed the infant to al-Noor, and said offhandedly, 'Give the child to his mother, and tell her that she will return to her quarters in the harem, and there await my pleasure.'

Over the following eighteen months Rebecca saw Osman only three or four times, and then at a distance as he came and went on affairs of war and state. Whenever he returned he would send al-Noor to fetch Ahmed, and would keep the child away for hours on end, until it was time for him to be fed.

The child flourished. Rebecca fancied that she saw in him a resemblance to her own father, and to Amber, which made her loneliness more acute. She had only Nazeera and the baby: the other women of the harem were silly, scatter-brained creatures. She missed her sisters, and thought of them when she awoke to another empty day, and when she composed herself to sleep with Ahmed at her bosom.

Then, slowly, she became aware that she wanted Osman Atalan to send for her. Her body had recovered from the damage of childbirth, except for the stretchmarks across her belly and the soft sag of her breasts. Sometimes when she awoke in the night and could not sleep again she thought of the men she had known, but her mind returned variably to Osman. She needed somebody to talk to, somebody to be with, somebody to make love to her, and nobody had done that with the same skill as Osman Atalan.

Then the rumour in the harem was that there was to be a great new *jihad*, a war against the Christian infidels of Abyssinia. Osman Atalan would lead the army, and Allah would go with him. Ahmed was now toddling and talking. She hoped that Osman would take them with him. She remembered how it had been at Gallabat when she had conceived. She thought about that a great deal. She had vivid dreams about it, of how he had looked and how he had felt inside her. Her loneliness was an ache deep within her. She devoted herself entirely to the child, but the nights were long.

Then the news ran through the harem. Osman was taking three wives and eight concubines with him to the *jihad*; Rebecca was chosen as one of the eight. Ahmed and Nazeera would go with her, but none of Osman's other children. She understood that he was interested solely in the child, and that she and Nazeera were merely Ahmed's nursemaids. Her empty body ached.

They rode to the Abyssinian border forty thousand strong, a mighty warlike array. Osman left Rebecca and his other women at Gallabat. He rushed into Abyssinia and struck with all his cavalry at the passes.

The Abyssinians were also a warlike nation, and warriors to the blood. Although they had been alerted by Ryder Courtney's warning, even they could not stand before the ferocity of Osman Atalan's attack. He drove hard for the mountain

345

passes at Minkti and Atbara, and seized them against desperate and courageous resistance. He slaughtered all the Abyssinian prisoners that he took, and led his army into the Minkti pass. They toiled up through bitter cold.

Ras Adal, the Abyssinian general, had not expected them to come so high and he made the mistake of allowing them to debouch unopposed on to the plain of Debra Sin before he attacked them.

The battle was fierce and bloody, but at last Ras Adal broke before the savagery of Osman's assault. He and all his army were driven into the river at their backs and most of them drowned. The entire province of Amhara fell to Osman, and he was able to advance unopposed to capture Gondar, the ancient capital of Abyssinia.

Gondar was the city in which Osman intended to set up his own capital, but he had never experienced a winter in the Abyssinian highlands. His Beja were men of the sands and deserts: they shivered, sickened and died. Osman abandoned his conquests, sacked and burned Gondar and led his men back to Gallabat. He arrived on a litter, drawn by his own warhorse, al-Buq. The cold of the mountains had entered his lungs and he was a sick man. They laid him on his *angareb* and waited for him to die.

Osman wheezed for breath. He choked and hawked and spat up slugs of greenish-yellow phlegm, 'Send for al-Jamal,' he ordered.

Rebecca came to his bedside and nursed him. She dosed him with a brew of selected herbs and roots that Nazeera prepared, and sweated him with hot stones. When his crisis came she brought

Ahmed to him. 'You cannot die, mighty Atalan. Your son needs his father.'

It took several weeks, but at last Osman was on the road to recovery. During his convalescence he sent for Rebecca on most evenings and resumed the long conversations with her as though they had never ceased. Rebecca was lonely no more.

As he grew stronger, he made love to her again, possessing her masterfully and completely, filling the aching emptiness deep inside her. He declared Ahmed his heir and, in the unpredictable fashion in which he often did things, sent for the mullah and made Rebecca his wife.

It was only when she lay beside him on the first night as his wife that she could bring herself to face the truth squarely. He had made her his slave, in body and in heart. He had snuffed out the last spark of her once indomitable spirit. The suffering he inflicted upon her so casually had become a drug that she could not live without. In a bizarre and unnatural way he had forced her to love him. She knew she could never be without him now.

*   *   *

Emperor John and all his subjects were infuriated by the capture of the province of Amhara and the sack of Gondar. With an army of more than a hundred thousand behind him he came down upon Gallabat to take his revenge. He sent a warning to Osman Atalan that he was coming, so he might not be seen as a sneaking coward. Osman decapitated his messenger and sent the man's head back to him.

Heavily outnumbered, Osman transformed the

347

town into a huge defensive zareba. He placed the women and children in the centre, and stood to meet the Abyssinian fury. It burst upon him. Al-Noor's division of four thousand men was almost wiped out, and al-Noor himself was gravely wounded. The exultant Abyssinians broke into the centre of the *zareba* where the women were, and the rape and slaughter began.

When Osman realized the day was lost, he leapt on to al-Buq, and spurred him forward, going for the head of the serpent. The Emperor had once been a legendary warrior, but he was a young man no longer. In his leopardskins, bronze cuirassier and the gold crown of the Negus on his head, he was tall and regal but his beard was more silver than black. He drew his sword when he saw Osman charging at him through the carnage. The Dervish commander cut down the bodyguard that tried to interpose themselves. He had learnt from Penrod Ballantyne, and he never took his eye from the Emperor's blade. His riposte was like a bolt of silver lightning.

'The Emperor is dead. The Negus has gone!' The cry went up from the Abyssinian host. The moment of complete victory had been transformed into defeat and rout by a single stroke of Osman Atalan's long blade.

Osman rode back to Omdurman with the heads of Emperor John and his generals carried on the lances of his bodyguard. They planted them at the entrance to Khalifat Abdullahi's palace.

Seven months later Rebecca gave birth to her second child, a girl. Osman was not sufficiently interested in a female to bother himself with a name for her. Rebecca named her Kahruba, which in Arabic means Amber. After some months Osman forgave her for bearing a girl, and resumed their nightly conversations and lovemaking. When Kahruba turned into a pretty little thing with smoked-honey hair, he sometimes stroked her head. Once he even took her up on the front of his saddle and ran al-Buq at full gallop. Kahruba squealed with glee, which caused Osman to remark as he handed her back to Rebecca, 'You erred grievously, wife. You should have made her a boy, for she has the heart of one.'

None of his other daughters received any sign of his affection. They were not allowed to speak to him, or to touch him. When Kahruba was six years old, at the feast of Kurban Bairam, she left the women and, with one finger in her mouth, she went to where Osman sat among his aggagiers. He watched her coldly as she approached. Undeterred she scrambled on to his lap.

Osman was flabbergasted. His aggagiers had difficulty in maintaining their sober expressions. Osman scowled at them as though daring any to laugh. Then he deliberately selected a sweetmeat from the bowl in front of him and placed it in the child's mouth. She retaliated by throwing both arms round his neck. However, this was going too far. Osman replaced her on the ground and slapped her little bottom. 'Be off with you, you shameless vixen!' he said.

*   *   *

Mr Hiram Steven Maxim sat on a low stool in the brilliant sunshine of the Nile delta. In front of him on a steel tripod was an ungainly-looking weapon with a thick water-jacketed barrel. On his left side stood a five-gallon water can, connected to the weapon by a sturdy rubber hose. At his right hand dozens of wooden crates of ammunition were piled high. His three assistants hovered about him. Despite the heat they wore thick tweed jackets and flat cloth caps. Mr Maxim had stripped down to his shirtsleeves, and his bowler hat was pushed to the back of his head. Since he had come from America to settle in England, he had adopted British ways and dress.

Now he rolled the unlit cigar from one side of his jaw to the other. 'Major Ballantyne,' he sang out. His accent still proclaimed that he had been born in Sangerville, Maine. 'Would you be good enough to note the time?' At a short distance behind him was a small group of uniformed officers. In the front rank stood the sirdar, General Horatio Herbert Kitchener, a stocky, powerful figure flanked by his staff.

'General, sir?' Penrod glanced at Kitchener for permission to reply.

'Carry on, Ballantyne.' Kitchener nodded.

'Time mark!' Penrod called out. Six hundred yards ahead of the machine-gun, at the foot of a high dun-coloured sand dune, was a line of fifty wooden models of the human form. They were dressed in Dervish *jibbas* and carried wooden spears. Mr Maxim leant forward and took hold of the firing handles. By squeezing the finger-grips he lifted the safety catch off the firing button.

'Commencing firing, now!' He thrust his thumbs down on the trigger button. The gun shuddered and roared. The separate shots were too rapid for the ear to distinguish. It was a prolonged thunder like a high waterfall in spate. The recoil of each shot kicked back the mechanism, and ejected the spent cartridge cases in a blur of glittering bronze. The forward stroke of the action reloaded the chamber, cocked and fired. It was too fast for the eye to follow the sequence.

Mr Maxim traversed the barrel. One after another the wooden figures exploded in a storm of splinters. The sands of the dune behind the targets boiled into sheets of dust. He reached the end of the line and traversed back again. The shattered remains of the targets hung from their frames. The returning torrent of bullets blew them to fragments.

The British officers watched in awed silence. The roar of the gun numbed their eardrums. They could not speak. They did not move. Mr Maxim's assistants had performed this demonstration numerous times and in many countries. They had been drilled to perfection. As one of the ammunition boxes emptied it was dragged away and a full one substituted. A fresh belt of ammunition was hitched to the end of the previous belt as it was sucked into the breech. There was no check, no jamming of the action, no diminution in the rate of fire. The water in the cooling jacket boiled, but the powerful emission of steam was drawn away through the pliable hose into the can of cold water. It was cooled and condensed. There was no steam cloud to betray the position of the gun to the enemy. The cooled water was recycled through the barrel jacket. The clamour of the gun continued without check. The final belt of ammunition was fed through the breech, and only when the last empty cartridge case was flung clear did silence fall.

'Time check,' Mr Maxim shouted.

'Three minutes and ten seconds.'

'Two thousand rounds in three minutes,' Mr Maxim announced proudly. 'Almost seven hundred rounds a minute, without a stoppage.'

'No stoppage,' Colonel Adams repeated. 'This is the end of cavalry as we know it.'

'It changes the face of warfare,' Penrod agreed. 'Just look at the accuracy.' He pointed to the row of targets. Splinters were spread over a wide area. Not even the poles that had supported the targets still stood upright. A thick cloud of dun-coloured dust kicked up by the stream of bullets hung in the air above the dunes.

'Now let the Dervish come!' murmured the sirdar, and his dark moustache seemed to stand erect, like the bristles on the back of an enraged wild boar.

Penrod and Adams rode back to Cairo together. They were both in high spirits, and when a jackal broke from the scrub at the side of the track they drew their sabres and rode it down. Penrod spurted ahead and turned back the drab terrier-like creature. Adams leant low out of the saddle and ran it through between the shoulders, then let its weight swing his blade back until the carcass slipped from the blade, rolled in the dust and at last lay still. 'Beats pig-sticking in the Punjab.' He laughed. When they reached the gates of the Gheziera Club, he said, 'Do you care for a peg?'

'Not this evening,' replied Penrod. 'I have guests from home to entertain.'

'Ah, yes! So I have heard. What does Miss Amber Benbrook think of your new pips?'

Penrod glanced down at the shiny new major's crowns on his epaulettes.

'If you remember her name, you must have received the invitation to the ball. It is her sixteenth birthday, you know. Will you be attending?'

'The remarkable young lady who wrote *Slaves of the Mahdi*?' Adams exclaimed. 'I would not miss it for the world. My wife would assassinate me if I so much as contemplated the idea.'

*   *   *

Amber's birthday ball was held at Shepheard's Hotel. The band of the new Egyptian army played until dawn. White-robed waiters served silver trays of brimming champagne glasses. Every commissioned officer of the army from the rank of ensign upwards, a hundred and fifteen in all, had accepted the invitation to attend. Their smart new dress uniforms made a handsome foil to the ballgowns of the ladies. Even the sirdar and Sir Evelyn Baring made a brief appearance, and each danced a Vienna waltz with Amber. They both left early, aware that their presence had an inhibiting effect on the festivities.

Ryder and Saffron had made the long circuitous journey down from the highlands of Abyssinia, across the desert by camel, up the Red Sea and through the Suez Canal to Alexandria to be there. Saffron's evening dress caused a mild sensation, even in this glittering company. She was two months pregnant, but of course that was not yet apparent.

At the beginning of the evening, after he had collected Amber and his sister-in-law Jane from the suite they were sharing on the top floor of the hotel, Penrod filled in Amber's dance card. He reserved fifteen of her twenty dances. She was a little peeved that he had been so restrained. At the stroke of midnight the band broke into a rousing rendition of 'For She's a Jolly Good Fellow'. The guests applauded wildly. The champagne flowed like the Nile, and everybody was in jovial, expansive mood.

Penrod climbed the bandstand with Amber on his arm. The band welcomed them with a long drumroll, and Penrod held up his hands for silence. He was only partially successful in achieving it while he proposed the birthday toast. They drank it with gusto, and Ryder Courtney burst into 'When You Were Sweet Sixteen'. The band and the rest of the guests picked up the tune. Amber blushed and clung to Penrod's arm.

At the end of the song he quietened them again. 'I have another announcement to make. Thank you!' The uproar subsided to a buzz of interest. 'My lords, ladies, and fellow officers, who fall into neither of the first two categories!' They hooted, and again he had to bring them to order. 'It gives me ineffable pleasure to inform you that Miss Amber Benbrook has consented to become my wife, and in so doing she has made me the happiest man in creation.'

A little later Colonel Sam Adams was smoking a quiet cigarette on the darkened terrace when he overheard the conversation of two young subalterns who had imbibed copious quantities of champagne.

'They say she has made herself a flash hundred thousand iron men from the book. Happiest man in creation? Ballantyne has that great gong stuck on his chest, pips on his shoulders, his own battalion, and to top it all the lucky blighter has dug himself a gold mine with his pork shovel. Why shouldn't he be happy?'

'Lieutenant Stuttaford.' A cold, familiar voice spoke from the shadows close at hand.

Pale with shock, Stuttaford came unsteadily to attention. 'Colonel Adams, sir!'

'Kindly present yourself at my office at ten o'clock tomorrow morning.'

By noon the next day Lieutenant Stuttaford, still suffering from a vile hangover, found himself packing for immediate departure to the desert outpost at Suakin, one of the most desolate and dreary postings in the Empire.

*   *   *

'The Egyptian army has always been considered a music-hall turn, the Gilbert and Sullivan opera of the Nile. The standing army at home, and those in the Indian Service snigger when they speak our name,' Penrod told the other members of the party. He and Ryder lolled against the transom of the felucca. Jane Ballantyne, Saffron and Amber sat on gaily-coloured cushions on the deck. They were sailing upstream in the hired felucca to climb to the summit of the pyramid of Cheops at Giza, and afterwards to picnic in the shadow of the Sphinx.

'How vulgar and silly of them.' Amber came immediately to his defence.

'In all truth they had good reason at one time,' Penrod admitted, 'but that was the old army, in the bad old days. Now the men are paid. The officers do not steal their rations, and turn tail and run at the first shot. The men are not beaten when they fall sick, but are sent to the doctor and the hospital. All of you must come to the review on Monday. You will see some parading and drilling that will astonish you.'

'My father was a colonel in the Black Watch, as you know, Penrod,' said Jane. 'I cannot claim to be a great expert, but I have read something of military affairs. Papa saw to that. As soon as we knew that we were coming to Cairo, Amber and I read every book about Egypt on the shelves of the library at Clercastle, as well as Sir Alfred Milner's excellent *England in Egypt*. Nowhere have I heard it suggested that the Egyptian *fellahin* are good soldierly material.'

'What you say is true. It was always unlikely that the rich and fertile delta, with its enervating climate, would produce warriors. The *fellahin* may be cruel and callous, but they are not fierce and bloodthirsty. On the other hand, they are stoic and strong. They meet pain and hardship with indifference. Theirs is a kind of docile courage that we more warlike peoples can only admire. They are obedient and honest, quick to learn and, above all, strong. What they lack in nerve they make up for in muscle.'

'Pen darling, that is all well and good about the Egyptians but tell us about your Arabs,' Amber interjected.

'Ah, but you know them well, my heart.' Penrod smiled tenderly at her. 'If the Egyptian *fellahin* are mastiffs, then the Arabs are Jack Russell terriers. They are intelligent and quick. They are venal and excitable. They do not lend themselves willingly to

356

discipline. You can never trust them entirely, but their courage is daunting. At Abu Klea they came against the square as if they gloried in death. If they give you their loyalty, and they seldom do, it is a link of steel that binds them to you. War is their way of life. They are warriors, and I respect them. Some I have learnt to love. Yakub is one of those.'

'Nazeera is another,' Amber agreed.

'Oh, I wonder what has become of her, and of our dear sister Rebecca.' Saffron shook her head sorrowfully. 'I dream of her most nights. Is there nobody in Military Intelligence who can discover this for us?'

'Believe me, I have tried diligently to find news of Rebecca. However, the Sudan is closed off from the world, as though in a steel casket. It slumbers in its own nightmare. Would that one day we have the will and the way to end the horror and set her people free. Rebecca is the first of those we would liberate.'

*   *   *

Rebecca sat with the other wives in the cloister of the inner courtyard of the palace of Osman Atalan. It was the cool of the evening and Osman was demonstrating to his followers the courage of his blue-eyed son. For many months Rebecca had known that her son faced this ordeal. She covered her face with her veil so that none of the other women would know of her fear.

Only three months previously Ahmed Habib abd Atalan had been circumcised. Rebecca had wept as she dressed his mutilated penis, but Nazeera had rebuked her: 'Ahmed is a man now. Be proud for

357

him, al-Jamal. Your tears will unman him.'

Now Ahmed stood before his father, trying to be brave. His head was bare and his fists were clenched at his side.

'Open your eyes, my son.' Osman's voice crackled. He tossed his sword into the air and it spun like a cartwheel before the hilt dropped back into his hand. 'Open your eyes. I want Allah and all the world to know that you are a man. I want you to show me, your father, your courage.'

Ahmed opened his eyes. They were no longer milky, but a dark blue like the African sky when stormclouds gather. His lower lip quivered and tiny droplets of perspiration dewed the upper. Osman flourished the long blade and cut at the side of his head with such force that the steel hummed in the air. The stroke could have bisected a grown man at the trunk. It swept past Ahmed's temple. His unruly coppery hair fluttered in the wind of its passage. The watching aggagiers growled with admiration. Ahmed swayed on his feet.

'You are my son,' Osman whispered. 'Hold fast!' He stroked the tip of his son's ear with the flat of the blade. Ahmed shrank away from the cool touch of steel.

'Do not move,' Osman warned him, 'Or I will cut it off.'

Ahmed leant forward and vomited on the ground at his feet.

An expression of contempt and shame crossed Osman's face, and was smoothed away immediately. 'Go back to your mother,' he said softly.

Ahmed tried to choke back his sobs. 'I do not feel well,' he murmured hopelessly, and wiped his mouth on the back of his hand.

Osman stepped back and glared at him. 'Go and sit with the women,' he ordered.

Ahmed ran to his mother and buried his face in Rebecca's skirt.

A tense silence held the watchers. Nobody spoke and nobody moved. They were barely able to draw breath. Osman was turning away when a small, delicate figure rose to her feet from among the ranks of seated women. Rebecca tried to hold her back, but Kahruba pushed away her hand and went to her father. He grounded the point of his blade and watched her stop in front of him. He studied her face, then demanded ominously, 'What disrespect is this? Why do you pester me so?'

'My father, I want to show you and Allah my courage,' said the child. She removed her headcloth and shook out her tawny hair.

'Go back to your mother. This is no childish game.'

'Exalted father, I do not wish to play games.' She looked straight into his eyes.

He raised the sword and stepped towards her, like a leopard stalking a gazelle. She stood her ground. Suddenly he cut, forehanded, at her face. The blade flashed inches from her eyes. She blinked, but stood like a statue.

He cut again, backhanded. A curl dropped from the loose mop of her hair, and floated to the ground at her bare feet. Behind her Rebecca cried out, 'Oh, my darling!'

Kahruba ignored her, and held her father's eyes steadfastly.

'You provoke me,' he said, and slowly traced the outline of her body with the blade. Never further than a finger's breadth from her flesh, the scalpel-sharp edge moved up from the outside of one knee, over her thigh, round the curve of her hip, along her arm and shoulder to the side of her neck. He touched her and she closed her eyes, then opened them as she felt the steel on her cheek. It moved up over the top of her head and down again to her other knee. She did not flinch.

Osman narrowed his eyes and brought the blade back along the same route, but faster, and then again, even faster. The steel dissolved into a silver blur. It danced in front of the child's eyes like a dragonfly. It hummed and whispered in her ears as it passed close to her tender skin. Rebecca was weeping silently, and Nazeera held her hand hard, but she, too, was close to tears. 'Do not make a sound,' she whispered. 'If Kahruba moves, she is dead.'

The dancing blade held Kahruba in a cage of light. Then, abruptly, it stopped, pointing at her right eye from the distance of an inch. The point advanced slowly, until it touched her lower lashes. The child blinked but did not pull away.

'Enough!' said Osman, and stepped back. He threw the sword to al-Noor, who snatched it out of the air. Then Osman stooped and picked up his daughter. He held her close to his chest, and looked around at their taut expressions. 'In this one, at least, my blood has bred true,' he told them. Then he tossed her high in the air, caught her as she fell back and carried her to Rebecca. 'Breed me another like this one,' he ordered, 'but, wife, this time make certain it is a boy.'

Later that evening Rebecca lay sprawled on his *angareb*. She still felt devastated by the events

360

of the day and by the controlled fury of his lovemaking, which had ended only minutes before. She had watched her daughter come close to death under the dancing silver blade, while she herself seemed to have come even closer.

She was stark naked, a vessel overflowing with his fresh seed, aching pleasurably where he had been deep inside her. The lovemaking had rendered her *harom*, unclean in the eyes of God. She should cover herself, or go immediately to bathe and cleanse her body, but she felt languorous and wanton. She opened her eyes and found that he had come back from the bedroom window and was standing over her. He was still half erect, his glans glistening with the juices of her body. As she studied him she felt herself becoming aroused once more. She knew, with sure feminine instinct, that he had just impregnated her again, and that she would be forced to many months of abstinence until she was delivered of the infant. She wanted him, but saw that now his seed was spent his restless mind had moved on to other concerns.

'There is aught that troubles you, my husband.' She sat up and covered herself with the light bedcloth.

'We spoke once of the steamer that runs on land, that travels on ribbons of steel,' he said.

'I recall that, my lord, but it was many years ago.'

'I wish to discuss this machine again. What was the name you gave it?'

'Railway engine,' she enunciated slowly and clearly.

He imitated her, but he lisped and garbled the sounds. He saw in her eyes that he had not succeeded. 'It is too difficult, this language of yours.' He shook his head angrily, hating to fail in anything he attempted. 'I shall call it the land steamer.'

'I shall understand what you mean. It is a better name than mine, more powerful and descriptive.' At times he was like a small boy and must be jollied along.

'How many men can travel upon this machine. Ten? Twenty? Surely not fifty?' he asked hopefully.

'If the land over which it passes is levelled it can carry many hundreds of men, perhaps as many as a thousand, perhaps many thousands.'

Osman looked alarmed. 'How far can this thing travel?'

'To the end of its lines.'

'But surely it cannot cross a great river like the Atbara? It must stop there.'

'It can, my lord.'

'I do not believe it. The Atbara is deep and wide. How is that possible?'

'They have men they call engineers who have the skills to build a bridge over it.'

'The Atbara? They cannot build over a river so wide.' He was trying desperately to convince himself. 'Where will they find tree trunks long and strong enough to span the Atbara?'

'They will make the bridge of steel, like the rails it runs upon. Like the blade of your sword,' Rebecca explained. 'But why do you ask these questions, my husband?'

'My spies in the north have sent a message that these God-cursed Englishmen have begun to lay these steel ribbons from Wadi Halfa south across the great bight of the river, towards Metemma and the Atbara.' Then, suddenly, his temper flared.

362

'They are devils, these infidel tribesmen of yours,' he shouted.

'They are no longer my tribesmen, exalted husband. Now I am of your tribe and no other.'

His anger subsided as suddenly as it had arisen.

'I am leaving at dawn tomorrow to go to the north and see this monstrosity with my own eyes,' he told her.

She dropped her eyes sadly: she would be alone again. Without him she was incomplete.

*   *   *

The year 1895 dawned and events were put in train that would change the history and face of Africa. British South Africa's conquests were consolidated under the new nation of Rhodesia, and almost immediately the predatory men who had brought it into existence attacked the Boer nation of the Transvaal, their neighbours to the south. It was a puny invasion under Dr Starr Jamieson that was immediately dubbed the Jamieson Raid. They had been promised support by their countrymen on the Witwatersrand goldfields, which never materialized, and the tiny band of aggressors capitulated to the Boers without firing a shot. However, the raid presaged the conflict between Boer and Briton that, only a few years later, would cost hundreds of thousands of lives, before the Transvaal and its fabulously rich goldfields came under the sway of Empire.

In England the Liberal Party of Gladstone and Lord Rosebery was ousted by a Conservative and Unionist administration under the Marquess of Salisbury. In opposition they had always been vociferously opposed to Gladstone's Egyptian policies. Now they had a massive majority in the House of Commons, and were in a position to change the direction of affairs in that crucial corner of the African continent.

The nation still smarted from the humiliation of Khartoum and the murder of General Gordon. Books such as *Slaves of the Mahdi* had set the mood for exonerating Gordon of shame. In the new Egypt, which was now virtually a colony of Great Britain, the tool was at hand in the shape of the new Egyptian army, reorganized, trained and equipped as no army in Africa before. The man to lead it was already at its helm in the person of Horatio Herbert Kitchener. Great Britain contemplated the prospect of repossessing the Sudan with increasing pleasure and enthusiasm.

By the beginning of 1896 Britain was ready to act. It needed only a spark to set off the conflagration. On 2 March, at the battle of Adowa, the Abyssinians inflicted a crushing defeat on Italy. Another European power had been thrashed by an African kingdom. This sent a clarion call to all colonial possessions. Almost immediately the gloomy forebodings of rebellion were fulfilled. The Dervish Khalifat Abdullahi threatened Kassala and raided Wadi Halfa. Reports reached Cairo of the gathering of a great Dervish army in Omdurman. Added to this, the French made covert hostile moves towards British possessions in Africa, especially in southern Sudan.

Thus a number of concurrent events had cast Great Britain in the role of far-seeing saviour of the world from anarchy, the avenger of Khartoum and Gordon, the protector of the Egyptian state.

364

The honour and pride of the Empire must be preserved.

The order went out from London to General Kitchener. He was to recapture the Sudan. He was to do it swiftly and, above all, cheaply. The attempts to rescue Gordon and destroy the Mahdi had cost Britain thirteen million pounds: defeat is always more costly than victory. Kitchener was allowed a little over one million pounds to succeed in the job that, thirteen years before, had been botched.

Kitchener summoned his senior officers and told them the momentous news. They were ecstatic. This was the culmination of years of gruelling training and desert skirmishes, and the laurels were at last within their reach. 'There will be more sweat and blisters than glory,' the sirdar cautioned them. Never one to seek popularity, he preferred to be feared rather than liked. 'From the twenty-second to the sixteenth parallel of north latitude we are faced with waterless desert. We will go to capture the Nile, but we cannot use that river as a means of access. The cataracts stand in our way. The only route open to us is the railway we will build to carry us overland into battle. We can use the river only in the final stage of our advance.' He regarded them with his cold misanthropic stare. 'There are no mountains to cross, the desert is level and good going. It will not be a matter so much of engineering technique as of hard work. We will not rely on private contractors. Our own engineers will do the job.'

'What about the Atbara river, sir? At its confluence with the Nile it is almost a thousand yards wide,' said Colonel Sam Adams.

'I have already called for tenders to supply the components for a bridge to be manufactured in sections that can be taken up on the railway trucks. Another call for tenders will soon be going out for the supply of steel-hulled river gunboats. They will be sent up by rail to the clear water above the fifth cataract. There, they will be reassembled and launched.'

The Egyptian officer corps was immediately plunged into a hurly-burly of planning and action.

*   *   *

There was only one respect in which the times and circumstances were not propitious. The delta of Egypt had been the bread basket of the Mediterranean since the time of Julius Caesar and Jesus Christ. For the first time in a hundred years the abundant fertility of its black alluvial soils had failed. The production of wheat and dhurra had fallen short of the needs of the civilian population, let alone those of a great expeditionary army.

'We are short of at least five thousand tons of the flour needed for the primary stage of the campaign,' the quartermaster general told the sirdar. 'After the first three months, we will require an additional fifteen hundred tons per month for the duration of hostilities.'

Kitchener frowned. Bread, the staple of any modern army—made from wholesome clean grain, and not too much hard biscuit—ensured the health of the troops. Now they were telling him that he did not have it.

'Come back tomorrow,' he told his quartermaster.

He went immediately to see Sir Evelyn Baring at the British Agency—it would have been political suicide for anybody to call it Government House, but that was what it was. Baring had championed Kitchener's appointment to commander-in-chief above the claims of better qualified men. Although they were not friends, they thought alike. Baring listened, then said, 'I think I know the man who can get your bread for you. He provisioned Gordon in Khartoum during the siege. Most fortuitously, he is in Cairo at this very moment.'

Within two hours a mystified Ryder Courtney found himself under Kitchener's reptilian stare.

'Can you do it?' Kitchener asked.

Ryder's business instincts clicked into place. 'Yes, I can. However, I will need four per cent commission for myself, General.'

'That is known as profiteering, Mr Courtney. I can offer you two and a half.'

'That is known as highway robbery, General,' Ryder replied.

Kitchener blinked. He was unaccustomed to being addressed in that fashion.

Ryder went on smoothly, 'However, in the name of patriotism I will accept your offer. On the condition that the army provides a suitable home in Cairo for me and my family, in addition to a stipend of two hundred pounds a month to cover my immediate expenses.'

Ryder rode back to Penrod's riverside home where he and Saffron had been guests since their arrival in Cairo. He was in jubilant mood. Saffron had been agitating: rather than return to Abyssinia, she wanted to remain in this civilized, salubrious city, where she could be close to Amber. When

Saffron agitated it was much like living on the slopes of an active volcano. Now her power to persuade was even more formidable than usual as she was pregnant again. Ryder had seen no good commercial sense in setting up business in Egypt, but Herbert Kitchener had just changed that.

Ryder left his horse with the groom in the stables and went down to the lawns above the riverbank. Jane Ballantyne, Amber and Saffron were taking tea in the summer-house. They were rereading and animatedly discussing the letter from Sebastian Hardy, which had arrived on the mail ship from England and had been delivered to Amber's suite at Shepheard's Hotel that morning.

Mr Hardy took great pleasure in informing Miss Amber Benbrook of the recent resuscitation of public interest in her book *Slaves of the Mahdi*, owing to the prospect of war against the evil Dervish Empire in Omdurman. The amounts paid by Macmillan Publishers in respect of royalties earned over the past three months amounted to £56,483 10*s*. 6*d*. In addition, Mr Hardy begged to inform her and the other beneficiaries that the investments he had made on behalf of the Benbrook family trust had been most favourably affected by the same considerations as the book. He had placed large sums in the common stock of the Vickers Company, which had purchased Mr Maxim's patent in his machine-gun. This investment had almost doubled in value. The value of assets of the trust now amounted to a little over three hundred thousand pounds. In addition Macmillan were eager to publish Amber's new manuscript, provisionally entitled *African Dreams and Nightmares*.

Ryder strode down the lawns, but the twins were so excited by Mr Hardy's good tidings that they were oblivious to his presence until his shadow fell over the tea-table. They looked up. 'What is all this laughter and high jinks?' he demanded. 'You know I cannot bear to see anybody having so much fun.'

Saffron jumped to her feet, a little ungainly under her maternal burden, and stood on tiptoe to embrace him. 'You will never guess what,' she whispered in his ear. 'You are married to a rich woman.'

'Indeed, I am married to a rich woman who resides permanently in Cairo, in a house paid for by General Kitchener and the Egyptian army.'

She leant back, holding him at arm's length, and stared at him in astonishment and delight. 'If this is another of your atrocious jokes, Ryder Courtney, I will . . .' She searched for a suitable threat. 'I will throw you into the Nile.'

He grinned complacently. 'Too early for a swim. Besides, you and I cannot waste precious time. We have to go hunting for our new home.'

He would tell her later that he must leave within days for the United States and Canada to negotiate for the purchase of twenty thousand tons of wheat. It was not the ideal time to break such news to a pregnant wife. At least she will have enough to keep her fully occupied in my absence. He had learnt by hard experience that when she was bored Saffron was more difficult to handle than the entire Dervish army.

*   *   *

The ground shook to the thunder of hoofs. Eight

369

horsemen raced each other down the long green field. The spectators shrieked and roared. The atmosphere was feverish and electric. Once again the Nile Cup and the honour of the Army polo team were at stake.

The white ball rolled over the uneven turf. Colonel Adams overhauled it swiftly, and leant low out of the saddle, mallet poised. His bay mare was as adept as her rider. She turned in neatly behind the bouncing ball, placing him in the perfect position to make the crossing shot. Mallet and ball met with a crisp thwack, and the ball sailed in a high arc over the heads of the opposing team, dropping directly in the path of Penrod's charging grey gelding. Penrod picked it up on the first bounce after it struck earth. He tapped it ahead, and his nimble pony chased after it, like a whippet behind a rabbit. Tap and tap again—the ball skipped towards the goalposts at the far end of the field. The other riders pursued the grey, their heels hammering into the ribs of their mounts, shouting and pumping the reins for greater speed, but they were unable to catch Penrod. He ran the ball between the posts, and the umpires waved their flags to signal a goal and the end of the match. Once again, the army had retained the Nile Cup against all comers.

Penrod rode back to the pony lines. Under her parasol, Amber was waiting for him. She watched him with pride and devotion. He was marvellously handsome and tanned, although there were crow's feet at the corners of his eyes from squinting into the desert glare. His body was lean and hard, tempered by years of hard riding and still harder fighting. He was no longer a youth, but a man

370

approaching his prime. He swung one booted leg over the pony's withers and dropped to the ground, landing like a cat. The grey trotted on to meet his grooms: he could smell the bucket of water and the bag of dhurra meal they had ready for him.

Amber ran to Penrod, and threw herself against his chest. 'I am so proud of you.'

'Then let's get married,' Penrod said, and kissed her.

She made the kiss endure, but when at last she must relinquish his lips, she laughed at him. 'We are getting married, you silly old thing, or have you forgotten?'

'I mean now. Immediately. At once. Not next year. We've waited far too long.'

She stared at him. 'You jest!' she accused him.

'Never been more serious in my life. In ten days I am away again into the desert. We have a spot of business to take care of in Omdurman. Let us be married before I go.'

They were swept up in the feverish madness of war when custom and convention no longer counted. Amber did not hesitate. 'Yes!' she said, and kissed him again. She had Saffron and Jane to help her with the arrangements. 'Yes! Oh, yes, please!'

*   *   *

Every pew in the cathedral was filled. They held the reception at the Gheziera Club. Sir Evelyn Baring placed the Agency houseboat at their disposal for the honeymoon.

They cruised upriver as far as Giza. In the evening they drank champagne and danced on

371

the deck, while before them rose the silhouette of the pyramids backlit by the sunset. Later, in the great stern cabin on the wide bed with green silk covers, Penrod led her gently along enchanted pathways to a mountain peak of whose existence she had only dreamed. He was a wonderful guide, patient and skilled, and experienced, oh, so very experienced.

*   *   *

Penrod left Amber in the care of Saffron and Jane, and took the steamer south to Aswan and Wadi Halfa to rejoin his regiment.

He found Yakub waiting for him at the river landing, wearing his new khaki uniform with panache. He stamped his feet as he saluted, his grin was infectious, and one eye rolled sideways. Yakub, the outcast, had a home at last. He wore the chevrons of a sergeant on the sleeve of the uniform of the Camel Corps of the Egyptian army. His turban had been replaced with a peaked cap and neck flap. He was still becoming accustomed to breeches and puttees rather than a long *galabiyya* so his stance was slightly bowlegged. 'Effendi, the peerless and faithful Sergeant Yakub looks upon your face with the same awe and devotion that the moon feels towards the sun.'

'My bags are in the cabin, O faithful and peerless one.'

They rode southwards on one of the flat-bed track-laying bogies of the new railway. The smoke from the engine stack blew back over them. The soot darkened Penrod's tanned skin and even Yakub turned a deeper brown while dust and sparks stung their eyes. At last the locomotive reached the railhead, and came to a hissing halt with clouds of steam billowing from her brakes.

The railway line had already been driven sixty-five miles into Dervish territory. Penrod's regiment was waiting for him and his orders were to scout the few small villages along the intended line of rail, then sweep the terrain ahead for the first sign of the Dervish cavalry, which they knew must already be on its way northwards to dispute the right of way.

Penrod found it good to breathe the hot, dry air of the desert again, and to have a camel under him. The excitement of the chase and the battle ahead made his nerves sing like copper telegraph lines in the wind. The sensation of being young, strong and alive was intoxicating.

They reached the village at the wells of Wadi Atira. Penrod opened the ranks of his squadron and they encircled the cluster of mud buildings, which were deserted and falling into ruins. There was one chilling reminder of the Dervish occupation: at the entrance to the village stood a makeshift but obviously effective gallows, made from telegraph poles that the army had abandoned when it withdrew after the fall of Khartoum. The skeletons of the souls who had perished upon it had been cleaned and polished by the abrasive, dust-laden wind. They still wore their chains.

Penrod moved forward past Tanjore where the desolation was similar. The old British fort at Akasha, relic of the Gordon relief expedition, was in ruins. The storerooms had been used by the Dervish as execution chambers: desiccated human carcasses lay in abandoned attitudes on a dusty floor, which was thick with the droppings of lizards and the shed skins of vipers and scorpions.

Penrod converted Akasha into an entrenched camp, a base from which the Camel Corps could sally out. He left two of his squadrons to hold the camp, and with the remainder of his regiment he pressed on into the Desert of the Mother of Stones to search for the Dervish.

While he scoured the land along the Nile, behind him the railhead reached Akasha and his rudimentary camp was transformed into an impregnable fortress and staging station, guarded by artillery and Maxim machine-gun detachments.

As Penrod's camels approached Firket, a few Bedouin galloped towards them, waving their arms and shouting that they were friendly. They reported to Penrod that, only hours before, they had been pursued by a marauding party of Dervish cavalry, and although they had escaped, five of their comrades had been overtaken and massacred. He sent a troop of his camels forward to scout the caravan route that led through a narrow boulder-strewn defile towards Firket five miles ahead. No sooner had they entered the defile than the troop commander found himself confronted by at least two hundred and fifty Dervish horsemen, supported closely by almost two thousand spearmen.

Trapped in the defile, the commander wheeled his men round in an attempt to extricate them and bring them back to the support of Penrod's main force. Before they could complete the manoeuvre the Dervish horses charged. Immediately both sides became entangled in wildest confusion, and covered by a dense fog of brown dust thrown up by the hoofs of the horses and the pads of the camels. In the tumult all words of command were drowned.

From the mouth of the defile Penrod saw that disaster was about to engulf his embattled squadron. 'Forward!' he shouted, and drew his sabre. 'Charge! Go straight at them!' With three troops of camels behind him, he crashed into the struggling mass of men and beasts. With his left hand he fired his Webley, and hacked with his sabre at the *jibba*-clad figures half hidden in the swirling curtains of dust.

For minutes the outcome hung in the balance, then the Dervish broke and scattered back behind the shields of their spearmen. They left eighteen of their dead lying on the sand and retreated towards Firket. Penrod sensed they were trying to lead him into a trap, and let them go.

Instead he turned aside and climbed Firket mountain. From the towering heights he glassed the town below, and saw immediately that his instinct had been true. He had found the main body of the Dervish army. It was massed among the mud-brick buildings, and the cavalry lines extended as far as the banks of the Nile a mile beyond the city.

'At a rough estimate three thousand horse, and only Allah knows how many spears,' he said grimly.

*   *   *

Osman Atalan arrived at Firket two weeks after the skirmish with the Egyptian Camel Corps. He had travelled fast, covering the distance from Omdurman in only fourteen days. He was accompanied by ten of his trusted aggagiers.

Since the first word on the British advance, and the commencement of the work on the railway line from Wadi Halfa, Firket had been under the command of the Emir Hammuda. Osman listened to the report of this indolent and careless man. He was appalled. 'He cares only for what lies between the buttocks of his pretty boys,' he told al-Noor. 'We must go forward ourselves to find the enemy and discover what they are planning.'

They came no closer to the village of Akasha than five miles before they were attacked by elements of the Camel Corps, and driven off with the loss of two good men. They made a wide circle round the village, and the next day captured two Bedouin coming from the direction of the village. Osman's aggagiers stripped and searched them. They found foreign cigarettes and tins of toffees with a picture of the English queen painted on the lids.

The aggagiers held down the Bedouin and sliced off the soles of their feet. Then they forced them to walk over the baking stones. This induced them to talk freely. They described the huge build-up of infidel troops and equipment at Firket.

Osman realized that this was the forward base from which the main infidel attack on Firket would be launched. He circled back through the Mother of Stones towards the Nile, coming in ten miles to the north of Akasha. He was searching for the railway line from Wadi Halfa that the Bedouin had reported. The railway had been in the forefront of his mind since al-Jamal had described it to him.

When he came upon it, it seemed innocuous, twin silver threads lying on the burning sands. He left al-Noor and the rest of his band on the crest of the dunes and rode down alone to inspect it. He dismounted, and warily approached the shining rails. They were fastened by fish-plates to heavy teak sleepers. He kicked the rail: it was solid and immovable. He knelt beside it and tried to lever out one of the iron bolts with the point of his dagger. The blade snapped in two.

He stood up and hurled away the hilt. 'Accursed thing of Shaitan! This is not an honourable way to make war.'

Even in his scorn and anger he became aware of a sound that trembled in the desert air, a distant susurration, like the breath of a sleeping giant. Osman stood upright on al-Buq's saddle, and gazed northwards along the line of rail. He saw a tiny feather of smoke on the horizon. As he watched, it drew closer, so rapidly that he was taken by surprise, the alien shape seeming to swell before his eyes as it rushed towards him. He knew that this was the land steamer of which al-Jamal had told him.

He swung al-Buq's head round and urged him into a gallop. He had a quarter of a mile to cover before he reached the foot of the dune. The machine was coming on apace. He looked ahead to the crest of the dune and saw his aggagiers on the skyline. They had dismounted and were holding their horses, allowing them to rest.

'Get down!' Osman roared as he raced across the open ground. 'Let not the infidel see you!' But his men were four hundred yards away and his voice did not carry to them. They stood and watched the approaching machine with amazement. Suddenly a blast of white steam shot up from the land steamer and it emitted a howl like a maddened jinn. Stupefied, making no effort to conceal themselves, they stood and stared at it. It was a mighty serpent, with a head that hissed, howled and shot out clouds of smoke and steam, and whose body seemed to reach back to the skyline.

'They have seen you!' Osman tried to warn them. 'Beware! Beware!' Now they could see that the rolling trucks were stacked with steel rails and crates. On the last they made out the heads of half a dozen men, who were crouched behind some strange contraption.

'Beware!' Osman was racing up the slip-face of the dune, almost at the top. His voice held a high, despairing note. Suddenly the yellow sands under the feet of the group of aggagiers and the hoofs of their horse exploded into flying clouds of dust. It was as though a *khamsin* wind had torn over them. The terrible sound of the Maxim gun followed close behind the spray of bullets. The troop of men and horse disintegrated, blown away like dead leaves.

The gun traversed back towards Osman, but before the dancing pattern of bullets reached him, al-Buq lunged over the crest. Osman swung down from the saddle. He was still stunned by the enormity and menace of the machine, but he ran to where his men lay. Most of them were dead. Only al-Noor and Mooman Digna were still on their feet. 'See to the others,' Osman ordered. He threw himself flat on the top of the dune and peered down the far side. He watched the long train of wagons wind away along the floor of the valley towards Akasha.

In the few moments that they had been exposed

to the fire of the Maxim gun, eight of his men had been killed outright, four were gravely wounded and would die. Four had survived. Five horses were untouched. Osman destroyed the wounded animals, left a waterskin with the wounded men to ease their passing, gathered up his surviving aggagiers and rode back to Firket.

Now that he had had his first glimpse of the juggernaut that was rolling down on them, he realized that his options were limited. There was little he could do to oppose and hold the enemy here at Firket. He determined to assemble and concentrate all his array on the banks of the Atbara river and strike the enemy there in overwhelming force.

He replaced the depraved and ineffectual Emir Hammuda with the Emir Azrak. This man was completely different from Hammuda: he was a fanatical devotee of the Mahdi; he had carried out many daring and brutal raids on the Turk and the infidel; his name was well known in Cairo, and he could expect little mercy if he were captured; he would fight to the death. Osman gave Azrak orders to delay the enemy at Firket for as long as possible, but at the last moment to fall back on the Atbara river with all his army. He left him, and rode back to Omdurman.

No sooner had Osman ridden away than Hammuda refused to accept that he had been replaced and engaged in a bitter dispute with Azrak, which left both men powerless.

While they wrangled the sirdar built up his base at Akasha. Men and equipment, supplies and munitions were brought down the railway line with machine-like efficiency. Then, with nine thousand

379

men under his personal command, General Kitchener fell upon the town of Firket. The Dervish were decimated and the survivors driven out helter-skelter. Hammuda died in the first charge. Azrak escaped with less than a thousand men and rode southwards to the confluence of the Atbara to meet Osman. With his Camel Corps Kitchener followed the fleeing Dervish along the riverbank, and captured hundreds of men and horses and great stores of grain.

Within weeks the entire Dervish province of Dongola had fallen to the sirdar. The juggernaut resumed its deliberate and ponderous advance southwards towards the Atbara river. Month after month and mile after weary mile the railway line unreeled like a silken thread across the desert. On most days the track advanced a mile or so, but on occasions up to three miles.

The workmen encountered unexpected hardships and setbacks. Cholera broke out and hundreds of graves were hastily dug in the empty desert. The first false flood of the inundation brought the 'green tide', all the sewerage that had settled on the exposed banks during the Low Nile, downstream. There was no other water to drink. Dysentery racked the army camps. Terrible thunderstorms poured out of a sky that usually never rained. Miles of track were washed away, miles more were swamped under six feet of water.

Zafir, the first of the new stern-wheel gunboats, was brought in sections from Wadi Halfa, and reassembled in a makeshift boatyard at Koshesh on the clear-water section above the cataracts. Her appearance was stately and impressive, and she was launched with General Kitchener and his staff on board. As the boilers built up a full head of steam there was an explosion like a salvo of heavy artillery as they burst. The *Zafir* was out of action until new boilers could be brought out from England and installed.

Yet the remorseless advance continued. The Dervish garrisons at Abu Hamed and Metemma were overrun, and driven back on the Atbara river. Here Kitchener bombarded Osman Atalan's great defensive *zareba*, then smashed it wide open with bullet and bayonet. The Arabs either fled or fought to the death. The black Sudanese troops who would fight as willingly for the infidel as they had for the Dervish were recruited into the sirdar's army.

Victory on the Atbara was decisive. Kitchener's expeditionary force went into summer quarters. He planned and mustered his powers and waited for the river to rise before the final advance on Omdurman.

Penrod, who had received a spear wound through the thigh during the fighting, was granted convalescent leave. He travelled back, by rail and river steamer from Aswan, to Cairo.

*   *   *

When Penrod limped into Cairo, Amber was beside herself with joy to have him at her side, and in her bed. Lady Jane Ballantyne had returned to Clercastle at the insistence of her husband. What had been planned as a three-month sojourn had extended to almost two years. Sir Peter had long ago tired of the bachelor existence.

Ryder Courtney had returned from a highly

successful visit to the United States and Canada. The wheat he had purchased was already offloading in Alexandria docks. He had arrived home just in time for the birth of his son. He had learnt that as soon as the Sudanese campaign ended, Sir Evelyn Baring would turn all his energy and the resources of the Khedive to the building of the great irrigation works on the upper Nile, which had been long projected. Almost two hundred thousand acres of rich black soil would be brought under permanent irrigation and would no longer be dependent on the annual inundation from the Nile. Ryder had purchased twenty thousand of these acres in a speculative move. It was a wise decision that, within ten years, would make him a cotton millionaire.

Penrod's wound healed cleanly, and he discovered that he had been gazetted for the Distinguished Service Order for his conduct in the battles of Firket and Atbara. Amber missed her moon, but on Saffron's advice she did not tell Penrod of this momentous occurrence. 'Wait until you are certain,' Saffron told her.

'What if he guesses the truth before I tell him?' Amber was nervous. 'He would take that hard.'

'My darling, Penrod is a man. He would not recognize a pregnancy if he tripped over it.'

With the approaching cool season heralding High Nile, and conditions conducive to resuming campaigning, Penrod kissed Amber farewell and, oblivious of his impending elevation to fatherhood, returned upriver to the great military camp on the Atbara.

*　　　*　　　*

When he arrived he found that the encampment now stretched for many miles along the riverbank, and the Nile itself resembled the port of some prosperous European city. It was a forest of masts and funnels. Feluccas and gyassas, barges, steamers and gunboats crowded the anchorage. There were six newly assembled armoured-screw gunboats. They were a hundred and forty feet long and twenty-four wide. They were armed with twelve- and six-pounder quick-firing guns, and with batteries of Maxim machine-guns on their upper decks. They were equipped with modern machinery: ammunition hoists, searchlights and steam winches. Yet they drew only thirty-nine inches of water, and their stern screws could drive them at speeds of up to twelve knots. In addition there were four elderly stern-wheel gunboats, dating from Chinese Gordon's era, which also carried twelve-pounders and Maxim guns.

The sirdar had asked London for first-line British troops to reinforce his already formidable new Egyptian army. His request had been granted and battalions of the Royal Warwickshires, Lincolns, Seaforth Highlanders, Cameron Highlanders, Grenadier Guards, Northumberland Fusiliers, Lancashire Fusiliers, the Rifle Brigade and the 21st Lancers had already joined and were encamped in the great *zareba*. The array of artillery was formidable and ranged from forty-pounder howitzers to field and horse batteries. The sirdar's large white tent stood on an eminence in the centre of the zareba, with the Egyptian flag waving on a tall staff above it.

Penrod found his camels fat and strong and his

men in much the same condition. Life in summer quarters, without the presence of their commander, had been restful. Penrod stirred them into action with a vengeance.

As the first green flood of the rising Nile had poured down through the Shabluka gorge, the grand advance began. Thirty thousand fighting men and their battle train moved southwards to the first staging camp at the entrance to the gorge. Here the mile-wide river was compressed into a mere two hundred yards between the black and precipitous cliffs. They were fifty-six miles from Khartoum and Omdurman. The next staging camp was only seven miles upstream opposite Royan Island above the gorge, but these were seven difficult and dangerous miles.

The gunboats thrashed their way up through the racing, whirling rapids, towing the barges behind them. The ill-fated gunboat *Zafir* now sprang a leak and sank by the bows in the jaws of the gorge. Her officers and men had barely time to escape with their lives.

For the infantry and cavalry the march to Royan Island was doubled in length. To avoid the rocky Shabluka hills they had to circle far out into the desert. Penrod's camels carried water for them in iron tanks.

Once they had reached Royan Island, the road to Omdurman was clear and open before them. The vast array of men, animals, boats and guns moved forward relentlessly, ponderously and menacingly.

At last only the low line of the Kerreri hills concealed the city of Omdurman from the binoculars of the British officers. There was still no sign of the Dervish. Perhaps they had abandoned the city and fled. The sirdar sent his cavalry to find out.

*   *   *

The Khalifat Abdullahi had assembled all his army at Omdurman. They numbered almost a hundred thousand. Abdullahi reviewed them before the city, on the wide plain below the Kerreri hills. The prophecy of one of the saintly mullahs on his deathbed was that a great battle would be fought upon the hills that would define the future of Mahdism and the land of Sudan.

Anyone looking upon the mighty Dervish array could not doubt the outcome of the battle. The galloping regiments were strung out over four miles, wave after wave of horsemen and massed black Sudanese spearmen. At the climax of the review, Abdullahi addressed them passionately. He charged them in the name of Allah and the Mahdi to do their duty. 'Before God, I swear to you that I will be in the forefront of the battle.'

The threat that the emirs and *khalifs* feared above all others was that presented by the gunboats. Their spies had reported the power of these vessels to them. Abdullahi devised a counter to this menace. Among his European captives still in Omdurman was an old German engineer. Abdullahi had him brought before him, and his chains were struck off. This was usually the prelude to execution and the German was prostrated with terror.

'I want you to build me explosive mines to lay in the river,' Abdullahi told him.

385

The old engineer was delighted to have this reprieve. He flung himself into the project with enthusiasm and energy. He filled two steel boilers each with a thousand pounds of gunpowder. As a detonator he fixed in them a loaded, cocked and charged pistol. To the pistol's triggers he attached a length of stout line. A firm tug on this would fire the pistol, and the discharge would ignite the explosive contents of the boiler.

The first massive mine was loaded on to one of the Dervish steamers, the *Ishmaelia*. With the German engineer and a hundred and fifty men on board it was taken out into mid-channel and lowered over the side. As it touched the bottom of the river the steamer's captain, for reasons he never had an opportunity to explain, decided to yank the trigger cord.

The efficacy of the mine was demonstrated convincingly to Abdullahi, his emirs and commanders who were watching from the shore. The *Ishmaelia*, with her captain, crew and the German engineer, was blown out of the water.

Once Abdullahi had recovered from the mild concussion induced by the explosion, he was delighted with his new weapon. He ordered the captain of one of his other steamers to place the second mine in the channel. This worthy had been as impressed as everybody else with the first demonstration. Wisely he took the precaution of flooding the mine with water before he took it on board. The mine, rendered harmless, was then laid in the channel of the Nile without further mishap. Abdullahi praised him effusively and showered him with rewards.

The Dervish commanders waited for the infidel

to come. Each day their spies brought reports of the slow but relentless approach. Better than anyone Osman Atalan understood the strength and determination of these stern new-age crusaders. When the infidel advance reached Merreh, only four miles beyond the Kerreri Hills, he rode out with al-Noor and Mooman Digna and gazed down from the heights upon the host. Through the dust they raised, he saw the marching columns and the lanceheads of the cavalry glittering in the sunlight. He watched the heliographs flashing messages he could not understand. Then he gazed at the flotilla of gunboats, beautiful and deadly, coming up the flow of the Nile. He rode back to his palace in Omdurman and called for his wives. 'I am sending you with all the children to the mosque at the oasis of Gedda. You will wait for me there. When the battle is won, I will come to find you.'

Rebecca and Nazeera packed their possessions on to the camels, gathered up the three children and, under an escort of aggagiers, left the town.

'Why do these infidels wish to hurt us?' Ahmed asked pitifully. 'What shall we do if they kill our exalted and beloved father?' Ahmed lacked the fine looks of his parents. His eyes were blue, but close-set and furtive. His front teeth protruded beyond his upper lip. This gave him the appearance of a large, ginger rodent.

'Do not snivel, my brother. Whatever Allah decrees, we must be brave and take care of our honoured mother.' Kahruba answered.

Rebecca felt her heart squeezed. They were so different: Ahmed plain-featured, timid and afraid; Kahruba beautiful, fearless and wild. She hugged the infant to her breast as she swayed on the camel saddle. Under the cotton sheet she had spread over her to protect her from the sun, her baby daughter lay listlessly against her bosom. The tiny body was hot and sweaty with the fever that consumed her. Omdurman was a plague city.

The little caravan of women and children reached the oasis an hour after dark.

'You will like it here,' Rebecca told Ahmed. 'This is where you were born. The mullahs are learned and wise. They will instruct you in many things.' Ahmed was a born scholar, hungry for knowledge. She did not bother to try to influence Kahruba. She was her own soul, and not amenable to any views that did not coincide with her own.

That night as she lay on the narrow *angareb*, holding her sick baby, Rebecca's mind turned to the twins. This had happened more often recently, ever since she had known that the Egyptian army was moving irresistibly southwards down the river towards them.

It was many years since she had parted from Amber, even longer since Saffron had run off through the dark streets of Khartoum. She still had a vivid picture of them in her mind. Her eyes stung with tears. What did they look like now. Were they married? Did they have children of their own? Were they even alive? Of course they would not recognize her. She knew she had become an Arab wife, drawn and haggard with childbirth, drab and aged with care. She sighed with regret, and the infant whimpered. Rebecca forced herself to remain still, to allow her baby to rest.

She was seized with a strange unfocused terror for what the next few days would bring. She had a premonition of disaster. The existence to which she had become inured, the world to which she now belonged, would be shattered, her husband dead, perhaps her children also. What was there still to hope for? What was there still to be endured?

At last she fell into a dark, numbed sleep. When she awoke the infant in her arms was cold and dead. Despair filled her soul.

*　　*　　*

The British and Egyptian cavalry moved forward together. The Nile lay on their left hand, and on it they could see the gunboats sailing up the stream in line astern. Before them stood the line of the Kerreri hills. Penrod's camels were on the right flank of the advance. They climbed the first slope, and came out abruptly on the crest. Spread below him, Penrod saw the confluence of the two great Niles, and between them the long-abandoned ruins of Khartoum.

Directly ahead, in Omdurman, rose the brown dome of a large building. It had not been there when Penrod had escaped. He knew, however, that this must be the tomb of the Mahdi in the centre of the city. Nothing else had changed.

The wide plain ahead was speckled with coarse clumps of thornbush, and enclosed on three sides by harsh, stony hills. In the centre of the plain, like another monument, was the conical Surgham Hill. Abutting the hill, a long low uneven ridge hid the fold of ground immediately beyond it. There was no sign of the Dervish. Obedient to his express orders, Penrod halted his troops on the high ground and they watched the squadron of British cavalry ride forward cautiously.

389

Suddenly there was movement. Hundreds of tiny specks left what appeared to be the walls of a *zareba* of thorn branches. It was the Dervish vanguard. They moved forward to meet the British cavalry. The front echelon of troopers dismounted and, at long range, opened fire with their carbines on the approaching Dervish. A few fell, and their comrades rode unhurriedly back to the *zareba*.

Then a remarkable transformation took place. The dark wall of the *zareba* came to life. It was not made of thornbush but of men, tens of thousands of Dervish warriors. Behind them another vast mass appeared over the low ridge in the centre of the plain. Like an infestation of locusts, they swarmed forward. Around and between their divisions individual horsemen rode back and forth, and squadrons of their wild cavalry swirled. Hundreds of banners waved above their ranks, and myriad spearheads glittered. Even at this distance Penrod could hear the booming of the war drums and the braying of the *ombeyas*.

Through his binoculars he searched the front ranks of this massive concentration of the enemy, and in the centre he picked out the distinctive scarlet and black war banner of Osman Atalan. 'So my enemy has come,' he whispered, reverting instinctively to Arabic.

Beside him, Sergeant Yakub grinned evilly and rolled his one eye. '*Kismet*,' he said. 'This has been written!'

Then their attention was diverted from the awe-inspiring spectacle of the Dervish advance to the river on their left. The flotilla of gunboats, with a crash of cannon, engaged the Dervish forts on both banks, which guarded the river approaches to the city. The Dervish guns responded, and the thunder of artillery echoed from the hills. But the fire from the gunboats was fast and deadly accurate. The embrasures of the forts were smashed to rubble and the guns behind them blown off their mountings. The Maxim guns scoured the rifle trenches on each side of the forts, and slaughtered the Dervish in them.

The British and Egyptian cavalry withdrew slowly ahead of the advancing Dervish army. In the meantime Kitchener's main army came marching up along the riverbank, and laagered around the tiny abandoned fishing village of Eigeiga. In this defensive position they awaited the first assault of the Dervish.

Suddenly the mass of advancing Dervish halted. They fired their rifles into the air, a salute and a challenge, but instead of coming on to the attack they lay down on the earth. By now it was late in the afternoon, and it was soon evident that they would not mount their main attack that day.

The flotilla of gunboats had reduced all the Dervish forts, and shelled the tomb of the Mahdi, destroying the dome. Now they dropped back down the current and anchored opposite the army zareba. Night fell.

*　　　*　　　*

At the rear of the Dervish army, Osman Atalan sat with the Khalifat Abdullahi at the small campfire in front of his tent. They were discussing the day's actions and skirmishes, and planning for the morrow. Suddenly, from the centre of the river, a huge cyclopean eye of brilliant light swept over them. Abdallahi sprang to his feet and shouted, 'What is this magic?'

'Exalted Abdullahi, the infidel are watching us.'

'Pull down my tent!' Abdullahi screamed. 'They will see it.' He covered his eyes with both hands, lest the light blind him, and threw himself on to the ground. He feared no man, but this was witchcraft.

*   *   *

Four miles apart the two great armies passed the hours of darkness in fitful slumber and constant vigilance, impatiently awaiting the dawn. At half past four in the morning the bugles of the river camp sounded the reveille. The drums and fifes joined in. The infantrymen and gunners stood to arms and the cavalry mounted up.

Before sunrise the cavalry patrols trotted forward. Because there had been no night attack they suspected that the Dervish had crept away during the hours of darkness, and that the hillside would be deserted. At the head of three troops of his camels, Penrod reached the crest of the slope in front of the zareba and looked down the back slope towards the city and Surgham Hill. Even in the dim light he could see that the dome of the Mahdi's tomb had been shot away by the gunboats. He searched the plain below him, and saw that it was covered with dark patches and streaks. Then the light strengthened with the swiftness of the African dawn.

Far from having absconded, the entire might of the Dervish army lay before him. It began to roll forward on a solid front almost five miles wide. Spear points shimmered above the ranks, and the

Dervish cavalry galloped before and about the slowly moving masses of men. Then the war drums began to beat, the ivory *ombeyas* blared, and the Dervish to cheer. The uproar was almost deafening.

As yet the Dervish masses were hidden from the main Egyptian army on the river, and the gunboats anchored behind them. However, the tumult carried to them. The attack developed swiftly. The Dervish legions were well disciplined and moved with purpose and determination. The British and Egyptian cavalry dropped back before them.

The Dervish front ranks, waving hundreds of huge coloured banners and beating the drums, topped the rise. Below them they saw the waiting infidel army. They did not hesitate, but fired their rifles into the air in challenge and rushed down the slope. The sirdar let them come, waiting until they were exposed on the open hillside. The ranges were accurately known to his gunners, and to the captains of the gunboats. However, it was not the British who opened the conflict. The Dervish had brought up a few ancient Krupps field cannon and their shells burst in front of the British zareba.

Immediately the gunboats and field batteries returned fire. The sky above the advancing Dervish masses was pocked with bursting puffs of shrapnel, like cotton pods opening in the sun. The sea of waving banners toppled and fell, like grass blown down by a whirlwind. Then they rose again as the men coming up behind the fallen lifted them high and charged forward.

The cavalry cleared the field to give the guns full play. The Dervish came on, but their ranks thinned steadily and they left the hillside thickly strewn with tiny inert figures. Then the Dervish were in range of the rifles and the Maxims. The slaughter mounted. The rifles grew so hot that they had to be exchanged with those of the reserve companies in the rear. The Maxims boiled away all the water in their reservoirs and were refilled from the water bottles of their crews.

The frontal attack had been planned, by Osman and Abdullahi, to allow their main forces to hook round the flanks and crush in to the sides of the infidel line. The men being massacred by the guns on the open ground were brave, but they were not the élite of the Dervish army. This was coming up behind the ridge.

Penrod had retired on to the flank, and was ready to deal with the survivors of the first charge when they tried to escape, when suddenly he was confronted by thousands of fresh enemy cavalry coming at him from over the crest of the ridge at close range. He must fly with his troops, and try to reach the safety of the lines before they were wiped out. They raced away but the Dervish and their excited clamour were close upon them. One of the gunboats, playing nursemaid, had been watching this dangerous situation develop. It dropped back down the river, and just as it seemed that Penrod's troops must be overtaken by overwhelming numbers of cavalry, it opened up with the deadly Maxims. The range was short and the results stunning. The Dervish cavalry fell in tangled masses, and their rear ranks pulled up and turned back. Penrod led his squadrons into the shelter of the zareba.

Now the sirdar could leave the zareba and begin the final assault towards the city. The Dervish were in full retreat and the way was open. The lines of cavalry, bayonets and guns crossed the ridge and moved down towards the shattered tomb of the Mahdi.

But the Dervish were not beaten. As the British lines neared Surgham Hill and the sandy ridge they found that Osman Atalan and the Khalifat had concealed the flower of their army in this fold of ground. Twenty-five thousand aggagiers and desert warriors burst out from ambush, and poured down on the British.

The fighting was terrible. The gunboats on the river could take no part in it. The British lancers were surprised by the close proximity of Osman's lurking aggagiers and were forced to charge straight at them. Savage, undisciplined infantry could not withstand the charge of British lancers, but these were horsemen. They ran forward to press the muzzles of their rifles against the flanks of the British horses, then fired; they hamstrung others with the long blades, they dragged the riders from their saddles.

The lancers suffered terrible casualties. Al-Noor killed three men. This short but bloody action was only a tiny cameo in the main battle that raged across the plain and around Surgham Hill.

The British and the Egyptians fought superbly. The brigades manoeuvred with parade-ground precision to meet every fresh charge. The officers directed their fire with cool expertise. The Maxims came up to exacerbate the slaughter. But the Dervish courage was inhuman. The fires of fanaticism were unquenchable. They charged and were shot down in tangled heaps, but immediately fresh hordes of *jibba*-bright figures sprang up, seemingly from the ground, and ran upon the guns and bayonets and died. From the gunsmoke that hung over their mangled corpses fresh figures charged forward.

And the Maxims sang the chorus.

By noon it was over. Abdullahi had fled the field, leaving almost half his army dead upon it. The British and the Egyptians had lost forty-eight men, almost half of whom were lancers who had died in the fatal two minutes of that brave but senseless charge.

*   *   *

Penrod was among the first men into the city of Omdurman. There were still small pockets of resistance among the pestilential hovels and stinking slums, but he ignored them and, with a troop of his men, rode to the palace of Osman Atalan. He dismounted in the courtyard. The buildings were deserted. He strode into them with his bared sabre in his hand, calling her name: 'Rebecca! Where are you?' His voice echoed through the empty rooms.

Suddenly he heard a furtive movement behind him, and whirled round just in time to deflect the dagger that had been aimed between his shoulder-blades. He flicked back his blade, catching his assailant as he struck again, slicing open his wrist to the bone. The Arab screamed and the dagger fell from his hand. With the point of the sabre to his throat Penrod pinned him to the wall behind him. He recognized him as one of Osman Atalan's aggagiers. 'Where are they?' Penrod demanded. 'Where are al-Jamal and Nazeera?' Clutching his wrist, the blood from his severed artery pumping sullenly, the Arab spat at him.

'Effendi.' Yakub spoke from behind Penrod's shoulder. 'Leave this one to me. He will speak to me.'

Penrod nodded. 'I will wait with the camels. Do not be long.'

'The remorseless Yakub will waste little time.'

Twice Penrod heard the captured Arab scream, the second time weaker than the first, but at last Yakub came out. 'The oasis of Gedda,' he said, and wiped the blade of his dagger on his camel's neck.

*   *   *

The oasis of Gedda lay in a basin of chalk hills. There was no surface water, only a single deep well with a coping of limestone. It was surrounded by a grove of date palms. The dome of the saint's tomb was separated from the taller dome of the mosque and the flat-roofed quarters of the mullahs.

As Penrod's troop rode in from the desert they saw a group of children playing among the palm trees, small, barefooted boys and girls in long, grubby robes. A copper-haired boy pursued the others, and they squealed with laughter and scattered before him. As soon as they saw the camel troop approaching they froze into silence and stared with huge dark eyes. Then the eldest boy turned and ran back towards the mosque. The others followed him. After they had disappeared the oasis seemed silent and deserted.

Penrod rode forward, and heard a horse whinny. The animal was standing behind the angle of the side wall. It was knee-haltered and had been feeding on a pile of cut fodder. It was a dark-coloured stallion. 'Al-Buq!'

He reined in well short of the front doors of the mosque, jumped down and threw the reins to Yakub. Then he unsheathed his sabre and walked forward slowly. The doors were wide open and the interior of the mosque was impenetrably dark in contrast to the bright sunlight without.

'Osman Atalan!' Penrod shouted, and the echoes from the hills mocked him. The silence persisted.

Then he saw dim movement in the gloom of the building's interior. Osman Atalan stepped out into the sunlight. His fierce and cruel features were inscrutable. He carried the long blade in his right hand, but he had no shield. 'I have come for you,' Penrod said.

'Yes,' Osman answered. Penrod saw the glint of silver threads in his beard. But his gaze was dark and unwavering. 'I expected you. I knew that you would come.'

'Nine years,' said Penrod.

'Too long,' Osman replied, 'but now it is time.' He came down the steps, and Penrod retreated ten paces to give him space to fight. They circled each other, a graceful minuet. Lightly they touched blades and the steel rang like fine crystal.

They circled again, watching each other's eyes, looking for any weakness that might have developed in the years since they had last fought. They found none. Osman moved like a cobra, tensed and poised for the strike. Penrod was his mongoose, quick and fluid.

They crossed and turned, and then as if at a signal, leapt at each other. Their blades slithered together. They broke apart, circled and came

398

together again. The silver blades blurred, glittered and clattered against each other. Penrod drove in hard, forcing Osman on to his back foot, keeping the pressure on him, the blades dancing. Osman stepped back, and then counter-attacked, just as furiously. Penrod gave ground to him, leading him on, making him buy each inch.

Penrod watched him carefully, then cut hard at his head. Osman blocked. Their blades were locked together. Now they both stood solidly and all their weight was on their sword wrists. Tiny beads of sweat popped out on their foreheads. They stared into each other's eyes and pushed. Penrod felt the sponginess in Osman's grip. To test him he broke the lock and jumped back.

As their blades disengaged Osman had a fleeting opening and tried for it, thrusting at Penrod's right elbow to disable his sword arm, but it was one of his old tricks and Penrod was ready for it. It seemed to him that Osman was slow. He hit the long blade and pirouetted clear.

Not slow. He changed his mind as they circled again. Just not as fast as he used to be. But, then, am I?

He feinted at Osman's face, then leant back, not making it obvious that he was inviting the riposte. Osman almost caught him. His counter-stroke came like thunder. Penrod just managed to turn it. Osman was at full extension, and there was the lag again, his old bad habit, slow on the recovery. Penrod hit him.

It was a glancing blow that skidded along Osman's ribcage under his arm. The point sliced down to the bone, but did not find the gap between the ribs. They circled again. Osman was bleeding

399

profusely. The blood loss must weaken him swiftly, and the damaged muscles would soon stiffen. He was running out of time and threw everything into the attack. He came with all his weight and skill. His blade turned to dancing light. It was cut and thrust high in the line of defence, then cross and go back-handed for the thigh, then at the head. He kept it up relentlessly, never breaking, never giving Penrod a chance to come on to his front foot, forcing him on to the defensive.

He cut Penrod high in the left shoulder. It was a light wound, and Osman was losing blood more heavily. Each fresh attack was less fiery, each recovery after the thrust just a little slower. Penrod let him expend himself, holding him off and waiting his moment. He watched Osman's eyes.

During the entire bout Osman had not gone for Penrod's hip. Penrod knew from experience that it was his favourite and most deadly stroke with which he had crippled innumerable enemies. At last Penrod offered it to him, turning his lower body into Osman's natural line.

Osman went for the opening, and once he was committed Penrod turned back so the razor edge slit the cloth of his jodhpurs but did not break the skin. Osman was fully extended and could not recover quickly enough.

Penrod hit him. His thrust split the sternum at the base of Osman's ribs and went on to transfix him cleanly as a fish on a skewer. Penrod felt his steel grate on his opponent's spinal column.

Osman froze, and Penrod stepped in close. He seized his opponent's sword wrist to prevent a last thrust. Their faces were only inches apart. Penrod's eyes were hard and cold. Osman's were dark with bitter rage, but slowly they became opaque as stones. The sword dropped from his hand. His legs buckled, but Penrod held his weight on the sabre. Osman opened his lips to speak, but a snake of dark blood trickled from the corner of his mouth and crawled down his chin.

Penrod relaxed his wrist and let him slide off the blade. He fell at Penrod's feet, and lay still upon his back with his arms spread wide.

As Penrod stepped back a woman screamed. He looked up. He became aware for the first time of the small group of Arab women and children huddled in the doorway of the mosque. He recognized the little ones as those who had run to hide as he rode up. But he knew none of the women.

'Nazeera!' It was Yakub's voice. He saw one of the women react, and then he recognized her. Nazeera held two children against her legs. One was the ugly copper-haired boy, and the other an exquisite little girl, a few years younger than the boy. Both children were weeping and trying to break out of Nazeera's grip, but she held them fast.

Then an Arab women left the group and came slowly down the steps towards him. She moved like a sleep-walker, and her eyes were fastened on the dead man at his feet. There was something dreadfully familiar about her. Instinctively Penrod backed away, still staring at her in fascination. Then he exclaimed, 'Rebecca!'

'No,' the stranger replied in English. 'Rebecca died long ago.' Her face was a pitiful travesty of that of the lovely young woman he had once known. She knelt beside Osman and picked up his sword. Then she looked up into Penrod's face. Her eyes were old and hopeless. 'Look after my children,' she said. 'You owe me that at least, Penrod Ballantyne.'

Before he understood what she intended and could move to prevent her, she reversed the sword. She placed the pommel on the hard ground and the point under her bottom ribs and fell forward upon it with all her weight. The length of the blade disappeared into her body, and she collapsed on top of Osman Atalan.

The children screamed, broke from Nazeera's grip, rushed down the steps and threw themselves on to the bodies of their parents. They wailed and shrieked. It was a dreadful sound that cut to the core of Penrod's being.

He sheathed his sabre, turned away and walked away towards the palm grove. As he passed Yakub he said, 'Bury Osman Atalan. Do not mutilate his body or take his head. Bury al-Jamal beside him. Nazeera and the children will come with us. They will ride my camel. I will ride al-Buq. When all is ready call me.'

He went into the grove and found a fallen palm trunk on which to sit. He was very tired, and the cut on his shoulder throbbed. He opened his tunic and folded his handkerchief over the wound.

The two children, the boy and the girl, must be Rebecca's, he realized. What will become of them? Then he remembered Amber and Saffron. They have two aunts who will fight over them. He smiled sadly. Of course, they will have Rebecca's share of the trust fund, and they have Nazeera. They will lack nothing.

Within the hour Yakub came to call him. On the way back to the mosque they stopped beside the newly filled double grave. 'Do you think she loved him, Yakub?'

'She was a Muslim wife,' Yakub replied. 'Of course she loved him. In God's eyes, she had no choice.'

They mounted up. Nazeera had the two children with her on the camel, and Yakub rode beside her. Penrod was on the stallion, and led them back to Omdurman.

* * *

Ahmed Habib abd Atalan, the son of Rebecca and Osman Atalan, became uglier as he grew older, but he was very clever. He attended Cairo University where he studied law. He fell in with a group of politically active fellow students, who were violently opposed to the British occupation of their country. He devoted the rest of his life to the same *jihad* against that hated nation and Empire as his father. He was a German supporter during both world wars and spied for Erwin Rommel in the second. He was an active member of the Revolutionary Command Council in the bloodless coup that ousted the Egyptian King Farouk, the British puppet.

Rebecca's daughter Kahruba remained small but she became more beautiful with every year that passed. At an early age she discovered in herself an extraordinary talent for dancing and acting. For twenty years she burned bright as a meteor across the stages of all the great theatres of Europe. With her wild, free spirit, she became a legend in her own lifetime. Her lovers, both men and women, were legion. Finally she married a French

403

industrialist, who manufactured motor-cars, and they lived together in regal state and pomp in their palatial mansion in Deauville.

The Khalifat Abdullahi escaped from Omdurman, but Penrod Ballantyne and his Camel Corps pursued him relentlessly for more than a year. In the end he deigned to run no further. With his wives and devotees around him he sat on a silk carpet in the centre of his camp in the remote wilderness. When the troops rushed in he offered no further resistance. They shot him dead where he sat.

The tomb of the Mahdi was razed to the ground. His remains were exhumed, and his skull was turned into an inkwell. It was presented to General Kitchener, who was horrified. He had it reburied in a secret grave in the wilderness.

After the battle of Omdurman Kitchener became the darling of the Empire. He was rewarded with a peerage and a huge money grant. When the Boers in South Africa inflicted a series of disastrous defeats on the British army, Kitchener was sent to retrieve the situation. He burnt the farms and herded the women and children into concentration camps. The Boers were crushed.

During the First World War, Kitchener was promoted to field marshal and commander-in-chief to steer the Empire through the most destructive war in all human history. In 1916 while he was on board the cruiser *Hampshire, en route* to Russia, the ship struck a German mine off the Orkneys. He drowned at the high noon of his career.

Sir Evelyn Baring became the 1st Earl of Cromer. He returned to England where he spent his days writing and, in the House of Lords, championing free trade.

Nazeera helped to raise all the children of the three Benbrook sisters. This occupied most of her time and energy, but what remained she divided impartially between Bacheet and Yakub.

Bacheet and Yakub pursued their vendetta for the rest of their lives. Bacheet was referred to by his rival as the Despicable Lecher. Yakub was the Jaalin Assassin. In their later years they took to frequenting the same coffee-house where they sat at opposite ends of the room, smoking their water-pipes, never addressing each other but deriving great comfort from their mutual antagonism. When Bacheet died of old age, Yakub never returned to the coffee-house.

Ryder Courtney's cotton acres flourished. He invested his millions in Transvaal gold and Mesopotamian oil. He doubled and redoubled his fortune. In time his mercantile influence encompassed almost all of Africa and the Mediterranean. But to Saffron he remained always a benign and indulgent husband.

General Sir Penrod Ballantyne went to South Africa on Kitchener's staff, and was present when the Boers surrendered at the peace of Vereeniging in the Transvaal. In the First World War he rode with Allenby's cavalry against the Ottoman Turks in Palestine. He fought at Gaza and Megiddo, where he won further honours. He continued to play first-class polo well into his seventies. He and Amber lived in their house on the Nile, and in it raised a large family.

Amber and Saffron outlived both their husbands. They grew ever closer as the years passed. Amber flourished as an author. Her novels faithfully captured the romance and mystery of Africa. She was twice nominated for the Nobel Prize for Literature. Saffron's marvellously colourful paintings were hung in galleries in New York, Paris and London. Her Nile series of paintings was eagerly sought by wealthy collectors on two continents, and commanded enormous prices. Picasso said of her, 'She paints the way a sunbird flies.'

But they are all gone now, for in Africa only the sun triumphs eternally.

GLOSSARY

Arab names will not go into English, exactly, for their consonants are not the same as ours, and their vowels, like ours, vary from district to district. There are scientific systems of transliteration, helpful to people who know enough Arabic not to need helping, but a wash out for the world. I spell my names anyhow, to show what rot the systems are.

T. E. Lawrence, *The Seven Pillars of Wisdom*

Abadan Riji—'One who never turns back'. Penrod Ballantyne's Arabic name

abd—slave

aggagiers—élite warriors of the Beja tribe of desert Arabs

Ammi—aunt

angareb—a native bed with leather thong lacing

Ansars—'The Helpers', warriors of the Mahdi

ardeb—Oriental measure of volume. Five *ardeb*s equal one cubic metre

asida—porridge of dhurra (*G.V.*) flavoured with chili

Bahr El Abiad—the White Nile

Bahr El Azrek—the Blue Nile

bombom—bullets or cannon shells

Beia—oath of allegiance required by the Mahdi from his Ansars

Beit el Mal—the treasury of the Mahdi

Buq, al—War Trumpet, Osman Atalan's charger

407

cantar—Oriental measure of weight: one cantar equals a hundredweight

djinni *see* Jinnee

dhurra—*Sorghum vulgare*; staple grain food of men and domestic animals

Effendi—lord, a title of respect

falja—a gap between the front top teeth; a mark of distinction, much admired in the Sudan and many Arabic countries

fellah (pl. *fellahin*)—Egyptian peasant

ferenghi—foreigner

Filfil—pepper, Saffron Benbrook's Arabic name

Franks—Europeans

galabiyya—traditional long Arabic robe

Hulu Mayya—Sweet Water, one of Osman Atalan's steeds

Jamal, al-—'the Beautiful One'; Rebecca Benbrook's Arabic name

jibba—the uniform of the Mahdists; long tunic decorated with multi-coloured patches

jihad—holy war

jinnee (pl. jinn)—a spirit from Muslim mythology, able to assume animal or human form and influence mankind, with supernatural powers

jiz—scarab or dung beetle

kufi—Muslim traditional skull cap

Karim, al-—'Kind and Generous'; variation of Ryder Courtney's Arabic name

kittar—bush with wicked hooked thorns

Kurban Bairam—Islamic festival of sacrifice, commemorating the sacrifice of the ram by Abraham in place of his son Isaac; one of the most important holidays in Islam

kurbash—whip made from hippo hide

khalifa—deputy of the Mahdi
khalifat—the senior and most powerful *khalifa*
khedive—the ruler of Egypt
mulazemin—the servants and retainers of an eminent Arab
Mahdi—'the Expected One', the successor to the Prophet Muhammad
Mahdist—follower of the Mahdi
Mahdiya—the rule of the Mahdi
nullah—dry or water-filled streambed
ombeya—war trumpet carved from a single elephant tusk
souk—bazaar
sitt—title of respect, equivalent to 'my lady' in English
Sakhawi, al-—'Generosity', Ryder Courtney's Arabic name
sirdar—the title of the commander-in-chief of the Egyptian Army
shufta—bandit
Tej—strong beer made from dhurra
Turk—derogatory term for Egyptian
Tirbi Kebir—the great graveyard, large salt pan in the Bight of the Nile
wadi—Gully or dried watercourse
Yom il Guma—Friday, the Muslim Sabbath
Zahra, al-—'The Flower', Amber Benbrook's Arabic name
zareba—fortified stockade of stones or thorn bush
zenana—women's quarters in an Arabic household